Eponymous

Eponymous

J. Eric Smith

Writers Club Press
San Jose New York Lincoln Shanghai

Eponymous

All Rights Reserved © 2001 by J. Eric Smith

No part of this book may be reproduced or transmitted in any form or by any means, graphic, electronic, or mechanical, including photocopying, recording, taping, or by any information storage or retrieval system, without the permission in writing from the publisher.

Writers Club Press
an imprint of iUniverse.com, Inc.

For information address:
iUniverse.com, Inc.
5220 S 16th, Ste. 200
Lincoln, NE 68512
www.iuniverse.com

The characters in this book are fictional and any resemblance to persons living or dead is purely coincidental.

ISBN: 0-595-17546-5

Printed in the United States of America

For the demons…fly away! be free!

Acknowledgements

Thanks to Marcia and Paige for patient reading, Xnet2 for idea bouncing, and all of the world's frustrated musicians (not to mention the critics who frustrate them) for inspiration.

Chapter One

By their words shall you know them.

Droning, jangling, blistering, bracing, loping, raging, keening. Seminal, transcendent, luminous, majestic, audacious, visionary, brash. Sell out, sold out, merch, indie, cred, biz, dud. Retro-, proto-, neo-, aggro-, post-, trans-, -esque. Ouvre, persona, sensibility, aesthetic, dialectic, genre, milieu. Eclectic. Erstwhile. Eponymous.

More than all the rest that last word: eponymous. That's the dead giveaway. You see that word, you know you've got one of them. No one else uses it. No one else needs to. No one else can. At least not correctly. Look it up. You'll see what I mean.

So who are these people who use such words?

They're the public gadflies who ladle the guilty over your pleasure, applying stringent intellectual standards to things most effectively appreciated by those who think about them the least.

They're the biting social parasites whose driving motivation is almost always to someday become one of the host organisms upon which they feed.

They're the deeply demented souls who live in a world where a packed stadium equals "lowest common denominator failure," while eight of their kind gathered in a space of their own making watching a nobody doing nothing anyone else wants to hear equals "artistic triumph."

They're the lowest, most desperate life form in the journalistic kingdom, the bottom-feeders who are willing to work in exchange for substandard salaries supplemented by free promotional materials—because if they're not willing to do so, then somebody else is.

In short: they're the music critics.

And I'm one of them.

And I think that I hate myself for it—as do a lot of other people I know.

Take the members of the many local bands I've casually bashed over the years from my critical home base in Albany, New York. They're my neighbors—and they're none too friendly as a rule, since few of them enjoyed having 100,000 or so of our other neighbors reading in the *Advocate* about how badly they blew, after they had bravely gotten up on stage to pour their hearts and souls into their little chosen art statements. For peanuts and beer, no less, if they were lucky—since most of them didn't even make that much after they factored in the costs of their equipment, transportation, rehearsal time and drug habits.

And see, there you go, that's one of the reasons that I think that I hate myself right there. I really should, at this stage in my life, be able to stop tossing out unkind and gross generalizations of just that type, right? But I can't. I just can't. I must not have gotten enough attention as a child. I must have gotten too much attention as a child. I must still be a child. But whatever the reason, that was an unfair comment for me to make, so let me set the record straight before I move on: many of the local bands that I've casually bashed over the years don't even bother to rehearse at all. Ha.

But the drug-addled local band members on the receiving end of my barb-rich bon mots aren't the only people who hate me. There are the nationally touring drug-addled band members that I excoriate, too, although they tend to be further away when the news hits and have little recourse but to send savage letters to the *Advocate*'s editor (who would be me, for music matters, very conveniently) and leave hateful messages on my voice mail. Until the next time they come to town, that is, when some of them (the ones with good memories) may occasionally choose to rile their audiences by taking my name in vain as part of their between-tune patter. I keep my hat down low at shows like that.

Then there are the always-enthusiastic bootlickers that make up the audiences at the shows I cover. They hate me too, and they tend to take things even more personally than do their stage-conquering heroes, largely as a way of proving their devotion—and sometimes to the point where they are more willing than the bands themselves to correct perceived injustices by issuing parking lot poundings to the offending critic. What have they got to lose, after all? They're not going to get a one-star review for poor use of a Doc Marten nor for unimaginative and repetitious deployment of a right jab to the kidney, now are they? Their actions speak louder than any words used to describe them after the fact.

To be fair once again, though, I have to note that critic beatings aren't always the fans' responsibility. I've got a nice knot on the bridge of my now-permanently-leftward-looking nose, for example, as a result of the pounding I invited after writing that a certain halter topped blonde backup vocalist was obviously using her throat for something other than singing when she auditioned for her band. How was I supposed to know that she was the burly bass player's wife? And how was I supposed to know that the cop who watched me take the beating a week later thought I deserved it? Fair's fair, I guess.

I was a little younger and a good deal stupider then, and I like to think that I've gotten better at watching my words (not to mention my back) as I've aged. I've also found that it doesn't hurt to have a well-planned escape route when entering and exiting a potentially hostile venue. Or at least it hurts less than the beatings. Well, except for that time when I climbed the chain-link fence behind the Heartland Club during a particularly hasty retreat and nearly hung myself as I leaped, seemingly to safety—little noticing in my rush that my sweatshirt's hood had become snagged on a fence post during my clamber up.

That night I definitely should have stood up to the two surly members of the self-proclaimed "evil black death metal band" that I had trashed the month before, describing their fare by evoking the sounds that an electric guitar would make if it were capable of projectile vomiting. Fighting back would have at least given me a less embarrassing way to explain the neck brace with which the emergency room nurse outfitted me, while my erstwhile attackers (who had cut me off the fence and driven me to the hospital)(eventually) chortled and guffawed and flirted with her.

And just for the record: I did give those guys a nice enthusiastic review the next time I saw them perform, mainly as a gesture of appreciation for deciding that I didn't deserve to die that night for my offenses, just to be hurt really badly. The members of that band still hate me, though.

As do the former members of my own band. Oh yes, I was in a band once, too—as was every other music critic in the world, since those who can, do, and those who can't, criticize. Mine was called Arctangent, and we got as far as signing a record contract with a major record label, but then went belly up soon thereafter, largely as a result of my own stupidity, although a nasty little substance abuse thing, and a manager, and some money (or the lack thereof), and a van and a bass guitar and a girlfriend all played their parts, too.

So not only do my former band-mates hate me, but the guys from the record company hate me too, and my (former) girlfriend really hates me, or at least that's what her parents and lawyers tell me, although I'm not sure that she's actually capable of hating me at this point. I don't know how strong, deep emotions like hatred are affected by severe brain injuries.

I haven't seen Kris (that's my ex-girlfriend, Kris Dennison's her name) for about two years now, since the day the orderlies physically removed me from the hospital room where she was recovering, badly, from the effects of one of my most impressive bouts of toxic stupidity.

I think that may have been the point when I really started hating myself, since up until that point it was more like a strong distaste, or a vague dissatisfaction. And if Kris does indeed hate me, then I'm sure she was well on her way towards a firm, emphatic dislike at that particular point in time, too, unless the morphine had taken that away.

Which is sad, because I loved Kris, I think, and I'm pretty sure that Kris loved me, once upon a time. And if blowing that good deal isn't enough of a rationale for my ongoing self-loathing, then I simply can't imagine what could be.

Although writing this little self-hurt book may help me think of some other explanations for it.

Chapter Two

Before I was a music critic, even before I was a musician, I was just a boy, just a boy, and my Mama would most gladly admit it, being the good Mama that she was, God rest her soul.

I was born and raised in Bridgefield, South Carolina, a seaside county seat that had (and has) been largely overlooked by aggressive developers otherwise keen to exploit the Palmetto State's coastal resources. Perhaps it was because Bridgefield lacked most of the things that aggressive developers seek when building those sorts of houses that are destined to be knocked back into the sea by the next hurricane.

We didn't have much of a port, for example, and what port we had reeked of the shrimp and brine and diesel fuel that continually leached off and out of our town's modest fishing fleet. We didn't have much of a beach to speak of, either, since we were located at the mouth of the Pocotaligo River, a fulsome black water estuary that ran both ways with the tides and didn't seem much inclined to lay down white, tourist-attracting sand where it needed to be laid.

We did have lots of thick, pungent mud along our coastline, though, most of it booby-trapped with oyster and mussel shells that would shred your feet if you were stupid enough to step on them without the heavy-duty waders with which we were all outfitted, almost from birth. And when the wind blew the right way in Bridgefield you could hear the sounds of young Marine Corps recruits being tortured across the water at the boot camp on Parris Island. Unless, that is, their sad sounds were drowned out instead by the endless roar of military fighter and cargo planes flying low overhead on their way to or from the Marine Corps Air Station at Beaufort. Idyllic island paradise it was not, although it was home, and that has to be worth something.

My parents named me Hutson Colcock Hay III. It wasn't a terribly imaginative name, since my grandfather and father shared it—and since my first, middle and last names were all culled from surnames of the stalwart families that had first settled Bridgefield's muck some 300 years before I arrived on the scene. The long local histories of the Hutsons, Colcocks and Hays spurred me to a brief childhood interest in genealogy, until I realized that the reason I bore those three names was because the members of those three families had been marrying each other, and not many other others, since first settling my home community. And a family tree just isn't much fun when it looks like a vine.

My moniker did pose some problems when it came to deciding what to call me, since I spent a good deal of time in the presence of both my father and my grandfather and there needed to be some way to distinguish between the three of us. Everyone referred to my grandfather as "Colonel," in recognition of the rank he wore during his service in the Army during World War II—and because Lieutenant Colonel Hutson Colcock Hay, Sr., United States Army Reserve (Retired), was too much of a mouthful. My father will be "Junior" to his dying day (even my sister and I call him that, since he just wasn't the "daddy" type), and in keeping with good Southern tradition as Junior's same-named son, I should by all rights have properly been called "Trey."

Fortunately, Junior and Mama were smart enough to realize that Trey Hay might cause me some problems down the line, although the alternate with which they chose to dub me wasn't a whole lot better: to this day, my family members refer to me as "Boy." I try not to let them speak to any of my grownup friends accordingly.

Family habits aside, however, Boy Hay wasn't likely to cut it when I started grade school at the John C. Calhoun Academy, Bridgefield's sole private school—which had opened the very same year that the hated Feds desegregated the town's public school system. Sending me to the Academy wasn't about race, though, Colonel and Junior regularly assured me over the years, it was just that a good Southern Gentlemen-in-training needed to go to a private academy for the sorts of moral and ethical education that the godless, prayer-free Bridgefield Central School District couldn't provide. And if the price of Calhoun Academy was well beyond the means of most of Bridgefield's minority families, well, then that was their problem, now, wasn't it? They could just go off and get themselves some education and improve their status in the community and earn enough money to send their young ones off to Calhoun with the privileged kids. I challenged the Catch-22 inherent in their logic once, but a sharp rap to the back of the head from Colonel ended that discussion quickly.

So upon arrival at the Academy, I suddenly and unexpectedly became Hutson Hay, although I aggravated teachers and students alike for weeks by failing to answer their calls of "Hutson," since no one had ever called me that before. Although actually they didn't call me Hutson then, exactly, either. No one seemed to apprehend the fact that my first name had a "t" in it, as they invariably defaulted with their soft Low Country drawls to "Huuuuuudson" with a "d". And I understood, even at such a tender age, that a name like "Huuuuuudson" immediately put me into the Bubba, Elmer, Cletus caste of moniker-challenged, low rent, white trash Southerners.

But what to do about it? I also understood even then that my middle name, "Colcock," was wholly unsuitable, as my fellow schoolboys would have had a field day with any name that was itself or contained a euphemism for "penis," as proven repeatedly by their treatment of my unfortunate friends Dick Hardee and Peter Gay. I wasn't about to become Cold Cock Hay to my friends and (worse) my enemies, no thank you very much. So I was Huuuuuudson for a few months, although I was none too pleased about it.

Fortunately, a brilliant insight culled from a Saturday afternoon matinee allowed me to reinvent myself in more self-pleasing terms. Like most boys in 1964, I was smitten by the exploits of Lassie, everyone's favorite movie dog, and his adventures with his hapless sidekick, Timmy Martin. (And I use "his" there intentionally because, dammit, Lassie was no girl to me, no matter what they called him, no matter what equipment he carried beneath his long, luxuriant fur). Could there have been a nobler creature in this world than Lassie? Could my own town's sorry-assed pack of roach eating dogs hold the proverbial candle to a magnificent beast like that big-screen collie? Could any of my human neighbors either, for that matter?

Then it occurred to me: the word "Collie" started the same way that "Colcock" did! I could legitimately adopt it as my nickname and assume all of the high-toned connotations and boy-tested popularity associated with everyone's favorite four-legged film star! But could "Collie" actually be used as a name? I pulled out my parents' musty old family dictionary that night and consulted the list of baby names in its appendix: there was no Collie (or Colcock), but there was indeed a Colin—and Collie could certainly be deployed as a nickname for that, right? I wouldn't be a weirdo for wanting a dog's name would I? Since that's what I could have been logically called if my parents had named me Colin Colcock Hay instead of Hutson the Third in the first place?

I read further to discover the meanings behind the name Colin and was immediately convinced that I'd chanced upon the perfect moniker: "Colin" was defined as "a youth" or "a whelp" or "a young hound." Hell, my parents already called me Boy, so Collie would just be a way of letting them do that in a different language, and I wanted to be a young hound like Lassie anyway, so the match seemed truly, divinely inspired.

I announced my intentions to take a new name that night at the dinner table and was virtually laughed out of the room by Junior and

Mama. Even my older sister, the equally-unfortunately-named Woodward Gregorie Hay (yes, all family names—leading her to be known as "Sister" around the house and "Wood Hay" everywhere else) muttered "Poor, poor Boy" as she sopped her biscuit about in the juice left by her country ham and steamed okra. You'd think that if anyone would have understood my desire for sensible self-definition, it would have been her, right? I mean, Wood Hay, for God's sake! What were Mama and Junior thinking?

Undeterred by the lack of family acceptance, however, I went to school the following Monday and brazenly informed teachers, friends and girls alike that from that point forward, I was to be referred to as "Collie Hay" if anyone wanted me to answer. A phone call to Mama by my homeroom teacher Miss Wilson elicited the expected "It's just a phase he's going through, humor him" response—but, to her credit, humor me Miss Wilson did. I loved her for that for years, even though she broke my heart in fourth grade by running off with Mr. Virgilio, Calhoun Academy's high school basketball coach. The slut.

Needless to say, however, the other boys weren't so acquiescent quite as quickly. I went through months of being called Wiener-Dog Hay, Toy Poodle Hay or Lassie Girl Hay (despite the fact that Lassie was a boy, dammit) before my entertainment value expired and the vicious first graders returned to their favorite pastime of tormenting Dick Hardee and Peter Gay instead. I was generally sympathetic to both of them after that, having been through the name-go-round myself.

And so there I was in 1964: a self-inventing first-grader named Collie Hay.

And here I am today: a self-defeating forty-two year old music critic still named Collie Hay, sitting in front of a computer, trying to figure out how I got from there to here, trying to decide whether here is a place that I want to be anymore.

Chapter Three

"What'cha writing?"

It's my room-mate Randy, sticking his head into my home office as he and my other room-mate Gerry are both apt to do any time they hear me typing in here. They can't stand not knowing what's going on, even if it's nothing.

"Book," I answer, truthfully.

"You're writing a book? A whole, real book?"

"Yep. Whole, real book."

"When did you start it?"

"Today."

"Huh," Randy concludes, stumped by this unexpected exchange. Normally when he or Gerry asks, I answer by grunting "review" or "interview" or "think piece" or "bio" or "letter" or some other mundane, monosyllabic response. This is news.

I hear Randy's footsteps receding down the hallway, then hear he and Gerry talking in the living room, just beneath the threshold of where I can understand what they're saying—although I know them well enough to fill in the blanks pretty accurately anyway. There's a moment of silence, then four feet head back towards my office, then pause at my door, shuffling.

Gerry, this time: "So what's the book about?"

"Us."

"You mean us, like, *us*? Like, me n' you n' Randy?"

"Yep. An' Kris n' Matt, too. And some stuff about Junior n' Sister an' her kids, and some other Bridgefield stuff, just to set the tone of the thing."

Randy's getting the idea now: "Are you gonna write about the band, too?"

"Yeah, the band's going to be in the book, too, I guess. And I think I'm gonna write about the *Advocate*. And Envirocorps."

"I hope he writes about when all three of us worked at Envirocorps," Randy notes to Gerry, as if I weren't there. "That would pretty cool, wouldn't it?"

"Yeh, really, that would be great," Gerry agrees. "And if he writes about when we were all at Envirocorps, then he'd probably have to write about the Treehouse, too, wouldn't he?"

To me, now: "Are you gonna write about the Treehouse, Collie?"

"Well, it would be hard for me to write about all of that other stuff without writing about the Treehouse, wouldn't it?"

"Uh, yeah, well, I guess so," Randy answers, mildly stung on Gerry's behalf. "We just didn't know if you were writing, like, a made-up story or a true story, 'cause if it's a made up story, then you wouldn't have to write about the Treehouse at all. That's all Gerry was asking, right, Gerry?"

"Yeh, that's all I was asking."

They're silent again. One of them shuffles. Randy probably, since he's bigger and his shuffles are a bit more audible than Gerry's accordingly. I've lived with Gerry and Randy for over fifteen years now, longer than anyone else in my life except for Junior and Mama and Sister, so I'm pretty well versed in their distinctive sounds, mannerisms and shuffles. Even when I'm not looking at them.

More shuffling. They don't want to bother me, but they want to bother me.

"The book's gonna talk about the accident, too," I offer, knowing that's one of the things that they want to ask.

"Oh, yeah, well, we kinda thought that it might, since it seems like you're writing a true story, now, the more you tell us, and not a made-up story," says Randy.

More shuffling. I stop typing and turn to look at them, side by side in the doorway, the top of the hulking 6'5" Randy's head nearly touching the low 19th century carved lintel, while the (maybe) 5'3" Gerry stands partially obscured by Randy's bulk. They're so extremely proportioned—and I'm so much the average between them—that it makes laundry day quite simple, since our disparate sizes make it pretty obvious as to who owns what, and we don't have to sort and separate before we go to the Laundromat.

They stand there together. They stare. I stare. They stare some more. I wait.

"So what are you gonna say about us?" blurts Gerry, finally, moving ever so slightly further behind Randy as he does.

"I'm gonna write about how you two are the best roommates and landlords in the whole wide world," I answer. "And how my every moment with you has been special, and how the Treehouse is the most fantastic place that I could ever live, and how I owe all of my success as a writer, and a man, and a human being to the two of you."

"Wow, thanks, Collie!"

"Yeh, thanks. Wow. That's so cool!"

That satisfies them, for now, and as I turn back towards the computer they head down the hall to the living room to discuss this most excellent new development in their lives. As they disappear out of earshot, I hear them bantering already about who's going to get the most print, never once bothering to wonder who I'm writing this book for in the first place, nor whether it would ever be published. I guess they've seen that all the other stuff I've written has been printed in the *Advocate* or in the liner notes of Arctangent's albums, so they assume that this latest project will no doubt see the light of day too. Somewhere.

And, honestly, I'm not exactly sure why or for whom I'm writing this book, either. I think I'm doing it partially because I've been making (or supplementing) my living as a writer for almost two decades, and I feel like I should probably have something more to show for that work than a pile of old *Advocates* moldering upstairs. And I also think it's partially because writing is the only way that I can actually get some facts and my thoughts about them in order, then do something about them and (more importantly) begin to believe that they actually happened. To me, no less.

Because if I don't (or can't) write about something, then it's generally not real to me—and I've reached a point where I want my life and my history to feel real. Or at least I think I do. Although the numb, dissociated approach that I've maintained over the years, drifting in an alcoholic haze, safe here in the Treehouse (that's what we call the converted 120-year old office building in Troy, New York, where we live), has been pretty damn effective to date.

But something's changed (or broken, more likely) inside me since the accident, and since Kris (through her lawyers) tossed me out of her suddenly fractured life, and since the band bit the dust. Now I don't have anything external to focus on and control and worry about and blame when things go wrong.

Now I just go to work, and come home, and go to work, and come home, and talk to Randy, and talk to Gerry, and talk to Randy and Gerry, and go to work, and come home, and go to work, and come home. And drink. And then talk to Randy and Gerry some more. And then drink again until I pass out and start the whole cycle all over again. Home is certainly comfortable, I guess, and work is comfortable, too, or at least easy, and Randy and Gerry are pretty thoroughly innocuous, so there's nothing really driving me or motivating me to look outwards or upwards or forwards at this point. The way Kris once did. Or the band. Or even my desire to escape from Bridgefield, if I go way, way back.

And the problem with not having an external source of inspiration in my life is that I'm spending an awful lot of time living inside my head these days—and I'm not sure I like the landscape here. So I'm hoping that if I can reproduce my internal landscape on paper and make it real for somebody else, then it'll become their problem, their burden, their landscape. Or at least our shared landscape. I might not mind it as much if someone else lived here.

Gerry yells at me from the living room: "Are you gonna write about Lindy, Collie? Is she gonna be in the book, too?"

"Yes, Lindy will be in the book, too. But I doubt that she'll be in it as much as you guys are, y'know, since you're pretty important characters, right? If that's okay with you, I mean, of course. I can cut your parts back a bit if you want and put more of Lindy in there…"

Randy and Gerry protest in unison: "Oh, no, Collie…you can write about us all you want…that's great, man…no problem with giving us big parts…let us know if you need us to help you remember anything…"

Pause. Pause. Pause. They're very, very predictable at this point. Pause. Pause. Pause…and…now: "Can we tell Lindy about the book, Collie?"

"Yes, Randy, you can tell Lindy about the book. Although I doubt that she's gonna care a whole lot, since she's heard most of the details before."

The front door to our apartment slams and I hear Randy and Gerry clumping up the stairs to Lindy Andersson's place. Patience and respect for other people's privacy are not among their strong suits. Patience and a willingness to be intruded upon are, however, two of Lindy's finer points, which is why Gerry and Randy both adore her so much. And I think she's fond of them, too, at least in the way that most people are fond of their pets. Or disabled children.

Lindy has not only heard most of my stories, but she's getting paid for fixing, or at least minimizing the damage associated with a lot of them as well. She's an attorney, and a resident of one of the Treehouse's three finished fourth floor apartments, which are conveniently located as far away as possible from the band's former studio-cum-crash-pad space on the first floor, and a respectable distance from the second floor digs where Gerry and Randy and I still live.

Our building's third floor has remained empty storage space for years, buffering Randy and Gerry's paying tenants from the mayhem that defined the Treehouse's bottom two floors for years. Randy and Gerry call the third floor the DMZ, after the demilitarized zone that still divides Korea between the side that Junior once took bullets for and the side that put the bullets into him. I periodically hear them dragging things around up there, trying to figure out how to make the space productive, how to connect Upper Treehouse and Lower Treehouse with something more than the creaky stairway umbilicus that currently links Lindy and other loft livers past, present and yet-to-come to our own second-floor world.

I kind of like having the DMZ empty, though. Since the band's studio space is now defunct and equally empty, I've actually got a pretty quiet, insulated, isolated space here on the second floor within which I can think, write or wallow, as appropriate. I still find myself drawn to the studio every now and then, mainly out of force of habit, I suppose, although I also find it a most conducive location for working up a fine pathetic, drunken wasted evening alone. I may have to start drinking in the DMZ, sometimes, just to mix things up a bit and create new challenges for myself as I try to make it to bed at 2 AM.

Gerry and Randy live here on the second floor with me, of course, but they're pretty much background noise at this point, somewhat like plumbing or heat or hot water: I notice them only when they're gone, or when they're not working properly. I do have to give the pair of them credit though: they've been bastions of stability and predictability in a world that's been distressingly dynamic otherwise.

Randy and Gerry were the first people I met when I started work at Envirocorps in 1984. Well, other than the human resources drone who had hired me that spring at the South Carolina Military Institute Alumni Job Fair in Ulmer, South Carolina, and gave me my "welcome aboard" speech at the start of my first Monday morning on the job in Troy, New York. Then showed me to my cubicle. Then vanished, leaving me with a pile of forms to complete and company propaganda materials to read.

Dr. Ernest Jaberg, I learned from said materials, was a South Carolina native, South Carolina Military Institute graduate and onetime Naval officer who had come to Albany to work on his doctorate in the mid '70s, then somehow never left. He established Envirocorps in a "technology park" built between Troy and Albany during the early '80s, when any mom and pop research shop could get a defense contract or three if they wanted it badly enough.

Despite having forsaken the land of his forefathers (or maybe sick with guilt from having done so), Dr. Jaberg was more than happy to hire other South Carolina Military Institute alumni for his growing company, on the strength of our gaudy class rings alone. It's the sole benefit I can claim to have experienced as a result of the miserable four years I spent playing soldier at South Carolina's foremost military academy. Well, other than learning how to hide booze really well, that is.

Dr. Jaberg's misguided patronage was a good thing for me, indeed, since I don't think anyone else would have hired me based on my actual academic performance at the South Carolina Military Institute, nor on the skills I learned while working for Junior at his music shop in Bridgefield. I had gotten some of my writings published by that point, however, and did have a degree in English—so I could use those factors to justify Envirocorps hiring me as a technical writer when I needed to think I'd earned my job for self-respect reasons.

But self-respect was running pretty low that first day after the Envirocorps human resources rah-rah speech. Dumped in my new cubicle, I turned on my word processor and sat there, clueless as to what I was actually supposed to be doing now that I was officially employed as a technical writer. I certainly wasn't about to get up and go ask anyone, of course, lest I look stupider than I actually felt I was. I figured someone would find me eventually and tell me to do something. Then I would do it.

Until that time arrived, however, I amused myself by adjusting my swivel chair, arranging the pencils and paper in my desk, turning the word processor on and off a couple of times and organizing the books in my shelf, first by height, then by color. Then I used the Yellow Pages to find a nearby motel, since I wasn't going to go apartment shopping until the following weekend and would need a place to go after this grueling 9-to-5 day had wound down.

So this was what a real job was all about, huh? Color me underwhelmed. Not to mention itchy: as the day progressed, I appeared to be developing a rash around my neck and underarms and belt-line from the new cotton-poly blend Oxford shirt that I'd bought, but not washed, in Jersey City, New Jersey the day before.

Kris was living in Jersey City at the time, so I'd spent the weekend there with her before driving up to Envirocorps that morning. And I had other things on my mind besides the wash that weekend, if you know what I mean—although all things considered and with 20/20 hindsight I figure that Kris probably would've enjoyed my company more if we had just done my shirts together. We hadn't been together for a while, so there were needs to be addressed. My biological ones taking precedent over all others, of course.

Kris had relocated from Bridgefield to Jersey City the winter before I moved north myself, sucked along by the wake of her departure, liberated by a death in the family. She had taken a job as an elementary school music teacher there (just like the one she'd had in Bridgefield) and was moonlighting with a series of small ensembles and community orchestras in the hopes of breaking it large as a bassoon player in the Big Apple and places beyond.

I understood those dreams. I had had them myself once upon a time, and I think I might have moved north thinking that I could vicariously ride her success as a musician, and not have to do all the hard work myself. Plus I wanted to be closer to Kris, of course, so I know that directly contributed to my decision to head north to the sprawling Albany-Schenectady-Troy metropolitan complex some three hours north of New York City. Well, that and wanting to escape Bridgefield after my mother died, I mean.

The so-called "Capital Region" (named after Albany, which, contrary to popular belief, is indeed the capital of New York, Manhattan be damned) was too disjointed to really be considered a true single urban entity, perched as its component pieces were in various loosely-connected geographic nooks and crannies, all defined by and mapped in relation to the junction of the historic Hudson and Mohawk Rivers.

And, yes, that would be that Mohawk River, of "Drums Along" fame, and that Hudson River, as in Henry and *Half Moon* and Sleepy Hollow and West Point and tainted fish. And yes, that Albany, as in the Erie Canal to Buffalo with a mule named Sal. And, yes, even that Schenectady, the birthplace of General Electric and font thereby of Thomas Edison's greatest industrial inventions, not to mention the inspiration for Kurt Vonnegut, Jr.'s (barely) fictional Ilium, New York.

Or was that the equally oppressive Troy, some ten miles east of Schenectady? I can't remember, exactly. Or maybe it was even Troy's sallow suburb Cohoes, where everything dies and nothing go-rows, as the old-timers liked to sing? Hard to say, come to think of it, although even those twin industrial wastelands along the Hudson had history on their sides.

Troy, the so-called Collar City, had been the home of Sam Wilson, meatpacker and Uncle to All America—after some creative

Revolutionary War soldiers decreed that the "U.S." in "U.S. Beef" stamped on their dinners stood for "Uncle Sam." And Cohoes was the home to the Harmony Mills, the most oppressive 19th Century manufacturing facilities never to have been featured in a Charles Dickens novel. Probably because they were too grim to be believable.

Hell, "Yankee Doodle" was even written around here, down the road a spell in Rensselaer, and there's a monument to Benedict Arnold's leg up the road a bit in Saratoga. So there's lots of ghosts up here in the Capital Region. And lots of dying cities and towns and counties and hamlets and farms and businesses, too. Troy probably being the most abysmal of the lot, with block after block of abandoned or quasi-rehabilitated buildings and street after street of potholes and windblown trash.

It reminded me of Bridgefield after I-95 diverted all the coastal traffic out of town that way, only it was colder and a little bit less fishy-smelling. I'm not sure I could have chosen to make my home in any of the Capital Region's other communities for that very reason, although I didn't know that when I left Jersey City for my first day on my first new job at Envirocorps.

Why did I pick Envirocorps in the Troy suburbs, besides the fact that Dr. Jaberg would have me, and no one else would? Or so I thought? Well, like a typically geographically-ignorant Southerner, I had assumed when I took the job that since New York was right next door to New Jersey, Kris and I were going to be neighbors again. It was going to be just like back in the good old days in Bridgefield, I imagined, when she had first started frequenting Junior's Music after moving down from Columbia. Sunshine and lollipops, every day.

At the end of that first weekend as a Jersey City Counter-Carpetbagger, however, I discovered that Troy was a lot further away from North Jersey than I had reckoned. A couple of hours further, in fact: I had to maintain a steady 80 miles per hour up the Jersey Turnpike and New York State Thruway to even make it to work on time on Monday. Barely.

And for what? I spent most of that day just staring dumbly at my word processor, waiting for someone to tell me what to do, scratching, scared, tired, nervous—until I finally heard footsteps coming down the aisle that led to my end-unit cubicle. Now that the moment of contact approached, however, I didn't want it anymore. I quickly turned to my word processor and started typing gibberish—random words, quick brown foxes, qwerties—just so I'd look busy to whoever happened to be heading my way.

I had never really worked for anyone besides Junior, after all, and I was desperate to make a good first impression on my new bosses and coworkers. My heart first raced, then sunk into my stomach, as the footsteps indeed stopped at the entrance to my cubicle, behind me, where I couldn't see who was watching me, or why. All I could hear was breathing. And shuffling.

"What'cha writing?" a deep male voice asked.

It was the worst question possible, since I wasn't writing anything and didn't know enough about what I was supposed to be doing to come up with any sort of proper answer.

I turned to face my accuser, keeping my body between him and the word processor screen so he wouldn't be able to see what was, or wasn't, on it. He was huge, and ominous, and I had no idea who he was or why he was there. My eyes darted to the plastic nametag he wore around his neck, just like mine, except that his said "Randall Coates" where mine said "Hutson Hay." The name meant nothing to me. Yet.

"Oh, well, nothing really...I'm just trying to get used to this new machine," I stammered, trying to save face. "I haven't really used one of these kinds of word processors before, so I was just kinda teaching myself, trying to figure out how it worked..."

I nearly leapt out of my own skin when a second head popped around the edge of my cubicle's opening, at what seemed to be about half the altitude of Randall Coates' ponderous mug. "Randy and I can show you how to work it," the small person offered, helpfully, eagerly.

"Yeh, me and Gerry can pretty much work any of the machines here, so we can help you with that. No problem."

"We're engineers here. And we've been here a long time. We know these machines."

"We do all the design and development work that guys like you will be writing about in the tech manuals."

"That's what you are, right? A tech manual guy?"

I mumbled in the affirmative as both Randall Coates and his small sidekick (whose badge read "Gerald Mekeel") joined me in my cubicle, more than filling the available room, more than crowding my own personal space.

"Your books sure are arranged nicely," Gerry observed.

"Yeh, I wonder if Jamie did that before he left," seconded Randy. "It doesn't really seem like the kind of thing he would have done, but maybe he got bored or something on his last day and thought he'd leave it nice and neat for Hudson."

"Collie," I blurted. "My name's Collie. Collie Hay."

"But your nametag says 'Hudson' on it, just like the river we can see from our house," noted Gerry, bending close to get a proper look.

"No. No, it doesn't. No, actually my nametag says 'Hutson' on it, not 'Hudson'—and that's my real first name, although I haven't used it since I was a kid. I prefer to be called Collie."

Randy: "You mean like the dog?"

Gerry, now looking at Randy: "Why would he want to be named after a dog? Is that what he means? Like Lassie or something?"

"Yeah, that's kinda strange, isn't it?"

"Uh huh, pretty strange. I wonder why he wants us to call him that? Did he say?"

I was speechless as I watched Gerry and Randy engage in one of what I now know to be one of their favorite pastimes: talking to each other about me (or anyone else) as if I (or anyone else) weren't there.

They turned and looked at me again. Silent. Shuffling.

"So where do you live," Gerry asked, breaking the silence that I sure as hell wasn't about to.

"Well, I don't actually have a place yet, to tell you the truth," I answered, telling the truth. "I've just moved into the area from South Carolina and I stayed at my girlfriend's house in New Jersey over the weekend. So I was gonna stay at the Best Western in Troy for the rest of the week, then see if I could find an apartment next weekend..."

Both Gerry and Randy leaned still closer towards me, their eyes brightening, almost in unison: "We have a place!"

"Yeah, a really great place..."

"With lots of space..."

"And it's cheap..."

"And we can make it look however you want it to look..."

"Since we own it..."

"And that means it's ours to play with..."

"So wanna come look at it?"

"Tonight?"

How could I get these guys out of my office besides agreeing to let them teach me word processing and then take me to their mysterious affordable abode? I sat, amused and amazed, while the two of them explained the function keys on my hulking NBI word processor for an hour, two voices, two minds, working almost as one.

I was just starting to get use to their back-and-forth pace when they startled me by springing up at almost the same moment and announcing, to each other, "Quittin' time," then literally bounding from my cubicle in their haste to retrieve their lunchboxes and backpacks from theirs. I gathered my own belongings and followed them nervously to the parking lot, climbing into the back of their monstrous early '70s vintage Oldsmobile Land Yacht, outfitted with vanity plates that read: "NJINEAR."

It only took about ten minutes to make it from the Greenbush Technology Park where Envirocorps was located to the converted four-story River Street office building in Troy's derelict downtown that Randy and Gerry called home. I got the overall gist of their story during that first ride, although it took several years before I actually got all the details—and even longer before I actually believed it was real and not some elaborate put-on. It went something like this.

Randall Coates and Gerry Mekeel had grown up next door to each other in suburban Colonie, just over the Hudson River from Troy, flush against Albany's West Side in a wooded neighborhood where they built an ever-larger series of treehouses as their construction skills grew with their sizes. Or at least with Randy's size, since Gerry has, evidently, always been the much, much smaller of the two, although I've never heard either of them remark upon the gross disparity in their physical builds. I'm not sure that they've ever noticed.

Upon graduating from Colonie Central High School, both with honors, Randy and Gerry went to the State University at Albany together. They both choose to pursue the still-new environmental engineering curriculum there, since Randy's dad had suggested that might be a growth industry someday, now that the government was getting around to cleaning up the messes it had made back in the '50s and '60s.

When the weather was nice, Randy and Gerry would ride their bikes to class in the morning, then home to their parents' houses in the evening, often studying together at night in their last great treehouse, a three-story job in Gerry's backyard. In the winter-time, Gerry's and Randy's moms would take turn ferrying the pair to and from campus, with the caveat that they'd only make one run each way per day, making it essential that they continue keeping their schedules aligned.

After finishing college, they both got jobs at Envirocorps within the first year of the company's inception, since Mr. Jaberg needed actual engineers at that point, and not just other South Carolina Military Institute graduates with whom he could share his Ulmer reminiscences. Randy and Gerry worked with the chemists and field analysts at Envirocorps to design remediation, decontamination and disposal schemes for some of the nastiest material humanity has ever created. By all accounts, and by the awards that decorate the walls of their cubicles, they're very good at what they do.

A couple of years later, Gerry's dad softly suggested that his fully-grown (or at least of-legal-age) son should begin thinking about getting his own place, since the senior Mekeels were beginning to contemplate moving south to someplace warm. Gerry immediately reported this distressing new development to Randy, and over candlelight in the Coates' backyard that night, the two compared their checkbooks, tallied their sums and planned for their next great partnership. Seeing as how they had few hobbies besides treehouse building, shared no expensive vices and both lived at home with their parents, their combined getting-thrown-out-of-the-nest-egg was surprisingly hefty. Even to them.

Randy and Gerry looked at dozens of homes in and around Colonie, Albany, Troy, Schenectady and their environs, but nothing that their frustrated real estate agent showed them caught their fancy. And the realtor's failure was understandable, after all, since she was showing them houses—and what they actually wanted (although they didn't know it at the time) was a giant play space where they could hammer and build and cut and paint to their heart's content, without scaring the neighbors.

Fortunately, their realtor happened to drive down Troy's derelict River Street while taking Randy and Gerry home to Colonie from another failed house viewing up the road in Lansingburgh. When the pair saw the boarded up Victorian-era storefront with the "For Sale" sign on its door, their karma alarms jangled in synchrony to let them know that they'd finally found their home. All four floors of it. And all for less than they would have paid to get a bungalow one-tenth the size in the suburbs. They dubbed it the Treehouse, and they began to build in it.

It was still something of a disaster when I first visited in 1984, with only the three river-view apartments on the fourth floor having been restored and re-finished, while the first three floors were still seething with possibilities and vermin. Gerry and Randy each had their own apartments on the fourth floor—and they offered me the third for a good chunk less than I had planned to spend on housing, thereby giving me more money for alcohol and trips to Jersey City. That seemed good to me.

So we shook hands, drove back to the office to pick up my car (still stuffed with all my belongings) and returned to the Treehouse—without me ever signing a lease or making any other sort of binding declaration that I was going to establish my domicile there. I commuted from the Treehouse to Envirocorps with Gerry and Randy almost every day for the next six years—and never once paid them for gas. Hell, when I left the company in 1988 and couldn't afford to pay even my paltry share of the rent, they refurbished part of the second floor of the Treehouse and let me move down there with them for free, so they could rent out our nicer, upstairs, river-view apartments to higher-paying customers, one of whom was (and remains) Lindy Andersson.

While I was teasing them earlier tonight when I told them what I was going to write about them in this manuscript, they really are the best roommates and landlords that a guy could ever ask for. I should probably tell them that with a straight face some time, although I'm sure they'd be mortified if I did. Oh well. They can read it in the book.

Chapter Four

Since 1953, my father has been the proprietor of Junior's Music, Bridgefield's sole instrument and sheet music shop. His store has come to carry a sort of a mythical status in Bridgefield as one of those community institutions that's as much a part of the town's collective consciousness as are shrimp, the tides, saw grass, Spanish moss and chiggers. And mud.

I don't think Junior imagined himself as a future music maven, however, when he left Bridgefield to attend the South Carolina Military Institute in 1945, while Colonel was overseas kicking Nazi ass and plundering Eastern Europe with aplomb. Note well, please, that Junior didn't have any other alternatives when it came to choosing his college: male Hays, Colcocks and Hutsons went to the South Carolina Military Institute as a matter of course. Self included, even, many years later. Much to my chagrin.

Colonel (still known as Hutson, or more likely Huuuuuudson, at the time) graduated from the South Carolina Military Institute in 1926, spent four years as a provisioning officer in the Marine Corps, then returned home to work at (and later run, when his own father died) the small family pharmacy through the Great Depression. When World War II got hopping with gusto in the early '40s, Colonel took the first steps toward earning his ultimate nickname by patriotically re-enrolling in the military, this time being commissioned as a Major in the U.S. Army.

He spent most of 1943, 1944 and 1945 in North Africa and Europe, earning a field promotion to Lieutenant Colonel along the way and thereby finally claiming the moniker he'd never let go of, peacetime be damned.

Grandma ran the pharmacy while he was gone—and made sure that Junior did everything he needed to do to get himself into the South Carolina Military Institute as well, just like his daddy and his daddy's daddy and all the other daddies before him. Colonel finally came home in late 1945, halfway through Junior's freshman year at the South Carolina Military Institute, figuring that by doing his part to win the war to end all wars, he'd created a world where other Hays, Colcocks and Hutsons wouldn't need to leave Bridgefield to fight foreign wars, ever again.

He was right about most things, was Colonel, (or at least he thought he was)—but this wasn't one of them. Unrest in Korea sparked into full-bore Cold War ugliness shortly after Junior graduated from the South Carolina Military Institute and accepted his own commission in the United State Marine Corps in 1949. Twenty-four months later, First Lieutenant Hay was off accordingly to follow Lieutenant Colonel Hay's footsteps as Bridgefield's official community representative to the conflicts abroad.

As was the custom in those oh-so-chaste-and-innocent days, Junior took his longtime sweetheart, eighteen-year-old Emmeline Colcock Woodward (a third cousin, once removed up the Colcock vine), to the altar a week before he deployed for Asia in 1951. They honeymooned in Savannah (an hour south of Bridgefield)—and then pretty Emme, still seven years removed from being my Mama, stood on the rail platform in Yemassee, no doubt waving her already-ubiquitous cigarette, as Junior boarded the train that took him out of her life for the next two years. She moved into Colonel and Grandma's house later that week—and never moved again.

While Colonel managed to complete his own European Adventure with nary a scrape nor scratch to speak of and Junior managed to keep himself intact through most of his two-year tour in Korea, the Hay luck had clearly been over-extended by April, 1953. Junior was shot in the shoulder and thigh that month during the Battle at Old Baldy—and was subsequently scooped up by the North Koreans and held as a prisoner of war for three weeks. He received minimal medical treatment beyond stanching his bleeding during that time and was riddled with infection and delirious with fever by the time he was traded back to the U.N. team, like a bleeding sack of flour, in the aftermath of the so-called "little switch" negotiations at Panmunjon. Junior always resented the fact that he wasn't traded as part of a more important sounding P.O.W. negotiation.

It was another four months, most of it spent in a hospital in Guam, before Junior made his way back home to Colonel, Grandma and Mama, honorably discharged from the Marines and with a nice Purple Heart to show for his efforts. Colonel regularly taunted Junior for not being quick enough to dodge the bullets the way he had when he was teaching Hitler a thing or three about the American way—but I think deep down inside he was jealous of Junior's wounds and medal. Colonel may have felt like a hero, but Junior limped like one.

When Junior finally did make it home, he had unlimited access to the Naval Hospital at Beaufort for the ongoing therapy that he needed for his shoulder and leg, and he also had a nice severance package from Uncle Sam that would tide him and Mama over for a spell. He didn't have a job, however, nor many prospects for one in Bridgefield since Colonel had all the help he needed (which would have been none) at the increasingly anachronistic and deteriorating drug store he ran on Bay Street, dispensing the fixes for what ailed you, along with an ever-expanding series of war stories. He didn't really need the business, after all, since his reserve pay and, later, military pension paid most of the bills.

So Junior's prospects around Bridgefield looked dim—until Old Sterling Smoaks of Smoaks' Music died later that fall without heir, leaving his shop (conveniently located directly across the street from Colonel's Drugstore) and his inventory in the hands of the county's probate court. In a fit of brilliance and foresight at that point, Colonel (who had watched the Smoakses selling sheet music, player piano rolls and the instruments needed to use them for twenty years) convinced—no, make that ordered—Junior to use his severance check to acquire the music business, posthaste.

Which his obedient son did, aided by a grateful probate judge, getting the "Junior's Music" sign up just in time for the 1953 holiday rush. Never mind the fact that he and Mama didn't have a musical bone between them and had to rely on bluff and misdirection, rather than product demonstration, when it came to moving his stock for the first few years they owned the store.

But move stock they did. And move stock he still does: Junior is 72 years old now, and happy as an oyster in mud as he sells ukuleles, clarinets, banjos and the occasional piano (all of which he's learned to play over the years) to Coosawhatchie County's finest. He also still rents out the fleet of violins that have provided shrill, teeth-hurting power to Bridgefield's school orchestras for nearly 50 years now. I played one of those violins myself during my Calhoun Academy days, and even helped Junior manage the rental program for four years after wasting an equal amount of time myself at the South Carolina Military Institute. I'll tell you one thing: there's nothing more depressing that being a repo man who takes violins away from little girls.

Mama helped Junior in the shop from the day they opened until a few months before she died from throat cancer in 1984. She was only 51 at the time of her unfortunate demise—but she loved her Pall Mall's right up until the end, did Mama. When her situation turned critical, we had to be especially vigilant to make sure that someone turned off her oxygen before she flicked her Zippo and blew the house apart.

Chapter Five

The band's studio is pretty much empty these days, everything but tatters of soundproofing material gone, some of our equipment destroyed in the accident and never brought home, the rest sold to pay my debt to society (and Kris) afterwards. Or at least some small part of my debt to society (and Kris). Or at least some small part of the legal expenses that I owe Lindy for helping me pay some small part of my debt to society. And Kris.

Gerry and Randy built the studio from scratch shortly after I started playing with Arctangent in 1988, thrilled to have a project suitable for the former first-floor retail space that anchored the Treehouse to Troy. That's always been one of the nice things about living with such eager busy building beavers: I have but to complain about some Treehouse shortcoming and the solution will be built, as long as it is suitably time-consuming and poses formidable challenges to entertain my extra-energetic engineers. It also never hurts that Gerry and Randy's generally ascetic lifestyles mean that they have cash and time to burn. Lucky me!

Security upgrades went in first, including bars on the storefront windows, bolts on the doors and a double-sealed vestibule (we called it the airlock) that let tenants access the main stairwell to their apartments without having to pass through the studio itself. That way we could leave our equipment in our rehearsal space without overly tempting any unscrupulous upstairs visitors, not to mention the crack heads and

Coosawhatchie County's pre-eminent rice and indigo farmers, once upon a time.

The only Carolina rice I eat now comes from a box, and I wouldn't recognize a piece of indigo if it snuck up and bit me in the ass. But we did have that music store, by God, and everyone in Coosawhatchie County knew that the Bridgefield Hay's were the ones you needed to see when little Delmas and Henrietta came of fiddle-playing age.

Ironically, however, the sneered-at Hardees did us one better when they hit the Interstate Lottery Jackpot: I-95 was unexpectedly built right down the middle of Hardeeville, immediately killing the Low Country's old Coastal Highway towns (including Bridgefield) while sending the value of the Hardee family holdings through the roof. Last I heard, in fact, Dick Hardee was a club golf pro in Florida, living in the beach-front palace his parents bought when they sold their previously-valueless land to the gas station and fast-food mavens who arrived in Hardeeville on the heels of the highway.

He's still white trash, though. Always will be. And he's still named Dick, so I've got that on him. Because I'm Collie, dammit. Collie Hay. Of the Bridgefield, Coosawhatchie County, South Carolina Hays. Junior's Boy. Sister's brother. Greg and Ward's uncle, even if I don't know which one's which. That's me.

Only no one up here in New York, with the possible exceptions of Randy and Gerry and maybe Lindy, seems to care. I'm not even sure that I do anymore, to be honest.

still—since I can't imagine a world that doesn't include a Hay-owned music shop in Bridgefield. Fortunately, Sister and Greg and Ward seem content where they are, so the guilt I feel about my own abdication from the family business is softened by that. Somewhat.

With Junior in the instrument-selling trade, I've been surrounded by music literally since my birth in 1958—and I have to confess that I've always associated music with really bad smells. For most of my childhood, Junior's Music shared a parking lot and a common trash disposal area with the Gay Shrimp Company, whose still-flopping-fresh fare ensured that Junior's customers remained awash in fishy aromas (not to mention Mama's clouds of acrid smoke) throughout their visits to the store.

I guess I should note here that Gay Shrimp was not named after the sexual orientation of its products, but rather after the Gay family, scions of poor Peter and one of the few Bridgefield tribes with as much historical clout as the Hutsons, Colcocks and Hays. I remain eternally grateful that they managed to keep themselves away from my family's breeding stock for the most part, since I still have nightmares about what it would have been like if I'd had to live my life as Trey Gay Hay.

I do have some Hardee blood in me, however, making Dick Hardee and I second-or-so cousins, but we didn't much talk about that as kids. Or at least I didn't. The Hardees of Hardeeville, you see, weren't generally considered to have been cut from the same skein of social cloth with which Mama and Junior's antecedents had knitted their single-pattern family quilt.

I think that snub had something to do with the fact that the Hardee forefathers hadn't been slave holders back in South Carolina's glorious antebellum past, while the Hutsons, Colcocks, Gregories, Woodwards and Hays had trafficked in human misery with aplomb. Southern families have long memories—and it didn't matter if we lived in a tiny house in dying coastal town now, what mattered is who we'd been:

My most vivid memory of Mama to this day is of how she was constantly spitting out bits of tobacco that had escaped from the butt ends of her filterless cigarettes, compulsively flicking her tongue and leaving small brown flecks of wet leaf on everything we owned. If there's a smoker's lounge in heaven, I'm sure she's got a fine new celestial Zippo in her apron up there to replace the one I pocketed when she died, not to mention a cherub or two to clean up her tobacco flecks. Which would make her happy, since Sister and I sure as hell never wanted to do it while she was with us.

Sister has helped out in other ways, though. Junior can't hear all that well anymore, so she and her 20-year old twin sons help out around the shop and generally handle most interactions with the public while Junior joyfully hammers out demo songs on the instruments of his customers' choice.

Oh, and get this: mine own dear sister Sister, shackled herself with the name Woodward Gregorie Hay, dubbed her own sons Gregorie Colcock Hay and Woodward Colcock Hay. I guess since her own family-name names were unisex, she felt it easiest to just pass them on for another generation, no muss, no fuss, no learning how to spell anything new.

Seeing as how she wasn't married when they were born (and never has been since) and was still living with Mama and Junior, however, that might have been a politic decision, since unmarried mothers were still sorely frowned upon in polite Bridgefield society. Even then, at the peak of the pre-AIDS disco era when everyone else everywhere else in the world was boinking with gusto.

Sister calls her now-grown sons Greg and Ward, since she's already staked her own claim to the Wood part of Woodward's name. And I have to confess that I still can't tell them apart, unless I visit them at the store when they've got their Junior's Music nametags on. I often wonder if they're going to change the name to Sister's Music when Junior goes to meet his maker, and then Greg and Ward's Music sometime later homeless folks who drifted by outside our building, blown by winds that no one else could feel.

We could still raise the interior blinds on the former storefront window, however, and when the occasion seemed to dictate it, we used to draw them up and play for the groups of vagrants that parked on the stoops of our block's many abandoned buildings. Our impromptu audiences didn't usually last long after they realized we were watching them watching us, though. Too creepy, even by their standards, I guess.

The next major studio improvement came when we properly soundproofed the entire first floor after the owners of the porn theatre two buildings down complained about audible, inappropriate beats making things hard (or, uh, soft) for their clientele. Then a bit later I complained myself within Gerry and Randy's hearing about how hard it was to get our speaker cabinets and drums in and out of the airlock. Hey presto! They blew out the back wall of the studio and put in a loading dock, scavenging steel security doors and authentic-looking rubber truck bumpers from a derelict warehouse in Cohoes. Who was going to miss them?

I think Arctangent's lead guitarist (and in-house technical geek) Brian Wellington was the next to complain: We had no restaurants within easy striking distance and he hated having to walk upstairs to his fourth floor apartment to store or prepare food while he was working. The kitchenette went in next to the loading dock access door, posthaste. Then when the piss smell drifting in from the loading dock (the easiest source of relief after a long beer-fueled rehearsal) got to be unappetizing, our manager-syncophant-vampire Matt Lawrence suggested that Gerry and Randy put in a small half bath with a ventilation fan against the back of the airlock. And they did.

And it was good: we could dig in and get comfortable for long stretches of time, rehearsing, recording, not rehearsing, not recording, all of our basic human needs met until day jobs or gigs intruded to make us leave our cozy little creative cocoon. With our creature comforts amply taken care of, Randy and Gerry began working with Brian to acquire and refurbish and install all of the electronic mixing and recording gear that turned what was originally intended to be rehearsal space into a proper, fully functional recording studio and hangout.

We called it Treehouse Studios—and we let other people come in and record in what we considered to be our most excellent space, for a nominal fee, of course, typically paid in trade for booze or pot or porn or equipment swaps and upgrades. Brian would engineer most of those sessions, although he wanted cash for his services, given his relatively low level of addictive, illicit or distasteful habits. Not to mention the fact that he actually paid Gerry and Randy rent.

We produced the Arctangent single and albums at Treehouse Studios, too, Brian and I tweaking knobs between performances, Gerry and Randy basking in a second-hand glow of coolness-by-association unimaginable to most engineers, Matt yelling "Rock and roll!" after each take, then passing out beers that he hadn't paid for. When he wasn't regaling whatever women happened to be in attendance with life-on-the-road tales, that is, even though we never got much further than a day's van ride from Albany.

But never mind those details: Matt believed more firmly in the whole decadent rock and roll dream thing than did all the rest of us combined, despite the fact that he had absolutely no rock and roll talent, credibility or taste to speak of, leaching them from Arctangent instead. And since none of us were mean or smart enough to make him go away, we let him suck our souls, taking as much credit as we did for our work over the years, using whatever infamy we accrued to better effect than we could use it ourselves.

Matt was persistent, though, I do have to give him that—and it got to the point fairly early on in the game where it was much easier to let him do what he wanted than it was to argue with him. So he shlepped our boxes. And he helped to book our shows. And he copied our posters and stapled them on telephone poles. And he sold merchandise at our concerts. And he slept in the studio when he didn't feel like driving home to his apartment in Albany, sometimes for days on end. And he drove our van when we went on the road.

Or at least he drove our van when we went out on the road most of the time. Had he done it all the time, I might not be writing this cheery little memento pre-mori. Had he done it all the time, I might still have a band and a studio. But he didn't, and so here I sit, one accident later, in an empty room that looks astonishingly spacious to me now with all of the Arctangent detritus removed. It's almost hard for me to believe that when the gear and Arctangent and the booze and the collected Arctangent buddies and honeys were in here, we used to have trouble creating enough space to reproduce our stage set-up. It's hard to imagine so much life in such a dead room, although I guess it's easy to imagine so much room in such a dead life. Mine, I mean.

"Hey asshole!"

It was the doorbell to the airlock, rigged by Brian to offer a series of digitally-processed curses, insults and epithets when pushed from the outside, since a gentle "ding-dong" wasn't likely to get people's attention when they were punishing guitars or shredding vocal cords within the studio's confines. Brian had used tapes of Matt's always-too-loud voice as his original source material. And every time I hear them now, I make a mental note to myself that I need to get them turned off or replaced. Then I erase the mental note, since I know I'll never do anything about it.

"Balls! Balls! Balls!"

The doorbell again. I guess whoever was out there wasn't going to let me mope around in the studio with my laptop computer and my bottles of vodka and orange juice this evening, the way I'd planned to do, now that this week's *Advocate* had been put to bed and gone to print earlier in the afternoon. It had been a few days since I'd told Randy and Gerry that I was writing a book, so I figured that I might ought to get something down on the computer so I could tell them that I was making progress, just in case they asked. Which they would.

"I'm coming," I yelled, as I always did, despite the fact that when the room was soundproofed, no one could ever hear me do it. I wasn't sure if they could now or not.

"Okay, but hurry it up," a muffled female voice replied from beyond the airlock, quickly nipping one rhetorical question in the bud, just as the doorbell erupted three more times in quick succession: "Bite me, Larry Dickman! Jeez n' flippin' peas! Nice socks, bitch!"

I opened the inside door of the airlock and lifted the cover of the peephole into the vestibule beyond. Someone had their finger over the lens on the other side.

"Just a second," I sighed and opened the next door, figuring that if someone knew the peephole was there, they had either been in the studio before or were determined to kill me eventually whether I let them in now or not.

"'bout time, Collie…what are you doing in there? Unclean acts? Crimes against nature? Covering up the evidence?"

It was Lindy. She still had her work suit on and her ubiquitous monster-sized briefcase at her side, so she was obviously stopping to see me before making it up to her apartment for the evening.

"I saw the light on," she noted, gesturing at the red bulb above the door, which was connected to the studio's interior lights as a way of letting people know when we were inside. That was another thing I needed to change, but never would. "Move! Let me in! Scoot!" she barked, picking up her case and shouldering past me into the studio.

I stepped aside to let her pass, since she was almost as tall as I was in heels, was devoted to some particularly rigorous form of yoga, and could have actually done some serious damage had she felt like shouldering, or wielding her briefcase, aggressively.

She dropped her case in the middle of the studio, turned round slowly, soaking in the nothingness, the change, the anti-ambiance, eyes coming to rest on my bottle, my other bottle and my computer.

"So, really, what are you doing down here all by your lonesome?"

"I dunno, nothin', I guess," I stammered. "Just, y'know, hanging out. Remembering. Thinking. That kind of stuff. It's quiet down here."

"It's quiet in your apartment too, when Randy and Gerry aren't home," Lindy replied. "I think you're down here wallowing. That's what I think."

"Well, yeah, I guess you could call it that. I was going to try to do some writing tonight, so I thought this could provide a little change of pace, some fresh inspiration or something…"

"No, you're just wallowing," she cut me off. "And getting drunk. Right?"

"Well…"

"Right."

She picked up my laptop and turned the blank screen towards me. "Not much writing going on here tonight, now, is there."

"I just got started a little…"

"Mmm hmmm…so is your book in here?"

I knew that Gerry and Randy had told Lindy about the book, but I wasn't sure that I wanted to let on that I knew she knew about it. I figured that confessing would either evoke a sad head shake or a tongue-lashing, since Lindy was still representing me in the case of Dennison v. Hay, and the sorts of confessional drivel that I was typing could, should and would be held against me if anyone knew they existed.

"Uhh…which book?"

She looked up at me, pinning me with her sharp, wide, brilliant blue eyes, which through years of legal practice she had developed into her key instruments of psychological torment and surgical character incision. I couldn't look away from her. No one could.

"You have more than one book in here, Collie?"

"No, no, not more than one. Not even one, really. Just thoughts. Ideas. Y'know…maybe more like a diary or something, not really a book, just kinda…"

"Gerry and Randy seem to think that you're writing a book about Kris? Is that one of the ideas?"

"It could be, I guess. Maybe. Write what you know, right? That's what you're supposed to do when you start a book."

"So you are starting a book?"

I was trapped. "Uh, yeah, I am. I'm writing a book. I want to write about Kris and the accident, and I want to write about the Treehouse, and I want to write about Junior, my dad, while he's still around, since he's kind of an interesting old dude, despite himself. And Sister too. And the military college. All that stuff. That's what I think I want to write about. So I thought I'd come down here and think about it for a while. And, uh, that's all. I guess. That's all."

I always had a hard time knowing when to stop talking with Lindy. She was silent for a moment after I finally ran out of steam, still staring at me, watching my face, no doubt honing in on key tics or wrinkles or looks that could tell her whether I was lying or not. I didn't think I was, but I couldn't be sure until she let me know one way or the other.

"I think that's a good idea, Collie," she said, finally. And surprisingly. "I think you need something to focus your attention, particularly since we're going to be done with your, uh, shall we say, delicate legal situation soon. And who knows? You might make some money on it, and that certainly can't hurt, given the way things seem to heading resolution-wise at this point."

"Oh, well, thanks…"

"Wait a minute, Collie, I'm not done. I think it's a good idea with two caveats. First, it can't turn into a wallow. You need to productively process what happened to you, maybe even using this book as a way of closing that chapter on your life and starting a new one, clean slate, tabula rasa, right?"

"Um. Okay. And what's the second caveat?"

"The second caveat is that you need to start figuring out what that new chapter in your life is going to be about. I don't want to have you finish the book and the case, on top of having already finished off the band and your relationship with Kris, then not have anything else to fill the spaces on your psychic bookshelf where all those things used to sit. You've got to figure out the 'what's next' part, because I don't want you sitting down here getting drunk and writing a 300 page suicide note. You got me? Start working on that happy epilog, mister, right now, unless you just want me to send your undoubtedly guilt-ridden manuscript to the insurance company, who would be very happy and interested to read it, and then wash my hands of the whole thing."

Lindy reached down to pick up my half-empty bottle of Stolichnaya as she finished, swishing it about rhythmically, intently as if it were a laboratory specimen jar and she a Nobel-hungry research assistant. Then she jabbed it at me accusingly.

"It would be really nice if your happy epilog didn't include this, Collie," she said, her voice and her eyes softening slightly as I recoiled involuntarily, while also tensing to jump if she dropped or tossed the bottle. "Really. If you haven't figured out that you've got a drinking problem after all you've been through, then maybe you really are as stupid and irredeemable as Kris and her family and their lawyers think you are."

I reached out to take the bottle from Lindy and set it down carefully on the floor against the wall. "So what do you think, Lindy?" I turned to face her, liquor safe for the moment from her hands, shoes, bag, wrath. "Do you think I'm stupid and irredeemable?"

"I wouldn't be representing you if I did, now, would I?" She retrieved her briefcase and headed for the airlock. "And we probably wouldn't have lasted as way-too-close neighbors all these years, would we, if I thought you were stupid and irredeemable? And I wouldn't be here talking to you now, would I, if I thought that?"

"You might be," I shot back, petulantly. "I'm a paying client, after all, so you've got to talk to me sometimes…but are we going to talk when the case is over?"

"Of course we are, Collie, although I'd suggest you not get up on your high horse about paying me, seeing as how you couldn't begin to afford me if I didn't want you to be able to. And seeing as how you haven't actually paid me anything yet anyway."

"You haven't won the case yet."

"And I'm not going to, you know that. I'm working to minimize the damage. Your damage. You can't win here. You lost a long time ago. But I'm still talking to you. And I'll still talk to you when I don't have to do so, as long as you're not wallowing. Or drunk. Or dead. We talked before you screwed up, so there's no reason to stop doing so afterwards. You didn't break my neck, after all, so I've got nothing to be mad at you about. Kris has got the rights on that locked up."

"Thanks a lot, that's very encouraging, Lindy."

"Hey, just the facts, man," she answered, in the airlock now. "You gonna stay down here and wallow and drink or are you going to help me get this briefcase up to the fourth floor?"

I picked up my laptop and started to retrieve my vodka and orange juice, but figured that it might be best to leave them where they were, sneaking back down later to get them when Lindy wasn't watching me.

"I'm coming up, now, I guess," I answered. "Gerry and Randy should be home soon and they're gonna come looking for me anyway, so I guess I may as well save 'em a trip back down the stairs."

"Okay. Here, take this. My feet are killing me and I don't feel like hauling it all the way up to North Korea. I need to complain about the stairs more, don't I? If I'm going to get Randy and Gerry to put in an elevator, I mean."

I took Lindy's case and followed her up three narrow flights of stairs, past the entrance to Chateau Gerry and Randy and Collie, past the door to the DMZ, up to the landing of the fourth floor where the Treehouse

Tenants lived. Lindy had the last apartment in the hall, the one that Gerry had lived in, way back when, although it wasn't recognizable anymore as his onetime snake ranch.

Dave McCormick, a dentist, lived in the middle apartment these days, a quiet guy and, we hoped, a harbinger of things to come in Troy: Randy was convinced that a dead city was definitely on the road to urban recovery when the dentists started moving back in. The first apartment right at the top of the stairs, on the other hand, was empty at this point: Brian had moved out when I started taking the studio apart. Randy was keeping the space open, holding out for another dentist.

Lindy unlocked her door, letting the scent of patchouli and god knows what other burning roots and leaves and oils drift out into the hallway. I set her case down inside her doorway and turned back down the hall. She called to me as I reached the top of the stairs.

"Collie?"

"Hmm?"

"Keep me posted on that happy epilog thing, okay?"

"Sure. It'll have to include a lawyer somewhere, I think, knowing me as well as I do and everything. Just in case you're interested, I mean."

"Only if you pay your bills this time and quit wallowing so damn much. But thanks for carrying the bag up. I'll talk to you soon."

"'kay. 'bye."

"'bye."

Her door closed. I headed back downstairs to see if I could cajole Randy or Gerry into making me some dinner. After I retrieved my vodka and orange juice.

Chapter Six

"Boy, I'm just glad that Colonel isn't here with us in the flesh to hear the blasphemous way you're talking right now," thundered Junior, in full Old Testament prophet-styled rage, slamming his fist on the checkered linoleum table in our kitchen, making Mama's mason jar ashtray jump with each concussion. "Although I keep expectin' him to strike you down where you sit from all the way up on high in his heavenly home…and I wouldn't blame him right now if he did, God rest his soul!"

My offense? I had suggested that Junior's beloved South Carolina Military Institute might not be the right college for me, seeing as how I wanted to be a musician or a writer or some other artsy thing. And seeing as how I wasn't at all interested in anything involving the guns, uniforms and short-haired, shouting men that defined life at a military college.

Which was putting it mildly for Junior's sake: I was actually somewhere quite beyond horrified at the thought of entering that rigidly conservative all-male institution after finishing up my secondary education in Bridgefield. I always had been adverse to such a course of action. I'd always said that I wasn't interested in the Institute accordingly. To Sister, to my friends, to everyone. Well, everyone except for Junior, that is, who had always been equally assured that I was going to his alma mater, and that he would be proud of me when I did.

Junior had been planning my future, as he saw it, for years—and I had never spoken back nor argued until that afternoon in the kitchen. I had wanted to tell him, mind you, for years: each time I caught sight of Junior's scars, in fact, I had contemplated telling him that I wanted nothing to do with the military school that had prepared him to star in a Korean turkey shoot. But I never mustered the courage that I needed to express that sentiment audibly—until I was overcome by the tantalizing reports of disco debauchery that had begun to reach the Low Country during my junior year at Calhoun Academy in 1974 and 1975.

My friends and I picked up on most of those decadent reports while loitering with bad intent over on Hilton Head Island, where all the beautiful rich played with each other (and sometimes with us) just down the coast a spell from Bridgefield. Well, geographically just down the coast, at least, since from a sociological standpoint, Hilton Head was actually light years removed from our little cultural wasteland there in the marsh. But the high society tidbits that I had overheard or (on lucky days) shared there steeled me with a firm resolve to get my slice of the hedonism that seemed to define the jet set world of the mid-'70s.

And what wasn't to love about all of that for a 17-year old boy? Loose women, plentiful pot, cheap cocaine, an endless gush of gin and tonics, sleeping all day, partying all night, writing the great American novel in my spare time, playing bass guitar with my musical heroes, Larry Graham and Verdine White and Bootsy Collins? Sign me up for that, right now, please!

Towards that nefarious end, I had surreptitiously sent off requests for information over the preceding six months to New York University, Manhattan College, Hunter College, Iona and half a dozen other schools in the New York metropolitan area. I figured if I could get admission to one of those fine institutions of higher learning, then that would put me right at the heart of the action in the Big Apple, where writers and musicians could be all that they could be, and more. My targeted arrival date was excitingly serendipitous, too, as I would be heading off for college during the bicentennial summer of '76, when New York City would be rocking with an entire planet's worth of party people, flown in special for the occasion.

The way I saw it, all the Hilton Head people would undoubtedly be there then, too, trading in the Low Country's summer swelter for the dark, cool cocktail lounges that dotted the Village (in my mind) or for the elegant torpor of the City's all-night discotheques. They'd recognize me, no doubt, and invite me into their new northerly world, sharing their secrets, their speed, their style, their sex. That's what I wanted. That was the future according to Collie.

But I couldn't tell Junior all that while rejecting the future he had planned for me. So I just stuck to my guns about wanting to be a writer or a musician, and not seeing the Military Institute as the best place to prepare me for such a career. He wasn't buying it.

"It don't matter what you want to be when you grow up, Boy," Junior countered as I fanned my collection of New York City-based college brochures out on the table. "You can be any damn thing you choose, once you got the education that you're gonna get at the Institute. Good Lord in heaven, look at me...I thank my Maker every morning for the gift of character and morality that I was given in Ulmer, 'cause that's what's made me such a successful businessman all these years. Colonel, too, may he sing with the angels, he was the best pharmacist you could ever want to have pourin' your pills, and he learned all that he needed to know about runnin' that drugstore at the Institute."

"Then how come he had to get that mail-order pill-pushin' degree when his daddy died and he took over the store?" I counter-countered, in my best surly teen voice. "And how come he had to go to that Marine Corps logistics school after he graduated from the Institute? And how come he had to back to school again when he rejoined the Army before the War? How come he didn't get all that information at the Institute? What good was the Institute if he had to go get all that other education so he could do his job and earn his keep?"

Junior was beet red by this point, trembling with apoplexy, eyes pointed upward at the kitchen's ceiling tiles, speaking to the dead. "Colonel, I hope you'll find it in your heart to forgive this stupid, stupid Boy for his disrespect and ignorance," he intoned. "He's jus' overcome with the heat of youth and doesn't know what he's sayin'. He's a good Boy, I know he is, in his heart, and I pray that you'll he'p me have the strength to show him the error of his ways. He'p me, Colonel, he'p me he'p him to understan' that his callin' is to follow in his daddy's footsteps, and in the footsteps of his daddy's daddy before him. Give me strength, Colonel. Lord knows I'm gonna need it with this one..."

Junior hadn't always prayed to Colonel. There was a time when a litany such as this one would have been made to our Lord Jesus Christ, the only begotten Son of God, our friend and Savior who walks with the angels and who's coming soon to take us all home, hallelujah! (That's how old Preacher Benson at the Pocotaligo River Baptist Church always referred to God's Boy, anyway, in a single high-speed stream of praise, faith and prophecy). But ever since Colonel had gone to the great barracks in the sky in 1973, Junior had taken to invoking his biological father's benevolence whenever he needed guidance from above. I guess he figured Colonel probably had less to do than the Creator of the Universe, and so was more likely to get involved in our day-to-day lives.

"Now you listen to me, Boy," said Junior, finished now with the spirits, but just starting in with me. "You know me an' Mama haven't been able to save the kinda money we need to pay for your college ourselves, seein' as how we've had to put all our spare cash into gettin' you and Sister educated right down there at Calhoun all these years."

(Unlike the nation's real service academies at West Point, Annapolis and Colorado Springs, the South Carolina Military Institute and its equally anachronistic sister school, the Virginia Military Academy, charged students for the privilege of torturing them. A good number of the cadets at those schools got free rides on R.O.T.C. scholarships, of course, but those scholarships came with related real military service tenures that I wasn't about to buy into—so I never applied for them, telling Junior my grades weren't good enough to do so.)

"I had hoped once 'pon a time that you'd do well enough in school to get one of them 'rot-sie' scholarships to use at the Institute," Junior continued. "But me an' you both know that ain't likely to happen in this lifetime, given your work habits…"

"I try as hard as I can," I protested, reacting strongly (as I always did) whenever Junior questioned my work ethic. Even if he was right. And even if I was the one who had intentionally scuttled any likelihood of earning the one of the coveted R.O.T.C. scholarships. "It's awful hard for me to do good at school, and help you with the store, and help Mama around the house, and do the school newspaper, and practice the bass…"

"Well, which one o' those seems like the one you shoulda dropped along the way, huh? That seems like a pretty obvious choice to me: if you gotta put down the bass guitar to get your grades up, I'd say that'd be a pretty fine investment in your future, don'tcha think?"

"You're the one that gave me the bass," I sulked. "I thought you wanted me to practice it."

"Yes I did and yes I do, and you may make a fine player some day—but it ain't gonna get you into the Institute or any other college, and that's what we're talkin' about today, ain't it? Don't go tryin' to change the subject on me, Boy, I'm too smart for you to do that, sure as eggs is eggs," Junior declaimed, hitting the kitchen table again for emphasis.

"So now you listen to me and you listen to me good," he continued, then once again turned his gaze heavenward. "And you hear my words, too, Colonel, you be my witness as I tell this ungrateful Boy how you've provided for him in your infinite wisdom and mercy. Same way you provided for me when I was a worthless boy myself, savin' up money through the Depression, sendin' home your soldier's battlefield pay so I could go to the Institute, just like you did, yes. An' same way you provided for me when I came home all broken and beaten from Korea.

There you were, prayin' to the Lord for wisdom, askin' Him to take care of me, watchin' Him take ol' Sterling Smoaks 'cross the River Jordan and leavin' the music store behind. You prayed for it! You saw it! You knew the Lord had provided an' answered your prayers for me! Holy providence! Blessed assurance! Amazing grace, how sweet the sound!"

Junior had worked himself into full evangelical lather by this point—and I've got to admit that he was pretty damn good and entertaining once he got going this way. He had picked up most of his style points from having watched Preacher Benson delivering the goods just about every Sunday for as long as I (or he) could remember. And while I know that Junior always envied that great Southern orator's command of both the English language and the mysteries of faith, I think that the Preacher himself would've approved of Junior's impromptu sermon that day. He was certainly getting my attention, I can assure you, and as he raved I carefully began to retrieve my offensive college brochures from the table, one by one, before Mama's cigarette jar spilled all over them.

"Colonel provided for us all his life, you spoiled, undeserving Boy," Junior continued. "And he's provided for you even in his death, bless his merciful soul in its heavenly home. You want to know how he did it, Boy? You want me to tell you what Colonel's done for you, so you can know what you're throwin' back in my face when you tell me you don't want to go to the Institute? An' all 'cause those little tittie girls that you like chasin' around Hilton Head don't go for the real men up there? Oh! Oh yeah! You surprised I know that, ain'tcha? You think I don't see right through you, you filthy Boy, you? I ain't as dumb as I look, now am I?"

I stifled the urge to answer "You can't be" and nodded sorrowfully, but by this time (and despite myself) I was actually mildly intrigued to learn how Colonel was providing for me from the great beyond, without me even knowing about it.

"So here's what you're turning your filthy, ungrateful, yellow back on, Boy 'o mine. If you are a Boy 'o mine, that is. Days like this could make me wonder about that, if your Mama wasn't the good an' faithful woman that she was, bless her heart," said Junior, lowering his voice for emphasis just as he lowered his body onto the chair across from mine, never once taking his eyes from mine.

"You remember when Colonel died and them people from Eckerds came and said they wanted to buy out his drugstore? Well, I wasn't about to give it to 'em, I was gonna fight to keep that store for the family—although I didn't know how I was gonna pay for all the repairs that old building needed, no sir. But then it occurred to me that the cash they was offerin' to jus' shut the bid'ness and knock down the building so's they could corner all'a Bridgefield's pill bid'ness was plenty 'nuff to cover the cost of four years worth o' schoolin' at the Institute. Plus some spendin' money for you while's you was there. And a li'l plum for me an' Mama to retire 'pon. And somethin' for Sister, too.

"So I took that money, I did. I let the store go an' I got the money we made from Colonel's lifetime o' hard work and sweat set aside, jus' so you can go to Ulmer and make a man o' y'se'f. And you gonna tell me you don't want that? Well, lemme tell you, Boy: That dog don't hunt. Not in these woods, he don't." He threw his hands heavenward for emphasis. "Thank you, Colonel!"

And then Junior sat back, spent. And I was speechless, although less from amazement at this revelation than from a vague disappointment at the story's anticlimax. I mean, that was it? Colonel died so that the people from Eckerds could send me to Junior's favorite college? That was Colonel's divine providence, his amazing grace, how sweet the sound, to save a wretch like me? It seemed a bit too convenient a story, especially since I knew that the pharmacy had been pretty much useless by the time Junior sold it—relieved that he'd been able to do so.

"Ah, c'mon, Junior, that's just a coincidence about the money n' everything," I finally blurted. "I mean, how come it ain't all for Sister to go to College somewhere? She hasn't got any money either, and she's 21 years old, and she's still livin' with you and Mama. How come it ain't for her to go to college, huh? Why does it have to be me? And why does it have to be the Institute..."

Junior lunged across the table and grabbed the skin under my chin with his long, wiry fingers, made strong by years of demonstrating musical instruments at the store. He pinched. Hard.

"Owww.... let go...you're hurtin' me..."

"Not nearly as bad as you're hurtin' my heart, Boy," Junior cut me off, pinching harder. "I can't believe you're talkin' to me this way. I can't believe you're talkin' about Colonel the way you are. So lemme make this all real simple for you, okay? Then you can tell me that you understand, and I might let you keep my name if you do that. 'cause otherwise I might have to smack the Hudson Colcock Hay right out of you, an' I don't really wanna do that, at least not today."

Junior paused, rearranging his fingers to get a better grip underneath my chin. My eyes were watering with a combination of pain and indignation by this point. "Here's how it goes. Sister's a girl. Sister don't need to go to college. Sister's gonna stay here and he'p me in the store, and she's gonna be happy to do it," Junior continued. "I got a big ol' bank account fulla money, though, and it's got your name written on it, and it's got 'South Carolina Military Institute' written on it. But if your name and 'South Carolina Military Institute' don't ever end up on a certain sheet o' paper together, then me n' Mama are gonna put ourselves a fat deposit down on a nice new little two-bedroom house that ain't gonna have no room in it for an ungrateful Boy.

"So here's the punchline, in case you haven't been able to tell that it's comin'," Junior concluded, flicking dismissively at the last brochure I had left on the table with his free hand. "There ain't no money in my bank account that's gonna get sent to no Hunter College, so if you want me payin' your way after you graduate from Calhoun, then you're gonna go to the Institute. Jus' the way I did. Jus' the way Colonel did. Jus' the way the Hays and Hutsons and Colcocks have done as long as there's been an Institute. It's what we do. It's what makes us what we are.

An' you can be a music salesman or a writer or a drugstore clerk or a bum, for all I care, after you get done there. But you ain't gettin' my blessin' for any of it unless you're gonna be a man and put on a uniform for four years and do us all proud."

Junior let me go. I collected my brochures, stood up and turned to leave the kitchen, figuring there was nothing left to be said by either one of us. I was wrong.

"Boy?"

"Sir?"

"You'll thank me for this some day, you gotta trust me on that, alright? Me n' yer Mama jus' want what's best for you—and hard as it is for y' to b'lieve, sometimes we knows more'n you do about what's gon' work an' what ain't. The Institute'll work for you, Boy. Ain't no Hunter College gonna do that. Y' un'erstan' what I'm sayin'?"

"Yes, sir, I understand. Thank you."

I mulled over the possibilities of how Hunter College could have worked for me, Junior aside, as I walked down the hall to my room, tossed my collection of brochures in the trash and accepted the inevitable: I was going to go to the South Carolina Military Institute in Ulmer. It's what us Hays did. And who was I to make a choice for myself when it came to an important family matter like this? Nobody, that's who.

Of course, this sudden change of events-yet-to-be was going to require another bit of creative self-redefinition, since I'd acted throughout my adolescence as though I were going to be a famous writing musician. Or a famous music writer. Or something else involving those two things that came most easily to me, those two reflexive behaviors that other folks generally recognized as my sole legitimate talents—which was fortunate, given that I wasn't much good at schoolwork, sports or physical labor.

My musical talent seems obviously preordained, I know, given that I virtually grew up in a music store. I never took lessons, but I always had my hands on the keyboards and guitars and violins and whatnots that Junior sold or leased, and I've always generally been able to make decent, pleasant, harmonious sounds on just about any instrument. Except for Kris' bassoon, that is. I never could get that double reed thing to work for me, and somehow it never felt right to me to be producing such a big, deep sound while straining to blow through such a little, tiny orifice. Kris made it look effortless, though, no strain, no pain as she produced beautiful, mournful, deep and resonant notes that seemed to emerge from the space around her as much as they did from her instrument.

I wasn't much interested in beautiful and mournful when I was a teenager, though—although I did like the deep and resonant bit. Watching Junior's customers over the years, I realized that almost every adolescent boy who entered the store, intent on getting his first instrument and starting his first band, purchased a guitar. And those who didn't buy guitars purchased drums. And those who couldn't afford drums bought microphones.

The bass guitar, on the other hand, was an instrument that seldom sold at Junior's Music, since it just didn't seem to have the babe-magnet appeal that its six-string treble counterpart enjoyed. And that anti-bass prejudice had an impact on the young bands in Bridgefield, as it does to this day in most American towns where rock stardom or athletic success seem to be the only ways to escape the dreaded curse of the fathers and the fathers' fathers before them. Every town in America—small, large, mid-sized, whatever—has got its share of those young bands, whether you're seeing or hearing them or not, since music is a far more egalitarian, easy to conquer pastime than varsity football and basketball and baseball are for most needy teenaged boys.

So almost all of those needy teenaged Bridgefield boys wanted to be Jimmy Page or John Bonham or Robert Plant when they grew up, while none of them wanted to play John Paul Jones. And as a result, most of Bridgefield's garage bands (or actually carport bands, since most houses in our town didn't have enclosed garages) played "Freebird" or

"Satisfaction" or "Whole Lotta Love" out of a multiple-guitar-plus-drums line-up, with the guy with the best hair screaming into a cheap microphone piped through a guitar amp.

If there was a bass player in a teenaged Bridgefield band, then he was the generally the worst guitar player who had been demoted, beneath even the dreaded "rhythm guitar" spot. Next step: out of the band completely. Or lyricist, if he was really desperate. And that totally guitar-centric worldview made it hard to make a name for yourself in Bridgefield's high school musical pantheon with an electric six-string accordingly, since the supply of teenaged guitarists far outweighed the demand for their services. You were unlikely to graduate from your carport to paying (or at least public) gigs unless you had some pretty awesome skills accordingly.

So in a fit of prescience, I picked up a bass guitar in the store when I was about 13, practiced it until I actually got good and started marketing myself to the older boys who regularly visited to ogle the latest model guitars and amps. I borrowed instruments from the store for a couple of years, until Junior bought me (or opted not to sell to someone else) a Fender Jazz Master as a Sweet Sixteenth birthday present. And it was a sweet instrument indeed, one that served me well until it was destroyed in the accident many years later, along with the musical careers of both Kris and Arctangent.

But long before Arctangent was making its minor mark with crazy industrial progressive rock sounds, most of Bridgefield's bands simply played refried Southern boogie rock or good-timey beach music when asked to perform at a party or school dance. So I learned that stuff just so I could fit in and get gigs and played regularly with a series of evolving (or devolving) high school bands right up until the time that I shaved my head and was sworn in at the Institute.

My real musical love back then when it came to the bass, however, was for the hard funk sounds being laid down by the likes of the Family Stone's Larry Graham, Earth, Wind and Fire's Verdine White and

Funkadelic's Bootsy Collins and Billy "Bass" Nelson. Had I attended Bridgefield's public schools, I might have been able to do something with the techniques I copped from those funk bass masters—although my whitebread peers at the Calhoun Academy were less than interested in exploring music made by or for the minority community in and around Bridgefield. Never mind that there were more of them than there were of us. And never mind that their music was better than ours was, too.

Playing the bass in public also opened many doors that I didn't even know how to knock upon prior to choosing an instrument. Chicks did indeed dig the boys in the band, and I lost my virginity after playing at a backyard bash when I was 14, succumbing to the wiles and whims of an older public school girl named Cindy Clark, who I knew vaguely from the Baptist Church's Youth Fellowship Group.

We got to know each other much better over the ensuing three years, however, before she ran off suddenly with a Marine Private (First Class), fresh out of boot camp, just a month of so before Junior shot me out of the saddle with the formal Institute proclamation. It was a tough summer, all the way around, that one was.

Cindy was a tall, spindly blonde with thick glasses and the sharpest cheek and hip bones I've ever encountered, even to this day, despite many, many opportunities to discover other more pointed ones over the years. I liked her angularity, the fact that it hurt when you bumped into her the wrong way. It made her seem dangerous. And hard. And her personality was suitably sharp as well: she refused to ever be publicly associated with me, a Calhoun Boy, and a younger one at that, and she publicly taunted me whenever the opportunity arose, never touching me with an audience about, never acknowledging my piteous puppy-dog stares.

But we got along just swell in private, thank you, where our needs more readily dovetailed and where social status—or the lack thereof—was no impediment at all to lust, true lust, just lust. Our dirty passion was fairly well hidden to all and sundry, since to most outside observers, Cindy and I actually both got increasingly pious and religious over the ensuing three years, neither of us ever missing a weekly Youth Group meeting at the Church.

But that was because we referred to (and treated) those seemingly innocuous meetings as "Youth Gropes"—and we became increasingly reliant upon them as we became increasingly enslaved to and dependent upon each other's bodies. The Youth Gropes ended around 9 PM every Sunday night, and when they were done, Cindy and I regularly coupled in parking lots, bushes and backyards all around town, occasionally even defiling the Pocataligo River Baptist Church's choir loft with our unclean desires. Nothing's more exciting than a secret, now, is it?

So I used Cindy for sex and Cindy used me for sex, although she could have gotten that from most anyone else in town, and with people that she wouldn't have minded being seen with in public even. Why did she stick with me, then? Well, I actually attribute the duration of our not-a-relationship relationship (three years is an eternity when you're a teen) to the fact that sex wasn't the only addictive thing that I was able to offer her.

Bridgefield's better bands (of which I was typically a member, being the only legitimate bass player in town) were generally able to acquire hefty quantities of mind-altering substances, both licit and illicit. Hilton Head was the chief local font for marijuana and cocaine and speed, while most of the clerks at the town's liquor store were happy to sell us all the beer and booze we wanted, seeing as how boys would be boys and all that.

The liquor stores did make us pay for their wares—as opposed to giving them away, the way they did for the football players—but we could generally keep ourselves in comfortable cash by reselling the drugs we scored or stole from the rich folks on Hilton Head. Surprised? Most people are when I tell them this, although I'm always counter-amazed at how most people think small towns are free from such urban scourges as drugs, alcohol and promiscuity. I mean, what else were we going to do if not those things? What else could we do? Small towns get dull without hallucinogens and breasts, after all.

And Cindy had breasts, and I had hallucinogens, so we kept ourselves mutually amused when we were together, each one satisfying the other's desires, whatever they might be. I often wonder what that Marine Corps Boot had to offer, accordingly, since enlisted men didn't generally have much money, and drugs were frowned upon in the Corps, even then. I suppose it may have been that Private Jarhead had a ticket out of Bridgefield for her, something that Cindy may have realized I didn't have at that point. Not that I'm bitter about it or anything. Much. But who lives in New York now, huh, Cindy? Not you.

So that was the life of Collie for most of my high school years. I smoked pot behind the gym, I played funk in my bedroom, I screwed Cindy in secret every Sunday and I dreamed of making it big someday by slinging my bass and singing the lyrics that had begun to fill my handwritten journals.

Some of those lyrics were actually published in the Calhoun Academy *Chronicle*, our school's in-house newspaper. I wrote for the *Chronicle* regularly and served as features editor during both my junior and senior years, putting myself into it with gusto after my English teacher, Mrs. Richardson, made a point of telling Junior and Mama what a fine writer she thought I was. Anything that was easy for me to do at school and that would win me good son points at home was a no-brainer, right? Plus, I figured that if the bass thing didn't play out, I could be a Pulitzer Prize winner instead. And while I didn't have much time to study anymore, no, I knew that it didn't matter, since I wasn't going to need good grades in algebra to be a respected writer or a famous bass player anyway.

Until Junior slammed the door in the face of my dreams while sitting across from me at the kitchen table during that horrible summer afternoon in '75. I mean, my entire public persona (well, for everyone except

Junior) was irrevocably altered at that point, since there was no good way to market myself as a cultural rabble-rouser while applying to (and eventually getting accepted by) the most conservative school in the state, if not the nation. I could have set out on my own, yes, defying my old man and making my own way at a school of my own choosing—but I knew I didn't have the heart or spine or soul to do it. Not to mention the resources.

So I knew I had but one more year to play the bass, to write, to find a new girl to screw, to smoke, to drink, to live, when you got right down to it. And I did those things with gusto my senior year accordingly, although my adventures all came with a whiff of hypocrisy, to others and to me, given the way we all knew they were going to end. Many of my longtime loser friends began to drift away from me that year, in fact, as I drifted ever closer to a date with orthodoxy and respectability. Rats can always tell when a ship's going down, after all, hitting the waves and swimming for safety long before they can be pulled down by the suction of the cracked hull as it spirals downward into oblivion.

And so it was that Collie Hay, rock star and writer, was fatally wounded on the linoleum kitchen table in Bridgefield, stabbed soundly by Junior with a poisoned knife of Colonel's making. The would-be cultural provocateur died one year later, finally polished off with a set of electric hair clippers in early July 1976, when instead of watching the tall ships sail into Manhattan, young Collie Hay passed through the portal of South Carolina's most esteemed military academy, head shaved bald.

I never would have imagined then that I would have been stupid (or strong) enough to revive that lost rock star and writer many years later and a thousand miles away. In New York, no less, but not in the City that bears the Empire State's name.

I never was good with that kind of detail stuff, though. Even the Institute couldn't change that.

Chapter Seven

My publisher, Anna Salocks, is perkier and more wound-up than usual as she opens the *Advocate*'s weekly editorial staff meeting at 10 AM sharp, too early in the morning on the day after Lindy gave me my happy ending epilog ultimatum in the studio.

"Okay, peoples, if I can have your attention for a couple of minutes before we get deep into editorializing, I've got a special little announcement to make today," she says, flipping her short blonde hair compulsively and waving her nail-bitten hands in the air, gesturing at the five unresponsive editorial staff members gathered around her conference table. "Listen up, listen up, listen up!"

I avert my eyes, sip my coffee and pretend Anna's talking to someone else. I'm not feeling all that well this morning, having stayed up late writing and drinking and wallowing last night, Lindy and her demands be damned. Which is pretty typical, actually, of what I do most nights before most of these meetings, except for the writing part, that is. The drinking and wallowing, on the other hand, are the keys to my release and decompression process each week after the paper goes to print, my two regular relaxation rituals before we start a new publishing cycle by gathering the editorial staff in Anna's office to plan the next week's issue.

We're an "alternative newsweekly," see, and while I understand the "newsweekly" part—all the news we've got, once each week—I'm not quite sure what we're an "alternative" to at this point. I know that when Anna founded the paper in the mid-'80s, she viewed the *Advocate*'s role as being the weekly paper that kept the staid daily papers and electronic media outlets honest, making her and her staff the reporters who watched the reporters. I used to periodically ask her if she thought there should be reporters watching the reporters who watch the reporters, just to keep us honest as well, but she would always tell me that I was just being an asshole whenever I brought that up, so I don't bother anymore.

To the *Advocate*'s credit, however, we do certainly provide some strongly opposing viewpoints to counter the mass-marketed, easy-to-swallow news that fills our airwaves and newsstands hereabouts. Not to mention far more extensive music, arts and film coverage and criticism than the dailies could ever afford to offer. Although despite those featured niceties, we're still somewhat predictable in our own way too: pick an issue, any issue, look to the left, there we are. Or at least there we are from an editorial standpoint, although art and advertising may not be quite as politically correct as our news items are.

We decry the exploitation of women, for instance, but we pay a good chunk of our weekly printing bills and freelance payments by running "adult services" advertisements in the back of the paper. We curse the tobacco industry even as we print full-page, four-color spreads for their products. We regularly rail against the twin blights of suburbia and consumerism while we drive to work in our gas-guzzlers from various far-flung cottage communities. We champion the plights and feel the pain of every disenfranchised and oppressed minority or ethnic group we encounter, despite the fact that we're a mostly white, middle-class-bred organization. We love the gay community to pieces, but we're all straight. Et cetera. Ad nauseum.

Anna sees no contradictions here, mind you, given her uncanny ability to compartmentalize the *Advocate*'s editorial, advertising, art and production departments—both in her head and in day-to-day office activities and business culture. Employees from those groups all talk to each other in casual, passing-in-the-hall sorts of ways, of course, but Anna discourages inter-departmental discussion of work items, lest an account representative spill some stinky beans about an advertising client, thereby inadvertently spinning an article being prepared by one of our writers. Or lest a production artist's confrontational full frontal nude cover shot come to the attention of the Evangelical Gospel Choir advertising a concert that week. Before we've collected their cash.

And collect cash we do, although not from our readers: some 40,000 copies of the *Advocate* are given away free each Thursday, their production (and our salaries) paid for solely by our advertisers, who want to reach the affluent, literate, socially-responsible-yet-hard-partying crowd that we tell them reads our paper. Which is, sort of, where I come in—since you can't have a paper with six pages of news and feature stories up front, then 100 pages of advertisements following. Nope, you need filler to balance out those advertisements, by God, things like movie reviews, art essays, social and civic calendars and (of course) music criticism out the proverbial wazoo.

And I write much of that advertising-balancing musical filler, although I also have a team of groveling freelancers who will pick up the records, shows and interviews that I can't or don't feel like doing myself. Brian wrote for me for a while, in fact, although I think he's so pissed off at me for dismantling the studio that he's not likely to do so again. Or at least not until he needs some extra cash for something. Like rent, maybe. Or food.

The other freelancers are ever eager, however, desperate to please and jockeying hard for the free concert tickets and petty cash I can toss their way in exchange for 500 words of overly-serious, often badly-written, always way-too-analytical drivel. Some of them have been around freelancing as long as I've been on staff at the paper, waiting for me to leave, or be fired, or die, or something, so that they can take my job and not have to beg for assignments anymore. I told you music critics were a pathetic bunch, didn't I?

"Alright, everybody, I'm particularly glad to see that Collie has joined us in a nicely punctual fashion today, looking as bright and cheery and chipper as he always does on Thursday mornings," Anna continues. She's standing behind me now, suddenly in touchy-feely mode, first rubbing my shoulders, then patting me on the head, each pat making me blink and wince as twinges of pain shoot between my eyes, ears and brain.

Anna's alluding to the fact that I'm usually the last one to arrive at the editorial staff meetings, surprise, surprise, although I have gotten fairly good at getting in right at 10 AM, having been read the riot act by my aggressively punctual publisher more times than I care to recall. She's a softie on a lot of things (the office is liberally visited by staff members' dogs and babies, for instance, and we've got a regular crew of homeless folks who stop by to get warm or cool in extreme weather) but woe unto the editor, writer or account representative that makes her wait. I've got enough problems without pissing her off over the small stuff, so I generally try to comply with this anal retentive facet of her machine-gun managerial style, as painful and difficult as that can be for me, particularly during these early morning editorial staff meeting mornings.

"Y'know, I think Collie may even have some idea about what my special announcement this morning might be, don'tcha Musicboy?"

"Uh, no. No, I'm not sure what you plan to announce this morning, Anna," I reply, nervously, wondering how this meeting has come to be focussed my way. "Hopefully not my resignation or my firing, since I don't think I've done anything to deserve either. At least not this week."

Chuckles from around the table. My stomach growls loudly and unpleasantly, and I fish about in my pocket for an antacid tablet or three, but have none. I hug my guts and try to burp discretely, but nothing's coming up. You think I'd know better than to drink on an empty stomach, but I didn't get any dinner last night since Gerry and Randy had gotten pizza at the office last night and didn't feel like cooking when they got home. And by that time, I didn't either. I figured the orange juice would tide me over, nutrition-wise, while I hammered away at my laptop, but this morning I'm thinking that the juice just made my stomach all that much more acid-laden and foul.

"Okay, Collie's playing coy, I guess," the clinically hyperactive Anna continues, making another two loops around the table before continuing. (She never sits during our meetings, just paces). "Well, that's fine, just fine, then. Let's see if he can play surprised after I spill the beans, too, even though I know that he won't be, really."

She hands me a card with the word "Musicboy" (her pet editorial name for me) printed on its cover in her instantly recognizable spastic scrawl. Had it been for Editor in Chief Carol Ziomek it would have read "Bossgirl." Arts Editor Rushton Chuta, Film and Theatre Editor Blaine Grenier and News Editor Julie Kirkland would have gotten "Artman," "Movieboy" and "Newsgirl" respectively. Anna was younger than I was, but she treated all of us (except maybe for grandfatherly Rushton) like her children. And we let her do it, although I'm not sure why. Maybe because she pays us, I guess, and lets us dress however we want around the office, kid-like, even when she wears sharp adult suits and severe grown-up power blouses every day. Or maybe it's because we're just afraid of her. That's more likely, come to think of it. Fear of mom. Mother does not approve. Get me the coat hanger, darling.

I start to open the card, looking around the table to see if anyone else knows what's up, but no one will make eye contact with me. My stomach growls again. My head hurts. Anna flits around the room unstoppably, pivoting on spiked heels as she reaches a wall and heading back the opposite way just as quickly as she had come.

The cover of the card reads "Happy Anniversary, Baby, Got You On My Mind" and features a picture of a happy couple frolicking through a meadow, an explosion of flowers and butterflies surrounding them. The word "Baby" has been crossed out and "Collie" has been written in above it. Anna's handwriting again.

I open the card. There's an old, old picture of Anna and I taped into the left-hand side of the card, while the Hallmark-ian doggerel on the right has been completely covered with white correcting tape, atop which the following message has been penned in purple magic marker: "Congratulations on ten years with the *Advocate*, Musicboy! We couldn't have done it without you! Smooches en regalia, Anna."

Ten years? Here? That long? Today? Holy shit. Wow. Today? Ten years? I'm not good with dates. I don't think in terms of time. I'm a fossil, and I wasn't even consciously aware that layers of journalistic sediment were squishing me in the editorial newsroom where I sat, day in, day out, aging. The others crane their necks to see the card, probably wondering why my face went ashen. I'm pretty sure they didn't know what was coming either, this being just an Anna special moment, not a full editorial staff special moment. And none of the other editorial staff members would have known about the anniversary anyway, since none of them were here when I arrived.

Ten years ago. Three years before Rush and Julie. Eight years before Carol. Nine years before Blaine. A long, long time ago. I sigh and hand the card to Julie who looks at it quickly and passes it on around the table.

"Tuesday was Collie's tenth anniversary with the paper," Anna explains to those who still can't see the card. "I didn't want to say anything to him before we finished this week's edition, though, since I wasn't sure whether or not he might go screaming off into the night if I reminded him of it. Now, at least, if he runs away, I've got a week to replace him. Ha, ha."

Anna coughs. The card circles around the table. Nobody comments.

"So, well, there we have it. Congratulations, Collie, Musicboy, old man, pal o' mine," Anna says as she sneaks up behind me again, wraps me in a quick, fragile hug and places a dry, cinnamon-flavored kiss on my unshaven cheek, then spins away again. I nod politely as she continues: "We've got cake coming at noon, so the other departments can share it with us, but I don't want you telling 'em about your stories yet when they do, got it?"

She points at each editor in turn, demanding acknowledgement.

"Yeh."

"Sure."

"Uh huh."

"Okay."

I'm the last to be pointed at, the last to reply: "I never talk to advertising and production, Anna, you know that. They don't like me and I don't like them, so we got nothin' to say to each other. So, um, jeez, while I appreciate the gesture and everything, do we have to do this whole cake thing at lunch? I mean, this sorta makes me feel kinda old and creepy, y'know?"

"You are old and creepy, Collie. And the cake's been ordered already. We got it on trade for a Central Bakery vertical eighth-page ad that's running this week, although you didn't hear that from me. So we're gonna get cake and we're gonna eat cake, whether you're with us while we do it or not," Anna answers, rhythmically tapping her fingers together beneath her chin, a gesture that I've learned over the years generally means her short patience is expiring. "But I'd certainly prefer that you be there, and I'm sure everyone else here would agree to that, wouldn't they?"

Murmurs of assent from the other editors, then a pause, then Blaine, Movieboy, our newest and youngest editor, all fractured syntax, dyed hair, tribal tattoos and body piercing speaks: "Dude, I can't imagine being here for that long. I mean, like, ten years ago, I was still in junior high school n' shit, still watchin' cartoons n' jerkin' off to Daphne on 'Scooby Doo' 'r somethin'. And I don' know where I'm gonna be in ten years, but hopefully by that time I've made my first million doin' somethin' wild, y'know what I'm sayin'? Like out in Hollywood or somethin'? Me n' the Brothers Coen n' David Lynch n' Tarantino n' that whole kooky film-maker thing, right?"

"Thanks for sharing, Blaine. I appreciate it, although I'm actually happy to be here still, lame old man that I am," I lie. "'cause, Anna coulda fired me about 100 times along the way and been justified for doing so and, uh, I could be dead too, right? So thank God for small favors. And cake."

"And antacid," I think, wishing I had a whole roll of chalky tablets to munch and that I didn't have to play nice during a lunchtime mandatory-fun office production. This anniversary thing is hitting me hard, perhaps because I've been reflecting and processing and wallowing so much lately anyway, without even having some nice convenient annual occasion to force me to do so. I mean, I haven't even celebrated my own birthday in years, leaving me grasping for dates whenever anyone asks me how old I am. "Old" being the operative word there, mind you, with the tenth anniversary of my marginal job at a marginal paper making me feel even older still than I did when I rolled out of bed this morning, slipped on yesterday's clothes and headed to work, a mere 40 minutes ago.

Old. I'm 42 years old. Hell, I already felt old when I took this job in 1990, especially since my idealistic, energetic boss was three years younger than I was, but was earning far more than she was (or is) paying me. And now ten years have gone by, which means that I have passed, or soon will pass, into my own lame middle ages. What do I have to show for it? Some cake. A lawsuit. A film-school graduate skate punk looking at me with sympathy. Not even enough money to throw a decent midlife crisis. Pathetic. Just really pathetic.

Julie reaches over and squeezes my hand, moving into my line of sight and forcing me to return her warm, friendly gaze, silently. I smile at her, despite myself. She's painfully shy and rarely speaks to anyone here face to face, unless she's answering a direct question that can't be addressed with a head nod or shake. But get her on the telephone with a news lead and, man, she can be absolutely savage, slicing through the bullshit and pinning her unsuspecting suspects as they wriggle and then fall still under the karmic chloroform she emanates through the phone line.

Most of Julie's victims are stunned accordingly when they meet her in the flesh after such a phone grilling, feeling totally neutered and emasculated as they stand before her in all of her seemingly-harmless, pony-tailed, bespectacled, bra-less, sandal-wearing, granola-scented, humane society-volunteering, Earth princess glory. No one makes the mistake of underestimating her more than once, though. Or if they do, they do so at their own peril.

"Okay, quick, quick, quick, let's get through the editorial business, shall we? Yes, we shall," Anna chirrups from over by the window behind her desk, monitoring the street beneath us, seeming to search for stories, just in case we don't have any. "Whaddya got, Movieboy, besides condescension for Collie?"

"Uh, big performance art thing up at Rensselaer, video installations, that kinda stuff. I'm doin' that one myself, an' I'm gonna cover that student play at SUNY, too. I got three films racked up with freelancers already, one of 'em left over from last week, so we're all set there."

"Uh huh, okay, okay, got any images for any of that?"

"We've got some promotional shots from one of the movies and from the video thingie, so I don't think we need to put any photographers on any of 'em," Blaine concludes.

"You good with that, Bossgirl?"

"That's fine," says Carol. "I'm sending one of the photographers out with Collie on Saturday and we've got some great images for the cover story that Julie's doing, so I think we're set, big picture image wise."

"What's Collie doing Saturday night?"

"Tom Jones at the Paramount," Carol answers for me. "Classic cheese, and he's always good for a panties-on-the-microphone shot or two."

"What else, Collie?"

"I got Tom on Saturday and I'm doing a folk show up at the Cohoes Coffee House Monday," I answer, looking at the picture in the card that's now been passed back to me, noting that Anna doesn't seem to have changed much in ten years, while I look much, much older. "The Paramount show will be the lead, with photos, Carol and I already got that set up. I've also got two other shows assigned to freelancers and I've got three record reviews in the hopper, ready to run if we need them this week, space-wise; I can also get a couple of more done by Tuesday if I have to. I did the think piece on album cover art two weeks ago, so want to wait another week before I do another one of those. And I've got two taped phone interviews with local bands in the can, so I just need to transcribe 'em and write 'em up whenever we want to use 'em."

Blaine again, sliding a metal stud planted in his eyebrow back and forth: "Who'dja interview?"

"Cobain Headstain and the Neatly Trimmed Triangles. The Triangles piece could be pretty interesting, they're actually thinking about what they're doing, and know how to talk about it. The Headstains are pretty much what you'd expect from their name, though. A one-joke piece, if that."

"You want Collie to write one of those up this week, Bossgirl?"

"Yeah, why don't we go ahead and go with the Triangles, Collie. I think we've got a decent photo of them already too, so we can get that in quick. That'll work, right?"

I grunt in the affirmative and scribble a note on the back of the card, knowing I won't be able to find it again by this afternoon. Carol will remind me, though. Her desk is next to mine, so she's pretty good about that stuff as part of her overall coordinators' duties for pulling the editorial section of the paper together each week. She's been with the paper for about two years now, and has provided a nice foil for Anna in our department—being slow moving, hard to anger and considerate, where Anna is not any of those things.

Carol's a lot bigger than Anna, too, both in height and build, so I think she could take our publisher in a catfight, if it ever came down to that. I daydream about them slugging it out sometimes, in fact, when I've got nothing else on my mind. And when the buxom Carol is dressed in just the right way to inspire such vile fantasies.

Anna's standing in her doorway now, back to us, watching the rest of the office, lest she miss something. "Who's got the cover again this week?"

"Me," says Julie.

"What is it?"

"Pollution. River. Activists. Governor."

"Uh huh, okay, that's good," Anna continues, having long ago figured out how to translate Julie's not-quite-answers. "Anything else this week, Newsgirl?"

"Bike path. Trains. Freelancers. Three."

"Good, thanks. Bossgirl, you got art lined up for all that?"

"Nice cover piece like I mentioned, yes, a really great, evocative photo of a culvert draining into the Hudson, and you can see the dead plants along the underside of it and everything, and there's a child's toy sailboat drifting into the frame, heading for the spillage. Worth a thousand words, easy, and Julie's already written about twice that, I think, so it's solid. And I think I'll send someone out to get some shots of people riding on the new trail along the Delaware and Hudson railbed for Julie's other story, too. Could be a nice counterpoint."

"What are you doing, Artman?"

"Exhibition of some newly-discovered works by one of the Hudson River School painters up at the Galleria Center in Troy," answers grandfatherly Rushton Chuta, the only Advocate staffer older than me and therefore entitled to have the word "man" in place of the word "boy" in his Anna-assigned nickname. "I think it's a tired, played out, over-hyped school of art, really, but these are new pieces, and people seem to want to see them, and they are local, sort of, so I want to check them out for myself, although I don't expect to like them. I will also be interviewing a new poet I heard at a slam last week and I would like to try to attend the Paige Duft Dance Ensemble recital this weekend, but only if Carol can get me a photographer, since I think that needs to be seen as well as written about, for reasons obvious to us all. I would hope."

The wiry, dusky, bald on top, furry on the chin, little-round-glasses-wearing Rush may or may not be Indian or Pakistani, depending on who's asking, and why. He's a regular on the local poetry slam circuit around here, a deeply talented foamer and raver—and an insanely private man who is all but certain that he's being taped, typed and targeted by nefarious, yet unseen, quasi-governmental elements. He owns no credit cards, refuses to pay taxes or vote, doesn't let anyone take his picture and does all of his shopping at Albany's sole independent cooperative grocery store, assured by the clerks that their produce comes straight from the farm, no third parties having touched his food. His paranoia can be contagious: I, for one, am certain that someday some men in black are indeed gonna bust into the *Advocate*'s offices and haul him away. I just hope I'm there when it happens.

"Can you get Rush a photographer, Bossgirl?"

"What night is the show?"

"I can go Friday or Sunday, not Saturday," answers Rush. "I have made plans. I don't intend to change them."

"I'll see if I can get someone to go with you on Sunday, then," concludes Carol. "Plan on going, and I'll let you know if I have any problems getting someone lined up."

Anna's anxious to get on to her weekly advertising staff meeting at this point: "Okay, what else? What's missing?"

"That's about it," wraps up Carol, our unofficial spokesperson for open-ended Anna questions. "The usual calendar kinds of stuff, some preview material, a little bit of space held for breaking Newsgirl stories early in the week, or for Collie's record reviews if nothing else pops up. Filler city, baby."

"Good, thanks, knock 'em dead," concludes Anna, waving her arms to clear us out of her office already. "I'll see you all at noon for cake, yes? Collie, yes?"

"Sure, Anna. See you at noon. High n' timely. You de baas, yes."

"Knock if off, Collie! You know I hate your southern white-bread slave imitation shit. And if you don't want cake, fine. That's an extra piece for me."

I smile and pat her on the back as I leave her office. "You don't eat cake, Anna, remember? It goes straight to your ass. And I'm sorry I was bitchy, I just wish you'd warned me before..."

But she was gone down the hall to rustle up the advertising staff for her next meeting before I could finish my sentence, me out of her mind, dirty money on it instead. She'd tire of the account reps in no time, too, then work her way through the art and production team, finishing just in time for our scheduled noon soiree, after which she would retire to her office to mull over her weekly rant on the publisher's commentary page.

Then she'd sign checks, leave to go the gym by 2 PM—and we wouldn't see her again until Monday. We never dared to ask what she did each Friday instead of coming to the office. I always figured that she slept for 24 hours straight, so she wouldn't have to do it again until the next week. Whatever the reason, we all enjoyed having the pressure let off our cooker every seventh day, so we didn't complain or question much, as long as Anna remembered to give us our signed paychecks before she left Thursday afternoon.

Which is generally best not left to chance, since from Anna's perspective giving us our checks on Monday means three more days of interest on the *Advocate*'s cash balance. So as the editorial staff files back into our collective work area, I ask "Who's supposed to remind Anna to sign our paychecks today?"

"I think it's the production department's turn," Carol answers. "Lemme check my book..."

She flips open her ubiquitous day-planner. "Yeah, it's production. I'll remind Jessica at Collie's anniversary party to keep an eye on Anna and make sure she doesn't get out without signing…"

"Bitch," mutters Blaine, for no particular reason, as he grabs the sports page and shuffles off down the hall to be the first into the single-seater men's room, as he does every week after the editorial staff meeting. He'll be gone for awhile, and Rush and I have taken to curtailing our coffee or tea drinking at the meeting to make sure we don't need to follow him any time soon.

"Do you remember what you agreed to do this morning, Collie?"

It's another of our weekly rituals: Carol making sure we do what we told Anna we were going to do. Or maybe it's just Carol making sure that I do what I told Anna I was going to do, since Julie and Rush and Blaine tend not to get as many reminders as I do.

"Hmm? Oh, uh, yeah, I think I wrote it down here somewhere, yeah, I'm, uh, going to…"

"Tom Jones. Cohoes Coffee House. Triangles."

"Right. Right. And cake at noon, yeah, I had that too, right."

This time I do indeed write it all down on my desk blotter, finding a white spot between all of the other little lists that I've written down on my desk blotter over the past two years after my weekly reminder from Carol. For the first eight years I was here, I didn't have such an effective system, which resulted in regular Wednesday eruptions when Anna popped in to see how something I'd agreed to produce was going, and I hadn't started it yet. I got pretty good after a while at issuing quick bullshit answers, then cranking our some piece of hack work, making sure I got a quote from somebody at the last minute, just to prove that it was my sources' fault, not mine, that I was late. It was nicer, these days, with Carol as my professional conscience and goad.

And so my work week is all laid out: this afternoon I'll touch base with the freelancers and photographers and confirm their schedules, then call the clubs to get them on the guest lists. Tomorrow, I'll transcribe and write my Neatly Trimmed Triangles interview. Tom Jones Saturday night, which will mean that I can come in late on Monday morning as compensation time, then write a record review or two on Monday and proof and edit anything the freelancers have submitted, then leave early, since I also have a concert on Monday night. Tuesday I'll write up my concert reviews and look at the week's press releases, make a few phone calls to writers and photographers to cover upcoming shows, assigning a few to myself, of course, generally the best of the lot, editor's prerogative. Wednesday will be final editing and assembly day, when I look at the other editors' work and they look at mine, and we tweak things, and prepare any last minutes filler, then ship the paper off to the printer.

And then I go home and drink and write and wallow, and we start the week all over again with another editorial staff meeting. As I've done for ten years. 520 weeks, 520 issues, although I figure I've missed probably 50 of those issues from vacation and touring and sickness and malfeasance. But still, I've done this dance, or variations thereon, some 470 times. Editors have come and gone, freelancers too, but Anna and I remain constant, the rocks upon which the *Advocate*'s editorial content has been built over the years. Or maybe Anna's the rock, and I'm just the lichen growing on the rock, coarse, furry, gray, hard to remove, drab, featureless, sucking sustenance from the very cold, bloodless heart of the stone itself.

That's a good analogy. I make a mental note to incorporate it into an interview or think piece soon. I wonder if the Neatly Trimmed Triangles have a personal parasite in their collective lives who could play lichen to their collective rock. The way I am to Anna. Or the way Matt was to me and Brian and the rest of Arctangent. A mineral leach. An energy vampire. A sustenance sucker.

But, no, I doubt the Neatly Trimmed Triangles have got one of those. They're too young, too fresh, too inexperienced. It takes a lot of time for lichen to take hold and wrap itself around a stone.

Ten years? Yeah, that would be enough to do it, no doubt about that. Give me another decade and I'll reduce Anna into a pile of rubble, just like I did to Kris.

Chapter Eight

The ideals of the South Carolina Military Institute are lofty ones indeed, with administrations past and present fully and earnestly dedicated to the intellectual stimulation, physical readiness, moral fitness and overall character development of the cadets entrusted to their care. The actual results that the Institute's military and civilian instructors achieve in pursuit of these lofty ideals, however, are a different matter altogether. Or at least they were in my case, although I'll admit that I may be the anomaly, the bad seed, the exception that defines the generally wholesome rule.

Sure, I was in fine physical condition during and shortly after my Institute time (push-ups and forced marches work on even the least willing flesh), but my morals, mind and character were as flaccid when I left as they were when I first passed through the Institute's main gate. They might actually have been worse at the end, in fact, since I spent most of that four year period conniving to be all that I wanted to be (which wasn't much), despite relentless pressure to be all that I could be (which was too much hard work). I had succumbed to Junior's will in attending his favorite academy of higher learning, but damned if I was going to embrace it.

The sad thing, looking back, is that if I'd exerted half as much effort on military drills and classes as I exerted trying to get out of them, then I'd have been regimental commander material, no doubt about it. But I didn't, and I wasn't. Instead, I became a master of the dodge, a brilliant practitioner in redirection, a doyen of denial, an artisan of fake illness and injury, a guru of work avoidance, a trailblazer in the under-appreciated field of leadership by contrast. So I can't say that I didn't learn anything valuable at the Institute, since those skills have actually been quite helpful over the past two decades, given the skeevy path over which my lazily opportunistic adulthood has meandered.

And I can also thank the Institute for helping me to develop one of my great, defining life skills, one of my unquestionably well-recognized talents, my gift, my calling, my art. I learned to drink in Ulmer, I did, like a champion, like a winner, like a man. I'd been little more than a dabbler in distillates before that time, an occasional, haphazard drunk, casual and amateurish in my tippling, cavalier in my commitment to the spirits that moved me, then and now. I took what was offered to me (drugs and alcohol alike) when on Hilton Head or when frequenting Bridgefield's look-the-other-way liquor stores as a teenager, but there was little rhyme, reason, logic or order in my program of self-medication and reality-obliteration.

But the entire life-style and schedule of the Institute—six days of rote, repetitive oppression followed by one day of liberty on the town at large—honed those drinking skills to a sharp, purposeful point. Because when you've only got 24 hours allocated each week for unsupervised fun, you get very, very efficient in pursuit of your chosen entertainment. Or intoxicants, if your primary entertainment objective is escape from the other six days of the week. And I was certainly cultivating escape from the Institute, believe you me, so I learned my drinking lessons well, eschewing the light-weight, over-priced fern bars that cultivated cadet contact right off the bat and heading instead for the seedier neighborhood joints where the real alcoholic masters practiced their art.

My drinking habits were shaped during my first two years at the Institute through devoted observations of those old masters, Buddha-like, stubbled, serene in the middle of their cigarette clouds, wrapped in piss-stained garments of denim and flannel and polyester that glowed like saffron when the neon lights were right. Cost efficiency was the underlying cornerstone principle for these professional drinkers, the ability to stretch your dollar well beyond its breaking point, or (better yet) to borrow two from someone else.

This facet of the Ulmer Drinking Academy program had great appeal for me, living, as I did, solely on the $100 of spending money Junior sent me on the first of each month (since cadets couldn't hold outside jobs, although we got room, board, uniforms and rifles as part of our tuition payments), supplemented by anything I managed to squirrel away working in the store during summers or Holiday breaks.

One of the first lessons I learned from Ulmer's Zen Winos was that beer was a no-no: its alcohol-content-to-cost ratio was quite poor, its water content was quite high, and time spent pissing diluted hops and barley was time not well spent in a bar. Unless you didn't bother to go to the bathroom for bladder drainage, that is, and I was not yet at that lofty level of self-absorbed alcoholic Nirvana.

High octane shots were the ticket, you see, and a professional drinker ordered as many of them as he could at once, then carried them away to a corner table, so he only had to tip the bartender for a single service. Happy hours were crucial, too, and the best happy hours were the ones where you ate free as long as you were paying for drinks, since that way you didn't have to spend money on food, and there's good, hearty sustenance to be acquired from giveaway pub-grub. A bit heavy on the starches and carbohydrates, yes, but calories were calories, and bread and fried food were often just the tickets when it came to sopping up or sustaining a sour mash stomach.

Cigarettes, too, were to be bummed, not bought, whenever possible. The easy marks were those regular nonsmokers who pretended to smoke only when they drank, playing with lit cigarettes as props or to keep their hands occupied while their minds wandered or their eyes roved the bar for sexual opportunity. Those sorts of people were always happy to share, since they didn't really want to (or were unable to) smoke a whole pack in an evening anyway, and the approach and ask helped break the ice, and gave them someone to talk with, lubricating the social organ and all that. Bonus points all round if the beggar and the begged-from were of opposite sexes.

You never approached a hardcore professional drinker for a gift cigarette, unless you wanted a lecture, or a fight, or a trade negotiation where one smoke would be proffered in exchange for one drink, a bad transaction on any account, unless you thought you could win the next round. It was okay to hit up a sloppy drunk amateur for a smoke, though, since they would want to bond, and buy you (and everyone else in the joint) drinks to show how much they loved you, after you lifted their Camels. You had to be careful with them, though, since if you bonded too closely or obviously, the bartender would assume it was your responsibility to get them out of the bar at closing time, which could get mean, and ugly, and embarrassing to all parties concerned. Watching grown men cry, even drunken grown men, has always made me uneasy. There but for the grace of God and Colonel, you know?

Somewhere near the beginning of my third year at the Institute I had another brilliant drinking insight: having learned my lessons well, I didn't even need to go to a bar to drink anymore, since my family lived close by and I had my own, private cell-cum-room at their house. After that point, I would just leave the Institute at noon on Saturday, buy a bottle of rum or vodka and a carton of orange juice at the package store near campus and start drinking right away during the 90-minute drive to Bridgefield. I also got to be quite adept at changing clothes while driving, shedding my uniform and replacing it with shorts, T-shirts, flip-flops. I didn't want to drive barefoot, after all, law-abiding citizen that I was and everything.

I'd be pleasantly tingled by the time I got home, would visit with Junior and Mama and Sister for a spell, then sit out in the backyard or walk down to the fishing docks (another hardcore drinker haunt) and sip with aplomb, free of charge. When I'd had enough (or run out of booze), I'd stagger home, yawn and wave at my parents and feign tiredness after a long week of good living, set the alarm clock in my room for 9 AM, collapse, spin, sleep. The next morning I would eat the free breakfast Mama made (along with a handful of aspirin, taken from Junior's medicine chest), dress in my uniform and leave at 10:15 sharp, just as Mama and Junior and Sister were heading off to church, expressing regrets that I couldn't join them.

"Tight schedule," I'd explain as I waved goodbye and roared back towards Ulmer. I would generally arrive back at the Institute fifteen minutes before noon meal formation, brush my teeth, shave, spray some deodorant in the air and walk through the cloud on my way to the central courtyard where we mustered at the end of each week's liberty. Sunday afternoon, which was supposed to be dedicated to unstructured athletic or academic pursuits within the Institute's confines, would instead provide time for me to sleep off my hangover. I would wake, refreshed, in time for evening meal formation at 6:30 PM, eat in the mess hall and attend (mandatory) evening chapel, a regular picture of mental, physical and moral fortitude, a fine flower of youth, promise and virtue.

I would retire to my room after chapel and proceed to stay up as late I needed to at night, well after curfew, towel stuffed under my door to keep patrolling sentries from seeing my desk lamp, to do the bare minimum studying needed to get me through the next day. Then sleep, then wake, then five-and-a-half days of drudgery avoidance, then a beautiful, cheap, refreshing day of drinking, and drinking, and drinking some more. It was a fine, efficient system, and with practice, I was able to execute it as well as it could humanly be executed. Maybe even better, since I was drinking with the divine by this point.

There were variations on the system every now and again, of course. Violations of any of the Institute's arcane rules and regulations could result in liberty being replaced by one of the school's equally arcane punishments. There were restriction musters (10 uniform inspections per 24 hour period), room tours (locked at your desk, studying, being excused only for meals) or area tours (marching around the campus in full uniform, carrying a rifle, 50 out of every 60 minutes, 8 hours each day). Bad news, each one, and during my first year, before I'd gotten my priorities straight, my desire to buck the Institute's will (fueled, no doubt, by frustration over my weakness in bucking my father's will a year earlier) resulted in regular liberty loss for one malfeasance or another.

But as I began to understand my true calling as a drinker, and knew that I needed my liberty time to pursue it more fully, I got more subtle and crafty in my subversion. Outwardly, I became an acceptable, but not model, cadet, most of the time, getting decent grades, doing decently at sports, looking decent in my uniform, being decent to my teachers, my company commander, my upper-class student officers. I generally did what I was asked to do, nothing more, nothing less, kept a relatively low profile except for when I spotted an opportunity to achieve maximum positive impact from minimum personal effort. I wrote for the school newspaper occasionally, as one example in that regard, both to keep my writing skills sharp and to show that I was willing to be a team player and rah-rah for the man, no matter how much I actually hated him.

Pent-up aggression and frustration would then be vented surreptitiously, by night, with no witnesses, through petty property crime, vandalism, graffiti, theft. A broken desk set here. A missing colors flag there. Odd reoccurring leaks in a toilet just above my Company Commander's office. Mysterious, ominous (and meaningless, but no one knew that) symbols and signs painted about the campus, in less than obvious places that made them more frightening to sensitive souls than they would have been had I emblazoned them across the Chapel altar. Subtle, pointless evil, never obvious, cheap sacrilege. And me by day, as bright-eyed and earnest as I got, outwardly aghast at such activities, inwardly smiling with satisfaction, counting the minutes until the weekend.

There were some weekends, once I got my liberty back, where the sex drive overpowered the alcohol lust, where all-night drinking sprees were interrupted by casual couplings, generally in terrifically inappropriate public or quasi-public places, continuing the tawdry tradition I'd begun with Cindy in high school. Although, as a general rule, I didn't strive for such liaisons when I went home to Bridgefield, but saved them for weekends in Ulmer instead, sometimes planning them, sometimes reacting to my family's requests that I not visit if they had other guests in town or were travelling themselves.

It generally wasn't all that difficult to get one's sexual urges met in Ulmer, if one stayed in a bar late enough and if one drank enough to get one's standards really, really low. No problems for me on any of those accounts. In time, I developed a pool of fairly dependable partners, most of them predictably available, most of them older, most of them moderately pleased to have a younger, clean, halfway-decent-looking male paying them attention, none of them expecting any sort of commitment or consolation from me the next day. Which was perfect, since the Institute's no-exit policies during the week precluded me from seeing or getting to know any of them in anything more than a sitting-at-the-bar, then screwing-in-the-alley sort of way. And when we were done with what we needed to do, we could go back into the bar, sit, and drink some more. Life was good. On Saturday nights, at least.

I probably would have started smuggling liquor (if not women) back into the Institute for other nights of the week at some point, except for the fact that I had a roommate, who definitely would not have approved of my doing so. Vance Collier, favorite son of tiny Walter's Crossroads in Mississippi, was willing to overlook such relatively minor infractions on my part as staying up past curfew or the occasional midnight reconnaissance raid, but booze or girls in the room would have pushed it a bit beyond his personal comfort level. It wasn't that Vance was prude about such things, mind you, but he did carry a healthy respect for the Institute's rigid honor policy, and that respect made him cautious accordingly.

And I understood this, completely, since one of the first military mantras we learned when we arrived in Ulmer was that "A cadet does not lie, cheat or steal, nor tolerate any cadet who does." It was the school's one inviolable rule. Being found guilty of an honor violation was an instant expulsion, no restriction musters, no room tours, no area tours, no diploma. This stringent absolutism in turn created a sick air of back-watching and vengeance-seeking among the cadets and the administration alike, since the easiest way for the school's staff to ferret out wrong-doing was to ask one cadet whether he knew if another cadet had committed a particular offense. Once such a question had been posed, everyone lost, particularly if any of the cadets in question had shared personal, private or compromising information with their friends, classmates or other fellow cadets.

Because it worked like this: if the first cadet, the one who got the question, knew of the offense and denied knowledge to protect his friend, then the actual offender owned him until the end of his Institute days. Because the actual offender could admit his guilt at any time, advise the school's honor board that his protector had lied, have said protector ousted, then take the relatively minor room tour or restriction muster punishment that came with the original offense. This created ample blackmail opportunity, needless to say, which was made even more reprehensible and vile from having stemmed from an initial attempt by one cadet to cover for another. One good turn did not necessarily earn another here, whether it was deserved or not.

Conversely, if a cadet adhered to the honor concept when questioned and ratted out another cadet about a rules violation, the informer would lose big that way, too. While he would still be on track to graduate, for the moment, he would invariably be subject to a retaliatory strike against his person, his property or his very presence at the Institute, if he could be spotted in a compromising honor position of his own. It was a bad, bad system, but very effective when used by the officers who ran the school as a way of ensuring that we cadets self-policed, or at least self-enforced, the Institute's rules and regulations, all in the name of honor and truth and fairness.

Never mind that none of us trusted each other. Not even Vance and I, completely, even though we lived together for almost four years. But no wonder, since we existed in a state of mutually assured destruction throughout that time. Each small, observed violation by one of us would be countered by an equal and opposite small, observed violation on the other's part, said violations escalating slowly over time, but never to the point where either of us would have been comfortable with liquor and ladies in our dormitory cell. Even though we both would have enjoyed having them there.

In a spirit of full disclosure here, I should note that while I kept my crimes secret from Vance to protect him from the honor board, I was often sharply accused and questioned directly about my own activities by those very same bastions of integrity—and lied to them regularly, without a lick of guilt. I never bought into the concept of honor for honor's sake, see, preferring instead to maintain my own unspoken honor code of convenience. It went something like this: "A cadet will lie, cheat or steal whenever he is fairly confident that he won't be caught doing so, and will tolerate any other cadet who does the same, so long as it's to his advantage to do so, and so long as he might be able to get something out of it through blackmail, later on."

Vance embraced the honor concept in a fashion somewhat closer to its intended form, consistent with his general overall reputation as straight shooter, military zealot, officer material. He wasn't a mindless automaton like some of our schoolmates, but he was certainly less than one standard deviation removed from the ideal, median cadet. Vance was also one of a relatively small number of cadets from outside of

South Carolina, having actually chosen to attend the Institute himself, as opposed to having being forced to go there by his father, which was how most of us had ended up in Ulmer.

Vance had always been a solid citizen and good athlete who desperately wanted to be a United States Marine Corps Officer and equally desperately wanted to attend a military academy on his way to that commission. Unfortunately for him, he didn't have the grades or connections necessary to win an appointment to one of the real service academies at West Point or Annapolis or Colorado Springs. He attended a year-long military preparatory school in Texas after graduating from high school in an attempt to better his grades and his chances with the A-league service schools, but his reapplications to Navy, Army and Air Force were rejected just as politely and curtly as were his first approaches.

Despite this setback, Vance didn't lose sight of his ultimate goal, licking his wounds, researching his options, finally applying, getting accepted and signing on as a cadet at Ulmer's finest finishing school. The good citizens of Walter's Crossroads threw a parade and barbecue for him at the high school football stadium where Vance had once made his neighbors proud. He had a picture of that farewell party on his desk that showed him standing modestly front and center while the collected and complete population of his home town, some 200 men, women and children, raised their hands, cheered or otherwise mugged for the photographer. I found the whole thing nauseatingly wholesome.

Needless to say, the staff at the Institute loved Vance, since he embraced everything they held dear and true and valuable, and was a living advertisement for just how far a young man from a small town could get with enough hard work and dedication and loving community support. No surprise, either, that my family adored Vance too; Junior seeing in him the hard-working, military-minded son he'd always wanted; Mama impressed that he always offered to light her cigarettes; Sister bedazzled by his piercing, dark to the point of being colorless eyes, strong, open features and wide-shouldered athlete's build. He was gracious and polite to all of them, and they appreciated it. He was basically the Anti-Collie, when push came right down to shove, yea verily and forsooth.

Junior, Mama and Sister would come up fairly regularly on Sunday afternoons (I wasn't about to blow my Saturday night liberty time with them) during my first year at the Institute, ostensibly to offer moral support, more likely to allow Junior to relive his glory days while Mama and Sister basked in the glow that was Vance. At some point during my sophomore year, however, their visits dwindled in both frequency and duration, in part no doubt because their presence during the periods of time when I regularly scheduled my weekly hangover recoveries caused me obvious, visible irritation, making their visits awkward and uncomfortable for everyone. I was sorry on some plane, but not a big one.

When I started coming home more often during my junior year, my family encouraged me to bring Vance with me, since his loved ones were so far away and he didn't have anyone to make him pancakes on Sunday morning, after all. I pondered the proposition, couldn't think of any good reason for saying "no" to their request and extended Vance an invitation to join me the next time I headed out to Bridgefield. He accepted gratefully, seemed to enjoy being with my family (more than I did, anyway), didn't much crimp my drink-sleep-eat routine and so won an ongoing open invitation to join my weekend road trips to the shore. He was a good passenger, I've got to say, regularly chipping in for gas money and occasionally even contributing to my weekly liquor buy, which kind of annoyed me, since then I felt compelled to share it with him.

Or at least in the beginning I felt that need to share, although even that decent compulsion left me once Vance's visits to Bridgefield became routine. We rarely saw each other once we got home, in fact, since he would go to the music store with Junior or walk on the beach with Sister or help Mama snap peas while I was out on the docks, catching up on the week's gossip with the winos. By the time I stumbled home at night, he would usually be curled up on the couch in the den, asleep already or still watching television, waving as I crossed the room on the way to my lair, me grunting back in recognition as I passed. We'd share the newspaper over breakfast Sunday mornings, him getting the sports page first, me getting the comics first, the two of us then switching, usually as Mama topped off our coffee and asked if we'd had enough to eat.

It was so positively, disgustingly domestic that I actually started to feel like I had a brother instead of a roommate after a while, and even more disgustingly, our family actually seemed to function a bit better as a five piece than it did as a foursome. Probably because all of us felt like we had to be on at least decent behavior when Vance was about, which was pretty much any time that I was about, thereby deferring or defusing any latent ugliness that might be festering below the surface as we sipped our coffee together each Sunday morning.

But all dull things must come to an end, and the season of our content was finally broken one Saturday afternoon during the autumn of my senior year when Sister unexpectedly appeared like an apparition on the docks where I sat drinking with Bridgefield's other vagrants.

"Collie?"

"Hey...what are you doing down here," I spat, literally and figuratively, instinctively sliding the brown bag holding that week's chosen libation (vodka) behind the barrel upon which I sat.

"I gotta talk to you, Collie."

"Umm, now? Here?"

"Well, now, yeah. I don't really care where."

Sister stared at me solemnly, then turned her gaze to the half-dozen other dock denizens gathered around the end of the pier. None of them could look her in the eye, and after about 30 seconds of scrutiny they realized they weren't wanted, raised themselves up, groaning, creaking, and shuffled off towards the harbormaster's shed. No one would stare at them while they drank there, of that they (and I) were sure.

Sister started again: "So, um, Collie?"

I braced myself for a lecture. I knew the only reason that Sister would have followed me to the docks was to give me a ration of shit about my sad lifestyle choices, then to rub my nose in the fact that I wasn't Vance and never would be. I acted nonchalant. I crossed my arms, squared my shoulders, prepared to raise hackles and voice quickly to cut Sister down where she stood, melting her in a pool of her own self-righteous juices. What authority did she have to criticize me? She was 25 years old, still living at home, dateless, largely friendless, clerking at Junior's Music, lonely, sad, forgotten. At least I had managed to fall out of the nest. Who cared if I'd been pushed, and Sister hadn't?

"Whaddya want, Sister? I mean, c'mon, go, say it, what?"

"Well, I don't really know how to say what I gotta say to you, Collie, so I guess I just gotta spit it out, huh?"

"Yes. Please. Spit. Now."

"I'm pregnant, Collie."

My ready-to-launch string of defensive words died in my mouth, slid down my throat, choked me, even as my head shot forward and my shoulders slumped as if I'd been punched in the gut. Mouth open, eyes wide, I stared into Sister's face as rivulets of tears erupted from the corners of her eyes and began coursing down her wide, sun-reddened cheeks. She pushed her straw-colored hair behind her ears reflexively and nervously, first the left side, then the right side, then shook her head so the hair fell out from behind her ears again, then wiped her cheeks with the back of her hand, then sighed, waiting for me to answer.

And I had nothing to say. Not a word of comfort. Not a word of compassion. Not even a decent word of surprise. I sat there like an idiot and stared, my brain overwhelmed by the heretofore-unimaginable image of my prematurely spinsterly older sister as an actively sexual human being. Or even as a human being at all, since I'd gotten to think of her the same way I was coming to think of Vance: as just another thing at the breakfast table dedicated to reducing the number of pancakes I got out of each batch Mama cooked. Then I had an image of Sister cooking pancakes for her own child, and I saw this child (who I immediately began thinking of as "Nephew") being every bit as sullen and ungrateful to Sister as I was to Mama and Junior.

It broke my heart. It broke my silence. It broke my trance. I rose from my barrel, walked over, took Sister in my arms and held her, whispering "Oh, Sister…Sister…oh…it'll be okay…it will…" in her ear as she clutched me tightly, her body wracked with sobs, her breath ragged as she wept. And I cried a little bit too, for her, for Junior and Mama and me, and for how badly I'd treated them all, and how badly I was going to treat them all again tomorrow, and for how badly Nephew was going to treat all of us when he came along.

As I look back on that moment on the dock, I think that I felt emotionally closer to Sister right then than I've felt to any other human being, under any other circumstances, at any other time. Because I realized then that she was every bit as much a victim of Bridgefield as I was, only she didn't get to run away six days a week to play soldier like I did. And while we'd been too far apart, age wise, to have much in common growing up, now we were both nominally adults, and now we could be allies as we faced a nominally adult world. I was glad she chose to confide in me. I loved her truly, like a brother should love his sister. For a few moments at least.

We stood there, hugging for several minutes, lost in that special moment, until I looked up and saw my shiftless drinking pals drifting around the parking lot, pointing in our direction and visibly guffawing. I started to get embarrassed, gently pushed Sister away, used my fingers to wipe the tears from her cheeks and tried to think of something else meaningful to say.

"So, uh, do you know who the father is?"

"Collie!" Sister slapped at my chest half-heartedly. "Of course I do, d'you think I'm some kinda slut or something? Why in the world would you ask me that?"

"I'm sorry, I said it badly.... what I meant to ask was: Who's the father?"

Sister looked at the ground, shuffled her feet, put her hands over her eyes, grimaced and finally whispered: "Vance."

Another psychic shot to the stomach. Another sudden inhalation and look of shock on my face. Another moment of stunned silence, although this one ending not with a wave of pity and empathy, but rather with a tsunami of rage and indignity.

"What?! You've got to be kidding me! What the hell did he do, rape you in the back yard or something? And after the way me n' y'all have been so good to him, treatin' him like..."

"Oh, Collie, shut up, shut up, shut up!" Sister cut me off. "Vance didn't rape me. Vance and I have been sleepin' together pretty much since you first started bringin' him home with you. An' I ain't been complainin' none about it, have I?"

"When? And how could y'all have been doing that without me knowin' about it?"

"After everyone else went to bed, you idiot, and after you stumbled home from sittin' out here drinkin' all day and passed out, most nights. We coulda been doin' it in the bed with you and you wouldn't o' known, bein' as drunk and stupid as you usually were by then..."

I let the mini-lecture slide. "Does Mama know?"

"No."

"Junior?"

"Gawd, no..."

"Well, uh, what about Vance."

"Yeah, Vance knows. I told him a coupla weeks ago. I had to tell him, don'tcha think?"

I suddenly became aware of the motion of the shrimp boats tied to the pier beside us and felt queasy, reaching out for my barrel and taking a seat on its edge, slapping it with my palm and gesturing for sister to sit next to me. She did, leaned against me, and I tried to decide if she felt heavier or not. I hadn't touched her in years, so it was hard to tell.

"Well, obviously, yeah, you had to tell Vance. But what the hell's he gonna do? And why the hell didn't he say anything to me about it? Jesus Christ, we've driven back and forth from Ulmer twice since then, and he never thought to tell me that he'd knocked up my sister? What the hell's that all about?"

"It's about that goddamn honor concept is what it is," Sister answered with a sigh. "Vance don't want you to know, although I told him I was gonna tell you sooner or later, or you was gonna find out when I started getting fat." Another sob erupted from her throat at that thought. "But I think he was secretly hopin' that I'd have a miscarriage, or decide to get an abortion, and then it would all be taken care of, nobody the wiser…"

"So he ain't plannin' to do the honorable thing by you, is he?"

"He can't," Sister answered, and began weeping again. "You know that cadets can't be married or have kids, so if we did get married, he'd have to quit the Institute, and I can't ask him to do that, after all he's been through to get this far…"

She was right. The very traditional, very archaic Institute was for single, childless males only, which resulted in an assembly-line stream of weddings on graduation day and the weeks that followed it. And I'd already seen half-a-dozen classmates fall by the wayside of their military studies after impregnating local girls who squealed to the administration as soon as they were scorned, although I hadn't thought of Vance being a likely victim in that regard, particularly with my own sister. He seemed too nice for that. It seemed like something that should have happened to me instead.

But that wasn't the problem at hand now, so I tried to focus again, for Sister's sake: "Okay, so the baby can't be due until sometime next spring, 'cause you're not showing yet, so why not have the baby, and Vance n' me n' you'll keep quiet about it, and then you and Vance can get married after graduation, when there's nothin' that the Institute can do about it."

Sister started crying harder. "I thought of that too, that's what I told Vance I wanted to do…but he said he don't want to get married at all. He don't love me that way, he said, an' while we've had a good time while he's in school an' everything, he said he don't want to be tied down just as he's startin' his military career, 'cause that's the most important thing to him, right now. He says he can send me money if I need it, he will do that, but that's all he can do for me. He says he wants me to take care of this, an' I know he means that he wants me to not have the baby…"

"Well, do you want to have the baby, Sister? I mean, maybe…"

She stopped me before I could get the sentence out of my mouth. "Of course I do, Collie, I want to have children, you know I always have. An' I may not get another chance, okay, this may be it for me. I mean, who's gonna want a woman who's still livin' at home with her parents when she's 24…"

"You're 25."

"…or whatever, 25, 35, it don't matter, nobody's wanted me all along, and now Vance don't want me either, but I want his baby, Collie, and I'm gonna have it, whether he wants me to or not. I just need you to help me tell Junior n' Mama, that's really all I need right now. Nothin' else. I just couldn't do it without havin' someone on my side when I did."

"When you gonna do it? Tell 'em, I mean?"

"I dunno, when do you think?"

"Well, if you want me around when you do, you're pretty much stuck with breakfast table talk, since that's about the only time we're all together, right?"

"Well, yeah, I guess. But this week Vance is here, too, and I don't…"

"I think that makes it all that much better, actually," I interrupted. "I think that's just the way you should do it: me n' him n' you at the breakfast table, me backin' you up, him havin' to say his piece and defend himself to Junior n' Mama, like the man that he ain't willin' to be for you."

"You think?" I could see that the idea appealed to Sister, too.

"Yeah, I do…let's feed Vance to Junior over breakfast tomorrow morning. Should be fun, don'tcha think?"

Sister smiled wanly. "Maybe not fun…but probably exciting, I will give you that."

"Okay, well…you prob'ly oughta get out o' here, then, before my friends over there in the parking lot start talkin' to someone besides each other. An' you don't need people whisperin' about how your brother got you pregnant or anything…"

"'kay, I'll see you back at the house, then," she said. "You gonna come home early tonight? Or stay out here all day?"

"I'll probably just stay out here. Don't want to tip Vance off that something's up, right?"

"Right. 'kay. Thanks, Collie. I'm glad I could talk to you about this."

"Mmm hmm," I acknowledged Sister's gratitude with a grunt, then reached behind my barrel for a swig of elixir to settle my nerves after this most unexpected and unpleasant encounter. Sister headed off down the pier, through the parking lot, up the road to our house, and the dock dwellers drifted back out on the pier as she passed them, grateful to be able to take a load off again. I raised my bottle their way in the universal gesture of toast, and they smiled, most of them toothlessly, and tipped their hats, bottles or chins back at me, reaffirming our silent brotherhood of dependency there on the docks of Bridgefield.

So it seemed like a good, tight, foolproof plan we'd come up with for addressing a pretty amorphous, conflict-laden situation. I felt like I contributed, like I'd helped, like I'd earned the right to drink in the sun for the rest of the day without guilt or bother. And true to my word, I didn't tip Vance off by changing any of my regular weekend routines. I rolled in at about 10:00 that night, grunted at Vance as he lay on the sofa in the den, went straight upstairs to my room, slammed the door (maybe a bit louder than usual, I concede that) and humped Morpheus with aplomb.

Until the alarm slammed me back into consciousness at 9 AM sharp the next morning, seemingly instantly, as if I'd never slept, as if my head had just hit my pillow, seconds earlier. Or at least as if my head had just hit the bed moments earlier, since I wasn't exactly pointed the right way, head on pillow, when I awoke, no doubt because I'd been trying to keep a hand on the floor to keep the room from spinning. So I laid in bed for a spell, disoriented as usual when I awoke, staring at the Earth, Wind and Fire and Brothers Johnson posters on my wall, untouched relics from my funky bass playing days, wondering who they were, and where I was, and why, and what I'd done to get here.

But then the smell of Mama's pancakes and crisp, sage sausage crept into my consciousness, and I remembered that I had breakfast plans, important ones, no less, groaned, felt the throb in my temples begin even as my feet touched the floor for the first time. I grabbed the pair of shorts and t-shirt that I'd been wearing all weekend, fished around in the pocket to see if I had any cigarettes left, found two, one broken, lit the other, inhaled, exhaled, felt the pain in my skull recede, but just a bit.

I dressed, shuffled over and opened the bedroom window (not that I needed to, since Mama generated enough smoke in the house that mine wasn't going to make any difference) and looked out at the back yard where Sister and I had once played (not with each other), and where Nephew would invariably while away his own childhood, in between trips to school and church and the music store. It was autumn, although you couldn't really tell since Mama's flowers were still blooming in Bridgefield's mild coastal climate, the blues and purples she favored defining the perimeter of her domain, shrubbery masking the chain link fence that kept the neighbor's dogs from snuffling out the bone meal in her bulb beds and excavating rhizome and corm alike as they rooted about for nonexistent tasty treats.

I saw that the impossible-to-kill fire ant nest in the back left corner of the yard was still hanging tough, its denizens and Mama seemingly having reached a détente of sorts over who was going to control that sector of turf. I made a mental point that I would tell Nephew someday that it was a very bad idea indeed to mess with the ants' tower, as I had discovered at a tender age myself after cracking it open with a bullwhip, raising a cloud of angry, stinging pismires into the air with each snap and recoil of the leather thong, enough of them landing on my arms and head to preclude me from ever trying that again.

But enough childhood memory mongering. Business beckoned. I tossed my cigarette out the window and into the rain gutter and tramped downstairs to the kitchen, where the family plus one awaited. I took my accustomed place, Junior across from me (both of us sitting exactly where we'd sat four years earlier when Junior had forcefully banished me to the Institute), Vance at my left, Sister at my right. Mama never sat down for breakfast, but instead picked at scraps and edges while she cooked for the rest of us, holding her cigarette dexterously with her left hand while pouring batter and flipping griddle cakes with the right.

I picked up the comics and waited for my first load of pancakes and coffee, glimpsing over the top of the paper at Sister and Junior, not wanting to look at Vance. I still couldn't tell by looking if Sister had put on any weight yet, although I noted that Junior was actually looking a bit doughy and soft of late, probably because Mama had adjusted her weekend breakfast recipes to accommodate a fifth mouth, and kept cooking that way, even on days when Vance and I weren't there. Junior also seemed to be nursing a bad tooth, his tongue working some spot behind his upper lip, worrying it, making him looked more pinched and pained than usual.

Sister wasted no time: "I got somethin' to tell y'all…"

Junior's eyes moved in her direction, but his head and body stayed still, except for the tooth-patrolling tongue, which seemed to have found the specific point of dental discomfort near the upper left canine. Vance and I continued to read our newspapers. Mama handled the conversational transition accordingly.

"What'cha gotta tell us, honey? Somethin' you read about in the paper this morning?"

"No, Mama, it ain't nothin' from the paper. An' it ain't nothin' that y'all are gonna like hearin', so you may want to sit down before I talk."

"I can't do that, baby, the pancakes'll burn. But I can hear from over here, so you just go ahead and tell us what's on your mind."

"Well, Mama, Junior…what I gotta tell y'all is that I'm gonna have a baby."

I heard Mama's spatula clank sharply against the griddle. I kept my eyes down for a moment, then looked up just in time to see Junior's tongue stop moving and his eyes shoot my way, narrowing.

"Did you know about this, Boy?"

"Well, uh, yessir…I did, but I thought it was best that Sister…"

"What'n the hell wouldja keep somethin' like this from me n' your Mama, Boy? What was you thinkin'? Sweet Colonel in Heaven I wonder about you sometime…"

There was no arguing with that, so I just turned my gaze Sister's way and furrowed my eyebrows to get her to go on with the rest of the news.

"Vance knew too," she continued. "About the baby, I mean, not that Collie knew…"

Vance sat his paper down on the table and sighed.

"Well how come everyone knew about this but me n' Mama, Sister? Don'tcha think we had a right to know, too?"

"Yeah, you do have a right to know, you do, that's why I'm tellin' you now," Sister paused. "But Vance had to know too, since he's the baby's daddy."

Mama let out a sharp little involuntary "ooo," set her spatula down, turned off the gas oven, walked over to the kitchen table and made little shoo gestures at me so I'd get up and let her have my seat. I meandered over to the other side of the kitchen and helped myself to one of her cigarettes, after picking up the pancakes left to burn on the griddle and setting them on the serving plate next to the stove.

"You gonna marry our baby, Vance?" Mama asked, her voice trembling. "Is that what this is about? You gonna marry our little Sister?"

"No, ma'am, Ms. Hay, that ain't my plan," Vance answered. "An' I'm sorry it ain't, for Wood and for you and for Mr. Hay, 'cause y'all have been nothin' but wonderful to me since I've been at the Institute. But Mr. Hay, I'm sure he knows what the rules are there: if I get married to Wood, then I gotta quit the Institute, and I can't see that bein' the best thing for me or for Wood or for the baby at this point. 'cause I don't have any prospects here, but I do have some good opportunities if I finish school and get my commission in the Marines, then I'll have a way to send some money home to y'all, but that's the best I can do if I can…"

I couldn't listen to this anymore. "Jesus flippin' Christ, Vance, quit making sad excuses. This ain't about the Institute an' it ain't about the Marines for you. It's about the fact that Sister, Wood, her," I pointed, "is good enough for you to screw on the sofa in a town where no one knows you when no one else's around, but you don't think she's officers wife material and you ain't willin' to take her outta here with you. I mean, you n' me been livin' together for almost four years, and you never once thought to tell me that you had something going with my sister? Or for my sister? Did it mean that little to you?"

Vance's expression never changed through my tirade, although Sister's face collapsed midway through it. "I didn't think what Wood and I did was any of your business, Collie," he answered. "And you can think what you want about my reasons for doin' what I want and need to do, but the bottom line is, and it always has been, that I wanna be a United States Marine, and that I wanna graduate from the Institute. I know that's hard for you to understand, since you don't have a clue about what you're doing there, or what you want to do when you finish."

I glared at Vance and tried to formulate a response, but Junior cut me off. "Vance is right, y'know."

Sister and I gaped at him in shock, before I finally blurted: "What? What do you mean Vance is right?"

"I mean, he's right about the Institute n' everything, n' about the fact that a man's gotta know what he wants out of life. And that Boy ain't got that kinda focus in life, 'bout nothin'. But I know what Vance wants for himself, I've heard him say it more times than I can count over the pas' three years. An' the education he gets at the Institute is gonna last him a lifetime, see, but if I make him quit to marry Sister now, then that marriage ain't gonna last longer'n the time it takes for the ink of that baby's birth certificate to dry. So if Vance's gotta choose between marryin' Sister and stayin' here or finishin' off at Ulmer and goin' off to be a Marine, he needs to go do the thing that's gonna get him what he wants outta life…"

"Oh my God, I, I can't believe what I'm hearing…" I stammered, aghast that my own father, and Sister's own father, would let Vance slip off the hook so easily, finding the Institute's honor easier to defend than that of his own flesh and blood. "I mean, who's gonna take care of Sister an' the baby if not Vance? Ain't nobody else I know gonna step in to raise another man's son, unless Sister's got some secret admirers I don't know about…"

"Boy, it ain't none of your business who's gonna take care of Sister, now, is it?" Junior turned to look at me again, his eyes darkening. "You ain't never been involved in her affairs before, you ain't never gonna be involved in her affairs again, so why don't you shut your trap an' let

Sister worry about that, if she is worried about it, but I doubt she is, 'cause she knows exactly who'll take care of her when she needs it, and for as long as she needs it too…"

"You an' the baby can stay here, sugar, your Daddy's right," Mama interrupted, taking Sister's hand in hers, then reaching to caress her hair and face. "You got nothin' to worry about as far as that goes…you our angel, and your baby will be our baby angel, we all gonna be okay, right?"

Sister nodded, although I couldn't tell if she was nodding sadly or appreciatively from where I stood. I shook my head in wonder at just how deranged my parents were, looked at the clock, looked at the stack of cold, ruined pancakes and announced: "Well, then, I'm glad we've all taken care of that. Now, y'all have to excuse me, 'cause I gotta get back to Ulmer, since I've got some fine education to attend to this afternoon. An' y'all might want to say 'bye' to Vance, too, since he ain't gonna be able to come home with me anymore, seein' as he's gotta focus on that Marine Corps commission and everything."

Sister fled the kitchen at that point, Mama following in her wake. Junior ignored me, turning instead to Vance. "I'm sorry this all happened this way, son. You got a great career ahead o' you, an' I'm sure that we're gonna have us one fine gran'chile, lookin' at how well you turned out." He rose, the two of them shook hands, and Junior retired to the backyard to sit in the swing where he did his best thinking, never once acknowledging my presence on his way out. Vance looked at me and shrugged. I shook my head in disgust and left to get my uniform.

We had a largely silent ride back to Ulmer, broken only when I noted, thinking out loud, and actually surprised to hear my voice when I did: "Y'know, I can still get you thrown out, whether you marry Sister or not. Just gettin' her pregnant's reason enough for them to separate you and send you home. The whole marriage thing is only gravy."

"Yeah, I know you can, Collie. Question is, are you going to?"

"I dunno."

And I didn't. Not then. Not for a long time after then, either. I thought about whether I was going to turn Vance in a couple of months later, when Sister found out that she was carrying twin boys, Nephews instead of Nephew. And I thought about it other weekends when I went home, too, alone, watching Sister get bigger every time I saw her, sometimes seeming to grow over the course of an afternoon while I sat on the pier, trying to think about nothing, thinking about Vance and Sister and the Institute and Junior and Mama instead.

And I thought about it pretty regularly while I was at school, sitting in the fourteen by twelve foot room that Vance and I shared, desks side by side, his bunk on top of mine, never saying a word beyond the obligatory "excuse me" that was necessary to negotiate such a cramped living space without inadvertently knocking each other over. Six months of near silence gave me a lot of time to think about it, in fact. Vance, too, no doubt.

I thought about Vance and the Institute and Sister a whole lot in March of 1980, when Sister gave birth to Greg and Ward, or Ward and Greg, who can tell, four weeks early, by Caesarian section. I saw them for the first time a couple of weeks later, and while they were still in the blob stage at that point and looked barely human to me, I cooed and made appropriate remarks about how this one looked like Junior and this one looked like Mama, and no one looked like Vance, who no one heard from, even after I left a birth announcement on his desk.

I asked Sister whether she wanted to hear from him. "No, I honestly don't at this point," she answered. "I mean, he said he'd send me money and everything, but I don't really need it, not enough that I wanna have to deal with him or anything. Let him go be a Marine, if that's what he really wants. I don't care anymore. I got the babies, they're beautiful, that's all I need right now."

A couple of weeks after that, Junior and Mama and Sister and the twins drove up to see me in Ulmer, and as we sat we on the lawn in front of the main barracks, azaleas in bloom under the drab red brick facade of my home for four years, each window thereon housing two drab, empty souls behind a screen of cheap institutional white Venetian blinds, my family scattered about on a picnic blanket in front me, Vance hiding somewhere in the Institute's inner sanctum behind me, the sheer monumental stupid wrongness of the whole situation came crashing down inside my soul. I mean, what kind of twisted, deranged lunatic would chose this antiquated, meaningless, soul-crushing pile of bricks and plaster and mindless tradition over this sweet, sweet loving woman here and her matched book-end babies as they lolled on the lawn, life-warming, soul-affirming, meaningful in all the ways that Institute and its regulations and its regimen could and would never be?

Such lunacy deserved punishment. I knew it, now, that someone had to suffer the way that Sister had suffered. That was the bottom line. Justice needed to be served. Vance needed to pay, to be revealed as the heartless military prick he was. I wondered, all of a sudden, what the kind and decent citizens of Walter's Crossroads would think if they found out that their Golden Boy had left a silver deposit in a honey pot far from home, then never bothered to pay the interest he owed on that account. They wouldn't approve. I owed it to them, too.

Now don't get me wrong: I didn't give a shit if Vance ever saw Sister or the babies, or if he ever sent them a cent, or if he became a general or a colonel or an Indian chief at some point down the road. I just wasn't going to let him choose the Institute over Sister, since being allowed such a choice somehow implied that the value of dogma and the value of a human life, or three human lives even, were comparable, and I knew that simply wasn't so, nor was it acceptable to believe that it was so.

And having reached such a conclusion, it took me very little time to vindicate Sister in the court of cosmic balance, even though no one else particularly wanted me to do so. Not even Sister. But never mind that, I knew that was just like how kidnap victims end up wanting to protect their kidnappers once the S.W.A.T. teams descend on the dungeon to rescue them. Sister would be grateful some day, and maybe we'd even be able to share another meaningful moment or two, like that day on the dock, once the whole thing was settled to my satisfaction.

So I went home the following weekend, rummaged around Sister's room, found the twins' birth certificate, with "Collier, Vance N." in the "father" line. I placed it in my desk drawer. I walked down to the far end of the barracks and requested an audience with the Commandant of Cadets. I advised him that Cadet Collier had impregnated my sister, who had since given birth to twins, who had received nary a visit nor a cent from their father.

The Commandant followed me back to our room. He asked Vance if my accusation was true. Vance had obviously been prepared for such a question as, without a delay, he denied paternity, questioned Sister's sanity and virtue, impugned my integrity and reliability, noted that we all had no idea who the boys' real father had been, but found it convenient to tag Vance, since he was a regular visitor to our sad little hovel in Bridgefield. He felt sorry for us all, he said, so he used to go home with me, since no one else would, and it was his duty to be good to me and my family, as a room mate, as a future leader of men. And look at how we were repaying his charity. What a world, what a world.

At this point I removed the birth certificate from my desk and handed it to the Commandant. At which point Vance noted that the certificate proved nothing, since Miss Hay could have lied to the hospital too. At which point I noted that blood tests could be arranged to sort out such ambiguities. At which point the Commandant announced that he'd seen and heard enough to convene an honor board to review Vance's case, particularly his troubling denial of paternity in the face of strong evidence to the contrary. At which point I smiled, because once that ball started rolling, someone was going to be flattened, and I was pretty certain that it was going to be Vance this time.

But I was wrong again. Rather than risk being discharged from the Institute for an honor violation, and thereby endangering his military career, Vance resigned voluntarily the next day, claiming family obligations back home in Mississippi. He was gone that evening, and I never saw him again, although I later heard from a classmate that he finished off his degree at a state college over the summer and was commissioned as a Second Lieutenant in the United States Marine Corps shortly thereafter. So much for my big scheme wrecking his life, although Vance's quasi-voluntary departure did relieve me on one front: I never had to tell Junior or Sister what I'd done to get him tossed out of the Institute, praise Colonel in heaven, Amen, Amen.

And after Vance was gone, things didn't really change all that much for me, since we hadn't been on speaking terms for some six months by that point anyway. Well, actually, one thing did change, I guess: I did drink in my room at the Institute regularly during the last month of school, since there was no one there to turn me in to the morality and propriety police. And I even brought a woman in with me once, mainly just to say I had, and because she thought it sounded exciting, and I have to admit that it was.

And then, after that monumental evening, I even managed to graduate, wonder of wonders, May 21st, 1980, number 214 in a class of 229. Not bad for a slug, and a liar, and a cheat, and a thief, and a drunk, huh? Nope, not bad at all. A round of drinks, all round, to celebrate. Here's to Collie Hay, graduate, avenging angel, life-wrecker, little brother and uncle extraordinaire.

And did I mention drunk?

Chapter Nine

"So what's with this zinger thing you've got going on all the time in here?" Lindy yells from our living room while I stand on the covered back porch, smoking and watching a lop-eared orange and black cat hunting garbage can gulls in the alleyway behind the Treehouse.

She had just finished reading the 180-some pages of book manuscript that I had ground out over a three-week period in May, year of our Lord Two Thousand and Naught, the month of my tenth anniversary at the *Advocate*, the month when the sun never shone on Troy. Or any other place in Upstate New York for that matter. So if the little celebration around my anniversary cake hadn't left me feeling tired and old and gray, then the weather certainly would have done the trick in its place. Combined, the two left a palpably oppressive weight on my soul, which I tried to excise, or at least shrug into a more comfortable carrying position, by spending my free time at home working on my book. Trying to make sense of something senseless. And trying to find something constructive to do to keep me from drinking and wallowing too much and too often.

Since the rain had started falling, Lindy had also spent a fair chunk of her spare time hanging out on our floor of the Treehouse. Up on her floor, you heard the rain on the roof, all the time, and the picture window view of the river was pretty grim under a vista of gray skies stretching westward as far as the eye could see. Pretty depressing place to be housebound by rain, for sure. Gerry and Randy and I had a terrifically comfortable leather sofa in our living room, too, so if Lindy was going to be inside reading, there wasn't a much better place to do it than here. Which was fine by me. I liked the company.

Lindy had been in the kitchen last night, Friday, hand-rolling ravioli with Randy (the more domestic of my engineers, yet still incongruous in his size XXL apron) when I had emerged from my office flipping through a thick sheaf of paper, representing the fruits of my labor as autobiographer to date. Randy and Gerry had been generally respectful, almost bashful, when inquiring about the book since I'd told them they were going to be in it, but Lindy had no such reservations, asking if she could read what I'd written, offering to edit if I needed it. I sneered at the mention of editing, since I myself was an editor and considered myself beyond rebuke or suggestion when it came to my own writing, but I did agree to let her read it, secretly pleased that she'd asked.

And now, the next afternoon, another dreary Saturday, intermittent drizzle still keeping us inside, humidity making us keep the windows open, high water on the Hudson leaving brackish tidal ponds all long River Street, the smell of brine and diesel fuel and wet Troy in the air, and Lindy yelling at me about zingers. What the hell is she talking about? I toss my cigarette into the alley, startling the cat, sending its target victim gull aloft into the dirty gray sky that perfectly camouflaged its dirty gray feathers, exhale deeply to clear the smoke from my lungs (Gerry and Randy weren't as forgiving as Mama once was about having their stuff smell like Marlboros) and return to the living room, where Lindy sprawls on her favorite sofa, stack of papers on the floor beneath her.

I act nonchalant and disinterested, although I'm pretty desperately interested in her opinions, on both what I've written and how I've written it. "What are you talking about, zingers?"

"Well, you know, you end each chapter with this sort of 'Oo, scary! What will he do next!' kind of foreshadowing thing, like a punch line, a zinger. Or a one-liner, maybe that's a better word. You turn into the master of one-liners whenever you've got to end a chapter. So what's with that? That's what I was asking."

Not exactly the sort of comment I was expecting. "Umm, well, I guess I just like to wrap things up, you know? I mean, a chapter break is an artificial construct anyway, it ain't like my life came in convenient, compartmentalized chunks that had nice, simple endings and beginnings, right? So if I'm gonna try to finalize some phase of my life after the fact, there's gotta be something that tells you that it's done, that a conclusion of some sort has been reached. Is that what you're talking about?"

"I guess that's part of it," she answers. "But it's also like you get all tongue in cheek, like you want to sort of shrug off the significance of what's come in the chapter up until that point. You seem to be making light of the things you've written, then promising nastier, darker, meaner fare in the next chapter, but then you hop back and forth from the past to the present, every other chapter, so you don't really capitalize on that sense of anticipation until a whole extra chapter later, but then you've put another zinger in there in between the two, so it's like the reader is anticipating a whole 'nother chapter ahead, not the one that they're reading at any given time, the way you've zinged them. Does that make any sense?"

"Well, no, it doesn't, actually. And, you know, all I'm trying to do is build anticipation, right?" I'm feeling pissy and mildly hurt now. "I mean, it's all about making a reader want to go on further than just to the page that immediately follows where he's at, isn't it?

"Maybe, maybe that's true," Lindy concedes. "But would you rather have people say that your book was a page-turner, or a chapter-turner?"

"Clever, nice zinger, nice one-liner. But I don't care what anyone calls it. I don't really plan on having anybody read it. You're reminding me of why I don't want to share it with people right now, in fact."

"Oh puh-lease, don't go turn into a baby on me now, for God's sake," Lindy sits up and shakes her finger at me. "As unbecoming as wallowing is on you, hypersensitivity to criticism is even less so. You dish it out all the time, so why can't you take it? And it's not that I don't like what you've done. I think what you've written is good, and interesting, and it all confirms that you're the awful, terrible excuse for a human animal that I've always suspected you of being. I just had that observation about your zingers. They seemed kind of rote after a while. Or forced. Or something. I thought maybe you'd want to fix that, or change it, whatever."

"Mmm…no. No, I don't think I want to change my zingers, but thanks." I start collecting my pile of papers from the floor and putting them back into neat order, noting some other stray red marks on their surfaces as I do. She edited. She really did edit. Bitch. I just wanted her to tell me it was wonderful as it was.

Maybe she just needs another invitation to do so. "Anything else you want to tell me about the book? Or just that one observation? Before I go back to my office to incorporate the multitude of comments you've felt compelled to scribble on my manuscript, I mean," I ask, sticking my head into the kitchen, then looking down the hall to see if Randy or Gerry are about, hoping to have an audience, or an ally, in my building snit. They aren't there. Damn.

"Well, do you really want to hear another comment, or do you just want to run off and sulk like a baby?"

"Oh, throw me another one, I can handle it. I'm a big boy," I bantered, although I didn't really feel like one.

"Okay. You've written eight chapters, almost 200 pages, and Kris hasn't appeared in one of them yet, except in passing mention, although I assume that your relationship with her and the whole accident and law suit thing are going to be a big part of the book, right?" She paused. "And Matt, too, for that matter…"

"I honestly don't know, Lindy," I answer, truthfully. "I mean, I hate to think that Kris is the defining element of my life. Or Matt, even worse. That would be kind of sad, don't you think? So I was sorta leaning towards spending more time writing about the band, and about being a music critic, or something a bit cheerier like that."

"That's fine, then, but you really haven't talked about those things either, have you? And I'm not sure I consider the band to be any cheerier a story than the Kris bit. On some plane, the way that ended and the way you guys blew the contract is even more stupid and pointless and depressing…"

"Thanks for the encouragement, then," I mutter, then speak more clearly before Lindy can catch her breath and continue down that vein. "I'm not done with the book yet, okay? And I think that in order to understand the Kris thing and to understand the band thing and to understand what music criticism means to me, you've gotta understand where I came from, and why those things happened to me the way they did. It's all background, that's what I'm writing now, the background stuff."

Lindy stands up, stretches, walks across the room and playfully squeezes my cheeks, giving me fish lips. "Maybe it's time to move to the foreground stuff, then," she says. "Maybe it's time to just go linear and tell the story the way it happened, get out of the whole then-now-then-now zinger oo-scary thing and lay it all out, the way it went, just the facts, man. Because when you get right down to it, the only thing happening in the right-here-right-now for you is that you're waiting for me to bail your sorry ass out the trouble you got yourself into. So how many times can you write that out before it gets boring?"

"I'll take that under advisement, Counselor…"

"You do that…" she says as she turns and walks into the kitchen, opens the refrigerator to see what's in it, then sticks her head up over the top of the door with an wicked glint in her eye, "…Boy."

"Ha ha."

"Ha ha, indeed, Huuuudson…."

"Ha ha, back atcha, Buh-lind-errr…" I over-pronounce the first and last syllables of her seldom-spoken proper Christian name, then bleat at her, "Baaaaaaaaa," thereby mocking her entire given name in one fell swoop, or at least its initials: B.A.A., Belinda Ann Andersson.

"Boy!"

"Buh-lind-errr! Baaaaaaa!"

She laughs and goes back to rummaging in the fridge. I figure if I act contrite, she might make me some dinner. I like it when people make me dinner. Or breakfast.

"Okay, you win, Bitchy Buh-lind-errr Baaaaaaaa, I'm sorry I got all defensive," I open. "I'm used to editing, not being edited…"

"Yeah, sure, you're a sensitive Girlie Man is what you are, Collie, or a sensitive Girlie Boy, rather, gonna let po' l'il weak ol' me get you all riled up with scathing criticism."

Okay, I can play along. "You're right, you're right, I'm weak and incapable of taking care of myself, helpless, a loafing blob, spineless, jelly in your hands, mud to scraped off the bottom of your boots." Time to cut to the chase. "In fact, I doubt I can even feed myself without help, so maybe in all your might and awesome power, you might want to whip up something quick and easy and set it a bowl on the floor so that I can…"

She doesn't buy it. The refrigerator door slams. "Nice try, but you need to go grocery shopping before I can cook here again. I don't make meals with mayonnaise and bologna and pickles, and that's all you've got in here now."

Lindy opens the door to the stairwell and waves, "I'm going back up to North Korea, so you can get crackin' on those edits."

"Bye. Thanks"

The door closes, then opens again. "Oh, one other thing…" Lindy starts, head popping around the jamb.

"What?"

"As your attorney, I hereby officially advise you not to share that whole chapter about the drinking thing with anyone…it wouldn't be good for your case."

"Sure. I ain't sharin' this with anyone any more anyway, remember?"

"Right," she snaps, gives me a thumbs up signal, closes the door, then opens it yet again.

"And one more thing…"

"Jesus, Lindy, what?"

"My apartment doesn't smell like patchouli. I don't burn that stuff. It's sandalwood you smell, dummy."

And this time the door closes, clicks, and her footsteps recede up the stairs to the fourth floor. I flip through the manuscript and note some of her suggestions and revisions. They're actually pretty good, most of them. I'm not going to tell her that, though. I'll just make the changes, toss her copy, and then claim that I'd caught the errors myself. If I ever let her see what I'm writing again, that is.

Gerry and Randy still aren't home, although I'm not sure where they've been all day. Maybe out shopping at the antique building supply store up the road, one of their favorite places, where they can spend entire weekends digging through old tiles and bolts and spigots and fixtures, looking to match or fix or augment something in our apartment, or in the Fourth Floor deluxe community models. Dr. Dave the Dentist up there shares their enthusiasm for historical renovation, so they've been spending a lot of time working on his apartment lately, or at least since Brian and I stopped having a studio for them to work on.

Wherever they're at, I hope they stop by the grocery store on their way home, since the pickings in the fridge are every bit as grim as Lindy had indicated. But I am hungry, so I fish a dill pickle out of the jar with my fingers, wrap it in a slice of bologna, then dip the whole thing into the jar of mayonnaise. Not bad. Not bad at all. I make another pickle and bologna burrito and eat it the same way, noting when I'm done, however, that there are now flecks of dill seeds and streaks of bologna fat and pickle juice sitting atop the tasty egg and vinegar emulsion in the mayonnaise jar. I cap the jar, shake vigorously, and open it again: no seeds, no crumbs, no flecks to be seen. No hurt, no foul, accordingly.

I return the bottle to the fridge. I sit on the couch where Lindy had been sitting. Her spot is still warm. But it's too quiet in here now. And I'm not drunk yet, which is generally a prerequisite to getting to that selfish point where I enjoy being by myself, sometimes to the point of hostility to anyone else who happens to be about. I usually retire to my office or the studio when I get to that point, so I can gnaw my own leg off in privacy if I want to, but still never escape from the insidious snare of addiction. I need to get started seriously on my drinking soon, come to think of it, if I'm going to get where I need to be by bedtime tonight. A late start can throw my whole schedule off if I'm not careful, but I'm a little bit sensitive about partaking too heavily when Lindy's about the house. Maybe I should just not drink today. Maybe, maybe…

I check the liquor cabinet to make sure there's enough there to do the job right, since there's no sense starting now if I'm gonna wind up at 10 o'clock tonight feeling unsatisfied with the quantity consumed, needing to go out to buy more, ideally to a bar, with rock bands, and women. Better to just do without for a day than to have to do that dance later this evening, especially since there's nothing going on tonight that would be worth reviewing in next week's paper, so it would be a wasted evening from a work standpoint.

But that's all a moot point anyway, since there's plenty of vodka here, and a little bit of rum in case things get rough later. That should tide me over fine, should I indeed commence drinking at this relatively late point in the day, rather than just waiting until tomorrow, when I can start over brunch, in keeping with my regular weekend schedule.

I ponder for a moment, not a long one, grab the bottle of nuclear potato juice and pour a long slug into a large, heavy-duty coffee mug, then head back through the living room to the porch again, to smoke, to drink, perchance to see if the cat has killed anything since last I looked. With all the water on the ground and dank warmth in the air, stuff down there is starting to stink pretty quickly this spring if nothing carries it away or nobody puts it into one of the dumpsters that line the alley, making trash pickup day one of the noisiest events imaginable hereabouts. I sleep through it most of the time, though. Practice, practice, practice.

I still feel like talking to someone, so I toss another cigarette into the alley, go back inside, grab the phone from off of its cradle in the corner of the living room and start dialing, the number of the family homestead in Bridgefield being the one that automatically pops to mind and finger. It's actually the only number I call these days, outside of work, since I can't call Kris anymore.

A deep male voice answers: "Hello?"

Toss the coin, take my chance. "Ward?"

"No, this is Greg."

"Oh, hey, Greg, I'm sorry…It's Collie."

"Hey, Collie, how you doin'?"

"Pretty good, pretty good, thanks, how 'bout you?" It only took seconds for the native South Carolina accent to begin creeping back to the surface once I started talking to my kinfolk in the coastal motherland.

"Good. Me n' Ward are doin' pretty good with our landscaping business this spring, lots of new golf courses goin' in up the coast near Charleston, so we been gettin' lots of contracts up there for that, makin' some pretty good money."

"Good for you two," I say, impressed, really. "Are y'all still workin' in the store at all, or just doin' the landscapin' now?"

"Nah, we still help Grampa Junior and Mama in the store. Mama won't let us out of that until we're makin' enough money so that she don't have to work there anymore either."

I see a fleeting vision of my mother in an oxygen tent, or maybe a shroud, asking Greg, or Ward, or Greg and Ward, for a cigarette, since it takes a moment, as it always does, for it to register that when Greg, or Ward, or Greg and Ward say "Mama," they really mean "Sister." She's been their mother for 20 years, but I still can't think of her as a parent, really. Much less one called "Mama."

"So, uh, is Sister around? Your Mama, I mean?"

"Yeah, she's here, hang on," I hear him yell "Mama! Collie for you!" despite the hand he has clamped over the phone mouthpiece. Then he's shouting at me again. "Good to talk to you, Collie!"

"You too, Greg. Tell Ward I said 'hey.'"

"Will do. 'bye."

"Bye."

"Here's Mama."

"'kay, thanks."

Sister took the phone from her son: "Hey."

"Hey."

"Greg says he n' Ward are doin' real well with their landscaping company, huh? That's pretty cool."

Sister pauses. "That was Ward, Collie."

"What? Well, that's who I thought it was when he answered the phone, but he said he was Greg…"

"They like screwing with you, Collie," Sister laughed. "They know you can't tell them apart."

"Well who can on the telephone?" I'm indignant. "Jesus, ain't like I can see them or anything."

"Would it help if you could?"

"No."

We both laugh, now.

"I didn't think so," Sister concludes, and I hear her take a drag on a cigarette at her end, a proper Hay Mama indeed, despite having watched her own mother die horribly from throat cancer a decade-and-a-half earlier. But, then, I should talk or criticize, right? "So what's goin' on?"

"Not much," I answer. "Workin'. Hangin' out. Oh, and, uh, I'm writin' a book."

"Oh yeah? Good for you, you need a project to get your mind off o' Kris an' all."

I pause, not sure whether I really want to get into this with Sister or not. What the hell, no guts, no glory, no spatter, no story. "Well, umm, sorta yeah, sorta no…I mean, the book is kinda about Kris, and some other stuff from real life, too, so it ain't really gettin' my mind off of the stuff as much as it's helpin' me figure out what all the stuff means to me."

It's Sister's turn to pause. "Like what other stuff."

"Y'know, stuff stuff, real stuff, like I just finished writin' about the Institute and Vance an'…"

Sister cut me off, quickly. "Collie Hay, don't you fuckin' dare tell me what I think you're gettin' ready to tell me."

"What?"

"You didn't write a book about Vance and me, did you?"

"Well, no, not a book about you, no," I fumble. "But, y'know, a chapter or so, yeah, I mean, how could I exclude all that?"

"Real easy like, since it ain't no one's business but my own, an' I don't want Greg and Ward havin' to read the Gospel Accordin' to Unca' Boy when it comes to explainin' where their father's at, or where he ain't at, these days."

"I'm not plannin' to let anyone read the book," I protest. "I'm just writin' it for myself, and when I wrote about the Institute n' you n' Vance, I was actually kinda reminded about the good stuff that came out of that, y'know? About how good I felt when you confided in me first, before Mama and Junior, that kinda stuff. So it's nice things, not bad things. I'm tryin' to pick the nice things out of my life, think about them for a change."

I'm lying now, of course, or at least not telling the whole truth, but I feel like I need a little bit of buy in, a little bit of validation, from Sister, especially having just revisited and acknowledged one of few precious, decent human moments of my life, which I had shared with her.

"I don't quite remember it like that, honestly," Sister retorts. "What I remember is that I had to track you down to the piers, and that while I needed someone to talk to, you just wanted me to hurry up and leave so you could finish drinkin' with the other bums down there."

Ouch. "Well, I'm sorry you felt like that, since that ain't what I was thinkin' at all." Well, maybe a little, but there was some legitimate compassion there, I don't think I'm making that up after the fact. Am I? Did I? Would I?

"Whatever, Collie, it was too long ago for us to be worryin' about it now, but I just don't want you gettin' Junior or the boys all stirred up about Vance and the Institute, alright?"

"What's to stir 'em up about?" I'm legitimately confused. "I mean, they know who their father is, right?"

"Yes, they do," she answers curtly. "But they don't know all the details about why he ain't here no more."

"Have you ever heard from him? I mean, has he ever tried to get in touch with you or to see the boys?"

"No," she pauses. "No, he hasn't. Except for once, about a month after you graduated, he wrote me then and told me that he wasn't able to send any money since you got him thrown out of the Institute."

"He left for a family emergency back in Mississippi, Sister," I shift into full denial mode. "Call the Institute, they'll look it up for you, it's in his record there, I'm sure. And if I was going to get him thrown out of the Institute, why would I have waited that long to do it? It doesn't make any sense."

"No, it doesn't, but then, what about you does," she answers with a sigh. "Look, whatever, Collie, I don't wanna fight about it, like I said, it's too long ago to worry about, an' I don't want you romanticizing it or telling your own version of the tale or anything, alright? I mean, I really prefer to not think about the Institute any more. Or Vance."

I'm not letting her off that easily, particularly since she's stung me again by letting me know, all these years later, that she was on to my role in Vance's exit from the Institute and her life. "How can you not think about it anymore living in that house? Doesn't Junior still talk about the Institute all the time?"

"No, not really, not like he used to," Sister answers. "Y'know, it took a lot o' screamin' on my part to stand up to Junior to keep him from insisting that Greg and Ward go there too. So since they, or I, decided that they were gonna stay here and the whole 'male Hays gotta go to Ulmer' thing has been proven bullshit, he kinda doesn't spend much time dwelling on it anymore. At least not with me, he may still harass the boys when I ain't around, I dunno about that. So I won that fight, which you lost, and outta respect for that fact, I'd really like you to promise me that you're not gonna rehash this old ground with anybody down here, when I'm the one that's gonna have to live with if you do. Okay?"

"Yeah, that's fine," I answer, pretty much beaten. "But what about just you? Do you want to read it yourself? Just to see what I've written?"

"No I don't. I lived it. I'm still livin' it. You ain't gonna be able to tell me nothin' about it that I don't know already."

"Okay, suit yourself. I was just tryin' to share."

There's silence on the line. I hear Sister smoking. I take the phone back out on the porch and light up a cigarette of my own. We smoke together, long distance, for a minute or so, before she feels like talking again.

"So what else is goin' on?"

"Nothin'. Still waitin' to see what happens with the civil suit. Lindy, that's my lawyer, she says she's tryin' to minimize the damage, but she doesn't think things look too good for me at this point."

"Huh. So what's that mean?"

"Probably that they're gonna rule against me, and that I'm gonna be liable for some huge sum of money that I don't have, so they're gonna make me sell everything I own that I haven't sold already, then take a chunk o' my paycheck each week to pay the difference, for the rest of my life."

"Jeez, that bites," Sister notes, astutely, succinctly.

"Yep, sure does. An' now you're tellin' me that I can't sell 'The Sister Hay Story' for a million dollars to the movies, so there goes that avenue of escape…"

"Nah, 'cause if you sold it to the movies, I'd take all the money myself."

"And what would you do with it then," I ask her.

"Oh, I dunno, maybe get Junior stuffed, mount him in the living room, burn down the Store, give the insurance money to Greg and Ward and then run away to Tahiti."

"Nah, I bet you'd just give it all to the South Carolina Military Institute Alumni Association, since you're such a closet cadet lover."

"Kiss my ass."

"I don't do sloppy seconds, honey, sorry."

She paused. "I was gonna say 'fuck you,' but I figured I'd be really settin' myself up with that, wouldn't I?"

"Yes you would."

"Okay. So I'll just say goodbye instead, then, how 'bout that?"

"That's fine," I answer. "I got work to do, justice to run from, books to write."

"I'll bet you do, you maniac, I'll bet you do."

"'kay. Tell Junior I said 'hey.'"

"I will," Sister says. "But I doubt that he'll hear me when I do. He never turns on his hearing aid anymore."

"Fine. It's the thought that counts anyway."

"Right."

"Right."

"'kay. Bye. Love you."

"Love you, too."

And a click. I look at the phone in my hand. Look at the now-empty vodka mug on the porch table. Look at my reflection in the glass door to the living room, see myself translucently, see our furniture through my features, see myself blanched and faded, a shadow, a wraith, a wisp of smoke and alcohol fumes. I look at my vodka mug again. There's more in the cabinet. I could have more now. I could. And it would be good, I would enjoy it. I really would.

But I wouldn't write much, or well, if I did. And it's occurring to me that maybe Lindy was right, that maybe it's time to set aside the background noise in my life, the cigarettes, the booze, the misery felt and misery inflicted, the ennui and the malaise and the zingers and get on with defining the foreground, with telling the real Collie Hay story, laying it all out, how I got from there to here, then to now, was to am. And always will be? Maybe. Maybe.

But the background is important, too, I can defend that because I think people need to know that I tried to wreck Vance's life (but failed, since he was resilient and had a fall-back plan), for instance, to fully appreciate the finer feats of long-term human destruction that I engaged in later, and the fact that I didn't learn from my mistakes the first time.

And the drinking thing, that colors every other thing that I've touched or made or been or thought for the past twenty years, so that's there too, and people need to know it, if they're going to know me. And I need to know it. This book is for me, I have to keep reminding myself of that.

And even the music critic stuff, that needs to be there, since the fact that I make my living by ripping apart other people's art is clearly indicative of the tenor of my personality, the meanness of my soul, the lack of creativity and craftsmanship in my own life, throwing rocks instead of mining them.

But now I'm getting weepy and pathetic. It's the stage where I'm at in my drinking cycle: I either need to drink more, fast, or start doing something else, soon, to get past this uncomfortable, unpleasant stage. Obliteration or action. Decisions. Decisions. I pick up my vodka mug, run my finger along its inner rim, toss it in the air to test its heft a couple of times, then fling it down into the alley below me, where it shatters dramatically, shards ricocheting impressively high back towards me. It occurs to me now that it was Gerry's coffee cup, in addition to being a nice symbol. Oh well, I need to write this thing, he needs to get a new coffee cup. I can't worry about that now. I need to get this thing done. I need to tell my story. I'm going to do it now.

But it's still going to take a while, zingers or not.

Chapter Ten

The South Carolina Military Institute's Class of 1980 graduated in May under a broiling Ulmer sun, sweating through our wool uniforms as we sat in the middle of the football field in our rickety old school stadium, our families, friends and other loved ones arrayed about us in the horse-shoe shaped bleachers. The open end of Cadet Stadium faced east, ostensibly to allow cooling sea breezes to work their way across the Low Country's marshes and fields, finally in due course to waft over the Institute's gridiron, where they would cool its athlete warriors as they blocked and ran and threw and tackled for tradition, for honor, for sixth or seventh place in the Eastern Independent Athletic Conference. Evidently, however, the breezes didn't show up when the football team wasn't playing.

I had been up all night the night before, celebrating my last weekend in Ulmer with all of my favorite winos, sluts, vagrants and barkeeps at O.P.'s Saloon, way out on Highway 301 towards Buford's Bridge, where drunk and disorderly was a way of life, not a criminal offense. Since I was only spending the first 20 days of May in Ulmer (graduation being the 21st), I had a decent chunk of my monthly $100 in Junior cash left to squander on my going-away party. So I ordered a big helping of take-out from Burnin' Pig Barbecue, smoked beef and pork, slaw, biscuits, greens, hush puppies, all the essentials, and took it all with me to O.P.'s, figuring that would be a good way of reminding the regulars that they needed to buy me more free drinks than usual, all night long.

My ploy worked. I spent the entire evening drinking and partying and eating, and I therefore spent most of my graduation day nodding in and out of consciousness, sweating alcohol and pig fat, trying to not let my head fall too far forward or to snore too loudly during the ceremony.

The Commandant of Cadets kicked off the whole shindig with a droning speech that put me under pretty quickly, right off the bat, blah blah blah duty, blah blah blah honor, blah blah blah fine young men, blah blah blah privilege, blah blah blah goddamned shiftless Hutson Hay framing the noble and ambitious Vance Collier (or did I dream that?), blah blah blah thank you.

Next up, our commencement speaker, General Paul Z. Pugh, United States Marine Corps (Retired), former commanding officer of the Marine Corps Recruit Depot at Parris Island, proud SCMI graduate, class of 1946. He'd been a senior during Junior's first year at the Institute, and my father held him in a perpetual position of awe and reverence accordingly, never mind what either of them had or hadn't accomplished during the ensuing 30-some years. My only sentient thought during his commencement speech, however, was to wonder what the "Z" in his name stood for? Zechariah? Ziggy? Zyklon-B? Hmm…I'd have to remember to look in Junior's yearbook someday. Or maybe not.

When the General finally left the stage, our valedictorian, Regimental Commander Rufus William Hampton IV (of both the Ridgeland and the Orangeburg Hamptons, a very well connected young man indeed), took the podium to offer some unctuous butt-licking words and was ceremonially recognized as our first graduate, to resounding applause. After Rufus, the other 49 honor graduates of my class were announced, each one walking to the stage for his diploma and a series of hearty handclasps from the Commandant and the General, applause dwindling steadily throughout the parade of very smart cadets as the audience grew weary of the repetitive spectacle unfolding before them.

And then it got even worse, for all parties concerned: the two-dozen or so cadet class officers who hadn't managed to reach the lofty academic ground occupied by the honors graduates were called forward, one by one, then those team captains and co-captains of the Institute's varsity sports teams who hadn't been recognized as members of the inner two circles, then, finally, the undistinguished rabble of our class, me smack dab drab in the middle of that latter group.

As best I could ascertain, the stadium was completely silent as my name was read, I walked up the stairs to the stage, shook hands, took my diploma and returned to my seat at the visiting team's 45-yard line. I wasn't terribly surprised, since I knew Junior would've disapproved of any gaudy public display of emotion, and I'm sure he had Mama and Sister (and maybe even babies Ward and Greg) well-prepared to beam proudly, silently, as I joined the long line of Hay men who had successfully navigated the Institute's hallowed, character-building halls.

Soon thereafter, Griffin M. Young (one of the few cadets to rank lower than me in the class standing and, not surprisingly, also one of the few that I ever saw in the bars around Ulmer, although we didn't speak to each other when our paths crossed there, respecting our rights to hide from reality, undisturbed) made his trek to and from the stage, this time to hearty applause again, since he represented the final member of our class to matriculate, and the end of a long, hot morning. In keeping with ancient and inviolable tradition, the 229 members of the Corps of Cadets then tossed our "covers" (that's the proper military word for "stupid looking hats") into the air in celebration, or release, or relief, and commencement was complete, as we stomped across a sea of white hats with black bills (it was considered bad luck to pick them up) on our way to meet our guests in the stadium bleachers.

Afterwards, some two-thirds of my class adjourned to the Institute's Chapel for commissioning ceremonies, where they were sworn in as officers in the Army, Air Force, Navy, Coast Guard or Marine Corps, signing away another four to six years of their lives in the process, depending on what kind of deals they'd struck with the recruiters or the ROTC programs that had paid for their education. And when commissioning was complete, the Chapel was turned into the Wedding Mart, where a long line of pent-up, horny cadets finally got to walk down the aisle with their respective beloved ones, eagerly signing away even longer chunks of their lives in the name of yet another form of servitude.

So it was a busy, life-changing day for a select group of promising young men, yes indeed it was. But for me? No great shakes, really, since I just went home to Bridgefield when it was all over, no commissioning, no wedding for me, thanks. Well, not directly home, exactly, not right away: first Junior and Mama and Sister and the babies and I went out to celebrate at the Burnin' Pig (I didn't have the heart to tell them I'd already eaten too much pork the night before), and Junior clapped me on the shoulder at the buffet line when no one was looking and told me he was proud, and that's when we all went home, in our separate cars. And I unloaded my suitcase and I went to bed.

Things were pretty much the same in Bridgefield as they'd been before I went to the Institute, except that now there were two babies in the house, and I had a Bachelor of Arts in English degree stuffed in the desk drawer with my old *Playboy* collection, and the kids who came into the music store (where I had immediately gone back to work upon arriving home) now wanted to be Eddie Van Halen instead of Jimmy Page. I occasionally tried to point out the importance of Michael Anthony's bass contributions to the overall Van Halen sound, but few of them were particularly interested in hearing me pitch the wonders of the four-string axe. Oh well, I made more on commissions when I sold them expensive guitars than I did when I sold them starter basses, so I wasn't much going to complain either way.

The dearth of new, up-and-coming Bridgefield bass players also made it fairly easy for me to get some decent, steady gigs with a variety of local and regional bands, many of them helmed by the same guys I'd been playing with, or in some cases competing with, four years earlier. But while the playing field remained fairly constant, what was actually being played on that field was dramatically, eye-openingly, somewhat depressingly different to me, since I discovered that having been cloistered from 1976 to 1980 meant that I had missed the most significant music revolution of my lifetime. And that had I actually moved to New York City in 1976, per my original plans, I would have been right there at ground zero when it happened.

But I didn't, or couldn't, follow those original plans, so I remained oblivious to the rise and fall of punk rock while slamming shooters at O.P.'s, I missed the subsequent commercialization of the revolution through New Wave and New Romantic filters while hanging out at the docks in Bridgefield, and the codification of the D.I.Y. ethic and the resultant twin demise of corporate disco and dinosaur rock were enigmas to me, since they didn't happen in my bedroom at home or in my barracks in Ulmer. I'd wondered about some of the safety pins and torn garments and bad haircuts that I'd seen in the store when I was home working in the summers, sure, but I'd just assumed that times were getting tougher in Bridgefield and the surrounding communities, not that a cultural revolution had reached the Low Country.

So there wasn't much call in 1980 for my previous public forte of funk-flavored bass stylings, nor in the pretentious sorts of progressive rock noodling in which I'd started to engage in my bedroom (having no outlet to perform it anywhere else) when I was home from the Institute, pretending I was Greg Lake or John Wetton, trying to avoid looking at my posters of Verdine White and Larry Graham while I betrayed the true funk bass cause to dabble in overly smart white boy pomp rock. Fortunately, however, the "anyone can play" ethos of the punk and its spawn meant that the new style bass parts were an awful lot simpler than the stuff I'd been accustomed to playing publicly four years earlier. So I could play songs by the Romantics or the Vapors or the Cars or

Blondie in clubs, and King Crimson or Funkadelic or Steely Dan in my bedroom, and still consider myself an artiste, despite all public evidence to the contrary.

I also started writing songs again during this time, taking four years worth of accumulated angst and creative energy and funneling it into a collection of dense, malign works that I wanted to play out for real audiences, but knew that I never could. At least not in Bridgefield. I made lots of tapes, though, and I got quite good at creating some pretty credible sounds on some pretty crappy equipment.

And so all those factors made it a fairly painless transition for me as I worked in the store by day, then put on the obligatory skinny tie and set about to bedazzle both high school kids in Bridgefield and bored New York socialites on Hilton Head alike by night, playing the more accessible New Wave hits of the early '80s just as rotely as I'd once played the Lynyrd Skynyrd or Fleetwood Mac covers before them. I even continued to take pay in alcohol, drugs or sexual favors, when the opportunities to do so presented themselves, just like the good old days, although as I got older and high school girls got younger, I did decide that it was best to just take my cash and run when playing the sorts of shows that they attended, lest temptation lead me to another sort of lock-up for four (or more) years.

But other than that, I was pretty undiscriminating and easy to please. I traded free coke and pot for cash for booze, then continued practicing my master drinking techniques, stretching my income while imploding my mind. And I continued the long-standing streak of meaningless sexual relationships that I'd begun with Cindy Clark during Youth Grope all those years before. With one twist: during the Youth Grope era, I'd felt bad that Cindy didn't want to be seen with me unless we were getting high or fondling each other, wondering about how unappealing I must have been on any meaningful plane for her to covet only my drugs and my body (with the latter being questionable, given the nature of the trade we were making). After I came home from the Institute, though, such a situation was optimal: many flings, no strings.

Life was good and simple and meaningless. At which point, drum roll please, enter Kristine Ravenel Dennison, of the Columbia Ravenels and Dennisons, both prominent High Country families of the Antebellum Era, making Kris a veritable modern day princess in the social circles where such historical things mattered.

Kris arrived in Bridgefield some time during the summer of 1981, a little more than a year after I had returned home from Ulmer. I'm a bit mushy on the exact date when Kris walked into my life, since she caused no immediate change to me (or it), and I had no sort of love-at-first-sight reaction to her, nor any premonition that she was different, the one for me, sunshine and lollipops and puppy dogs forever and ever, amen.

It wasn't like that. At all. In fact, it wasn't much of anything, at the beginning, except for an occasional business transaction, some muted nice talk as we exchanged money and goods. And to be honest, I really didn't notice her at first because my scamming sensors weren't at all attuned towards well-dressed, clean, polite young women when they walked into Junior's Music, although a chunky blonde in a halter top and cut-off shorts trailing an aroma of cigarette smoke and sweat would've caught my attention right away, dirty opportunity presenting itself for the taking.

Kris had grown up in the Columbia suburbs before attending Winthrop College in Rock Hill, right up by the North Carolina border, earning her music degree then staying on to complete her teacher's certificate. Like many sensitive, well-bred, academically-minded souls, she wanted to make a difference as a teacher, so (perhaps having watched Jon Voight in *Conrack* one too many times) instead of taking a cushy position in a private academy somewhere in or around Columbia, she looked for a challenging, meaningful job, a place where she could lift the disenfranchised locals out of their cultural mire and grace them with the gift of music. Bridgefield obviously fit the ticket.

So Kris had moved her modest belongings into a small cottage-style house down at the end of Bay Street, overlooking the marsh, and spent the summer of 1981 acclimating herself to the humidity, the poverty, the insularity of Low Country South Carolina. I imagine that it didn't take her long to find Junior's Music as part of that acclimation process, since we provided the instruments that her students would be playing in the upcoming year. I'm vaguely aware (or am fabricating memories, it's hard to tell which) of her being in the store maybe half-a-dozen times doing school stuff before we actually spoke—although not about the school's music, but about Kris' own music.

I was behind the counter at the store, reading *Rolling Stone*, trying to catch up on four years worth of lost music history, when the bell over the door jingled. I glanced up, quickly decided that the professional-looking woman entering the store didn't appear to have a high probability of being a shoplifter, went back to my magazine, waited for her to deposit product on the shelf in front of me. But she didn't. She walked straight to my register.

"Hi."

I looked up, surprised. "Hi. Can I help you?"

"I hope so," she paused. "You wouldn't by any chance happen to sell bassoon supplies, would you?"

Now, there was a question that I'd never been asked during a lifetime spent hanging out in a music store, since neither the Calhoun Academy nor Bridgefield's public schools offered bassoon as an orchestra instrument.

"No, sorry, we don't," I answered. "But I might be able to check a catalog and see if we can order you something, if you want. What is it that you're looking for?"

"Reed cane. Or just a finished reed even, for now" she answered. "And I'm embarrassed, because a good bassoon player should never run out of reeds, but I haven't had a chance to get any cane to make new ones since I moved to Bridgefield, and I just split my last whole reed this morning, so I need a new one. Quickly, if possible, since I don't like to go a day without playing, y'know what I mean?"

"Yeah, I do," I answered as I rooted around under the counter for the appropriate musical equipment catalog. "I play the bass, and I get kinda itchy if I don't touch it for a while, too, although I can't claim to play it every day..."

Then Kris really surprised and impressed me. "Right, right, you're a bassist. I thought that it was you that I saw playing in the band out at the Fripp Island Country Club a couple of weeks ago."

Wow. She'd noticed me. She'd connected me from place A to place B, with only a minor hint to help her. I stood up and actually looked at her for the first time,

She was tall, almost as tall as me, with a swimmer's or a runner's sort of tight body, posture impeccable, making her an ideal living clothes rack, everything looking just the way the designers intended when she put it on. She had shoulder-length brown hair, full, worn loose, moving as she moved, and sometimes seeming to move on its own when she didn't. She smiled easily, with lots of teeth, and she had stunning charcoal-colored eyes, which were easy to see, since she looked at people when she talked to them.

Unlike me. I couldn't return that gaze, dropping my eyes back to the catalog now open on the counter. "Umm...okay, this company sells oboe and bassoon reeds...is that what you want? Or did you say you made your own?"

"I make my own when I can get decent reed cane," she answered. "There's a place up in Charlotte that I used to be able to order it from when I lived in Rock Hill, but I haven't been up there in a few months. But I could buy a couple of manufactured reeds now, if that's all you can find, then get some cane later..."

I wasn't going to let her go without making a stronger effort to satisfy her needs, though. "Let me call another shop we sometimes do trade with up in Charleston," I told her, reaching for the phone before she could comment. "Hang on one sec…"

Three rings before an answer, fortunately the right one: "McCreedy Music, can I help you?"

It was Jeff McCreedy, like me a second generation music store drone, now managing the family business himself since his father had retired to West Palm Beach a couple of years earlier. "Dude, it's Collie at Junior's."

"Collie, what's cookin'?"

"Lookin' for some reed cane for a bassoon, man."

"Some what?"

"Reed cane," I cupped the phone and hissed this time, just in case I was saying the wrong thing, not wanting to embarrass myself in front of my interesting new customer.

"What the hell's that?"

"Dude, I dunno, it's what people make reeds out of, I guess."

"Oh, oh…I get it," I could almost hear the light bulb snapping on over Jeff's head. "Like the wood that they make the reeds out of, it must be cane, right?"

"Yeah, yeah," more urgently now, like I was scoring drugs or something. "You got any? Or know anyplace I can get some?"

"Nah, man, most double-reed players are pretty weird about their reeds, make 'em themselves or get 'em direct from some secret double-reed player cartel or something, so I don't really do a lot of business in that sort of stuff," Jeff answered. "I got lots of sax and clarinet reeds, and wood to make 'em, but not much as far as doubles go. Hang on, let me check the catalog…"

"Don't bother, I checked all mine, I doubt you have anything I don't."

"Alright, then," pause. "So, like, good luck n' stuff."

"Right, thanks."

For nothing. I hung up on Jeff and returned my attention to Kris. "Sorry, he's all out right now," I explained, assuming the masterly air of a man who trafficked in bassoon reed cane on a regular basis. "Do you want me to order some of these reeds in here for you, then maybe you can give me the name of the place you get the cane from and I can get it for you at wholesale price or something?"

"Thanks, thanks, that would be great," she smiled at me, such a smile, and I think I may have even blushed. "Got something I can write on?"

I handed her a receipt pad and she wrote the name of the music store in Charlotte, something hoity-toity sounding, no doubt specializing in all sorts of arcane instrumentation that we'd never, ever hear in lowly Bridgefield. Then she wrote "Kris Dennison" beneath it, and her phone number. "I'll be in here pretty regularly, but if you want to call me when the reeds get in, or if you can get the cane, that'd be great," she explained.

"Why?" I asked, letting the question hang, watching the surprised look on Kris' face, then realizing what an idiot I was. "I mean, why will you be in here regularly? Not why should I call you."

"Oh, I get it, sorry, I was confused," she laughed and her hair moved all around, wow. "I'll be in here a lot, 'cause I'm the new music teacher at Bridgefield Elementary, and you're the only music store in Bridgefield, or at least the only one I've found so far."

"Nope, we're it, not only in Bridgefield but in all of Coosawhatchie County," I told her. "So we see all the music teachers here, all the time."

"Great then, so I guess I'll talk to you soon," Kris answered. She pointed at the sign taped to cabinet reading "Make checks payable to Junior's Music" and asked "So, are you Junior?"

"No, no, Junior's my dad, I'm his son, Collie."

"Pleased to meet you, Collie," Kris stuck her hand out to shake, so I mark that as the first time we touched, very significant, and nice.

"Likewise," I didn't want her to leave. I didn't want her to leave. I didn't want her to leave. What to say? What to say? "Y'know, I'd love to hear you play sometime," I finally blurted. "I'm honestly not sure that I've ever heard anyone play the bassoon."

"You never had to listen to Prokofiev's 'Peter and the Wolf' in elementary school," she asked.

"Umm, jeez, maybe I did, I dunno. Been awhile, right?" I laughed nervously.

"Well, if you could remember it, the bassoon played the part of the grumpy old grandfather," Kris continued. "So it's kind of a grumpy old grandfather of an instrument, I guess, although it also occasionally gets to play the star, briefly, like in Stravinsky's 'Rite of Spring.'"

"Umm…"

"Or did you ever hear the jazz-rock group Henry Cow?"

"Umm…" this was getting embarrassing now.

"They have a bassoon player named Lindsay Cooper, who uses the instrument in a more rock oriented way, pretty neat stuff," she concluded. "But anyway, I gotta scoot. Thanks, again, Collie…and I hope I get to hear you play again soon, too."

"Right," I could speak again, familiar ground, gig promotion time. "Stop by Hughes' Tavern this Saturday, I'll be playing there, should be fun." But there won't be any of that Stravinsky there. And not that Lindsay Cow person either. But I didn't tell Kris that.

"Alright, maybe I will, thanks."

And she was gone. And I wanted her back. So I ordered three bassoon reeds from my regular instrument supplier, then called the music store in Charlotte that Kris had recommended and chatted with them about wholesale suppliers for reed cane. I learned that you could buy the stuff in tube form, raw, dried for at least two years, with a standard 25mm diameter, ready to be split into four pieces for reed fabrication. Or that you could buy cane in varying stages of processing, depending on how much time you wanted to spend making your reed: there was gouged cane, and gouged and shaped cane, and gouged, shaped and profiled cane.

Then, of course, the Charlotte clerk informed me that you could just buy a reed and save yourself all that fabrication time altogether, but I scoffed at that suggestion, by now a true and fervent believer in the importance of making one's own bassoon reeds. So I asked where they got that raw tube cane stuff and learned that it came from France, from some plantation, where they grew what my Charlotte counterpart assured me was the finest tube cane that money could buy. He was more than happy to provide the number, which I was more than happy to call, despite the fact that Junior would be less than happy when he got the phone bill a month later.

But I needed that tube cane, and so I dialed. A man answered the phone, making noises that I assumed were French, which was completely incomprehensible to me, Ugly American that I was (and remain). So I asked (in English) if anyone spoke English there and was remarkably, pleasantly surprised to discover that the manager of the reed cane plantation (the very man who had answered the phone) did indeed speak the Queen's tongue. He did much of his business in the Anglophone world, he remarked, and was quite pleasant and efficient as he took my order for one kilogram of bassoon tube cane, guaranteeing that no piece would be shorter than 150 millimeters in length.

I had no clue, mind you, about how much a kilogram was, nor how long 150 millimeters was, nor whether I had bought Kris eight reeds worth of cane or 800. No matter, though: I owed Monsieur Plantation Manager a mere $175 by the time we'd calculated airmail postage and traded American Express card numbers to complete our transaction. If Junior got too crazy about the expense (not to mention the long-distance phone call), I'd just eat the cost myself, since I'd be willing to pay at least that much to have Kris gush in enthusiasm and admiration at my initiative and thoughtfulness.

I thought about Kris' reaction (or my expectation of Kris' reaction) for the rest of the week, only occasionally thinking about how nice it would be to sleep with her, which was odd, since normally if I thought about a woman at all, that was all I thought about. I thought about calling her and reminding her that I had a gig on Saturday, and then telling her what I'd done for her, but I figured the effect would be better if I had my kilogram of reed canes in hand when I did, so she could rush down and get them straight away, and praise me, lots, when she did.

So I didn't call, and I was actually jittery as we took the stage at Hughes, looking out over the derelicts and the dancing girls, hoping against hope to see Kris there. No such luck, alas. I made a mental note that she had seen me at the Country Club out on Fripp Island the last time, so maybe Hughes just wasn't the sort of place that she would go on a Saturday night. Or maybe she had a date, and he was taking her to someplace nice, not to a dive like Hughes. I worried about it all night, and my performance suffered accordingly. Not that anyone in the crowd noticed, but my bandmates did, shooting me withering looks all night as I fumbled with my bass, thinking about bassoon reeds.

The canes showed up the following Tuesday. The box was big, but not obnoxiously so, although I doubted that Kris would ever have to buy another piece of cane, if each one of these little tubes could be split into four reeds. Then I started to wonder whether the stuff was perishable, particularly in Bridgefield's dank, damp climate, so that Kris would have to make hundreds of reeds all at once or throw the spoiled, moldy, rotten old canes that she couldn't use away, cursing the fact that I made her buy them all from me in the first place. Could I just give them to her? Would that be too weird? Probably.

I called her that afternoon, still undecided about my approach. She answered on the first ring: "Yes?"

"Kris? Hi, it's Collie. Collie, from Junior's Music."

"Oh, hi, Collie. What's going on?"

"I've got a package for you here, just wanted to call and let you know…"

"Great," she interrupted, "my reeds are here!"

Her reeds. Oops, I'd forgotten that I'd ordered those, too. They hadn't arrived yet, actually. "Umm, well, sorta, yeah, not the reeds, the finished ones I mean, but I did get you some reed cane, like you were talking about, so you could make your own."

"Oh, fantastic! Did my store in Charlotte ship some down to you?"

"No, not exactly," I wasn't sure now how much I wanted to tell her. "I mean, I did talk to them, but they referred me to this other place, so I called there, and ordered the canes from there instead."

"What place," Kris asked.

"Umm…." I looked at the packing slip on the counter in front of me. "Plantation Tubulaire de Ver, I think that's how you say it."

"In France?!"

"Yeah, they told me that's where the best canes came from."

"They're right," she responded with a laugh. "That's why I never bought mine there. I always had the store order for me from some catalog company out in Washington State somewhere. Wow. French tube canes. Nice." A pause. "How many did you order?"

"Oh, I dunno, the box is pretty big, there's a bunch of 'em in here," I answered. "They sold them to me by weight, so I bought a kilogram. That's a couple of pounds worth, I think."

Kris laughed enthusiastically, and long, although I couldn't tell whether she was laughing at me for being a moron or in delight at having a lifetime's supply of reed cane. I could almost hear her eyes watering in mirth over the phone line, and I was getting decidedly uncomfortable when she finally got herself under control and could speak again.

"Wow, Collie, I'm, uh, speechless, I guess," she said, still chortling. "That's some kind of customer service, I've got to tell you. Dare I ask how much I owe you for all that cane?"

"Umm, how 'bout if I say nothin', if I offer 'em as a gift, a welcome to Bridgefield from Junior's Music," I kept on quickly, before she object or interrupt. "Since I'm gonna be takin' lots and lots and lots of your money over the years, seeing as how we're the only music store in town and everything."

"I couldn't ask you to do that. They had to be expensive, weren't they?"

"Not too bad, no," I answered. "You can pay me for the pre-made reeds at retail mark-up price when they come in, but just take these off my hands…'cause no one else is ever gonna need bassoon reed cane in Bridgefield, if the last 20 years of business is any indicator."

Kris laughed again, and thought for a moment, than finally said, "Okay, I will. Thank you. That's really, really sweet of you. Really kind. I appreciate it."

"When can you stop by to pick 'em up?" I asked, pumping my fist in the air.

"You gonna be around later tonight?"

"Sure, we're open 'til eight tonight, so stop by anytime before then."

"Okay, thanks again, see you then."

"Right. See you. Bye"

I had actually been planning to leave before dinner that night so that Junior and Mama could close up the store, but I called them at home and told them my plans had changed, and that they could stay home, and that I'd close myself. Junior was suspicious, but he finally acquiesced after he couldn't get a handle around any sort of nefarious conduct or activity on my part. So I was all by my lonesome in the shop when Kris showed up around seven, and I handed her the box of cane, and we both had a good laugh about how much of it there was, and I felt really decent, really normal, really swell about myself.

In fact, I think that bassoon reed cane acquisition may have been the first really selfless, nice thing that I'd done for another human being, certainly as an adult, although I suppose I might have been nice as a young child, it's hard to remember so far back. And it wasn't really selfless, I guess, since it made me feel good, but that's okay, I think, since it was a clean sort of good feeling, quasi-selfless maybe, not dirty and cheap like my other human contacts.

As Kris was leaving the store, I called out to her, "I was sorry to miss you last Saturday night at Hughes…we played a good set," I lied, since she couldn't prove otherwise, "and I think you would've had a good time."

"Yeah, I actually drove by there," she said, sheepishly, "but it's really not the kinda place that I feel comfortable going into by myself. I mean, I wanted to hear you play, but I didn't want to sit at the bar and have to deal with all the drunks mauling me, y'know?"

"Well, sure, I can understand that," I answered, not understanding at all. What was the point of going to a bar if not to maul or be mauled?

Then Kris surprised me yet again. "I mean, I'd feel fine if you and I went together," she said. "And I could meet some of the people you know and stuff, so I had someone to talk to, and so I could tell people I was with you if they startled hassling me or anything."

My heart skipped a beat as I immediately reached for my appointment book to see when my next performance was due. "Ummm, we're playing again this Saturday, actually, back out at Fripp Island," I told her, trying not to let my voice quaver. "They're having some kind of golf tournament out there, then a party, with dancing and everything, afterwards. If you want, I could pick you up for that and give you a lift out. We'd have to get there a little early for sound check, then just hang out for a while, but maybe there'll be some people I know or something, if you want to do that."

I was pretty sure that I wouldn't really know anyone out there, since the kind of folks with whom I fraternized generally didn't do the country club thing, but that was ideal, since I didn't want anyone giving Kris the straight Collie skinny anyway. At worst, she could hang out with the band girlfriends, but only after I warned their significant others to muzzle them, ix-nay on the ollie-Cay ories-stay. It seemed like a good plan, although I'd had those before, and they generally weren't.

"Sure, that would be great," Kris answered, jerking me back to the present, nicely. "What time do you want to pick me up?"

"How 'bout six, just to be safe."

"Six it is…here's my address, and you've got my phone number, right?"

"Right, right, thanks, great, okay…see you Saturday."

"See you Saturday."

Which came, and which was pretty damn wonderful, I've got to admit. We chatted on the way over to the club, Kris noting that she really hadn't met many people in Bridgefield yet, expressing her gratitude for me having sort of gone out of my way to be decent to her. The band soundchecked while Kris talked to some other members of the entourage, and some of the club members who happened to be about the room while we warmed up, then we had a couple of hours to hang out, and watch the sun go down, and talk, and get to know one another.

This was normally the time that I spent drinking before a show, of course, but I didn't want to do that (or not too much of it with Kris there), and I honestly didn't really feel like I missed it, much, since I was so enjoying all the other stimulation being thrown my way. And then we played, and Kris watched me all night long, dancing by herself during appropriate numbers, when the floor was appropriately crowded, and I couldn't help but notice that she was, objectively speaking, the best looking woman in the room, and I couldn't help but swell with pride since she was, subjectively speaking, there with me.

After our set, we visited some more with the other guys in the band and I drove her back to Bridgefield, parking in her driveway, where she leaned over, kissed me on the cheek and thanked me for a lovely evening. I watched her until she was safely in her house, feeling like some sort of Ward Cleaver clone, doing the just and noble thing, and then I drove home, chain-smoked a dozen cigarettes on the back porch (she didn't smoke, so that was out too while we were together) and went to bed. Happy. Really happy. Really feeling like a grown-up, doing a grown-up thing with another grown-up. It was a new feeling, but a really good one, and I wanted more of it.

So I started calling Kris whenever we had a show coming up, and she generally joined me, although after school started in the fall, she would usually beg off on weeknight gigs, for the sake of the kids and everything, and that was fine, too, since those would be the nights I'd smoke like a chimney, get hammered when the show was done, and fuck bar sluts in my car. But I felt guilty about that, I did, particularly after Kris' usual evening-ending kiss on the cheek graduated to a nice lingering mouth-to-mouth kiss somewhere early that fall, and since I hadn't been smoking that night, I could taste Kris when I kissed her, and she was sweet, and lovely, not sour with alcohol and nicotine. She smelled nice, too, something floral, maybe fruity, I couldn't really tell, I just knew that it wasn't sweat or dried puke or anything else that I was used to smelling under such circumstances.

And then one Saturday night, probably October or November of 1981 I'd guess, a nice cool autumn evening, perfect for sleeping with the windows open, we pulled up in Kris' driveway, and she tossed her hair fetchingly, and smiled compellingly, and asked me if I wanted to come in and see her house. I did, I did, yes, and we went in, and she showed me her living room, and her kitchen, and where the bathroom was, just in case I needed it, and then her bedroom, outfitted with the first futon I'd ever seen, and pillows everywhere, and a big dressing mirror, and flowers, flowers that smelled like Kris tasted, which was sweet, very sweet indeed. And I did taste Kris that night, I did, her lips, her neck, her shoulders, her body, her skin, all of it, and she mine, as we stripped down and dropped and rolled on her futon, extinguishing no flames while we did so.

While my relationship with Kris had been demure and virginal to this point, her aggressive, I-know-what-I-want performance in bed that night led me to believe that she'd acquired that knowledge through some extensive, hands-on experience, belying her nice girl exterior, you bet. Which was actually good for me, since my romantic style was obviously fairly course and rough, given my own experiences to date, and I wasn't sure I could pull off the sensitive Casanova thing with her. Moot point, thankfully.

When we were done, I started to get out of bed to gather my belongings, since I was used to rapid escapes during the rare occasions when I had sex in a bed, lest someone's husband get home before I got out, but Kris held my arm and curled up against me and seemed to fall fast asleep, fast. So I relaxed, and stared at the ceiling, and smelled the flowers, and counted my good fortune, and eventually drifted into dreamland myself, as content and at peace as I'd ever been, or at least could ever remember being.

I woke to the sound of water running in the bathroom, so I smiled, stretched, lolled about on the futon languorously, yawned, thought that maybe we could spend the morning as we'd spent the evening before, shuddered in a paroxysm of satisfaction as I did so. Then Kris stuck her head into the bedroom.

"Hey, Collie, wanna go to church with me this morning?"

Whoa! Not at all the morning-after greeting I'd been anticipating, not by a long shot. I pretended I didn't hear her, so I had time to fabricate an appropriate answer. "Umm…what?"

"Will you go to church with me this morning?"

I thought that's what she'd said. "Uh, I really don't have appropriate church clothes here, Kris, so I'd have to go home and get some, and, uh, I doubt we have time for that, right?"

"Sure we do," she answered. "It's only about seven right now. We got two and a half-hours before Bible study starts, and three and a half before the regular service. So we can have breakfast here, then you can go over to your house and get dressed, then swing back by here on the way to church. We can skip Bible study, if you want."

"Yeh, yeh, that would probably be best," I stammered. "So, uh, what church do you go to, Kris?"

"Pocotaligo River Baptist. You ever go to that one?"

"Sure, yeah, that's where my family goes, yeah. I been there," I reached for my pants and started dressing as Kris disappeared back into the bathroom. "Umm…so do you, like, go to church every week, or is this just sort of us having to go get good with the Lord after last night or something?"

She laughed. God, I loved that laugh. "No, Collie, I go every week, or whenever I can," she shouted from the bathroom. "I've sinned worse than this, believe me, so I don't need to cleanse my soul or anything. I just like having a couple of hours a week to be quiet, and listen, and think about God or whatever, just get centered, y'know?" I didn't. I hadn't heard that term before. She popped into the bedroom again, "And I just thought it would be nice to spend some more time with you today, okay?"

And I couldn't argue with that, now, could I. So we ate breakfast at her house, pancakes, just like Mama made (but, then, how different could Bisquick get?), and good coffee, and fruit. I'd never eaten fruit at breakfast before, I don't think. I usually got sausage or bacon or country ham. Not fruit. It was good, though, sweet, like everything in Kris' world, totally changed the dynamic of the meal to not have that weird combination of maple and salt and smokehouse flavors with each bite of your syrup-covered breakfast meat.

And then I went home, and Junior and Mama and Sister and the twins were having their breakfast, and they invited me to join them, and I told them I'd eaten already, and went upstairs and showered and put on nice clothes, church clothes, and went back downstairs and told them I would see them soon at church. Mama and Junior looked shocked, since I hadn't been to church with them since leaving to go to the Institute, but Sister, without even looking up while she shoveled gruel into Ward or Greg's mouth, cut right to the chase.

"Collie's got a new girlfriend," she said. And I smiled and waved to them all and left to go back to Kris' house. And we went to church together, and sat near the front, and I felt the eyes of every soul in the room upon me, although my eyes kept wandering up to the choir loft where Cindy and I had once nuzzled and stroked, and when Kris took my hand after the introductory hymn, I actually became visibly, uncomfortably, inappropriately aroused. Fortunately it passed before I had to stand to sing the next hymn.

But it came back when we returned to Kris' house, and to her futon, that afternoon. And many afternoons that followed that afternoon, as I took to spending most Saturday nights at her house, and some Fridays and the occasional weeknight too, kids be damned. Junior and Mama were tickled pink, needless to say, that I had a nice girlfriend. Well, any girlfriend at all would have tickled them, I think, but they were especially pleased that I had one who made me go to church, and who came by the store and was pleasant and courteous to Junior, pretending (or maybe not, she may really have been that nice) to enjoy his rambling stories and instrument demonstrations.

And so it went for the next eighteen months or so, a period that I've got to consider the happiest of my life. Kris and I went to many, many shows together, some where I was playing, some where I wasn't. I started keeping my bass at her house, and she let me hold her bassoon, and showed me how she made reeds, and we even played together at her house sometimes. She taught me some classical songs. I taught her some of the songs I'd written. And I loved the way our low-range instruments joined together beautifully, the treble range filled, if at all, by our voices, talking, singing, exploring, sometimes wordlessly, sometimes pouring out words inspired one by the other.

I actually became monogamous during that period, too, eschewing cheap bar encounters even on nights when Kris wasn't with me, much to some of my regulars' chagrin. I still drank, but less, although still more than Kris, and most other people, but not as much as I once had, and never out on the docks anymore, and rarely by myself. I tried to quit smoking, since Kris was a healthy sort who ran regularly, sometimes tapping on the window of the store as she passed on her way up the road, all legs and arms and hair and teeth, but that addiction was hard to curtail completely.

I was honest about that with Kris, though, and told her that I smoked when I was in clubs, and when she wasn't there, since I was getting so much second-hand smoke anyway and needed to do it in self-defense, which she seemed to accept, as long I didn't taste like smoke when she was kissing me.

And they were glorious kisses, worth not smoking for. Glorious days. Glorious Kris. Glorious Collie, even, if you can imagine such a thing, for eighteen glorious months. And then just when I expected it to go on forever, just when I thought I could count on it being my end all and be all, it all came tumbling down, like a house of cards, like the Walls of Jericho, like a drunk taking a fall down three flights of stairs, feeling nothing the whole way down.

Chapter Eleven

"Jesus Christ, Mama, what the hell was that about?!"

It was May of 1983, and I had just walked into the kitchen, where Mama was sitting at the table, with a bowl of bread and warm milk sop in front of her—and I saw her make the most horrible-looking face that I've ever seen on another living human being. It was something out of a nightmare, her eyes clinched tight, her mouth pulled down in a rictus grin, her left hand in her hair, seemingly trying to pull her ear off underneath, tendons in her neck taut, her body shivering.

"Oh, hey Boy," she looked up at me with an abashed look on her face, after the spasm had passed. "I wish you wouldn't take the Lord's name in vain, you know that upsets me when you do that."

"I'm sorry, but that look on your face when I came in scared me. What were you doing? Is everything alright?"

She didn't answer, but got up from the table and took her bowl of mush to the sink, emptying it, running the garbage disposal, not answering.

"Mama, answer me," I said, trying to stanch the hint of panic creeping into my voice. "How come you were making that face?"

"It ain't nothin', Boy, I got a sore throat's all, so it kinda hurts a bit when I swallow."

"Are you sick?"

"No, no I'm fine," she said, puttering at the sink, her back to me. "I'm fine, my throat hurts is all."

"Well if it's hurtin' bad enough to make you look like that, I think you oughta get a doctor to look at it," I thought for a moment. "Has it been like this for awhile? Or did it just start?"

"Mmmm…it's been sore for a little bit, but it's okay, don't get all worried about it," she finally turned to look at me, and her eyes were wet and red. "Lemme make you some breakfast, you look hungry."

And she did, and I watched her while she fried the pancakes, and she never cut a piece for herself, or nibbled at the scraps as she normally did. Or as she normally had done; I wasn't sure how long since I'd seen her do it, come to think of it. In fact, I wasn't sure how long it'd been since I'd seen her eat at all. She didn't usually sit with us, but served and sampled while she worked. But not today. And not recently, as best I could recall.

After breakfast I went and found Sister watching TV in the den with Greg and Ward. "How long's it been since you've seen Mama eat?" I asked.

"What are you talkin' about, Collie?"

"How long's it been since you've seen Mama eat anything," I repeated. "I walked in on her eatin' her sop this morning and she was making a face like it was killin' her, like her head was gonna explode or something. And as soon as I walked in, she threw her food away and tried to distract me. But I got to thinkin' that I haven't actually seen her eat in a long time, like she's hiding from us when she does it, and if she's makin' the face I saw this mornin', then I can understand why."

"I dunno," Sister paused in thought. "I can't remember. But have you looked in her bathroom recently?"

"No, why?"

"Go look," Sister said. "Go look in her trashcan, see what's in there."

I made sure Mama was still in the kitchen and slipped into her bathroom, and picked up her trashcan. An empty hairspray can. The

"Homes" section of last Sunday's *Bridgefield Reporter*. And underneath, a nest of small rolled up balls of tissue paper. I fished one out with the toilet cleaner brush and set it on the floor, then used the brush handle to unroll it. There was a clot of dried blood and phlegm inside. I literally ran back to the den.

"What the fuck is that in there, Sister?"

"Watch you language around the boys, Collie," Sister snapped. "It's blood. She's been coughing up blood for awhile, I think. I saw her do it once a month or so ago, and she told me she had an upset stomach, and not to worry about it. And I figured she's a big girl, so I didn't make a stink about it. But I went in there to borrow some deodorant from her a few days ago and saw all the little bloody tissues in there, so I assumed she must still be coughing it up from somewhere."

I was dumbfounded. "Well, Jesus, why didn't you tell me? I mean, that ain't right for someone her age to be coughing up blood."

"It ain't right for anyone any age to be coughing up blood. But I can't make her do anything she don't want to do, and she seems fine otherwise, I guess, so I didn't think it was a big deal."

"Didja tell Junior?"

"That would be making it a big deal, now, wouldn't it?" she said.

Junior was already down at the store, so I dressed, drove over and waited until there were no customers in the store, then asked him "Is everything okay with Mama?"

"Whaddya mean, Boy?"

"I mean, is she sick or something? I haven't seen her eat in ages, and I saw her gagging something horrible this morning while she was having her sop, and Sister says she's been coughing up blood for awhile, and none o' that's right. So have you noticed this stuff? Do you think she's okay?"

He was silent for a moment. "I saw her cough blood one time, yes, I did, a little while ago, but she said she had an upset stomach, so I thought maybe she had a little ulcer or something, and she was takin' some bismuth or some kaolin or something for it, and she said it made it feel better. So I didn't bother her about it none."

"Well I think you should bother her about it, I think she's got somethin' wrong with her. Ask her to eat in front of you and watch what happens if you don't believe me."

"I'm sure it ain't nothin' big, Boy, so don't go gettin' her all worried and upset, hear? I'll talk to her and see what's wrong when I get home tonight."

I held Junior to his word, and as soon as got into the house, I called Mama and told her that he and I needed to talk to her. She was on the porch, smoking, looking slightly pained, but nothing like what I'd seen earlier in the day. We sat with her and Junior asked how she was feeling, and she said fine, she just had a little sore throat, and he asked if she was still coughing some blood, and she said yes, but it wasn't a big deal, and Junior looked at me as if that closed the case.

But it didn't. I went back in the house and called Doctor Talbot, our longtime family physician and another fine product of the South Carolina Military Institute, at home, told him I was worried about Mama and gave him a rundown on her symptoms. And I finally got some vindication in my concern: he said that most certainly sounded serious, and asked me to put Mama on the phone. She wouldn't come, so he asked for Junior, and after a long series of uh-huhs and yessirs and yeps, Junior hung up the phone, turned to me and said "Y'happy now? Doc Talbot says Mama's got to come in and see him tomorrow. "

"Well, good," I replied. "And, yes, I am happy that you're talkin' some sense about this now, although you're actin' like its my fault that she's sick, an' it ain't. I just seem to be the only one that's concerned about it."

"Ain't you a good Boy, then," Junior answered with a scowl. "You sorely concerned about your Mama now, just like a good Boy should be. Well, I hope you didn't have any plans tomorrow, 'cause you're gonna have to open the store and be there until me an' your Mama get back from the doctor's office, an' when the doctor gets done tellin' her she's fine, I may just decide that we need to come home an' rest anyway, so you should plan on bein' there all day tomorrow."

"Fine with me."

"Good, then. Fine with you." And he stomped off to his bedroom in a huff, as I stomped upstairs to mine wrapped in a blinding corona of righteous indignation.

I opened the store the next morning, and dealt with customers in a distracted fashion, waiting for Mama and Junior to show up, or call, but they didn't. Sister did, though, around three o'clock that afternoon.

"You gotta come home, Collie," she whispered.

"I can't, there's no one else here."

"Then close up the store, you idiot," she answered, louder this time. "You have got to come home, do you understand me?"

"Why? What's going on?"

"Whaddya think, Collie? Jesus Christ…"

"Is Mama okay?"

But Sister had hung up on me. I put the "Closed" sign on the door, with a quickly scrawled note underneath it saying "Back at 10 tomorrow, sorry for any inconvenience," hopped in my battered, unwashed Buick Skylark and roared home.

"Where's Mama?" I shouted as I entered the house.

"She's in her bedroom, packing her bag, Boy," Junior answered from the kitchen. "Get in here and shut your mouth for a second."

I did as I was told. Junior and Sister were in the kitchen, Sister wiping her eyes, Junior chewing his lip and drumming on the tabletop. I bit my own lip and waited for someone to speak.

"Doc Talbot says Mama's got to go to the hospital in Savannah for some tests, and some observations," Junior finally said. "He says there's something wrong with her throat, she got sores in there, and she got some nodes that are all swollen in her neck and her chest and under her arms, and they did a chest X-ray and there's somethin' in her lungs they want to go look at some more."

"What does he think it is?" I asked, sorry now on some plane that I'd made this an issue, wishing now that I'd just let it go away on its accord.

"He don't wanna say yet," Junior answered. "He got some ideas, but he don't wanna say."

Sister looked up at me and shook her head, "She's got cancer, Collie, that's what it is. It's pretty goddamned obvious, ain't it? What with her smokin' so much, so long and everything?"

I was literally, physically stunned that Sister would speak that word, a wave of nausea shaking my body, my hands and jaw clinching involuntarily, the air being forced from my lungs. I turned a chair around and sat, head down between my knees, feeling like I was going to faint. And as clarity returned, I had an image of Mama suffering, and it was unbearable, and I started to cry, for Mama, for me, and for what a horrible, unworthy son I'd been to her, and that now it was going to be too late for me to do anything about it.

"I ain't dead yet, y'all don't need to go on like that," Mama said, walking into the kitchen behind me. "I'm gonna go out front and have a cigarette, and then your Daddy's gon' take me to the hospital, and y'all can come see me tomorrow, after the tests is done an' everything, an' after you get someone to look after Greg an' Ward, alright?"

I started to make a comment about the smoking, about how stupid it was for Mama to be lighting a Winston just before she was off to the hospital to find out how a million Winstons before this one had destroyed her body, but Junior shot me such a withering, scathing, don't-you-dare look that I bit off my words, and a chunk of cheek in the process. Instead I stood up, wiped my face, walked over and hugged Mama, who hugged me back and said "You a good Boy, son," which made me cry all that much more. And then she walked out front, bag in hand, lit a Winston and waited for Junior to take her to her doom.

Sister was right. It was cancer. It had started in her throat, the doctors figured, and had spread to her lungs and was now vigorously romping into her lymphatic system, from which there'd be no return. They gave her maybe three months to live without treatment, maybe a year to eighteen months with an aggressive regimen of chemotherapy to stanch the spread of the disease, although it was far beyond the point of operability or where she would ever be likely to fully recover from it.

She was a trooper, Mama was, and she said she wanted to watch Greg and Ward grow for as long as she could, so she elected to receive the treatment, which was every bit as nightmarish for her and all of us as I'd ever read it to be. She was violently sick, confused, in mind-scrambling pain after the first couple of chemo sessions, and it got worse as time went by and both her disease and its antidote took their toll on her. We would take her to Savannah for treatments, then try to get her home and in bed as quickly as possible, although we rarely made it to the house before the vomiting and delirium started.

I wish in hindsight, however, that I could have handled the situation half as well as she did, but instead I turned horrible, too, not towards Mama, but towards everyone else in my life, Kris included. While Kris had been wonderful and compassionate and kind and understanding in the beginning, even volunteering to help out in the store after school and on weekends, her patience was finite—and my ability to test it was apparently infinite.

I got weepy and needy at first, clinging to Kris, putting my burdens on her, expecting her to carry them for me, until I felt like taking them back. Then I began to invade her space, trying to stay out of my own house whenever I could get away with it, showing up on her doorstep most evenings after Mama had finally been drugged into slumber, expecting her to take me in and comfort me. I was wholly unsympathetic to any need that Kris might have, complaining bitterly when she went home to Columbia for a week towards the end of summer, chastising her for abandoning me in my time of need, and generally remaining surly any other time she was gone from Bridgefield for more than a day or two.

I stopped going to church with Kris, since I wanted nothing to do with the God of Pocotaligo River Baptist Church if He would, or even could, do what He was doing to Mama, despite her regular attendance in His house, Sunday in, Sunday out. And I started drinking more heavily, even when I was out with Kris, seeking escape the only way I knew how, since prayer and faith were out of question at this point. And smoking, too, sneaking out of a room when Kris was in it to have a cigarette, despite what they'd done to Mama with God's good blessing, then feigning innocence when she smelled tobacco on my breath.

And one night, I even took a bottle of vodka to her house, and was in her kitchen pouring myself a drink when she walked in and declared that I was absolutely forbidden to drink in her home, ever. So I went out in her back yard and drank out there instead, and she locked her doors and put down her blinds and wouldn't answer when I rang or banged or yelled, and I finally gave up and fell asleep on her back porch, amidst a pile of cigarette butts. She woke me the next morning by hitting me in the head with the back door, repeatedly, trying to get me to move so she could get out to empty her trash. She wouldn't say a word to me, and I left and went home to drink some more, and to listen to Mama crying in her sleep.

So I probably shouldn't have been surprised when the other shoe dropped that November. "I'm leaving, Collie," Kris announced simply one evening when I had showed up, haggard and smelly at her doorstep.

"You're leaving me?" I repeated, dumbstruck.

"Yes, I'm leaving you. And I'm leaving Bridgefield."

What to say? What to do? How could she leave? "But what about the school? Aren't you on contract all year? How can you leave now? What about the kids?"

"I'm leaving at the end of the semester, December 19," she answered. "I'll lose some money, and I have to pay the school back for some of the benefits costs that they've already spent for me, but I can't stand it here anymore. You're literally making my life a living, breathing hell on Earth here, and this town is just too goddamned small for me to be able to get, and stay, away from you. So I'm sorry about your mother, and I'm sorry that you're not going to have a place to hide from your mother, but I'm leaving."

Wreckage. Catastrophe. Doom. Sorrow. Despair. "Can I come see you in Columbia sometime?" I finally whimpered.

"I'm not going back to Columbia," Kris answered.

"Where are you going?"

"I'm going to Jersey City, New Jersey. One of my mother's cousins teaches up there, and her school's music teacher died, so they had a vacancy and she called and thought it would be a great job for me, so I applied."

"And they just took you? Sight unseen?"

"No, Collie, they didn't take me sight unseen," she answered, shaking her head. "I went up there and interviewed four weeks ago, but since you could barely stand to have me out of town at all, I figured it best not to tell you where I was going. Or maybe you didn't notice I was gone?"

I was starting to wonder if I was dreaming, or if I'd somehow had a reaction to handling Mama's pain killers, since those words coming out of Kris' mouth were too surreal to actually be happening. My brain seized at that point, accordingly, totally confused, unable to deal with stimulus, so I started laughing.

"What's so funny," Kris asked, sourly.

"What the hell are you gonna do in New Jersey?"

"I'm gonna teach and I'm gonna make a difference while I do it," she answered. "And I'm going to play my bassoon, hopefully with an orchestra, or at least some sort of ensemble where I can make some money doing the other thing that I love to do, besides teaching. And there aren't any orchestras in Bridgefield, Collie, in case you haven't noticed. Although there are plenty of them in New York City. That's the real reason I wanna try this. I want to be a musician, like you, but not like you, either, a real musician, playing real music for a real ensemble, not some bar band night job for a bunch of drunks."

That hurt, and I was clutching for straws now, grasping thin air and flailing. "New York City's not in New Jersey, Kris…"

"It's right across the river, no further than Hilton Head or Fripp Island are from here, and you certainly manage to play in those places just fine, so why can't I live in Jersey City and play in New York? And you don't need to answer that question," she concluded, anticipating my next move quite accurately.

Now it was time for me to get mad. And childish. And petty. And mean. "Well, you sure as hell aren't taking all of those cane things that I gave you to New Jersey, Kris. I ain't gonna let you do that. They belong to the store, to me, they stay here."

Kris stormed out of the room at this point, returning moments later with a familiar looking cardboard box. "Fine," she yelled, "here's your canes. Have 'em all." And she threw one at me. And then another. And they hurt. I began to beat a retreat, slinking out the door as Kris continued to hurl reed cane after reed cane at me, chasing me off her porch, down her driveway, into the road. "Keep your damn canes, Collie," she screamed again. "And here's a box for 'em too," she added, flinging that as well. "And just for the record, these canes sucked, you got taken to the cleaners, you stupid, stupid asshole."

I don't think I'd ever heard Kris curse before, but I was certainly getting a mouthful over this one. I started to pick up the canes scattered about the lawn, then thought better of it and drifted off down the road, back to home, back to Mama, back to the bottle. And the cigarettes. And just to cement the end of my contract with Kris, I went out that very same night to Hughes Tavern, and I picked up a grotesque gargoyle of a female drunk, and I took her out into the alley behind the bar and buried my face in her crotch, drowning myself in stink and dirt and sickness and the foul taste of abject rottenness and misery.

When I finally dragged myself home, reeking of body-odor and beer and swill, Sister was still awake in the den, watching TV. "What'd you do tonight?" she asked.

I growled at her and started to head upstairs.

"Kris called," she continued. I stopped and stared at her. "She said to tell you that if you ever set foot on her property again, she's going to call the police to have you removed. I stayed up to tell you that, just in case you were thinking about going over there again."

I muttered a string of obscenities, at Kris, at Sister, at life. "Hey, don't shoot the messenger," Sister said. "I'm just passing on the word. Suit yourself and head back over there and spend the rest of the night in jail. See if I care."

But I didn't have the strength to do it, and I was beginning to feel ill, so I went to the bathroom and made myself puke and crawled down the hall to my room, not making it all the way to my bed, spending the night passed out on the floor instead, dreaming of Kris.

While she may have starred in my dreams, Kris did a fine job of avoiding me in real life for the remainder of the time that she was in Bridgefield. I know she stopped by the store a couple of times for work stuff, Sister told me that, but she never seemed to do it while I was there, looking for my car before she visited or peeking in the window to make sure I was out, no doubt. I pined for her, sitting in the store sighing, staring at the door, waiting for her to enter and tell me that it was all a joke, she was fine, I was fine, we were fine, hallelujah. But she never came. Or at least not while I was there.

I missed her horribly and desperately wanted to go throw myself at her feet to beg for mercy, but it occurred to me that maybe if I played things cool, maybe if I didn't chase her, then maybe she would realize that she wanted me back all by herself. Maybe she'd even apologize for how rotten she'd been to me. Yeah, that would be great, I could make her beg for mercy, sure. So I didn't call her. And I didn't go to her house. And I behaved badly on a regular basis, because I could. And Kris never visited. And Kris never called. And then the semester ended, and the day that she was to supposed to be moving out of Bridgefield came, and passed, and was gone. And Kris with it.

And then the phone rang.

"Hey."

I nearly choked on the bowl of cereal I was eating when I realized that it was Kris on the line. I'd been eating a lot of cereal lately, since no one was cooking for me anymore. "Hey, hey...where are you?" I asked, hoping against hope that she was still here in Bridgefield.

No such luck. "Durham, North Carolina," she answered.

I was trying to sound breezy, trying to pretend that we didn't really have anything to talk about, hoping we could keep things casual, so she could just hurry up and come home and get back to taking care of me in the style to which I'd become accustomed. "So what are you doing up there? In Durham, I mean?"

"Just stopping over. In a hotel. I stayed with my family in Columbia last night, hung out with them this morning, wanted to get a little ways on the road today so my trip tomorrow wasn't so long."

Then silence for a moment, before she continued, "So how's your mother."

"Umm...y'know, she's dying, right? She has some okay days, more bad days," I wasn't sure how much Kris really wanted to know, but I figured I'd give her the full skinny, just in case. "They got her on oxygen now most of the time, although we don't let her take it outside with her when she goes to sit on the porch to smoke. An' the pain medications make her loopy, and she's lost almost all of her hair, an' they're talking about putting a feeding tube in her stomach since it's gotten so hard for her to swallow anything other than liquids. But other than all that, she's fine."

But who cared? I wanted to know how Kris was. I wanted Kris to know how I was. I wanted her to ask, but she didn't seem to be inclined to do so, so I fired the first salvo instead. "So, how are you? Are you doing okay? Ready for this move?"

"I'm fine, Collie," she answered, but she didn't really sound it. "I'm nervous about the move, of course, since it's kind of a big deal, moving up to the city and everything. And I think it'll be kinda hard to be so far away from my family. And from Bridgefield…"

"And from me?" I interjected, hopefully, desperately.

Kris chuckled. "No, no I think it'll be easier being far away from you actually," she said. "I think right now I like you in the abstract more than I like you in the flesh."

Well, that was a start, I guess. "So you're telling me you love me for my mind, not my body?"

"Something like that, yes," she answered, not seeming to realize that I was joking. "I love the fact that you can get up on stage and play music. And write it. And be good at it. I love the way you love music. I love the way you were with me in the beginning, how thoughtful and considerate you were. I love talking to you," a pause, "Like how we're talking now. I love all that. And I miss it all. Very much."

"Then how come you waited until you were ten hours away to call me, then?" I asked.

"Because I can't see those things when I'm actually looking at you anymore, Collie," Kris replied, matter-of-factly. "All I see is smoke and drunkenness and anger and bitterness, and I don't want to see those things. I want to imagine the Collie I fell in love with when I talk to you, not be confronted by the reality of the Collie that you became."

"What if I went back to being the old Collie?"

"Do you think you could?" Kris retorted. "I mean, is it possible to go back like that?"

"I dunno, maybe," I sighed. "Y'know, maybe when Mama's thing is finally over, it'll be easier for me to get things under control myself. I dunno. I mean, without you here all I see in my future is a lifetime spent working in the store and playing lame cover tunes in creepy little neighborhood bars or lounge-lizarding around in the country clubs or whatever. Y'know, and as long as that's all I'm doing, then it's gonna be real hard to quit drinking and smoking and whatever, since that's so much a part of the lifestyle. But then, if I quit playing out, and all I've got to look forward to for the rest of my life is working in Junior's Music, then I ain't sure that I want to try to take better care of myself, since I might live longer that way and extend the nightmare."

"Was that different when I was there?" Kris asked.

"Well, yeah, of course, I mean, I could do all those things, but instead of coming home and going to bed in my parents' house every night, I could go be with you, and it made me feel like an adult somehow, a real person, living the way that real people are supposed to live. I mean, how sad is it that I'm 25 years old and I still live in my parents' house? How sad is that?"

"Pretty sad, yeah, I gotta agree to that," Kris answered. "So why don't you move out?"

"'cause if I'm not moving in with someone else, there ain't no point in doing so. I'd just take my bedroom here and put it somewhere else, and I'd still be all alone, except that I wouldn't have anyone to cook for me, or clean the place." I looked around the increasingly dirty kitchen and sighed again. "Not that I have anyone doing that for me now, for that matter."

More silence on the line. "Well, anyway, I'd better let you go," Kris finally said. "Will you write me when I get to New Jersey? I'm going to be lonely there, with just my mom's cousin around, and you made me feel welcome in Bridgefield at first, so maybe you can help me get settled up there, too."

"Sure, if you give me your address," which she did. "And your phone number?"

"No, I'm not sure I want to give you that yet, Collie," she answered. "Let's just write to each other for a while. Let's deal at that level, real basic, pen pals, remind each other why we liked each other once…"

"I still like you, Kris, you know that…"

"Yeah, I do, but I sure wasn't liking you very much when you were out in my backyard pissing in my azalea bushes a couple of months ago."

She had me there. "Okay, I'll write. But will you call me when it's okay for me to call you, too?"

"Maybe," answered Kris.

Which was okay with me, since at least that meant there was something to hope for in the future. Things weren't quite as rosy as far as Mama was concerned. She was spending more and more time in the hospital and less and less time at home, although she was adamant that she was going to die in her own bed, so in a perverse scheme to attempt to acquiesce with her wishes, Junior typically brought her home when she was at her worst, just in case, then took her back to the hospital to rest when she was feeling better. She had quit the chemotherapy treatments in October and elected to pass on radiation therapy. There wasn't any point. She understood that by then. Hell, even Ward and Greg understood that by then.

They did finally put a feeding tube in Mama's stomach just after Christmas, since she'd gotten where it was all but impossible to get food down, and hold it down when it got there. She was emaciated by this point, looking more like a 1,000 year old crone than a woman of fifty, which she was, hard as it was for me to believe. That seemed pretty damn young to be this sick, even with her smoking habits, so I started to worry about whether there was something more to her illness than cigarettes, like maybe we had some genetic thing that I was going to find out I had someday, or maybe we lived on top of some toxic waste dump that was slowly frying all of our chromosomes and mutating all of our mitochondrion, whatever they were. I took to checking the glands in my throat regularly, a habit which continues to this day, health awareness for a moment, before I go smoke a pack of cigarettes and do things to my lungs that I can't palpate or pulse. Out of sight, out of mind, as they say.

In early January, the doctors installed an oxygen tent over Mama's bed, since she was getting too weak to pick up the mask and place it over her face when she needed it, which was pretty much all the time by now. I'd never much thought about euthanasia, about mercy killing, before that point, but let me assure you that I was all in favor of it at this stage, since Mama lingered far beyond the point where she was enjoying lingering, and far beyond the point where we enjoyed having her linger. There wasn't a lot of quality time spent in the house towards the end. We didn't all bond, and share, and make death a beautiful experience. Death was horrible, no two ways about it, and dying was even worse.

But dying seemed to be what Mama did best these days, and she kept right on doing it, all the way through January. Towards the end of the month, the hospital staff began talking about making arrangements for hospice care in our house, and I couldn't figure what they were on about, since I thought they were talking about those cheap hotels where kids stayed when they went to Europe. Sister explained it to me at some point though, I think before I'd embarrassed myself by asking the question out loud.

After that point, we had a nurse around the house pretty much all the time, putting something in this tube, taking something out of that tube, putting this other tube into an entirely different place altogether. Preacher Benson started hanging around a lot, too, he and Junior sitting on the back porch together, not saying much of anything, me doing my best to avoid them both when they were there together, since I wasn't much inclined towards spiritual things then, and wouldn't have been much inclined to discuss them with Junior and Preacher Benson had I been. They'd both caught me in too many sins to serve as spiritual advisors in my time of need, so I just did without.

Or I wrote long letters to Kris in lieu of face-to-face counseling. And she wrote letters back, not as long, but nice, thoughtful, always noting that Mama and I were in her prayers. And Junior and Sister and the twins too. And I drank, I did, I have to admit it, although I was chaste during this period, largely because watching the putrefaction of a human body day after day made it hard for me to want to touch another one, even a healthy one, and there weren't many of those in Bridgefield's bars to start with.

And then Mama died, on Abraham Lincoln's birthday no less, emancipated at last from the worries of the flesh. But no bang, not in her case. No whimper, either, or at least no whimper that I was around to hear. I was at the store with Junior when it happened, Sister calling us to tell it us it was over, us both stunned, then relieved, then saddened, then relieved again that her struggle was finally over. She had deserved better, which made us sad again.

We closed the store, drove home, sat in the room with Mama for a couple of seconds, her not looking much different than she had when she had been alive the day before. Sister and the Nurse said it happened quick, just like a switch was flicked and Mama decided she didn't want to live anymore, so she didn't. One loud sustained beep on one of the countless machines to which she was wired, and that was all she wrote. Her heart had just had enough. I don't blame it.

They came and took her body away a short while later, and we had a service at the Baptist Church a few days after that, and then we buried her in the old family plot at Stony Creek, some thirty miles inland, where you can dig six feet without hitting water. There were about 50 people at the graveside services, some cousins and aunts and uncles who I hadn't seen since I was a child, some friends of Mama's from the Church, some customers of the Store who had grown accustomed to seeing Mama smoking and spitting bits of tobacco while she demonstrated her ukulele technique.

I had to stand up in front, right by the grave, with all of those people looking at me as they put Mama into the ground. I didn't feel sympathy in their gazes either, but rather disapproval, disappointment, distress at how Sister and I had turned out, and how it must have hurt Mama, and driven her to an early grave. I glanced over at Junior at one point in the service and had one of those revelatory moments of epiphany: Junior looked like an old man now, even though he was only 54. I didn't know if Junior had just become an old man since Mama had died, or if he'd been one for a while, and I just hadn't noticed. But either way I was sad for him, although not because he'd lost his wife, but because he was an old man now, and it occurred to me that he probably realized it himself, and that it bothered him.

We had people over to the house after the burial for a potluck dinner put together by the church ladies, with a bit of help and support from Sister. By seven that night, though, everyone was gone, and it was just Junior and Sister and me and the twins left to begin going through Mama's stuff and making arrangements to have her hospital equipment taken out of the house.

We did pretty good on the second of those items, getting most of it out within a day or two, probably because there were other people who needed it, but we never really made much of a mark on Mama's belongings. Most of them are still there in her half of Junior's closet, in fact, since he hasn't had anything else that he's needed to put in there during the past 16 years. He still sleeps on his own side of the bed, too.

I wrote Kris a day or two after the funeral, a relatively short note explaining what had happened and explaining that I didn't have it in me at the moment to pen a long one. She called me three days later, for the first time since we had spoken when she had stopped in Durham, and we talked for nearly two hours, and I cried, and she cried, and when we were done crying, she gave me her phone number, but told me not to over-use it, and said that she still wanted me to write to her, that those words were important, both to her and (she suspected) to me as well.

After the dust settled from Mama's passing, things went back to being the ways things were in Bridgefield for me, just the way that they'd gone back to normal after I came home from the Institute: I worked in the store, I played in the bands, I drank, I smoke, I caroused. Life, such as it was, went on.

And it began to dawn on me, around this time, that maybe that's all there was to life, such as it was: the occasional catastrophe interrupting a long, steady stream of colorless, featureless normalcy and complacency. I mean, I knew that it was only a matter of time before I'd have to watch Junior go to meet his maker, or at least his Colonel, at which point I'd grieve, then go back to the music store. It was questionable as to whether I'd get to watch Sister die or not; she was older, but I lived a less healthy lifestyle.

And what else was there to look forward to? I might get married someday, maybe, but that seemed a long shot, since I hadn't been able to even start thinking about matrimony seriously when Kris was here, and I didn't anticipate having another opportunity like that one dropped into my lap. Plus, I'd cuckolded enough husbands in my time to make me pretty thoroughly leery about ever wanting to become one myself, since I'd experienced firsthand just how powerful the thrill of the strange, the allure of the different could be. I'd much prefer to be the fled to than the fled from, all things considered.

All these factors left me feeling flat, peaked, existentially strung out, drawn and quartered. And surly, mainly, that was the main thing that I became, at least outwardly, letting my disgust, distaste and disdain for everything that life threw my way ooze out my pores, waft across the room on my breath, sully and taint everything that I touched, anti-Midas style. I expected, somehow, that people would see my malaise as justified, and that they'd want to help me overcome it, engaging me, rousting me from my apathy and ennui, doing for me what I couldn't do for myself.

And it happened, sort of, although not quite the way that I'd hoped or imagined it might.

"Boy, I'm gettin' awful tired of you mopin' aroun' the store, depressin' the customers," Junior announced one evening as we closed up shop. "Y'know, that kinda behavior just ain't good for sales, people wanna buy music instruments 'cause music makes 'em happy. An' you clearly ain't happy, which is fine, long as you look happy when customers come in. But you can't seem to even do that, an' that's somethin' gotta be fixed."

"No, I'm not happy, you're right," I answered candidly. "But how would you feel if you saw your entire life laid out in front of you by the time you were in your mid-'20s, a life built aroun' workin' in your daddy's store an' livin' in your daddy's house? I mean, that's kinda depressin', don'tcha think?"

"No, no I don't," he paused. "I was happy to be able to look forward like that, after havin' been shot up an' held as a prisoner o' war by the time I was your age. But here's the point you seem to be missin': ain't nobody makin' you stay here in the store except y'self. An' ain't nobody makin' you stay here in Bridgefiel' either, except y'self. An' to be honest, the reason I sent you to the Institute was so you'd have a chance to do somethin' new, somethin' different. Colonel, bless his sweet soul in heaven, went there an' came home to be a pharmacist. I went there an' came home to be a music instrument dealer. You went there, an' you came home an' did exactly what you did before you left. So that's your own fault, an' I ain't gonna have you mopin' aroun' here like an ungrateful servant, like a whipped, beaten slave, if you're gonna stay. If you ain't happy here, then leave."

I was shocked that such a notion would even enter his head, much less leave his mouth, much less when I was around. "But you need me here to help out, especially since Mama's gone, I mean," I blurted. "Who's gonna help you with the store if I go away?"

"Sister's boys gonna be goin' to school next year, so she can he'p me more. An' I can hire someone, same way I always did when you was at school. Ain't a big deal, Boy, ain't no one makin' your play the martyr, 'cept yourself."

"But what else can I do in Bridgefield besides work here? Or play in bands, like I'm doin'? I mean, you know I'd love to do that full time, but it don't pay."

"Probably nothin' you could do here otherwise, I'd agree with that," Junior answered, always candid. "Too many people know you here. Too many people seen you sittin' out on the piers, drinkin'. Too many people seen you actin' like an idiot in the bars, too, messin' with other people's wives an' whatnot."

He knew about that? Wow. "So what can I do, then?"

"You can leave Bridgefiel', that's what you can do. In fact, I saw in the Institute alumni news that they was doin' a job fair up in Ulmer in a couple o' weeks, for graduates lookin' to start careers, or to start new careers, workin' with other graduates," Junior said, reaching under the counter and fishing out the magazine as he spoke. "Right here, see?"

He handed me the magazine, applicable page dog-eared. "So you want me to leave, that's what you're saying?"

"Yes, Boy, that's what I'm saying," he answered. "You can always come back here if things don't work out, but you at least need to try to have your own life, instead of reliving mine and resentin' it. That ain't doin' nobody no good, an' it's bad for business, too."

I was horrified by this conversation on one plane, but on another I felt like I'd been given dispensation, freed from the ties that bound, offered the opportunity to finally do what I had planned to do in 1976, to go become a writer, or a musician, somewhere that mattered. I called Kris and asked for her advice that night, and she was cautiously optimistic, noting that she had experienced some difficulties moving into new, strange communities, but they'd brought new rewards, new challenges, new chances to be something different, to escape from the preconceived notions under which one's family, friends and community held one.

So I went to the Institute job fair. I walked around the gymnasium and looked at the display booths and shook hands with all sorts of corporate recruiters and shills and pimps and peons. Most of the companies represented at the fair were based in South Carolina, the Institute's fruit generally not falling far from the tree. But there were a few from more far flung locales, including Envirocorps, in Troy, New York, just north of the State Capitol in Albany. They had four technical writer slots to fill, and they were hungry for Institute graduates, the very dogmatic Dr. Ernest Jaberg having sent his Human Resources Drone south with strict instructions to bring the crème of South Carolina's youth back to join the Envirocorps team, failure not acceptable.

I talked with the Human Resources Drone (I have to think of him in Capitals, since I never knew his Name), who explained the duties of the technical writer and seemed suitably impressed with my English degree and the fact that I'd written for my high school and college newspapers. The Drone gave me a writing test, editing facts, correcting grammar, putting together proper paragraphs from a jumble of sentences, clauses and words, that sort of thing. He talked about the nature of the company's work, and how Envirocorps was a pioneering interest in hazardous waste remediation throughout New York State, which was evidently in desperate need of some serious cleaning up.

I didn't really care much about that, visions of Manhattan and regular soirees with Kris, just across the river, filling my head by this time. The Drone noted that Envirocorps wouldn't be able to pay my relocation expenses to Troy, but I told him that was okay since I could fit everything I owned in my car. He talked about company benefits, a whole new world to me, and alluded to some salary figures that seemed astronomical to me at the time, since I'd never had to pay for my own room and board and didn't realize how quickly money could be spent by those who did. He told me he'd have to make some phone calls back to the home office, and that he'd be in touch soon.

And he wasn't fooling. By the time I made it home, some two hours later, there was a message from another Human Resources Drone up in Troy, calling to extend an employment offer on behalf of Dr. Jaberg and all his staff at Envirocorps. I accepted before I'd even told anyone else that I'd been contemplating a job in New York. So they didn't get the crème of South Carolina's youth, or anything close to it, but they did get me, filling one of their four available slots, and evidently gladly—since no one else was crazy enough to move to New York.

When Junior got home that night, I told him that I'd be moving in July, to New York, and he seemed stunned by the fact that I'd managed to find a job so quickly, so effortlessly, although in my ignorance at the time I didn't understand why he reacted that way, since I thought this was how it happened for everyone, once they decided to play grownup. Sister took it in stride since, like me, she probably just assumed that when one wanted a job, one just went out and got it. Our insularity and ignorance was charming, looking back on it now.

I called Kris that night to share my news, and she was equally surprised, although it was hard for me to ascertain whether she was pleased or frightened by the news. She asked me if I was going to be able to handle New York, having never seen it; she, at least, had flown up to Jersey City for an interview before moving there, so she had some sense of what she was getting into. I told her I'd be fine, assuming a worldly air, acting as if moving to New York was the easiest, most natural thing I could do, despite the fact that the only time I'd ever set foot outside of South Carolina to date was to visit Savannah and its surrounding suburban or beach communities, all of them less than 90 minutes from home.

But the die was cast, and in a matter of weeks I found myself heading north on Interstate 95, stuffed with the cake and ice cream that Sister brought to the store for my going-away party. I had all my clothes, my record albums, my stereo, my bass guitar, my practice amp (I had to sell my concert stack, since it was too big to move) and my toiletries stuffed in my Buick, making it ride low on its shocks, making me feel every bump in the highway emphatically as I tooled northward, each jolt putting me that much further away from everything I'd known up to and including that point.

By three o'clock that afternoon, I was further away from home than I'd ever been. By four, I entered the State of North Carolina for the first time. I thought I might stay in Durham, since there'd be some nice symmetry with Kris' own northbound exodus that way, but when I looked at the map, I realized that it wasn't on Interstate 95, and I wasn't about to risk getting lost by leaving the only major highway I knew. I stopped in Fayetteville instead, and went out that night and was amazed at how much like Bridgefield that city was, little realizing that most small cities located near major military installations looked that way, bars, pawn shops and porn dealers within easy reach of the soldiers stationed therein.

I drove to Philadelphia the next day, which looked very different than Fayetteville and Bridgefield. I'd finally entered a new world. I went and saw the Liberty Bell, stood there for a moment, thinking "Well, there's the Liberty Bell, huh" then went out and got drunk. I slept late the next morning, showered, brushed my teeth three or four times so I'd be fresh, then drove the remaining two hours to Kris' house in Jersey City, getting there mid-afternoon Saturday. She lived in a small town-house complex, much different from her cottage on Bay Street on the outside, but inside, it was just like old times, flowers and futon, pillows and passion, fruit at breakfast, then Church, then more pillows and passion.

We never even made it into New York City during that first visit. I figured I'd have plenty of chances to see the Big Apple properly later. And then it was Monday morning, and I was whizzing northward on the New York State Thruway, finally realizing that Troy and Jersey City weren't neighbors at all, or New York City either, for that matter. I skidded into the Envirocorps parking lot with minutes to spare, rushed in, was indoctrinated, stamped, processed, greeted and deposited in my cubicle.

Eight hours later I had a Treehouse, a Gerry, a Randy and an entirely new life. Who could have imagined?

Chapter Twelve

My first month at Envirocorps was a blur of over-stimulation, as I was learning the basics of environmental remediation, the nuances of technical writing and the day-to-day subtleties associated with working for a business that wasn't owned by my family. It should probably come as no surprise that the last item was the hardest for me: I was used to coming and going as I pleased, dressing the way I wanted, being as surly as I felt and saying whatever happened to be on my mind at any given time. Such behavior doesn't fly, alas, in a workplace where personal and professional lives are generally segregated, and it took a few rebukes from coworkers and supervisors alike before I began to understand that certain rules of decorum applied once I passed through the maze of potted trees that lined Envirocorps' stylish foyer.

But I'd learned to keep a low profile at the Institute, and having already been so trained I was quickly able to vanish into relative obscurity at Envirocorps as well, just by adhering to certain innocuous work tenets. Showing up on time, for instance, or wearing decently professional-looking clothes, and not reeking of alcohol and smoke during the workday. Or not hitting on or flirting with my coworkers, particularly ones far more senior than I in the company. They generally didn't appreciate it, and didn't mind telling me so.

Those basic grown-up skills mastered, I was then able to focus on the actual meat of my job at Envirocorps: turning the incomprehensible babblings of our engineers into text that an average contractor or businessperson could understand.

Dr. Jaberg employed half-a-dozen field engineers who traveled throughout New York State, studying some of its most lethal and toxic sites, as well as some more relatively benign locales that may have been tainted with oil, or fuel, or antifreeze, or the odd stray bit of radiation during the days when such things could be dumped pretty much wherever one found it convenient to dump them. The field engineers, in turn, would work with developmental engineers (guys like Randy and Gerry), chemists and our token physicist to create methodologies for (at worst) neutralizing the nastiness in place or (in an ideal situation) taking the offending materials away for proper disposal in someone else's backyard.

Our technical team was pretty creative, I'll give them that, coming up with all sorts of containment and glassification and cement packaging schemes to help make the Empire State the kind of place that families could live and grow without fear of genetic mutation. But as a general rule, Envirocorps employees weren't the ones who actually went in and dug up the dirt: our field engineers would go back and supervise, yes, but the real work was done by the owners of the tainted fields, or by contractors hired by those same environmental slum lords, lest we be the ones sued when something blew up or caused someone to melt into a pile of bone and ooze on a work site.

Which was where I came in: I wrote the "how to do it" manuals that accompanied the glass and the potions and the cement and the kilns and the shovels and the bags and the radiation shielding. It wasn't a bad gig, all things considered, since once I'd written things, the engineers and chemists and token physicist would review the final product before it went out the door, and their signatures were the ones on the documents, so if the family of the melted construction worker managed to get a lawsuit past the contractor, then past the owner of the land, then into Envirocorps, I figured I'd be the last one to be burned at the stake.

Plus once I'd written about how to cook one chemical into glass, I could pretty much cut and paste and use the same words to describe the procedure associated with turning some other chemical into glass, so I only put in about six months of truly original work during my entire time at Envirocorps. Which was kind of sweet, since it meant I didn't have to think a lot when I was there at the office, freeing my mind up to ponder such pressing questions as what I'd like to drink when I got home that night, or what I'd like to do to Mandy over in the secretarial pool.

My cubicle was pretty nice too, fairly well isolated, yet open enough so that I could hear anyone coming before they could see me daydreaming. I didn't even have to think much about how I got to and from the office: Randy and Gerry provided me free transportation, although they tended to stay later than I might have chosen otherwise. But that made me look good, too: I was an eager work beaver, yessir, slaving away at my work station in the evening when all the other drones had gone home, making a point of saying "howdy" to Dr. Jaberg whenever he walked by at night, just so he'd know I was there. A little brown-nosing never hurts, as long as your peers aren't around to see you do it. I'd learned that at the Institute too.

So after the culture shock subsided, and life in New York began to take on its own predictable rhythms, and I survived my first winter (another savage eye-opening experience for one as warm-blooded as I), I began to actually start feeling like I was going home when I went back to the Treehouse, instead of going to a temporary hospice, or hostel, or whatever those things are called. Gerry and Randy and I weren't all living together at the beginning, each of us still having our own apartments up in North Korea (although we still just called it the Fourth Floor at the time), our second floor snake ranch and the first floor studio still years away in front of us. So I actually had a fair amount of privacy at night when I wanted it, which was another relatively novel and pleasant experience. I'd always wanted to walk around my house naked, just to save on the amount of laundry I had to do. Now I could.

Kris and I talked a lot more now, since the long distance bills weren't quite as long, and we'd generally try to get together once a month or so at one of our places, although after about a year, we generally defaulted to her place, ostensibly so we could go into New York City, but also probably because my housecleaning skills weren't all that they should have been.

So the relationship sort of fell into a routine as well: we were getting along fairly decently, we enjoyed each other's company, we had good sex, we were comfortable, we didn't see each often enough to crowd each other's space. But we didn't really go anywhere as a couple accordingly, since force minus friction produces nothing, or so our token physicist used to say.

Kris and I also began to slowly drift apart as far as music (once our binding passion) was concerned: I wasn't making it anymore, while Kris was going out of her way to play her bassoon for anyone who would have her. She developed a fairly dependable, reliable set of venues for her music (much as I had done in Bridgefield), playing with a couple of small community ensembles in and around Jersey City, doing weddings, church ceremonies, community gatherings, that sort of things. There were also a number of school programs in North Jersey where bassoon was offered as an orchestra instrument, so that Kris could earn some money teaching high school students in the evening as well.

She hadn't yet managed to penetrate the A-league musical outfits in Manhattan yet, but she was still trying. My bass guitar, on the other hand, was gathering dust under my bed, since I didn't have the time or the heart to go make all sorts of new connections in the Capital Region— especially since they had always come to me in the past, working there in the music store where everyone had to shop if they wanted to play.

So where music used to be one of the things that Kris and I talked and enthused about when we were together, I didn't have anything to say about it anymore once I'd settled in Troy. Other than to make vague noises of approval regarding Kris' accomplishments, that is, once I'd given up on being a bassist and taken to the life of the technical writer instead.

We went on this way for nearly three years, although by the beginning of 1987, it began to get harder to schedule my trips down to Jersey City for one reason or another: Kris would have a recital, or a school function, or a field trip, or some reason or another that it wasn't convenient for me to be at her place over the weekend. But that was okay with me, since by that time I had enough experience and tenure at Envirocorps to be able to take advantage of the newer female employees who had arrived—but who hadn't yet learned that it wasn't a good idea to date (or sleep with, who am I kidding?) coworkers, particularly nasty old Collie Hay down in Tech Pubs.

That fact alone should have made Kris' next surprise announcement all the more understandable and predicable, if not palatable.

"I got engaged, Collie," she announced shortly after I arrived at her house one Saturday during the Spring of 1987, wheedling my way into a trip down to Jersey City the night before, since I had no other action pending at home. I didn't get what she was saying at first, though, since I assumed she was using some industry term for having signed on with a symphony or something.

"Wow, congratulation," I said, by way of vague noise of approval, digging in her refrigerator as I did so. "With who?"

"With, or, uh, to a guy named Mark," she paused, waiting for me to stop rooting through her food, waiting for me to have the sort of reaction that she had been expecting me to have. "Mark Bartos. He's a theology professor at Seton Hall. I met him when I was playing over there. I've known him for about a year now. He wants me to marry him."

"What?!" I pulled a bag of cherries out the refrigerator as I turned to face Kris, finally realizing what she was talking about, dropping the small red fruits on the floor as I did. They bounced. "What are you talking about? How can you be getting married?"

"Like this," she said, holding out her left hand so I could see the rock poised there, which I never would have noticed had she not pointed it out, being a guy and everything. "Mark proposed last weekend. I said yes. So we're getting married. In July."

"Jesus, Kris, you just said you've only known him for a year, I mean, how can you marry someone after you've only known him for so short a time? We've been together for, what, almost six years? What about me? Why would you marry this guy when you wouldn't marry me?"

"You never asked me to marry you, Collie," she answered, astutely and correctly, and, to be honest, the thought of proposing had never seriously occurred to me either. I had always liked having my cake and eating it—not to mention eating other cakes—too much to contemplate the big commitment. But I would have married Kris right there on the spot that day, just to keep her from tying the knot with some other guy. How's that for spite?

"To tell you the truth," Kris continued as I gaped, "I'm not sure that I would have said 'yes' if you had asked me to marry you. I value our time together, I really do, and you mean so much to me, and I just hope that we can still be friends, that's all."

"Well, why the hell did you let me come down here this weekend, then?" I asked, finally bending to pick up cherries and starting to toss them in the trashcan.

"Don't throw those away, they're expensive. Just rinse them off and put them back in the refrigerator where you found them," Kris ordered. I wasn't feeling orderable, though, so I just tossed them in the sink. "I let you come down here because I wanted to tell you in person," she continued. "I thought I owed you that. I guess I must have been wrong. I guess you assumed I was just feeling horny, and wanted you to come down to give me what I needed, right?"

Well, yeah, that was pretty much the way I'd seen it. "No, it's not that at all," I lied. "I came down so we can spend time together. I enjoy your company, that part of it included. I thought you felt the same way."

"I do. I do enjoy your company," Kris said. "But you know as well as I do that we're not going anywhere. And we're getting further apart all of the time: we just really don't have that much in common anymore, and the whole long-distance relationship thing is getting to be a drag. So we just get together out of habit, out of routine, when we don't have anything else to do. We're comfortable with each other. Maybe it's because we remind each other of home in South Carolina…"

She seemed inclined to go on this way for a while. I wasn't interested in listening though, so I cut her off with the rudest question I could muster. "Does he have a big cock?"

"Define big," she shot back, without missing a beat.

"Bigger than mine."

"If that's big, then yes," she said with a cruel smile. "But that has nothing to do with this. It really doesn't. In fact, I think that I'm actually looking forward to a relationship that's based on something more than cock at this stage in my life, Collie. Mark appreciates my music. He wants to hear me play. He wants to see me succeed. And we have so much in common: we go to Church together, we like the same sorts of music and plays, and the same kinds of foods, all that kind of stuff. He's just got a real wealth of life experience and he's willing to share it with me, and I'm willing to accept his offer."

"What's he done that I haven't done?" I pouted.

"Got a doctorate in theology, for starters," Kris answered. "And a couple of decades worth of maturity on you, too, which I'm beginning to appreciate more and more."

"What do you mean by that?"

"He's in his early fifties, that's what I mean," she answered, and braced herself for my predicable response.

"Oh, God, Kris, you're marrying some old man who wants to have a young piece of arm candy, that's what you're doing," I tried to do some math in my head, failed, decided to make a general statement instead. "He's got to be almost as old as my dad. I mean, can you see my dad dating someone as young as you?"

"I'm not that young anymore, and neither are you. We're both pushing 30, and it seems to me that that's a good age to start getting on with your life, trying to decide what it is you want to be when you grow up…"

"Is he rich? Is that it?"

"He's comfortable. But that's not it, either. I'm not marrying him for his dick or his money. I'm marrying because I love him, and he makes me very happy, and he believes in me. What don't you get about that?"

"I don't get how you could have been sleeping with me over the past year while you were falling in love with my father, that's what I don't get," I told her, ready to wound her at this point. But she was always better at that than I was.

"Consider them mercy fucks, Collie," she said. "From me to you. You're welcome."

"Am I going to get one this weekend?" I asked, cutting straight to the lowest common denominator.

"No. No, you're not."

"Then I guess I'd better be on my way, then," I said, walking out to the living room to get my bag, which I'd dropped on the floor by her sofa. "Good luck to you and Dr. Churchmaster the Elder."

"It's late, Collie," she had her hand on my arm now. "You don't have to go. I still want to be with you this weekend, just not that way…"

"I can be with Gerry and Randy if I'm going to be with someone not that way, Kris," I pulled my arm free. "I'll get out of your hair so you can have Uncle Theology over to count his money and figure out which arm you'll look best on when he's out showing you off to all of his other old friends."

"That hurts, Collie. That's really hurtful," she said, and her voice choked on the last word, and I could see tears welling up in her eyes.

"Join the club then, Kris. You've got to learn to take it if you're going to dish it out."

And I left, hitting the road northbound, but getting only as far as Paterson, New Jersey, some fifteen minutes away, before I decided I didn't want to drive anymore, stopped and took a room at the Holiday Inn there, and proceeded to get sloppy drunk in the lounge, hoping to pick up some bar trash while I was there. No such luck, though: I struck out in Paterson just as I'd struck out in Troy and Jersey City for the weekend. But at least here I had a swimming pool to jump into, fully dressed, once frustration got the better of me. So there was that. That was good.

And it was also good to have Gerry and Randy around when I got home the next morning, since I'd never really had any male friends with whom I could commiserate when things went rotten in my life.

"So that Kris, she's a real bitch, right?"

Gerry laid it out nice and simple a couple of nights later as he and I sat on barstools in Randy's kitchen, while Randy chopped and sliced and diced something together for dinner.

"Definitely a real bitch," Randy agreed without turning away from his cutting board. "Real bitch. Maybe the worst bitch ever."

"You think the worst ever? Really? I mean, there've been some pretty bad bitches sometimes along the way, haven't there?" Gerry was thinking hard, talking while he did it. "I mean, some really, really bad ones. And you think she may be the worst ever, huh?"

I could certainly make a case for it, but figured I'd let Randy and Gerry think out loud and make my case for me.

"Well, like, what could you do worse than call someone to come to your house, three hours away, then tell them that you're marrying someone else instead? That's pretty heinous, I think," Randy said, tossing a handful of chopped vegetables into a pan of olive oil for emphasis.

"Well, she could have called him down there, told him that she was marrying someone else, and then killed him," Gerry offered. "That would have been worse."

"Maybe not," I opined. "I mean, if Kris killed me, then I wouldn't have to feel bad about what she did to me anymore, right?"

"Yeah, that's true," Gerry agreed. "So this may be the worse thing a bitch could do. Maybe Randy's right."

"Of course I am," Randy concluded, stirring the sizzling onions and peppers and celery in his saucepan, filling the room with salivation-inducing aromas. "Question, though, is how's Collie gonna get back at Kris for being such a bitch? He can't just take it lying down," Randy glanced over his shoulder at me. "Or sitting down, or whatever."

"I'm not big on vengeance," I offered. "I mean, I think Kris probably wanted to have her cake and eat it too, to marry Minister Mark and still have me be around to offer moral support or whatever, so I've probably punished her enough just by stomping out and leaving her there all teary and everything. That's probably enough."

Gerry didn't think so: 'What if Collie killed her?"

"Nah, that wouldn't work," the more pragmatic Randy countered. "Because he'd still be alive and he'd still feel bad, so she still would win, she still would be the high bitch queen and everything. Unless he killed himself, too…"

"…a suicide pact!"

"No, that would be more like a murder/suicide, I think, since she wouldn't kill herself, he'd kill her instead."

"And then no one's left to feel bad."

"Right."

"Right."

They both looked at me, waiting for my agreement. "Well, sure, in theory, you guys are absolutely right," I assented. "But I would have had to kill her right away for it to work. If I go down there and pop her now, then it's premeditated, and I get in more trouble that way."

"But you kill yourself, too, so it doesn't matter," Gerry observed, astutely.

"Yeah, but what if I chicken out," I countered. "Or what if I miss. I put the gun up to my head and pull the trigger and my hand jerks and all I do is take off my ear or something. Then I'm totally screwed: premeditated murder, lots of guilt, one ear. I think I'm better just letting her ride."

Gerry couldn't argue that one, but Randy didn't seem quite ready to let the revenge concept go. He'd added tomatoes and dried herbs to his sauce, so the whole thing was smelling rich and earthy now, simply screaming out to have a chunk of hearty bread dipped in it. "You could get back at Kris by doing music, couldn't you?"

"Whaddya mean?"

"Well, she said that one of the reasons that she didn't want to be with you anymore was because you weren't doing anything with your music," Randy said, slowly and deliberately, as was his style when he was thinking, or stirring, or both. "So if you started doing music again, and you got all rich and famous doing it, then maybe she'd realize that she gave up on you too soon, that she dropped you just when you were ready to make it big…"

"Yeah, then she'd feel really bad, really stupid," Gerry added, getting the drift by now. "That bitch! He'll show her a thing or two about music!"

"Yeah, I think he'll definitely be able to say that he wins if he does that."

"Right, put her in her place and everything."

"Where she belongs, 'cause she's not going to be as good at music as he is."

"No way."

"Can't happen."

"Nope. Good plan, Randy."

"Thanks."

I was silent throughout the exchange, as I generally remained whenever Gerry and Randy started talking about me as if I weren't there, figuring the shock of me speaking unexpectedly could be dangerous to all parties concerned. And normally I was also silent because they tended to be patently ludicrous when they thought out loud, particularly about me—but in this case, I was silent because their argument had a strange appeal, a certain logic that fit my passive-aggressive persona. There was a definite allure in their plan, both from the standpoint of it giving me the impetus I needed to start playing music again, and from the standpoint of allowing me to partake of vengeance upon Kris in a slightly more palatable fashion than murder/suicide.

So after double servings of Randy's magnificent spaghetti sauce ladled over noodles (he'd tell me it was actually marinara con linguine or something, but it'll always be spaghetti sauce on noodles to me, low-rent uncultured white trash that I am), I retired to my apartment, got my bass out from under my bed, plugged in the practice amp and played. I was rusty, but it felt nice, and it did make me itch to stand up on stage again, and watch people moving to the lines I laid out beneath them. I'd need to get a new bass cabinet before I could play out, of course, unless I did the coffee house thing, but the granola set wasn't particularly appealing to me, so I nixed that concept right up front.

It took me nearly a year to set aside enough money to be able to get the equipment I wanted and needed to keep myself out of that coffee house circuit, though, and even then the rig that I scored was a second hand one, offered on consignment at one of the area's many impersonal, look-alike shopping mall music stores. I got an invitation to Kris' wedding in the mail while I was saving, which inspired me to put a bit more out of each paycheck than I'd originally been planning, then got a Christmas card that winter signed "Love, Kris and Mark" that almost inspired me to give up drinking, just to accumulate cash quicker. Emphasis on almost.

I'd finally built up the boodle I needed in early 1988, acquiring a monster used Ampeg cabinet stuffed with eight twelve-inch speakers, then scoring a pre-amp and my own monitor speaker as well, since the ones clubs tended to use tended to suck. Jerry and Randy helped me cart the gear home, and we set it up in the storefront of the first floor, where the studio would ultimately be built, and I offered them an improvisational solo set that rattled windows up and down our block, eliciting the first of many complaints from the porno theatre up the road. But that was okay, because the music also made a toothless drunk stop in front of the store, where he shuffled and gyrated to the sounds I crafted, creating nearly-visible aroma contrails as he twirled—and I knew that if I could make that sorry excuse for a human being move, then I'd still be able to work my magic on the (slightly) nicer looking specimens of humanity that tended to frequent rock clubs and bars.

I couldn't do it by myself, though, so needed to make some quality contacts with other musicians in the area. The mall music stores tended to have bulletin boards with "players wanted" notes tacked up in a patchwork of index-carded dreams, most soon be shattered, but I was so put off by the cookie-cutter nature of all those mercantile outlets that I couldn't help but believe that the musicians who advertised there had to be cut from similar sterile molds themselves. So I started skimming the back pages of *The Advocate* instead, figuring that the then-relatively-new underground newspaper might provide a more appropriate advertising venue for the musicians who actually mattered hereabouts.

And mattering was important to me this time. I'd played in enough cover bands to know that I could make decent money if I chose to join one again, and perhaps get a good reputation in my own community, but never manage to go anywhere with it, since every other community in America had its own competent cover bands as well. I didn't want to play my ass off and get stuck in Troy, much as I'd gotten myself stuck in

Bridgefield before, by not pushing myself musically, by acquiescing to popular tastes instead of making some small effort to define them.

Unfortunately, most of the advertisements appearing in the back of the *Advocate* seemed to be for working cover bands, or for bands that defined their original sounds by comparing them to the sorts of lowest common denominator acts to which cover bands tended to turn for material. Around March of 1988, however, just about the time when I didn't think I could stand another day of the snow and cold, just when I thought I might hang up this whole New York adventure altogether, one advertisement caught my eye: "Guitarist and keyboardist looking for rhythm section to help put the progress back in progressive rock. Chops a must. Brains help. Serious inquiries only. Call Brian and George, 866-2121."

I'd been playing classic progressive rock in my bedroom for years, and certainly had to the chops to do so publicly, although I'd always assumed that no one would want to hear me do it. Brains? Well, I suppose I could lay claim to those. While sober, at least. So I might have been a match—but I didn't call that week: I got busy at work, distracted by booze, something happened, I don't know what, life hurried on, destination unknown. When I picked up the *Advocate* a week later, though, the advertisement had changed: "Guitarist, keyboardist and drummer looking for bassist to help put the progress back in progressive rock. Chops a must. Brains help. Serious inquiries only. Call Brian, George and Steve, 866-2121."

I realized then that I didn't want to let this opportunity go just yet, so I whim-called the number that night. A woman answered. I asked for Brian, George or Steve, heard her shout "Brian" with her hand over the mouthpiece, then got a quiet "Hello?" from my future lead guitarist, although it took a little while for me to tease much more out of him, since his spoken communication skills were a bit on the inadequate side. Brian finally got around to asking about my background, though, and I fudged the truth by describing the extent of my public performing experience, but implying that I'd been playing King Crimson and

Genesis in the pubs of Bridgefield, instead of Kool and the Gang and the Romantics.

Brian also asked how old I was, and I had to think for a moment before remembering that my 30th birthday was coming up in three months. That seemed old, so I lied and told him I was 26 instead. He grunted, and noted that their new drummer was an older guy too, like me. So I was dealing with a kid. Fine. I could deal with kids. I was a kid once, and played with adults regularly, and was damn good at it, sometimes making them sound better than they had any right to be on their own. Maybe Brian and George and Steve (who I assumed was the new older guy drummer) could do the same for me. I arranged to meet them to jam at their rehearsal space in Clifton Park (one of the Capital Region's sterile northern suburbs) the following Saturday.

I had to borrow Gerry and Randy's car to do so, equipment hanging out the trunk with bungee cords and rope wrapped around everything to keep it from flying out onto the highway as I gently crept northwards across the Mohawk River. Brian had given me directions, and not having spent much time in Clifton Park I assumed I was going be meeting him in some converted loft, or warehouse, or industrial space—so was moderately surprised and mildly disappointed when I got the appointed place and discovered instead that it was a garage attached to a house on a street where all the other garages and houses looked just the same, only with slightly different shades of brown and green and ivory paint on their windows and doors.

I could hear noise from the garage, although the door was locked shut, so I walked to the front door of the house and rang instead. A matronly middle-aged woman answered, asked if she could help me; I recognized her voice as having been the same one I had briefly spoken with on the phone earlier in the week and told her I was there for the rehearsal. She invited me in, asked me to take my shoes off in the foyer, then led me through the house to the garage, holding the door for me as I entered, shutting it behind me as she left.

"Thanks, Ms. Wellington," shouted a mildly dazed-looking kid behind a bank of keyboards, shaking his dark, shoulder length brown hair out of his face as he did, it falling right back in front of his eyes again as soon as he'd finished.

My eyes swept the doublewide garage, a silver, recent-model Audi parked on one side. There was the keyboardist and his rig. There was a drum kit with a lumpy-looking, Elvis-sideburn-wearing proletariat of a drummer behind it, face blank. And there was another kid playing with a hand-full of wires on the floor, a painfully skinny kid this one, with a shock of black curly hair that seemed to be as wide as his shoulders, and a wispy little set of stringy whiskers on his lip and chin, the rest of his face smooth, unshaven, probably never needing to be shaved.

The skinny kid stood after the keyboardist shouted. He didn't look at me, but did sort of raise a hand in greeting, then mumbled: "I see you've met my mother."

"Uh, yeah, I did, thanks," I answered. "Umm…can we open this garage door so I can get my gear in here?" I was actually sort of hoping that they'd say "no" at this point, so I could just leave. But the skinny guitarist, who I assumed was Brian, reached over and pushed a button on the wall, and the door opened to reveal my car outside, speakers popping out of the trunk.

"Whoa! Rock n' roll!" shouted the keyboardist, leaping out of his seat and rushing down the driveway to admire my stacks. "Wow! This is gonna be loud, man. Excellent!"

I appreciated his enthusiasm, if not his maturity. "Help me get this stuff out, alright?"

"Oh, sure, yeah, here," he reached over and helped me lift, and together we rolled the gear into the garage, Brian and the drummer never moving to help. "I'm George, by the way," the keyboardist continued as we went back for a second trip. "George Kellenberger. The drummer is Steve Pettit, or Stephen, actually, is what he likes to be called, but no one calls him that. And you met Brian, right? The guitar player?"

"I haven't met him, no," I answered. "But I spoke with him on the phone. He's the one who invited me up here."

"Right, right, I knew that," George continued. "We hear good things about you. And you've certainly got some nice gear, so that's half the war right there, right?"

"Half the battle," said Brian, softly, as he plugged his guitar into a series of silver boxes that looked like effects pedals, except that they had raw solder on their surfaces instead of product logos. He stood, stepped on a couple of them, strummed his guitar and looked up to see me watching him. "I made these," he said. "I want a certain sound, and the ones you can buy in stored never sound quite right to me. So I made my own."

"Brian's an electronics genius, man," George said. "He can make all sorts of stuff, whatever you need, don't ever bother buying anything again, 'cause he'll just take care of you, and it costs a lot less and the stuff he makes is better than the stuff you buy, he's right about that."

"It sounds alright," said Stephen, or Steve, making me jump since I'd forgotten he was sitting there.

"That's a compliment coming from Steve," George said, with a nervous laugh and a quick glance over at the drummer. "Steve usually hates everything."

Steve didn't respond. He and George and Brian just looked at me instead. I figured I needed to take charge of the situation, since none of them seemed able or willing to run an audition.

"So how do you want me to do this?" I asked. "Brian told me you guys were interested in doing some original progressive stuff. Do you wanna just jam? Do you want me to play a solo piece just so you can see what I can do? Or something else?"

No answer. Finally Steve said, "Just do whatever you want. They don't know what they're looking for. They'll jump in if they can."

Okay...I could see that this wasn't likely to go anywhere, so I plugged in my bass and figured I'd run through an improvisation based on some

King Crimson riffs, since if they knew progressive, they'd know that stuff. I played about a minute of "Larks Tongue in Aspic, Part II" all by myself, but just as I'd decided to wrap it up and call this whole exercise a bust, George began to lay down a deep, resonant, wobbling synthesizer line beneath my busy bass patterns. I simplified my run, leaving the core pattern of "Larks Tongue" to follow George's lead and make it easier for Brian and Steve to cut in.

I looked over at George's gear and noticed what he was playing for the first time: he had the obligatory late model Korg keyboard there in his rack, but was currently working on a beat up old Prophet V synthesizer, the greatest noisemaker I'd ever encountered, in Junior's Music or onstage. I was impressed, both at his taste and his technique. He and I began to lock nicely when another voice began to swell, Brian pulling a painfully ripe sustained note out of his guitar, creating a sinus-wobbling drone, a background wail, a technological scream the likes of which I've never heard before.

I'd pulled into a straight 4/4 cadence by this time, building it around the original chord pattern George had crafted on the back on the King Crimson figure that I'd thoughtlessly, haphazardly tossed out onto the garage floor minutes before. Brian and George began to trade runs and lines atop my foundation, and it was clear that they'd been playing together for quite some time, having a strong intuitive feel for where the other was going before the other had actually realized it, much less played it. They were making some beautiful, powerful noises, captivating me, as much as I'd expected to be underwhelmed, if not offended.

We needed a beat, though, and I kept creating come-in opportunities for Steve, who sat, looking bored, watching the three of us play. Finally realizing that he wasn't going to take the improvisational bait, I shifted into my well-practiced music director role and began working Brian and George towards a crescendo, a wrap-up, returning to where we had started, then cutting it all off quickly and decisively. It took a moment before they realized what I was doing (not surprising, since I doubt they'd played with anyone else), but once they got clued in to my intentions, they began to follow my leads, working with me, taking our unstructured first number to a logical, satisfying conclusion.

I smiled despite myself when it was done. George was a bit more enthusiastic: "Dude, that freakin' rocked!"

"That was nice," Brian agreed, playing with his boxes on the floor.

"It was alright," noted Steve. "I couldn't really get into it, though. Kind of noodling, not my thing." He paused, before rising and announcing "I gotta piss," then disappearing into the house.

I reached into my pocket to fish out a celebratory cigarette, but as soon as the pack emerged, Brian stood and pointed at me: "You can't do that in here. Or in the yard. My parents don't want anyone smoking on their property."

Yeesh. I put the pack away and rhythmically tapped my fingers on the top of my bass cabinet instead. "So what's with Steve? Does he actually play drums or what?" I asked, by way of making conversation.

"Oh yeah, he's real good," George answered. "He's played in, like, ten bands in Albany over the past few years, and he played in some back in Wisconsin—that's where he grew up—before he moved here. He's got lots of connections and stuff, all the stuff we don't have at all."

My extensive musical experience told me there was a problem here, although it seemed that George and Brian may not have noticed it, assuming that it was normal for drummers to change bands every six months: "Any idea why he's not with any of those bands anymore? I mean, ten bands is a lot, particularly if you're not counting the ones he played with in Wisconsin…" I tossed out open-endedly.

"It's because he's an asshole," Brian answered simply. "A total asshole. But he's a good drummer, when you find something he wants to play, and he knows all the club owners and promoters, so he can get us in the door at some places, I think."

"And then we can kick him out," George continued.

"Yeah, he's our meal ticket now, and no one else will have him at the moment, so we've got to humor him for awhile until we're good enough to have other people want to play with us," Brian continued. "We can't make it out of the suburbs without someone like him."

"Or him" George said, pointing my direction. "He's got experience. And connections."

"My connections won't do you any good up here," I corrected. "Although my experience might, there you're right. We'll see."

Steve returned as we spoke, taking his place behind his drum kit, expressionless, rubbing his hands on his thighs as if to dry to piss off of them. "So now what?" he asked, flatly.

"Wanna do 'Jerusalem' again?" George asked. "That sounded pretty good last week."

"Do you know 'Jerusalem?'" Brian asked me.

"You mean the Emerson, Lake and Palmer song?" I countered, surprised that these barely post-adolescent players even knew the song, much less wanted to play it.

"Yeah, although it's like the English national anthem or something," George answered for Brian. "We figured we'd play some things by other people that we all knew for a while, just to get used to playing together, then we could start working out some original stuff. Me n' Brian have written some songs, n' maybe we can all work on some stuff together."

It was an odd audition song, but I did know it, vaguely, so after a little faux organ intro by George, Steve finally began playing his drums and we stumbled through the chord structure a couple of times until I had the gist of the thing. By about our fifth run-through, it sounded fairly crunchy, and I could at last begin to understand Steve's appeal as a drummer, since he was precise, powerful and emphatic behind the skins. I had just begun to lose myself in the groove when I was brought back to reality by a horrible sound.

"And did those feet," the horrible noise went, "….in ancient times…walk upon England's mountains green…"

It was George. He was singing. He was bad. I couldn't help but to start laughing, and when I did I lost my place, and the song sputtered and died.

"Sorry about that, I lost my place," I said, still grinning. "Umm…I wasn't expecting George's vocal stylings on that song, I guess. They took me by surprise."

"Yeah, he sucks," noted Steve, rudely but in this case, accurately.

"Were you planning to sing publicly, George?" I asked.

He was red-faced by this time, although I couldn't tell if it was out of shame or rage. "I dunno, I guess so," he said. "Maybe. I mean, I sing better than Brian does."

I could believe that, since I had a hard time imagining Brian being able to generate enough wind in his pipe cleaner of a chest to be able to speak loudly, much less sing. "Well, I don't wanna hurt your feelings, George," I explained. "But you're not going to be able to sing like that for a paying audience."

"So we need to find a singer, you think?" Brian asked.

"Yeah, yeah, I do," I answered. "Or get George some singing lessons," I looked over at the dejected keyboardist. "No offense or anything, man. You really are a brilliant player, I can see that already. But singin' ain't your strong point."

"Think he can do any better?" the always helpful Steve inquired, to no one in particular.

"I've sung backup vocals with a lot of bands," I answered, looking right at him. "So, yeah, I do think I could do better, although I'd prefer not to be the lead vocalist, since I'd rather concentrate on the bass."

"Let's try it with you singing, then," Brian said.

"Fine, we can do that," I agreed. "You got the words to this song written down somewhere?"

George handed me a sheet from atop his keyboard rack, and I taped it to the side of my cabinet. We launched into "Jerusalem" again, and I sang it, and it was fine, nothing special, nothing awful, but functional.

"That did sound better," George admitted, sheepishly. "You can sing pretty good."

"Thanks," I said. "I hate these words, but thanks."

We puttered around with a couple of other vintage '70s progressive art-rock type numbers before we began to jam a bit, and Brian and George trotted out a couple of their original numbers. They were interesting, but they were terribly knotty, all fractured time signatures and skewed rhythms. I praised the originality of the work (figuring I needed to build George back up after bursting his vocal bubble), but explained that I thought it would work much better with real audiences if we could take the chord structures and get them to work within more straightforward rhythmic parameters—since people at bars and clubs wanted to be able to tap their toes, or bob their heads, or dance, and there was no way any of those things were going to happen atop an 11/7 time signature.

Steve agreed with me, as the other half of the veteran component in the ensemble, and he and I began to lay down some fairly beat heavy rhythms, trying to get Brian and George to force their leads into a club friendly groove. And I give them credit for great technical proficiency as they were, for the most part, able to make the switches I was pushing, stretching here, contracting there, pulling their wild adventures in time management into some recognizable, presentable structure, without losing the exploratory nature of their creations. I was beginning to see true potential here.

But then the lights of the garage flickered on and off half-a-dozen times and George and Brian stood and began to unplug their instruments.

"That means it's quitting time," Steve explained.

"Brian's parents only let him have the garage on Saturdays, from noon 'til six in the evening," George added. "They don't want to bother the neighbors at dinner time."

"So where else do you rehearse during the week?" I asked, amazed.

"Umm, in my bedroom, George and I," Brian answered. "We haven't had to worry about it with a rhythm section yet."

"Well, we need to worry about it, if we're gonna do this," I told them, knowing that I was interested in at least another session or two, figuring that Brian and George weren't going to turn me away if I wanted to be there. "Steve'll tell you, too, I think, that you can't make a band work on one rehearsal a week. It'll take us months and months to get going that way. Don't you know of any other rehearsal spaces around here?"

"There's some space in Albany," George said. "We looked into it, but it's expensive to rent space, and I'd kinda worry about my stuff being down there without anyone there to keep an eye on it or anything."

"Let me talk to my landlords, then," I told them. "I live in Troy, and we've got a big, old, open office building with lots of space in it. And if we rehearsed there, it would be a shorter drive for everyone, I think." Me especially.

"How much will they charge us?" Brian asked, frugal right from the get-go.

"Maybe nothing," I answered. "They're pretty good guys about stuff like that."

George and Brian looked at me appreciatively as we began to pack our gear. Steve sat in the back and stared, then said "Tell him what the band's called."

"We were going to," George said. "We just hadn't gotten around to it."

"Arctangent," Brian muttered, not looking at me, scowling at Steve.

"What?" I couldn't hear him, or wasn't sure I'd heard him correctly, since that seemed an odd name for a band, to say the least.

"Arctangent," George seconded. "Me n' Brian decided a long, long time ago that that's what we wanted our band to be called. We think it sounds cool. Kinda smart. Kinda technical. So we're Arctangent."

"Not subject to negotiation," concluded Brian.

"Is that the stupidest thing you've ever heard or what?" Steve said, looking my way.

I had decided that I didn't like Steve much by this time, and that Brian and George had something going for them that I might be able to exploit, so I figured I wouldn't waste a silver bullet on an issue about which I didn't much care, one way or the other. I'd played in bands with worse names than Arctangent, after all, groups with names like the Sumter Creek Sunshine Band or the Bay Street Beachmasters or the Knights of White Rappin'.

"No, whatever, it's fine," I said, ignoring Steve, nodding at George and Brian instead. "It's your band, after all."

And in that moment, and with that phrase, I had them. And in that moment, and with that phrase, I also took the band away from them. Even if they didn't know it at the time, they let me do it—because I'd stood up for them, classic friendless nerds both, against a real Albany musician, a guy who regularly appeared in the pages of *The Advocate* with one band or another. Brian and George had never played in public, but in their minds, they arrived as musicians that day, the day that another real musician acknowledged that they were a band. Only by telling them that it was their band, I made it my band instead—since I'd made its existence contingent upon my approval. I'd learned a thing or two about the power of flattery at the Institute and Envirocorps, after all.

Gerry and Randy were thrilled, of course, at the prospect of having a rock band rehearsing in the Treehouse, so by the next weekend, they'd put in some basic security features, added some outlets and done some other needed electrical work on the first floor so that we could haul the other guys' gear down and set it up in a semblance of how it would look, feel and sound on stage. As we pulled out of Brian's driveway with our last load that afternoon, Brian's mother standing in the door watching, disapproval writ large on her face, I made of point of lighting a cigarette, taking a long luxurious drag and blowing it out the window as I waved to her. She didn't wave back. She hated me already. I was working quick in those days.

But Brian needed me as a bad influence, I think, since he was 20 years old, still living at home, still spending most of his time alone in his bedroom listening to music recorded when he was in diapers, still largely friendless, certainly a virgin, a sad specimen indeed—except for the fact that his lack of vices and social incompetence had allowed him to become both an electronics wizard and a guitar genius with all the spare time he had on his hands. He and George, a loser of a slightly less painful variety, had met in Junior High School (no doubt at an A/V Club meeting or a Chess Tournament or some other such embarrassing thing), striking up an affinity based on shared creepy loser interests, and beginning to play together—sometimes in Brian's bedroom, sometimes in George's—soon thereafter.

George had only a crummy Casio keyboard in those days, but Brian found the Prophet V (broken at the time) in a pawn shop and managed to love it back to life, no doubt modifying it for the better while he was at it. George's parents, impressed at their son's seeming discovery of a creative (maybe even marketable) talent, bought him the Korg when he graduated from high school. At that point, he and Brian had had to move into the garage, since the amps, effects, guitars and keyboards were no longer particularly mobile, and could no longer be conveniently packed into a bedroom space. One year later, they felt confident enough to place their first advertisement, picking up Steve in its first week, me in its second. Not a bad batting average, all things considered.

Once we moved into the Treehouse, I was able to put them all on a regular rehearsal schedule, Tuesday nights, Thursday nights, Saturday afternoons. Since we could lock things up and leave them, we were able to get in, get to work, and get out fairly quickly. While we never actually formally agreed that I was going to be the singer, and we never actually ever stopped talking about needing to get one sometime, I ended up in front of the microphone by default—which also served to simplify our fare a bit more than we might have chosen to do otherwise, since I couldn't sing and play insane bass figures at the same time.

This bothered George and Brian a bit, but I knew it was a smart move on any objective basis, since the simpler the music was, the easier it would be for audiences to connect with it. And us. And I also knew that if they went and hired a singer, they'd end up with some shrieking Geddy Lee or Jon Anderson clone, singing about fairies and dragons and hobbits and whatnot, whereas I had done backups for long enough to be able to keep things out of the dog whistle range, and to sing with a bit of force and enthusiasm, instead of delivering lyrics in a state of twee ethereal distraction.

We worked up a cover of Roxy Music's "Editions of You," which I held up as a landmark example of the type of music we could, and should, produce: a hammering beat, exceptional guitar and synthesizer solos, clever chord structures, urgent vocals, cynical world-weary lyrics. Brian wanted to keep "Jerusalem" in the set, too, and while I agreed that we did a great job with it instrumentally, I hated singing William Blake's sickeningly Anglophile words. I mean, Troy had plenty of dark Satanic mills, sure, but the whole lamb of God bit and the building Jerusalem in England's green and pleasant land stuff left me cold, and then some.

So I decided I'd write and sing something else, although I didn't tell anyone that before stepping up to the microphone at one rehearsal and letting loose with a nasty, hateful stream of blasphemy designed to preserve the tune's structure and intensity, but to dedicate it to something more relevant and close to my heart than chariots of fire and arrows of desire. I wasn't really a fan of the God of Abraham at that point, remember, seeing as what he'd done to my mother and everything. So my new lyrics went like this:

And did those feet in ancient times
Walk the Dead Sea in hobnailed boots?
And was the holy Lamb of God
Boiled in a pot with herbs and roots?
And did the countenance malign

Blast life from these occluded plains?
And did the magical prophets worship here,
Amidst these rattling bones and chains?

Bring me my vat of boiling oil,
Bring me my arrows of disease,
Bring me my lance and pike and sword,
Bring me my dirty needles please.
We shall call forth that endless night.
We shall spill rage upon the land.
So blow the horns and break the seals:
The kingdom of Baal is now at hand.

I didn't look at any of the others as I sang, keeping my back to them, listening to hear them falter or pause. But none of them did, they just kept rumbling along behind me, and when I hit the "kingdom of Baal" line, George sprayed the most spine-chilling, tooth-grinding squall of white noise and subsonic undertones that I'd ever heard atop Brian's circular guitar figure, and I knew they'd bought the change, and I knew we'd made something special.

When we finished, George leapt from his stool, pumping his fist, exclaiming, "Dude, that was absolutely freakin' evil! It rocked, man! Lemme see those words."

"Kinda scary, Collie," Brian said, with a painful-looking grin on his pinched face.

"It was okay," Steve added, a rare compliment from the King of Blah. "Where'd you get it?"

"I wrote it, man," I said, enthused despite myself. "I can't stand that old William Blake shit anymore, so if we're gonna do that song, we're gonna do it that way."

"Is it still called 'Jerusalem' then?" George asked, reading my scrawled lyric sheet.

"Nah, I don't think so," I answered. "I think we should call it 'Baal' now, doesn't that work better?"

"Works for me," said Brian, crossing out "Jerusalem" on the set list at his feet, writing "Ball" in its place.

"Two A's, Brian," I said. "B-A-A-L. A really nasty Old Testament God, if I remember Preacher Benson's fire and brimstone services right."

We also put together a dozen originals over that spring and summer, half of them rearranged leftovers from Brian and George's bedroom songwriting sessions, four of them originals that I brought to the table from my own private creative moments, two of them ("Tapeworm" and "Swirling Pool of Dysfunction," cheery numbers both) collaborative efforts resulting from jams between Brian and George and I. (Steve didn't jam, so he got no songwriting credit). With "Baal" and "Editions of You," that gave us 14 songs that we could deliver in just under an hour. It was a bit much for an opening act, and a bit short for a headliner, so we could pinch or pull whichever way we needed, based on circumstance.

We finally had Steve cash in his community connections in September 1988, booking three opening sets in quick succession at the Heartland Club, the Britannica Lounge and Humphrey's, then ostensibly headlining a "Three Band, Three Buck" night at the Quail Tavern, although playing the third slot just meant we could go longer, but with fewer people in the audience. Crowd response was decent to good in all cases, with "Baal" and "Editions of You" getting the best reaction (familiarity, even faint, breeds response in rock and roll clubs), and "Tapeworm" and a George-Brian composition called "The Microscope Show" emerging as the other cornerstone moments in the set.

We got our first mention in press, too, in the *Advocate* (of course), on the day we played the Quail Tavern. Critic-publisher Anna Salocks, in a larger review of Love and Rockets (for whom we opened when we played at Humphrey's), gave us a couple of lines of praise at the end of her article:

"Acclaimed area drummer Stephen Pettit's new project, Arctangent, played an interesting opening set that evoked some odd mix of Wire and Roxy Music, whose 'Editions of You' the local quartet covered to good effect. Pettit and Arctangent's bassist (who also sang) worked together well, creating a thick, rich bottom that a younger (not to mention scared) looking guitar and keyboard duo decorated with some technically impressive noise and filigree. Not like anything else I've seen around here, and worth paying attention to accordingly."

Brian and George were embarrassed by Anna's (accurate) observations, and I was annoyed that Steve hadn't bothered to tell anyone our names while getting us booked, but the gist of the review was positive, reason to celebrate, which we did that night at the end of our spacious and effective Quail Tavern set, then again later at the Treehouse, listening to the sound board tape I'd made. We sounded good. We really did. And you could hear people's applause picked up on my vocal microphone, and that alone sounded better than anything I'd heard in ages, certainly since listening to Kris say "I'm getting married."

So Arctangent existed in the public domain now, with official media sanction, and we were original, and we were interesting, and we were worth noticing. Look it up if you don't believe me. And had my name actually appeared in Anna's review, I would have clipped it and sent it to Kris the very day it was issued. I cut it out and put it on my bulletin board at Envirocorps instead, impressing Pam the postal girl so much that we had to lock the doors of the company mailroom the next night and let our passions flow, rain or sleet or hail be damned. There'd be other reviews for Kris. Later.

Chapter Thirteen

All of Stephen Pettit's bands had to fire him eventually. Except for Arctangent—but that was only because he spared us the inevitable necessity by announcing, just before a gig in February of 1989, that he was moving back home to Wisconsin, family business, y'know, didn't want to talk about it, taking off soon. We were stunned, for a minute or two, but then we got over it, and throughout the set Brian and George and I looked at each other and grinned, knowing that the rhythmically-gifted sack of karmic cancer sitting behind us was going to be far away sometime soon.

And when Steve said soon, he meant soon: he played out the set that evening, took his equipment home (instead of to the rehearsal space) after the show and vanished from our lives that very night. Brian and I stopped by his apartment complex a couple of days later and looked in his window (Steve lived on a first floor courtyard, where he could watch the women swimming in the pool from his easy chair), just to make sure he wasn't dead in there or something. But the place was stripped. Steve and his car and his furniture were gone. We thought this was good.

So good, in fact, that we had an impromptu party that night in the rehearsal space to celebrate our unexpected loss, Randy and Gerry joining Brian and George and a couple of local bar girls and I for drinks and loud music and some good pot I'd been given at Steve's last gig and even a light-hearted, laugh-inducing contest to see who could come up with the most obnoxious Steve story. We unanimously awarded the evening's prize to George when he recalled Steve locking himself in the Wellingtons' bathroom after a practice, then walking into the kitchen as the Wellingtons were sitting down for their dinner and asking if they had a plunger, noting that he'd clogged the toilet with a particularly robust bowel movement. By the time Mrs. Wellington returned from the basement with the plumber's helper, however, Steve had driven off, assuming that the Wellingtons would take care of the problem, since it was their bathroom and everything. Brian couldn't remember whether anyone ate anything that night or not—but he knew that he himself went hungry, appetite suppressed beyond recovery.

I laughed until I almost soiled my own pants at the memory, relishing (now that I didn't have to deal with it anymore) the fundamental vileness that was Steve. We also all had a good laugh as we worked on the text for the advertisement that we planned to place in *The Advocate* to see if we could rustle up a new drummer in short order. We finally settled on something simple, yet mildly amusing nonetheless: "Arctangent wants a drummer. Assholes need not apply. Call Brian at 866-2121." We didn't need to say anything more than that by this point, since we'd established our name about town already—and everyone knew that Steve was an asshole, so we didn't have to explain that bit either.

We didn't have quite as easy a time filling the drum stool as we might have liked, though, in large part because I was playing an active role in the selection process this time—as opposed to letting Brian and George pick the first person who replied to their advertisements, the way they had done with Steve and me. So we took a little hiatus from performing and auditioned eight people in the Treehouse over the next three weeks (a different one for each rehearsal), some older, some younger, some technical players, some power players, one female, one electronic percussion geek, one sad kid who showed up without a kit at all, thinking we'd provide him one.

We finally settled on Barry Swinton, who had gone to the same suburban high school that had spawned George and Brian, although he had graduated three years earlier than they had and had no recollection of ever having seen them before. He was by far the tallest musician I've ever worked with, six-foot-six at least (although his posture was bad, so it was hard to measure him exactly), with a mop of shoulder length blonde hair cut bowl-around-the-head style. He was a smart, technically gifted drummer who could keep a beat while never seeming to actually play on the quarter notes, arms and legs gyrating spasmodically as if he was chasing something that he was never going to catch, no matter how hard he tried.

Barry also had ten years worth of piano lessons behind him, so he understood the melodic side of the musical equation as well as he did the rhythmic one, which made him a valuable songwriting asset for Arctangent. We actually began to write as a four piece as soon as he joined the band, since he enjoyed the experimental jam component of our rehearsals and was willing to bring in his own themes and motifs for the rest of us to knock around as we cobbled together new material or modified arrangements of older songs to fit his more limber style.

We felt that we couldn't let Steve's departure go unmentioned in public, though, so one night after we'd pulled together a nice, propulsive new instrumental that Brian had written, I went home, did some research in Gerry's *World Almanac and Book of Facts* and wrote lyrics that explained exactly how much Steve's departure had meant to all of us, and what we figured he would make of himself in Wisconsin:

He's going to Wisconsin
And building himself a new life
He's buying himself a farmhouse
And finding a blonde wife

He's going to be a Lutheran
He's making his own cheese curds
He's going to Wisconsin
To be a man of fewer words

He's going to see the Packers
He'll vacation at the Dells
He'll have to buy a new tractor
The best one that John Deere sells

He's going to Wisconsin
He's leaving New York behind
He'll stay a night in Chicago
With a friend, if he don't mind

He's buying himself a parka
He'll surely be needing a plow
To put on the front of his tractor
Or yoke to the back of his cow

He'll probably be quite happy
With family and heifers and such
He's going to Wisconsin
We hate him so very much

We played "Wisconsin" live for the first time at our debut concert with Barry in the band, a mid-March 1989 show at the Britannica Lounge. The gaggle of other musicians in the crowd stood and gave us one of the heartiest rounds of applause we'd ever received when the song ended, since most of them had played with Steve, too, and hated him just as much as we did. It became an instant staple of our sets accordingly.

That first show with our new drummer also marked another milestone in the Arctangent's evolution, although we didn't realize it at the time. Barry's older sister Bridget (a strikingly tall blonde, like her brother, but with a better haircut) showed up to watch the show with a boyfriend du jour, thereby formally introducing musical hustler Matt Lawrence to the band, although (as we later learned), he'd been watching us for quite some time from the shadows, observing yet unobserved.

With 20/20 hindsight in effect, I think we actually got a taste of how Matt operated that very first night: since we rarely saw Bridget after that show, I have to think that he probably asked her out (or got her to take him out) just to have an easy, casual, non-obsessive way of approaching us. Matt knew we'd be less suspicious of him that way, since Bridget had a reason to be there—and he was with Bridget. He knew how to get what he wanted, did Matt, and wasn't averse to being a user of the most heinous variety when pursuing his targeted objectives. And that's one of the nicer things I can say about him.

Matt and Bridget stood right in front of the stage throughout our set that evening, Bridget watching Barry and looking bored, Matt bobbing his head, pumping his fist, yelling "woo hoo" at the end of most songs. It was an impressive display of fan enthusiasm, no two ways about it. The couple then joined us in the basement band room behind and beneath the stage after the show—along with Randy and Gerry, who generally didn't miss a concert unless they were travelling or wrapped too deeply in Treehouse construction projects to be able to leave when we were playing. It made them feel dangerous when they hung out at places like the Britannica Lounge. They liked that feeling.

Introductions were exchanged all round in the ready room as we toweled off and rummaged in the cooler for refreshments. Matt enthused about the set at length while Gerry, Randy and Brian stood in the corner of the room talking electronics, George lay on the floor, breathing hard and staring into space, Barry tapped out a cadence on the broken coffee table next to George, Bridget continued to look bored and I sat on the couch and drank, figuring I'd earned the right tonight for playing and singing a fabulous set. (Of course, if we'd played a bad show, I'd have had to drink to drown my disappointment but logic and rationalization are important to a drunk, so I always had a reason when I had a bottle).

We waited for about fifteen minutes, until such crowd as was in the room had dispersed, before Barry uncurled his impossibly long spine, stretched and said "Time to go schlep the gear, dudes."

But before any of us could make it up from our comfortable spots, Matt was out the door and up the stairs, yelling "I can help, lemme give you a hand," while Barry looked bemused and followed him up to the stage.

And Matt did indeed give us a hand that night, helping Barry and George pack their gear, rolling and pushing and hauling all of our stacks and other assorted big black boxes out to our line of cars and pick-up trucks in the back alley behind the club. And then he followed us back to the Treehouse and helped us unload everything there, setting it up in the rehearsal space, loudly admiring Gerry and Randy's property as he did. Bridget had disappeared somewhere between the Britannica and the Treehouse, but Matt didn't seem to mind. He was hauling Arctangent's boxes. That seemed to be enough for him for the evening.

I wasn't complaining, mind you: I was happy to have another body to move gear, as we were short on that front as a rule, me having banned Brian from touching heavy equipment anymore, since every time he tried to lift or sling or drag, he ended up bruising or breaking some part of his terribly frail body, and it just wasn't worth the risk to have our guitarist playing with splints on his fingers. So, y'know, if this guy Matt wanted to carry my amp, more power to him. And if he wanted to hang out in the rehearsal room late into the evening and praise me and my music after George and Brian and Barry went home and Randy and Gerry went up to the Fourth Floor, well, who was I to argue with that? It was nice to have someone to drink with, after all, as Matt's company meant that I wasn't an alcoholic, since alcoholics only drank alone, right?

I was shaken awake there in the studio several hours later by a concerned-looking Gerry, who hissed "Collie! Collie! We're going to be late for work" as he pulled me off the couch and propelled me towards the stairs. I couldn't remember falling asleep, or passing out, or whatever I had done, but I did remember talking late and I turned to make sure I hadn't dreamt those conversations—and sure enough, like Little Red Riding Hood in Baby Bear's bed, there was Matt, sprawled out at the foot of my bass cabinet, snoring. I had a twinge of concern about leaving him there, but Gerry was insistent, and I acceded to his prods and dragged myself upstairs to shower and get ready for another thrilling day at Envirocorps.

Needless to say, I wasn't very productive once I got there, so just after lunch, in an effort to avoid doing any real work for the day, I called Barry and asked him about that guy who had followed us home the night before, vaguely recalling that he had something to do with the drummer's Amazon sister Bridget. Barry said Matt was okay, as best he could ascertain, a regular sort of enthusiastic parasite around some of the clubs in town, working at the door, sweeping up after shows, doing whatever needed to be done that no one else would do. He also worked in the used record store way out on Central Avenue towards Colonie, and occasionally was spotted at traders' conventions in the area with boxes of rare discs that he'd no doubt purloined from his sometime place of employment.

Barry's suggestion of purloining gave me a twinge, since we, or I, had left this relative stranger in our rehearsal space with some very expensive, hard-to-replace custom gear. I started to get nervous, which made me even less productive, so at about two o'clock I trotted down to Randy's office and asked if I could take his car out for the afternoon to run some errands, then come back and pick him and Gerry up before dinner time. He agreed, but he made me promise to stop by the home repair store while I was out to pick up some insulation or something that he and Gerry needed to finish the loading dock entrance. I told him I would, but I knew that I wouldn't. I took his car anyway.

Matt was nowhere to be found when I got home, but everything in the rehearsal space seemed to be in its proper place, so I figured that my lapse of common sense hadn't hurt us in any way. I went up to my apartment, cursing each step on each flight of stairs as I ascended, set my clock for five thirty, napped until being jolted awake again by the alarm at the appointed hour, brushed my teeth, drove back to Envirocorps, stopped by Randy's office, handed him his car keys and said "Sorry, man, I didn't have enough time to make that stop for you. Want me to try again later tonight?"

"No, that's okay, me n' Gerry can go take care of it later, thanks for trying, though," he said, just the way I knew he would. His predictability was such a comfort sometimes.

I didn't think much about Matt again until Arctangent played at the Quail Tavern the following Thursday and, lo and behold, there he was, front and center, digging the show to a nearly unhealthy, almost distracting extent. No sign of Bridget, though, so he didn't seem to be at the show out of girlfriend family obligations, the way he was the first time. He was at the show for us—and I wasn't quite sure how I felt about that, seeing as how he was male and didn't seem to have anything I wanted or needed.

It struck me then, as I looked down on Matt from the stage, that he was put together like a pile of inverted triangles. He had a wide forehead with side-parted straight brown hair sweeping across its top, prominent eyes, his face tapering quickly to a pointed chin, praying mantis like. Under a long neck, he had then wide shoulders and a robust chest tapering quickly again to a narrow waist, beneath which powerful looking thighs dwindled into oddly-skinny ankles, making it look as if he should topple over at the slightest push. I didn't recall him looking so much like a geometry project gone bad the last time I'd seen him, but it could have been the angle from which I was looking at him. It was weird in either case, and kind of disturbing.

I looked away from Matt as we launched into "Shotgun" (one of four new songs we'd worked up collectively since Barry joined the band), staring into the stage lights instead so I couldn't see anything for a few moments, hoping he'd be gone when my vision returned. But when next I looked down, he was still there, looking back at me intently, bobbing his head to the rhythms Barry and I were laying down from the stage. No surprise, then, that when we were done with our set, he was there at the side of the stage, ready to help us break down, pack up and transport our gear home once again.

As we settled in at the Treehouse (the airlock and the soundproofing were done by this point, and the loading dock was nearly completed, although the kitchenette, half bath and studio isolation booth were still only in the dreaming-about-it stage), I decided that we couldn't let Matt unilaterally join our entourage without at least a cursory challenge, and Brian, George and Barry seemed unable or unwilling to ask any questions about a gift horse that carried heavy amps without being asked. So I took the leap on their behalf.

"Y'know, we all appreciate you helping with our gear and everything, Matt" I began. "But I gotta ask you something, 'cause we're not really used to having people go out of their way to do things for us."

"Sure, man, anything," Matt said, sitting on other end of the sofa, leaning forward, eyes wide, hanging on my every word. "What's on your mind?"

"What do you want from us?"

Matt's faced clouded, briefly, thought-wrinkles forming on his forehead, then he brightened again, along with the light bulb that seemed to have popped on inside his skull. "I don't want anything from you guys, that's not what it's all about at all," he said. "I'm more into what I can do for you guys, since I think you're the best band I've heard around here—and I've been looking for a band to work with, someone to help out with all the shitty little jobs and stuff that you shouldn't have to do. Roadie stuff. Selling merch. Booking, dealing with scumbag promoters, those kinds of things."

I watched the other three puff perceptibly as Matt pegged us as Albany's best band, but as a master of brown-nosing and flattery myself, I wasn't particularly impressed.

"Okay, that's fine, but I still gotta ask: what's in it for you? Are you a masochist? Do you want to have people walk all over you? Are you looking to get paid? 'cause none of us are making much money at this point, and I don't think any of us would be much interested in sharing any of it with you right now if we did, you know what I mean?"

Brian's head snapped up as I mentioned money, and sharing it. "I know what you mean, absolutely," Matt answered, without a pause this time, looking at Brian as if to comfort away his very frugal fears. "But it's really simple: I've always wanted to be in a band. It's all I've ever wanted to do. But I can't sing, and I'm a terrible guitar player, and I learned both of those things the hard way, trying to do them both and getting laughed at and rejected by everyone I auditioned for. But I love the whole rock and roll thing, y'know? I love live performances. I love travelling. I love making deals, working with people to get the word out, to get them to come to shows, to sell them stuff when they're there.

"And I've been doing that kind of stuff, working for clubs, record stores, whatever it takes, just trying to get myself into the business one way or the other," he continued. "I know everybody in this town who's got anything to do with music, including the music critics, who you need to know, too. I've got connections around here, and as much as you may have hated Steve, he had them too—and now that he's gone, you need someone who can weasel their way into a club or get their calls returned if you want to do something other than play a weekly residency at the Quail for the next five years."

"But how do you have all of these connections," I pressed. "What do you have that I don't, I mean?"

"Lots of time on my hands," Matt said. "You've got a full time job. You've got to rehearse on nights when you're not playing out. I can come and go pretty much as I need to. I can hang out at the back door of a club all afternoon so the owner can't avoid me."

He stopped talking suddenly, sat back on the couch, looked thoughtful for a moment, then leaned forward again, this time with a curious grin on his face. "Plus I know how to get stuff," he said. "People take my calls 'cause I get them stuff."

"What kind of stuff?"

"What do you want?"

"I don't want anything," I told him. "I just want to know what you're getting for other people that makes them return your calls."

"Whatever they want," he said, still cryptic, still grinning.

"Like drugs, you mean? Or women? Or guns? What are we talking about here?"

Matt refused to be pinned down. "Whatever they want. And whatever you want. I can get it. People appreciate that. I can do a lot for your band, believe me."

I have to admit that I was intrigued. Barry and George and Brian were over on the other side of the room, pretending to look at George's synthesizer, but I could tell that they were listening too—and none of them were giving me the sorts of body language that was telling me to end this impromptu interview on the spot.

"Okay, let's cut to the chase, then," I said. "Tell me in concrete terms: what do you want from us? What do we have to give you to have you help us out with your connections?"

"I really don't need much," Matt answered. "I need you to cover my expenses: if I spend some money for you, I need you to reimburse me, but I won't spend money for you unless you give me approval ahead of time."

"Okay, that's reasonable."

"And then I just want you to give me the chance to prove myself to you," he continued. "I want you to let me work for you for one year, covering my expenses, like I said, but otherwise just as a volunteer, doing whatever I can do, schedule permitting."

"Alright. And then what, if we decide that you're good to your word, and good for the band?"

"Then I want to be your manager," said Matt, tossing his dream card on the table. "I want to manage you guys, on contract, get a cut of what you're going to make—because I believe that you have a better chance of getting out of Albany, and taking me with you, than anyone else I've heard around here. But I don't think you can do it without someone working in your corner, so I think you need me as much as I need you."

This was getting kind of heavy, so I tried to lighten the discussion a bit by shaking my head in an aw-shucks fashion and saying "I'll bet you tell that to all the other bands."

He didn't take the joke. "No, I don't," he said, defensively. "In fact, I've only made this offer to two other bands, ever."

"What did they say?"

"They both said 'no,'" Matt answered. "And they're both gone, now. Steve was in one of them, in fact. They folded up right after they threw him out. They didn't get lucky and find a better drummer with a decent personality, the way you did. And the other band just wanted to do things themselves, and they plugged along for another year or so, and things never moved forward or back for them, and they just eventually gave up out of boredom. Both of them needed someone on their team. Neither of them recognized it, or neither of them thought I was the right guy. And now they're gone."

"Well you must not have held up your end of the deal during the one-year trial period for them to say no, right?"

"Wrong. I didn't offer them that. I just told them that I wanted to be their manager right away, and they couldn't understand how they could give anyone any money since they weren't making any themselves, although I tried to explain that they needed to spend money if they wanted to make money, but they weren't buying it," Matt said, shaking his head. "And I could tell that you weren't going to be able to see it, either, so that's why I'm offering you my services for free for a year. I'm that confident that you'll be successful, and that I'll be able to make up my time investment in money, many times over, in a few years."

I stood up and gestured at Matt to do the same. "We need to talk about it privately, just the four of us, plus maybe Gerry and Randy, since they've got a stake in what we're doing, too," I told him. "So let us talk, and we'll call you..."

"No, I'll call you back," he interrupted. "Tomorrow night. It's hard to get in touch with me sometimes, so it'll be easier this way."

"Okay, fine, whatever works for you," I mumbled as I opened the airlock. "We'll talk to you tomorrow night. Call Brian's house, that's the best way to get hold of us, or at least Brian, and he can pass on what we've decided. Let me get his number for you..."

"I've got it," Matt said, surprising me. "It was in the *Advocate* ad you placed when you hired Barry. I wrote it down, since I was planning to call you some time, once you'd gotten going again with a new drummer. I knew Steve wouldn't agree to work with me, based on his reaction when I approached the other band he played in."

"That's a pretty good recommendation on some plane," I noted. "I mean, an enemy of Steve's is a friend of ours, right?"

"Then you've got a lot of friends in town," Matt agreed, reaching into his pocket as he did, pulling out two superbly rolled, deliciously fat joints and passing them to me. "Just a sample of the kind of stuff I can get. Enjoy 'em while you decide. I'll call Brian tomorrow."

I closed the airlock doors behind Matt and re-entered the rehearsal room to find Barry, Brian and George lined up on the sofa, all eyes on me.

"Thanks for all the help and support in that conversation, guys," I said sarcastically. "Really made me feel like you were all really well invested in things here."

"It didn't sound like you needed us, Collie," George said. "We didn't want to screw up your negotiation or anything. You're the one with this kind of experience, not us."

"I don't have experience with managers," I said. "And I don't know the local scene all that well, so I need you to tell me whether this guy's legitimate or not."

"He's been around for a while, and he does seem to work pretty hard, I have seen that," Barry offered. "I mean, already he's helped us twice hauling gear, and that's the most annoying thing we have to do, if you ask me, so I'd be happy to throw him ten bucks a night just to handle load-in and load-out."

"Is he dating your sister or something?" I poked.

"I'm not sure," Barry answered. "I've only seen them together a couple of times, so I don't think it's anything serious if they are. She works at the college bookstore at Siena, so maybe Matt was just trying to get in good with her so he could get some free textbooks for some club owner working on a masters degree or something. Or maybe he's her pimp. I really don't know."

"If he's pimping your sister, then I want to include her in any arrangement we make with him," I noted with a smile, then nodded at Brian and George. "What about you guys?"

"I think what he said about having to spend money to make money makes sense," George said. "I mean, we haven't reinvested anything in the band so far, and we're doing okay, I guess, but we're still playing the same places we played from the beginning—and I'm not sure how to go about moving on to something different or bigger."

"And it would be nice to actually make some money doing this," added the ever practical Brian. "So maybe we just let this guy do his thing for a year, watch him to learn his tricks, then drop him when his time's up and start doing the stuff ourselves. That way, the only money we've spent is the expenses that he says he needs, and we'd spend those anyway if we knew what it was we were supposed to be spending them on."

"Nice, Brian, very nice," I said sarcastically, although I liked his nefarious logic. "What about all this stuff about 'being able to get things' and all that? Are we gonna get in trouble if this guy's a pusher or something?" I held up Matt's gift joints for the others to see. "I mean, personally, I don't mind having someone that can get me stuff like this when I want it, but what about you guys?"

No one answered, but they all had squirrelly little grins on their faces, making it evidently clear that they were as intrigued by the concept of having a band fixer-gopher-getter-mule as I was. "Do we want to give Matt a test, maybe?" I pressed, wanting at least some affirmation from the rest of them, so I wouldn't take the sole blame if it blew up. "Maybe see if he can get Brian a seventeen-year old Filipino virgin or something like that? See if Matt can get him laid, maybe?"

Brian reddened. "I don't need his help doing that. I'm fine on my own."

We all laughed at his hollow machismo, Brian joining us himself eventually. How much action could he be getting out there in his parents' house in Clifton Park, after all? "So we're agreed that we want to give Matt a try, then?" I asked when the frivolity had dissipated. "But we'll let Brian take care of his own poontang needs, yes?"

"Works for me."

"I'm game."

"Fine."

"Alright, then," I concluded. "Brian, you let him know when he calls you tomorrow night, and tell him we want him to be at the next rehearsal to discuss his plan of action."

And Matt did indeed show up at the next rehearsal with a plan. We needed "merch," he explained. Things that people could buy at shows and take home to share with their friends, making us money and providing a public relations function at the same time. Matt arranged for our next concert to taped right off the sound board, for starters, then went off and had 1,000 copies made with a simple, typed sleeve, noting the titles of the 12 songs then in our repertoire, our names and contact information. Brian wondered whether it was legal for us to put "Editions of You" on the tape without advance authorization, but Matt insisted—noting that if Bryan Ferry came and sued us over it, it would be great press, all around. We agreed, and left it on the tape.

We also had some stickers and t-shirts printed over the next month, simple things, marginal quality in both cases—but, like the tapes, cheap to produce and easy to move at shows. And amazingly enough, to us at least, we started turning a profit on this stuff fairly early on. Matt, who worked our sales table at concerts, became our de facto treasurer, not only handling the merchandise but also making sure we got our guarantee and any share of the door proceeds due to us at evening's end. We decided that since we weren't paying Matt, we would divide profits into five equal parts: one for each band member, one for the band itself, to be spent by Matt on promotions, merchandise or equipment upgrades, when necessary.

Matt started printing posters and flyers and handbills for our shows with his new spare cash, and for bigger shows even took out paid advertising in the *Advocate*. That, in turn, got the paper ever more interested in us, earning us several small concert reviews and a nice little mini-review of our live tape in the local scene section. Anna wrote the piece, actually using all of our names this time and calling my vocals "seasoned, authoritative, mature." I figured that just meant that I was old and smoked and drank too much, but I liked the way she put it better.

Matt marked the end of his one-year trial period by getting us booked at the biggest show we'd played to date, a huge college concert series in the prison-like gymnasium at the State University of New York's Albany campus. Any thoughts that Brian (or I) had had about learning his tricks and booting him were gone by this point, since we had no idea what he did, or how he did it, or who he did it with—and we weren't really willing to put the work in to learn. So we actually sat down at our next rehearsal and created a contract of sorts, the first written documentation of the fact that Arctangent existed as a business entity, that it was bigger than just the four of us onstage.

The one-page written agreement described the band members' duties (write, play, sing), Matt's assignments (book, schlep, sell) and laid out a financial formula that split our earnings six ways, one share for each performer, one share for Matt, one share for the band expense fund. The band members' percentages went down from our previous spoken agreement, but Matt assured us that we would be making more money since he'd be able to devote more time to our cause now—so the net we would be pocketing would be larger. We all signed it without a lot of discussion or without seeking any legal or professional review of what we were doing, thereby setting an unfortunate band precedent that would come to haunt us later when the record companies came knocking upon the Treehouse door. Chalk one up to Matt's power of persuasion, even then.

By May of 1990, Arctangent had become a big enough fish in our own small pond to merit a feature interview in the *Advocate*. Matt arranged the logistics and insisted that Anna do the piece on our own turf, actually driving down to Albany to pick her up and bring her and her photographer back to the Treehouse to conduct the interview portion of the article. Anna interrogated us in the rehearsal studio on the first floor, pacing, nibbling her nails, shoving her tape recorder in respondents' faces to make sure she captured our words, intimidating Brian and George to no end, leaving Barry and I to handle most of the talking once they shut down.

We were gracious, attributing the band's genesis to George and Brian's vision, thanking Randy and Gerry (who lurked in the airlock, giggling, while the interview was conducted), lauding praise on the local club owners and audiences who had helped us get where we were, blah blah blah. We never mentioned Matt, though. Even then, I think we knew that he was best kept in the shadows, that he had serious loose cannon potential, that the general public shouldn't connect him with us, in case he blew up while they were watching. I also never mentioned Kris, nor that I had gotten involved in this project as a way to tweak her, nor that I had actually started sending her our press clips, without comment or explanation, just wanting her to see them, hoping that her own clips weren't better than ours.

We also bitched about our jobs—mine with Envirocorps, Brian's at Radio Shack, George's at a leather goods store in the Colonie shopping mall, Barry's at his father's hardware store—noting that it was going to be hard for us to take the proverbial "next step" with the band while tied down with such mundane, soul-crushing regular day-to-day tedium. Anna was intrigued by the Envirocorps thing, no doubt because it seemed so incongruous a job for a rock musician, so we talked about that at length, and about technical writing as compared to (what we called) "real writing." That then brought up Gerry and Randy, and how I moved here from South Carolina, and Junior's Music and the Institute and all the other cover bands I'd played with before, and life in Bridgefield compared to life in Albany and Troy. It was a nice conversation, even if I did all the talking.

And that being the case, I suppose I shouldn't have been too terribly surprised when the final article presented Arctangent as the culmination of the interesting and unusual (when compared to most local musicians) Collie Hay story, with George and Brian and Barry playing distinctly supporting roles. Even the band photo supported this view: the four of us stood in front of the Treehouse, me closest to the camera, Barry and Brian to my right, George a little further back to the left, looking away from the lens, Gerry and Randy barely visible, like ghosts, deep in the background inside the building, looking out as us as we posed. I apologized to everyone when the article ran, but only George seemed to take it hard, and then only for a day or two, so I figured that the others had probably come to the conclusion that I was the voice and face of the band anyway, this just confirming it.

I was terribly surprised, however, at the next phone call I received from Anna, a couple of weeks later.

"Collie? Anna. *Advocate*," she opened, staccato style. "Still want out of that dead end tech writing job you told me about?"

"Uh…yeah, I guess so," I stammered. "Why?"

"Need to expand here," she answered. "If I want to make this paper work for the long run, I've got to stop spending so much time writing and spend more time on business development. So I'm looking to hire a pair of writer-editors right now, maybe more later. I'd like you to do music writing: you know the scene, but you're not so ingrained in it as to have lost your objectivity. And I like the way your mind works. I think we could work together well. I'd need to see some writing samples and everything, but I'm more concerned with office chemistry than I am with technique at this point. I can teach you technique. I can't teach myself to like you if I don't."

"Wow, I'm not sure what to say," I told Anna. "I mean, this is really sudden and everything. Do you need an answer right now? Or do we need to talk about pay and stuff first? I don't know how something like this is supposed to work."

"I can't pay you much, I've got to tell you that right up front," she said. "$25,000 a year, plus benefits, plus expenses. But, more importantly for you, I think, a very flexible schedule that may allow you to do a lot more with Arctangent than you can do right now. I don't really care when you're in the office, as long as you're on time for scheduled meetings and you show up to assignments and you meet deadlines. And that expenses line is a big benefit to you, too, if you spend any money on concerts or records or anything—since you'll get all those things for free now."

I vaguely heard the last part of her pitch, but I was unfortunately focused hard on the first thing she said, that little money thing that appeared to me, on the surface, to be an immediate deal buster. "That would be a big pay cut for me," I told her, crestfallen. "I make, like, $38,000 per year now and I'm not sure that I could even pay my bills if I earned what you're talking about. I mean, I don't even have much of anything left over each month now after I pay my rent and other stuff like that."

"And drink," I thought, but didn't say that to Anna.

"Right, I knew it would be a pay cut for you," Anna pressed on. "But think about whether you want to have a comfortable tech writing job that pays marginally well but keeps you from chasing the big bucks with your band—or whether you want to figure out how to make what I can offer work for you, so you can pursue your music the way you want to."

She paused, probably not for effect, although it worked that way whether she intended it to or not. "You told me in the interview that when you were a kid in the music store, you dreamed of being a writer or a musician," she continued, finally. "Well, here's your chance, pal o' mine, Collie o' Carolina: I'm giving you your dream. You think about that and call me back by close of business tomorrow to set up a meeting to discuss details, okay?"

"Okay, I'll think about it," I said. "And thank you, Anna. Really. This is very, very cool of you, and I appreciate the offer, whether I take it or not."

"Right. 'bye," said Anna, hanging up before I could answer.

I wasn't even quite sure how to assess her offer, since I had no idea where my current, seemingly adequate paycheck went. There was rent, of course, and car insurance and food and concerts and records and clothes. Gas for the car, too, although that wasn't much, since I rode to work with Gerry and Randy all the time.

So that all didn't seem to add up to $38,000 per year, even after taxes had been pulled out of my gross income. I did buy cocaine and pot occasionally, which could get a bit expensive. What else? Drinking? Did I spend that much on drinking? Was that possible? Maybe.

I sat on my bed for about an hour trying to run numbers to see what I could cut to make ends meet within Anna's offer, but I wasn't getting anywhere, so I trotted down the hall to see if Gerry and Randy were around, figuring they could help me work it all out. I knocked on both of their doors and received no answer from either apartment, so I went back to my own apartment, looked out the window and checked to see whether their car was parked in its accustomed alley spot. It was. They were in the building somewhere.

I walked down the stairwell, listening for movement or voices. Nothing on the third floor, but as I approached the landing of the second floor, I heard activity inside the large, seldom-used storage space directly above Arctangent's rehearsal room. I pushed the door open and found Randy and Gerry inside, most of the junk that had occupied the store room pushed back against the far wall, the floor marked with tape as the engineers paced and measured and muttered to each other.

"Hey," I said, after standing in the door for a couple of minutes waiting for Gerry and Randy to notice me.

"Hey, Collie."

"Hi, Collie, what'cha doin'?"

"Watchin' you guys," I answered. "What are you doing?"

"We're thinking about moving down here to the second floor," Gerry answered. "So we're just measuring and marking and doing all that kind of stuff. Planning. Seeing if we can do it."

"Why do you want to move down here?"

"So we can rent our apartments upstairs," said Randy, as if it were the most obvious thing in the world.

I still didn't get it. "Well, why not just put apartments down here, then, instead of giving up the nicer ones on the fourth floor?"

"Because the noise from downstairs would bother the tenants," Gerry said. "We can't ask anyone to pay for this floor if you guys are playing downstairs, right?"

"And we don't want apartments here," Randy added. "We're thinking about just making one really, really big apartment, and sharing it, so we don't have to put in as many kitchen and bathroom fixtures and stuff."

"Won't the noise bother you guys, though?"

"We're usually with you when you're playing," Randy offered. "So it shouldn't be much of a problem for us, I don't think. We're used to it. You're noisy up in your apartment, anyway, with the stereo going and everything."

"Really noisy," said Gerry.

"Do you think he doesn't realize how much noise he makes?" asked Randy, looking at Gerry now, zoning me out.

"Probably not."

"We would know if it was us, right?"

"Yes, I think we would. Wouldn't we?"

"Probably. But maybe he doesn't."

"No, probably not. You're right."

They both looked at me. "We're used to noise," Gerry said, presenting the results of their dialog as if I hadn't heard it the first time. "But you'll have to be quieter if we rent those apartments up there to someone else."

"Maybe we should market them to people who are hard of hearing," suggested Randy. "They wouldn't mind."

"There's not too many of them, though," countered Gerry. "We couldn't count on a steady stream of deaf tenants, I don't think."

"I'll try to be quieter," I said. "Whether you guys move down here or not."

"Okay."

"Okay, thanks, Collie."

"No problem," I said, then watched them taping and hammering and measuring for a few minutes more before saying, "I got a job offer today."

I thought that would get their attention, but it didn't seem to phase them. "Which one?" asked Gerry. "That new publications supervisor position or the one in the tech library that's been empty since Adam retired?"

"Neither one," I answered. "Anna Salocks from the *Advocate* called and asked if I'd come write for the paper."

"That's cool, Collie," Randy said. "But will you have enough time to do that and the band after work?"

"No, no, this would be work," I went on. "I would do this instead of Envirocorps. I'd go work at the *Advocate* during the day, then be able to do more with the band at night than I can right now."

Now they were paying attention. Randy spoke first. "You're leaving Envirocorps?"

"Probably not, no," I said. "Anna can't offer me enough money to make it possible for me to go, I don't think. I was gonna talk to you guys to see what you thought, since you're better with money than I am."

"What's she offering?" asked Gerry.

"$25,000 a year," I told him. "So that's like a $13,000 pay cut a year, although I'll get all of my concert tickets and albums and stuff for free."

"How much do you spend on that now?" Randy asked me, as he set his tools down and walked over to the far end of the room, staring up into middle distance thoughtfully.

"I dunno, I usually buy three or four records a week, I guess," I answered. So that's like 40 dollars a week or so, and maybe one concert a week, five or ten bucks there, say."

"So he spends about 50 dollars a week on music stuff," Randy said to Gerry. "So that's, what…"

"About $2,500 a year, say," Gerry finished.

"So that helps some," said Randy.

"Right, but he's got about $10,500 to go, still."

"Right."

"But his taxes will be lower with lower pay, right?"

"Yes, they would be. Does he get any tax return now?"

Gerry looked over at me. "Do you get a tax return each year?"

"Yeah, about $1,000 last year," I answered. "It's like Christmas in April for me, nice to get a big check like that to go out and spend…"

"He's having too much tax withheld," Gerry said to Randy, ignoring me once he'd gotten the information he needed. "He needs to adjust that, so his paycheck will increase a little bit, so that'll help ends meet throughout the year."

"Particularly if he's just frittering away the return when he gets it," added Randy, as they both looked my way, disapprovingly.

"So if he spread that $1,000 out over the year, then he's only got about $9,500 to make up," Gerry continued. "And I wonder if he's taking into account money that he makes with the band?"

"Are you taking into account money you make with the band?" Randy asked me.

"No, I just usually spend that when I get it," I answered. "I don't really know how much I make, to tell you the truth."

"But he could save it up and use that for bills, too," Randy said to Gerry. "So that could be a couple of thousand dollars there."

"And if the band starts to play more often, then that amount of money could go up," Gerry noted. "And he said he could do more with the band in this new job."

"So let's say about $2,500 there, so now he's got, like, $7,000 or so to make up, right?"

"Right. I wonder what else he spends his money on?"

I answered the question before one of them could ask me directly. "Food, rent, car stuff, entertainment, insurance, general expenses, that kind of stuff. Nothing big."

They heard me, but didn't acknowledge me, since they hadn't spoken to me before I spoke to them. "How much do we charge him for rent?"

"Four fifty each month," Gerry said. "Same thing he's been paying for six years now."

"So that's, what, nine hundred, forty-five hundred plus nine-hundred again…"

"$5,400 a year," answered Gerry, always better at math than his larger counterpart.

"So that would get close to doing it, if we cancelled his rent," noted Randy. "He'd have to find something else to squeeze, but he should be able to make up $1,500 or so a year, right?"

"Right, right," Gerry started pacing now, an idea almost visibly germinating in his head. "And we could cancel his rent by making him move down here with us, then rent out his apartment upstairs for more money!"

"Yeah, we could probably get six hundred for each of them up there now, eighteen hundred a month, instead of four-fifty now."

"And bringing him down here with us would fix the problem of noise that we have with him being up there."

"Right, 'cause we're used to it."

"Yeah, we're used to it."

"And, y'know what? If we all split the food bills down here together, instead of stocking three separate refrigerators and pantries and everything, then I bet he could save enough money to make up the difference right there, without doing anything else," Randy continued, on a roll now. "So that takes care of him, makes it possible for him to take that job if he wants it…"

"And we make more money upstairs, and don't have a noise problem for our new tenants," Gerry concluded. "So that works for everyone."

"Right."

"Right."

I stood speechless, dumbfounded, amazed as I always was when Gerry and Randy retreated into their own private world and emerged with some bizarre, yet wholly workable solution to a seemingly insurmountable problem. "Ummm…you want me to move down here with you guys?" I finally asked, when their logic train seemed to have run all the way around the bend and back.

"Sure," answered Randy.

"And not pay rent?" I went on, wanting to make sure I understood this all.

"Right," said Gerry. "We won't pay rent to live here, so if you're living here with us, why should you pay?"

"Because I don't pay the mortgage on the building?" I suggested.

"Neither do we, anymore," said Randy.

"We paid it off a while ago," added Gerry.

"It wasn't much," continued Randy. "The building was cheap and we put a lot of cash down."

And that seemed to be that. Randy and Gerry went back to work, ignoring me again, Randy noting to Gerry that they'd need to put an extra wall in to make my room, Gerry in turn wondering if I'd need my own office to write in, and if I did whether it would go on this floor or downstairs. I left them there at that point, not wanting to answer a question I hadn't been asked, not wanting to break the spell of good fortune that my trip to the second floor appeared to have produced. I tiptoed back up the fourth floor, called the *Advocate* and told Anna I didn't need to think about it overnight, but would be happy to come in at her convenience to work out the details of my employment.

I went to her office the next day and was quickly introduced to the concept of trade accounts as we went out for a fabulous lunch at one of Albany's better restaurants (one I'd never even contemplated setting foot in before, given its fancy reputation), then settled the bill in exchange for reduced advertising rates in the next month's paper. Anna told me that the *Advocate* had trade accounts with over 100 local businesses—and that as long as my expenses were business related, I was welcome to take advantage of them as an employee of the paper. I was far more impressed by that than I was by the dental and medical coverage, since I didn't go to the dentist or the doctor as a general rule, but I did eat lunch a lot.

After our meal, we went back to the *Advocate* offices and Anna showed me my workspace, far larger, far nicer than my cell at Envirocorps. (Of course, a few years later when I was sharing it with four other people, it didn't seem quite as spacious, but it was still comfortable). We agreed that I would start at the paper in four weeks, giving me time to settle my affairs at my current job and take a little time off between one employer and the other. I drove back to Envirocorps after lunch, went immediately to the Human Resources Department, stood in the door and announced: "I quit…in two weeks."

My announcement generated more paperwork that afternoon and in the days that followed: official letters of resignation, performance reviews, exit interviews, security briefings about proprietary and classified information to which I may have had access, all those sorts of things. Gerry and Randy even arranged a little going away party for me at lunch on my last Friday at Envirocorps, with cake and a card signed by a surprising number of employees, some of whom I wasn't even sure I knew.

Dr. Jaberg even stopped by to wish me well and to announce to all and sundry gathered that I had done the South Carolina Military Institute proud through my hard work and dedication to the Envirocorps cause, while the people I actually worked with regularly rolled their eyes and shook their heads, smiling at me as they did. There were handshakes and a few hugs and kisses when we were done, and Dr. Jaberg said I could take the afternoon off, so I packed up my desk, loaded my possessions into a box and walked out of Envirocorps for the last time.

The security inspector took my building badge as I left, and when I drove back around the loop in front of the lobby, I noticed him reprogramming the access codes, no doubt to preclude me from coming back and shooting the place up. I smiled at the notion, and in pleasant anticipation of working in an office where there were no security codes, no building badges, no guards waiting at the doors to make sure I belonged each day, no ties, no dress pants, no shaving or haircuts if I didn't want them. It all seemed like so little to ask, but it seemed like so much to have, since I'd been deprived of those basic lazy-man's rights for six odd years.

I used my unexpected two weeks of vacation to drive down to Bridgefield, visiting for only the fourth time since moving to New York six years before. The other three trips had been for the Christmas holidays (every other year, whether I needed to or not) though, so this was the first time I'd returned to the sticky, humid miasma into which my hometown turned from June to September each year. It was also the last time I made a summer trip down there accordingly: without my noticing it, my body's cooling and heating mechanisms had adjusted to my more northerly habitation, making me a biological Yankee, if not a spiritual or emotional one.

So I spent as much of my time as possible at the music store (which was centrally air-conditioned) instead of the house (which relied on a couple of inadequate window units for environmental control). Junior and Sister ran the store much as it had always been run, and the parade of teenagers attempting to actualize their rock and roll dreams rolled through much as it had always rolled through, except that now all the boys looked like R.E.M. clones instead of Duran Duran clones—and there were a few more girls coming through the store than there used to be. Twenty percent of the total traffic now, maybe, and many of them looking at guitars and basses instead of flutes and clarinets and tambourines. That was progress.

Greg and Ward, ten years old now, hung around the store too, much as I'd done all those years ago. That made me nostalgic, and sad, since they seemed so fresh and oblivious to the depravities and pain that life was going to throw their way in a few short years. I suppose I'd looked like that to other adults when I was that age too, although in reality I know that I was cynical and bitter all the way back to the earliest days of my childhood. Maybe Greg and Ward were too, who could tell? I tried to picture them standing one on either side of Sister's deathbed as she begged them to turn off her oxygen so she could light one more smoke, then watching her go to meet her great reward, orphans now, even through their father was still alive somewhere. It seemed to me that they would handle it better than I did, maybe splitting the grief between them in ways that Sister and I never could.

I saw a few of my old band mates that summer in Bridgefield, too, stopping by for strings or sticks or picks, telling me that work was good for cover bands with all the new country clubs and resorts opening all up and down the coast on either side of Bridgefield. I probably swelled visibly when I explained to them that I was singing and playing original music now, in New York no less, at which point most of them excused themselves and went on with their shopping, after exchanging the obligatory nice-to-see-you-again-mans. Envy was a beautiful thing, when you were the one inspiring it.

After such visitors left, I generally critiqued their appearances to Sister if she happened to be within earshot. "Damn, Billy's gotten bald," I might say. Or "Jesus Christ, did you see Floyd? He's almost completely gray. Looks like an old man!" Or "Wow, Ray looks like he's been doing some heavy duty coke or crack or something…there was no soul behind those eyes anymore, y'know, like it ran out his nose with his mucous membranes or something?" Sister would generally just nod and walk away, until one day when I must have hit a particularly sensitive nerve or whispered on a particularly bad day.

"Will you fuckin' knock that off, Boy," she snapped. "'cause I don't know how long it's been since you looked in the mirror, but you're lookin' a helluva lot older than you used to too. You think you're exempt from age? I don't: I see gray hairs on the side of your head, blood vessels in your nose that tell me you been drinkin' too much, a beer gut that all but confirms that fact and bad posture and skinny arms that tell me you been spendin' way too much time sittin' at a desk liftin' words instead of doin' real work like real men do. So get over y'self, okay? You ain't no specimen either."

I started to counter-critique Sister, but thought better of it. She'd actually aged moderately well, her figure holding up, her hair still pretty, although she was hard looking about the eyes and she'd started developing those lines on her upper lips that smokers got from inhaling too long and too hard. I'd still have done her, in other words, if she wasn't my sister. So I didn't criticize, since I didn't think I could win by (or was justified in) doing so. And I kept my observations to myself after that, or shared with them Junior, whose hearing was going even then, so he'd generally just nod and smile, regardless of what I had said to him.

So it was just like old times, for a spell, only better—since I knew it was temporary, not a life sentence. And when it started to get old, I drove north again, retracing my original route (except for the stop in Jersey City), arriving back in Troy two days before I was scheduled to start at the *Advocate*. Upon returning to the Treehouse, I was pleased to find that Gerry and Randy had actually made some impressive progress on the second floor while I was gone, framing all of the rooms, drywalling some of them, getting plumbing fixtures in place for the kitchen and bathroom.

They had decided to give me two small rooms at the back of the apartment: one for my bed, one for my office, the two with a door between them and their own separate doors onto the main hallway. Our communal bathroom was going to be across the hall from my suite, with Randy's room next door to mine and Gerry's next to the bathroom, both of them the same size as my two rooms combined. Our hall opened into a large living room area, L-shaped so that we could set up a dining room situation in the shorter end of it, off of which the kitchen could be readily accessed.

Each floor of the Treehouse had a back deck-cum-fire-escape on its backside, overlooking the alley, and Randy and Gerry were in the process of opening a bigger space in the wall of the second floor's main living area so that we could have sliding glass door access to what passed for a back yard in Troy. That way, I could see inside to the living room and wouldn't feel lonely while I was out there smoking, they noted coyly. I got the hint, although I didn't always follow it.

Matt had also been a busy boy while I was away, booking us on three big outdoor summer concerts, one in Albany, one in Saratoga Springs, one in Manchester, Vermont, our first out-of-state performance. That latter show was on a Sunday, and we didn't make it back until nearly two in the morning—but I slept until eleven the next day and rolled into work at the *Advocate* at noon and no one batted an eye. Same thing happened whenever I reviewed a concert: late arrival was expected the next morning, unless it was editorial staff meeting day, for which tardiness was not tolerated.

Those meetings weren't as long in the beginning as they are now, though, since the participants' lists consisted of just Anna and I and Brennan Baxter, the original Artgirl to my Musicboy. We didn't pick up a Newsperson or a Filmperson until the paper's next growth spurt in the mid-'90s, and we didn't get a Bossperson for a few years after that, when I got too undependable even for Anna to deal with and an intermediary (or replacement, if required) was deemed necessary. So we had fewer things to discuss, fewer pages to fill, fewer freelancers to manage. But Anna still went berserk if I was late for a meeting on Thursday mornings, so I generally made every effort possible to be there, you bet.

Brennan was a small, pudgy, freckled brunette tomboy type—and one of the most sexually aggressive human beings I have ever encountered.

We fooled around on and off (timing and location solely at her discretion) for the first two years that I worked at the *Advocate*, until Brennan left on short notice to move to Seattle, lured by the prospect of those rugged, dirty looking flannel grunge boys and girls, all available for her pleasure, all on her demand.

I have to admit that I was somewhat relieved when Brennan left, although I missed her acerbic writing, so I actually used her as a freelance record reviewer for many years after her departure from the office, valuing her up-close-and-personal expertise of the latest sounds coming out of the Pacific Northwest. I knew her well enough to generally be able to tell which artists she'd slept with just by the tone and tenor of her reviews.

I wondered if Kris knew me well enough to read between the lines of the reviews that I sent to her, generally compiling a package every month or so of things I'd written, or things that had been written about me or Arctangent, never adding a single remark, never penning a single explanatory comment, just mailing them, as was, for her perusal.

In the beginning, I assumed that I'd hear from her at some point, but she never responded to the packages, just send me sterile Christmas and Birthday cards in the appropriate season signed by both her and her old man of a husband. I suppose she was doing the same thing to me that I was doing to her, just letting me know she was still alive and still married, rubbing my face in that fact, although I have to think that my gloating was far more powerful and (hopefully) more painful for her than hers was to me. But I couldn't be sure, since she was just as passive-aggressive and stubborn as I was.

Back at the homestead, Gerry and Randy finished off the second floor in October of 1990. I helped them move their stuff (and my stuff) down to our new digs that month, then tried to help them repaint and repair the damage I'd done to my old place, but they weren't much interested in my offer, since they somehow got something therapeutic out of doing things like that themselves, whereas I required direction and maintenance and oversight—and was more trouble than I was worth accordingly. I didn't protest too much at being excluded, though, since it looked like a lot of hard work, and I wasn't really much for work at all, particularly the hard variety.

The apartments went on the market for rent just before Christmas that year, and Brian surprised us all by being the first tenant to sign a lease, finally fleeing his mother and his father in Clifton Park. He made some noise about the rent, since he knew I wasn't paying any, but Gerry and Randy (rightly) noted that I'd paid rent for six years already, and I didn't have my own place anymore, and all of us got free use of the first floor—which logic Brian understood very clearly, since losing the rehearsal room would have sent us back to a garage somewhere, maybe even the one at his parents' house. It was worth $600 a month just to avoid that, even to Brian, who had gone to full time at Radio Shack in order to finance his exciting new life as a free man in Troy, unfettered and alive.

The rest of us benefited from having Brian in the Treehouse on a regular basis, too, since that proximity allowed him to work with Randy and Gerry to turn the rehearsal space into a proper studio during the course of his first year as a tenant. Brian got along quite well with Randy and Gerry, in fact, since he spoke the language of engineers, talking capacitance and impedance and load-bearing members and the like, thereby becoming the first and only person I ever saw fall into Gerry and Randy's mode of talking amongst themselves as if there was no one else around them. I could see from the beginning, however, that George harbored some resentment about that fact, since up until that point he had been Brian's special geek friend. I figured they'd work it out eventually.

The Treehouse got its second new tenant just after the holidays, when yet another uber-nerd named Mike Koonz and his collection of computers moved in. He lived upstairs for nearly three years, too geeky even for Randy and Gerry and Brian to befriend, mocked ruthlessly by Matt and Barry and I for his stereotypical tape-repaired plastic glasses, white socks with black shoes, poor personal hygiene and resultant body odor, and total lack of ability with members of the opposite sex. Shortly after he moved out, we read in the main Albany daily newspaper that he had sold a proprietary computer-mapping-related software application to Microsoft for several million dollars, and was retiring to Orlando, Florida at the age of 29, planning to spend as much time at the EPCOT Center as he could. He who laughs last, and all that, indeed.

We didn't fill the last apartment for another couple of months, although when we did we filled it for the long haul. Lindy Andersson moved into the Treehouse in March 1991 and she's still there today, thank God, since without all those years of close cohabitation with her, I doubt that I could have gotten her (or anyone else) to handle my legal affairs after the accident. Especially since the case remains so cut and dried against me and I'm so incredibly broke at this point that she's not likely to see much of a return—emotional, legal or financial—no matter how the whole thing turns out in the end.

Chapter Fourteen

My first year at the *Advocate* was eye opening on a variety of planes.

I learned the hard way, for instance, that there were certain things you could (or should) say in a review and certain things you couldn't (or shouldn't) say in a review. It took having my nose broken by an irate husband and then hanging myself on a fence while fleeing a death metal band before I really internalized that fact, but once I grasped the concept, I grasped it good. Unfortunately, each of those injuries (both of them impacting my ability to sing as they did) cost Arctangent a few scheduled gigs and the money that went with them, but at least Matt was able to get me some absolutely fabulous pain-killers to numb the pain, the sting and the embarrassment that I felt.

And Matt wasn't the only one procuring mind-altering substances for me all of a sudden. As a music critic and (maybe more importantly) as the editor who assigned reviews and decided which shows would be previewed and which ones wouldn't, any number of musicians, club owners, promoters, managers and agents decided that I was worthy of ass-kissing and happy-making. And they all quickly realized that the quickest way to my heart was through my addictions—to alcohol, to other illicit drugs, to sex, to food, to whatever hedonistic, body-pleasing buttons they could, and did, push when dealing with me. I liked it that way, I did, I have to admit it.

It also didn't hurt Arctangent any to have me making assignments to freelancers and photographers. I couldn't actually assign anyone to cover us directly, mind you, but as we played opening sets for a growing number of national or international touring bands, I had growing number of opportunities to make assignments for reviews of those headliners—and the writers, wanting to stay on my good side, weren't about to miss the opportunity to say nice things about the opening acts in such circumstances, now were they?

Sometimes I ran their words (always, in the spirit of full-disclosure, adding "*Advocate* staffer" in front on my own name any time it was mentioned), sometimes I didn't, but it certainly didn't hurt my ego either way to have a regular stream of praise for my night job rolling across the desk at my day job, month after month after month.

I started taking the raw articles back to the Treehouse to share with the other guys, so they could see what people were saying if I chose not to use it in the paper. Brian generally didn't react as much to what was being said as he did to how poorly it was being presented in its pre-edited state, noting that he could do better if given the chance.

So I gave him that chance, taking him on as a freelancer late in the summer of 1991, just around the time that he and Gerry and Randy had finished installing the basic sound components for what was soon to be dubbed Treehouse Studios, using money from the band's investment fund, supplies cadged from Brian's Radio Shack job and my connections in the music community—since I generally knew when other studios or bands were going under and was able to score equipment at fire sale prices accordingly.

I have to admit that Brian surprised me with his effectiveness as a freelancer, since he communicated so poorly in speaking situations, but was tight, punchy and insightful in print. He was also willing to work harder than most of my other freelancers, and having him there in the Treehouse meant that if I screwed up and missed making an assignment, I could generally get him to go do it on close to zero advance notice, since Brian liked making money. Plus I knew his day job and band schedules, so it made it easy for me to plan concerts for him weeks, sometimes months, in advance—and I wouldn't have to remind him when the day actually arrived, since he was more organized than I was in keeping calendars and knowing where he was supposed to be at any given moment.

Matt also changed the way he dealt with me, since now I was not only one of his charges, but was also one of the key portals for pursuing his own objectives, personal and otherwise. He'd always been generous in "getting stuff" for the band, but he also started making regular appearances at the *Advocate* offices, making special drop-offs for me and me alone, usually pot, sometimes cocaine (I was afraid of needles, so it never got any harder than that) reminding me that there was always more where that came from. And he wasn't exaggerating, believe me, I tested him.

By the fall of 1991, Matt decreed that we needed something more formal looking for our merch table than our now long-in-the-tooth live tape. He wanted a single, on vinyl, something that we could sell and ship off to radio stations, something that looked professional, thereby making his schmooze and squeeze jobs easier. So Brian, Barry, George and I went into and formally christened Treehouse Studios as a working facility that October, recording a new and improved studio version of "Baal," still our most popular concert staple, as the A-side of our first single.

Since we wanted to give folks who already had our live tape a reason to buy this single as well, we filled the B-side with "Monster Badge," an early Brian and George composition that had fallen out of the live setlist during the Steve era, in large part because he wouldn't play it the way that Brian and George wanted it played. Barry had no problem delivering the Burundi beats that they desired, however, and I also thought it politically prudent to put something with a strong George presence on the single—since he had grown increasingly distant from the rest of the band as Brian had established new, George-free relationships, first with Gerry and Randy at the Treehouse, then with me at the *Advocate*.

Matt made the arrangements to have the single mastered and pressed in New York City the next month. I actually saw "Baal" b/w "Monster Badge" for the first time at the office, since Matt opted to mail me a copy as an editor before he showed me one as a band member. I'll give him credit for dramatic flair: it literally made me feel light-headed to be going through a pile of mail, unsuspecting, coming across my own band's record, carrying just as much weight and import and clout as any of the others I had received that day.

I put "Baal" on the turntable I kept by my desk for sampling such offerings—and it sounded just as good, just as professional, just as real as the things I was receiving from real record companies, from real bands. It was a sublime moment: Anna had promised to deliver me my childhood dream of being a writer and musician, and there I sat, both at the same time, just fifteen years later and 150 miles further north than I had expected.

We had a listening party at the Treehouse on our next rehearsal night, playing the single over and over again, getting drunker and drunker and sillier and sillier as the night went on, fortunately remembering to cover up most of the expensive electronic equipment before things got too sloppy, blessedly having just finished installing the inside bathroom, so we didn't have go out on the loading dock and freeze each time nature beckoned. Randy and Gerry and Matt were there that night, of course, as they always were, and Lindy and Mike Koonz actually joined us at some point, too, along with a couple of *Advocate* advertising staffers I'd invited over (both of them female), Barry's fiancée Janice and George's new-ish girlfriend Ingrid.

I was actually quite glad to see Ingrid there that night, glad to see George establishing a relationship with someone outside the band to balance any discomfort he was feeling with Brian, particularly knowing that if Ingrid was taking care of him physically, then he'd quickly realize just how relatively unimportant his purely cerebral relationship with Brian had been.

I was knocking these thoughts around in my head at some point during the evening—but alcohol and ecstasy had evidently linked my tongue on a hardwire loop with my brain, so I was surprised to suddenly realize that Lindy was sitting on the couch with me, answering my observations, presumably not from reading my mind.

"I don't think it works that way, Collie," she was saying. "I mean, it's good that he's getting laid and everything, yeah, but if he's feeling like a spare tire in the band these days, or like he's not part of the inner circle, he's gonna leave anyway. Maybe just so he can have more spare time to fuck Ingrid, see?"

I was confused and disoriented by this point, unsure of what I'd said, unsure of what Lindy was saying. "So, do you think George was fucking Brian before? Is that what you mean?"

"No, no, I don't think they were doing that," she answered. "I think they were just really good friends, and that during their formative years, they didn't really have any other friends. And being ostracized that way, I'm sure that their friendship was really, really important to them, probably more so for George even than Brian, since Brian's so acutely self-winding that he probably needs other people less than George does. So I'm sure that George doesn't even know exactly what he misses, just that something's gone."

"Uh huh," I nodded, trying to see down Lindy's blouse as she sat back on the sofa and watched the room around her.

She didn't notice. "In some ways, it's probably the same thing that happened with Gerry and Randy when they were young," she continued. "I mean, can you imagine how Gerry would feel if Randy suddenly decided that he had some new friends and new work that were more important than Gerry? I think that may be what George is feeling." She looked back at me as my eyes snapped up to meet hers. "And my guess, with what little you've told me, is that George blames you for all of it, since it was still his band and Brian was still his best friend until you came along. I can see that in Ingrid's body language towards you…she's clearly not predisposed to like you."

I wanted her to look away again so I could stare at her chest some more, but she seemed to be waiting for an answer, most likely one beyond my muddled brain's capability at the moment. I kept coming back to the lowest common denominator accordingly. "So you think Gerry and Randy are queer, then?"

"If anyone would know that, it's you," she said. "You're the one who lives with them in the house of lost boys."

Good point. "I don't think they're a couple, no," I slurred, looking for them with the drug-addled thought that I might want to make sure they weren't engaged in some unexpected carnal act in the middle of the studio before I went on. "They both love women, I know that, but they're both the kind of guys that women love back, too much." That wasn't making sense. "They're the kind of guys that women like to have as friends: they're sweet, they're nice, they're helpful, but in general girls don't get all riled up over the thought of getting nasty with Randy or bumping uglies with Gerry. In fact, I don't think that thought even enters the heads of most women Randy and Gerry meet, since most women think of them as children, or puppy dogs, or something like that…"

Lindy laughed, and my vision spun, and the room wobbled, so I unexpectedly (to me and Lindy both, no doubt) leaned over on the sofa and put my head in her lap. She patted me on the back of my head, and I smelled the scent of incense that clung to her clothes, maybe even to her skin, and smiled, and shifted my weight to get more comfortable, even as I heard Lindy saying, from far away, as in a dream, "Don't get any ideas down there, Mister Hay, since I think of you as a puppy dog, too, albeit a dangerous one that hasn't had its shots…"

And the party swirled on as I swirled out on the sofa, waking as I so often did the next morning, confused about where I was and how I got there, laying still, trying to figure out if any parts of my body hurt, reviewing the tapes in my head, trying to ascertain which ones were dream rolls and which ones had captured reality. Lindy's smell was all that lingered, that—and something about how George hated me. Or was it Ingrid? Or both of them? Didn't matter, I needed to get to work.

And fortunately it wasn't an editorial staff meeting day, so I was able to wobble in around lunch time, drawing knowing looks and wry grins from Deanna and Patricia in advertising as I stumbled by their cubicles. I'd asked them over last night hoping to get lucky with one or the other. Or maybe even both. I wondered if anyone had done so in my stead. Brian maybe? Gerry and Randy? Was there a big nasty foursome up on the second floor last night while I slumbered in the studio? I'd never know, although I doubted it, since neither Deanna nor Patricia seemed like the puppy petting types.

I still had a copy of "Baal" on my desk and, since I didn't feel particularly productive quite yet, I spent about a half an hour wrapping it back up in heavy cardboard, addressing it to Kris and shipping it off to Jersey City. I'd been a bit remiss in my passive-aggressive mailings of late, letting a couple of months at a time pass before sending Kris a care package, sometimes so involved in that day-to-day minutia of being a writer and a musician that I forgot that I was doing at least the latter of those two jobs in an effort to spite her. It had been almost four and a half years since she'd gotten married, after all, so the strength and power of my venom had abated quite a bit, although I still liked to fang her every now and again, just on principle.

Interestingly, this one shipment finally brought a response of sorts: I received my annual Christmas Card from Jersey City a couple of weeks later, and there was actually a message inscribed inside it. "Dear Collie," it read. "That song is truly evil." I knew which one she was talking about. "But I have to admit…I loved it." Huh! Wasn't expecting that.

"Merry Christmas and Happy New Year." Back to platitudes, right, keep it comfortable. "Best, Kris."

Not "Kris and Mark," mind you. Just "Kris." I wasn't sure what to read into that. Was "Baal" so evil that Mark refused to let her put his name to the card? Had he forbidden her to write to me, ever again, leading her to have to sneak a note off from outside her house somewhere? Was it because she was writing a personal opinion, not an official family opinion? Was it because Mark had been hit by a bus the month before, leaving Kris a lonely, but wealthy, New Jersey widow? Or was it just because Kris was a lot more grown-up than I was, and was finally willing to take the lead in establishing some more normalized relationships between us?

I contemplated contacting her, sending her something personal in return, just to get a better understanding of where she stood, what she was up to, but I was diverted to more pressing matters a couple of days later when George showed up at rehearsal and announced, as Lindy had predicted, I think, that he was leaving the band. He wanted to spend more time with Ingrid, he said, and she really didn't like the whole Treehouse environment where he had to spend so much of his time as a band member. He was thinking about going to college, too, since he wasn't going to be able to be a keyboard player in a band for the rest of his life, or so he figured.

We argued and wheedled and cajoled a bit, and the news expectedly hit Brian a bit harder than it did Barry and I, but it was pretty clear that George's mind was made up—and that it was too late for Brian to atone for his cardinal sin of growing up and making new friends. So once we had all accepted the fact that George was indeed going to be departing, we got right straight back to business and had Matt write up an amended band contract that terminated George's share in our partnership and eliminated any claim that he might have on our future earnings.

He balked at the latter part, and wrote on the bottom of the page in a surprisingly girlish looking script: "If you make any money with any songs that I wrote, then I get a fair share as a songwriter." We looked at each other and shrugged, then started to sign—until Barry reminded us that "Monster Badge," the flip-side to "Baal," bore George's songwriting credit, which could cause a problem if we were planning to keep selling and marketing it.

George shot Barry a sour glance, no doubt feeling like he was about to get away with something up until that point, although there may have been more to the look than that: the two of them hadn't been getting along particularly well for a while now, probably since Barry had sarcastically referred to George's beloved as "Ingrid Ono" one night when she was sulking over some perceived slight or another in the ready room at the Heartland Club.

Matt asked George how much he thought, realistically, that his share from that single might be, since he, Matt, didn't really see any of us making much money on the thing. George said he figured he could have counted on a couple of hundred bucks at least, at which point Matt took the strongbox that held the band's expense cash, handed George two crumpled hundred dollar bills and wrote in "George is square with us for any share of money made on 'Monster Badge'" at the bottom of the contract amendment.

And then we all put our signatures at the bottom of the page, writing George out of the band, assuming that it was all fair, square and legal, never once thinking to take an extra five minutes to call Lindy and get her legal opinion, one that I know now she would have offered readily, gladly and freely. None of us really thought that way, though. Or maybe Matt did, but I'm sure he was the only one, and it was in his best interests to keep us dependent on his business advice. Which we were willing to do, since Matt had done fine by us at this point, personal annoyances aside, and we'd learned that when we questioned his recommendations we ended up spending a lot of time arguing and posturing—then doing what he had wanted to do in the first place anyway.

Matt had generally stayed out of the musical side of the business, though, until George left and Brian, Barry and I started contemplating replacements.

"You don't need anyone else," Matt interjected over the studio intercom from the control booth (shades of the taped doorbell that Brian would shortly install) as we argued the pros and cons of putting out an advertisement or simply making someone an offer. "You're not going to be able to play the songs George wrote anymore any way, and that's the most keyboard-heavy stuff in your current set list. So look at this as an opportunity to increase your share in the profit."

"And yours," I shouted back at Matt. "Don't go getting all altruistic on us. You make out like a bandit too if we don't replace George."

He had entered the studio space by this time so we didn't have to yell through the soundproofing. "Maybe," he agreed. "But that's really not why I'm saying this. I think you guys can get tighter as a three piece, really let Brian emerge as a no-shit guitar god instead of burying his work under a bunch of keyboard noise. And besides, Barry can play keyboards…"

"Not while I'm playing drums," Barry interrupted.

"No kidding," Matt continued. "But you can program sequencers or we can use tapes or whatever, so you don't actually have to have someone up on stage doing it for you."

"Like Rush," Brian noted. "They're a three-piece, but they use tapes when you see them live."

I didn't like the idea of tapes and told the others that, although I was more amenable to having Barry armed with a synthesizer by his drum kit, triggering appropriate sequences or rhythms to add some depth to our live sound. We knocked the idea around for another hour or so, and we never really reached a resolution on the subject (or not for a long time afterwards at least), but we did move forward as a three piece, in much the same way that we'd moved forward with me being the vocalist three years earlier. Necessity and laziness are indeed the parents of invention.

But that point aside, George's timing couldn't have been any worse. We'd sent "Baal" to just about every radio station in the Northeast and Matt had been aggressively courting clubs in New York City, Montreal, Boston and Syracuse to broaden our geographic reach and put us in markets where we'd be more likely to make an impression on the secret high priests of the music industry. One of the Albany commercial rock stations picked the song up for airplay almost immediately, not terribly surprising given our successful track record to date in the market and my ability to spin us as we needed to be spun in the local press.

More surprisingly, however, was the fact that several college stations and even one commercial (although low-rated) station in the New York metropolitan area picked up "Baal" during the early months of 1992, finally generating a faint groundswell of interest among club owners and promoters there. We just had to figure out what we were going to play when we got there, since Matt said we had to drop the George co-penned "Microscope Show," "Shotgun", "Tapeworm," "Swirling Pool of Dysfunction" and "Monster Badge" (which we'd just started playing again right as we put the single out) from our set list, lest George show up and want a share of the door for the evening.

I didn't think George would do that, mind you, but I was willing to go along with Matt since some of the first replacement songs we worked up as a trio were older numbers that I'd written before Arctangent, but that hadn't stuck for one reason or another the first time we'd tried them out. I was particularly fond of "Love and Hate and Us" (guess who I wrote it about?), "Lamprey," "My Garish Life," "Suffer Me" and a cheery little number called "Makeup" that was probably also about Kris, and maybe even a little bit about me, although a bit more obliquely and symbolically so than the strident, obvious "Love and Hate and Us." The lyrics, as it turned out, were more prophetic than I'd ever imagined:

She hides her face behind a makeup veil
She paints her face, she paints it on a veil

Before a mirror on a rusty nail

She passes him and all he sees are eyes
She sits and eats and all he sees are eyes
Communicates with gestures she with sighs

She strips away the veil at night alone
She strips away the veil and stands alone
Reaches down to dial the telephone

Awake in bed, she's lying on her back
Awake in bed, unmoving on her back
With the kitchen door ajar a crack

He comes and feels the scars around her eyes
He comes and feels the scars around her eyes
Touches them and cries and cries and cries

Brian brought a couple of new songs ("There But For" and "Kill Thing") to the table as well, and we still had our stalwarts, "Baal" and "Wisconsin" and "Editions of You," none of which George had written, although we had to rearrange them heavily to make them work without his keyboards. (And by the time we were done with that, I'm not even sure that anyone could have traced "Baal"'s origins back to "Jerusalem" any more, so fundamentally had we stripped down and the rebuilt the original work). That gave us ten songs, and we built in a couple of time-killing jam sections for Brian to start maximizing his improvisational guitar skills, Matt assuring us that that would bring all sorts of new, virtuoso-loving fans to our concerts, once word hit the street as to just how good a player Brian actually was.

We tested the new set and the new line-up at a couple of low profile shows in Albany before giving Matt the green light to continue trying to get us shows in markets outside of our home town. He vanished for almost a week at that point, then reappeared in the studio one night with a schedule far more ambitious and aggressive than anything we'd dared to date: fourteen days starting in mid-April and featuring shows at small or mid-sized clubs in Springfield, Pittsfield, Northampton, Poughkeepsie, Storrs, Hartford, Newport, Providence, Islip, Hempstead, Trenton and culminating (best of all) with an opening set for a four-band bill at the legendary CBGB's in New York City.

We'd never traveled for more than two days at a time prior to this trip and had never played more than three shows in a single week—so Matt's proposed agenda constituted a fundamental shift in mindset as far as our concept of touring was concerned. We planned to rent a van, figuring we'd either sleep in it with our gear or rely on the kindness of strangers we met at shows, leaving Matt in the van to guard the gear instead. Matt agreed, in concept, and he also planned on being the road show's driver, letting us rest while we traveled, then sleeping while we set up our gear and otherwise wasted time before sound checks or gigs themselves, then working late to ensure we got paid and that all the equipment we took into the club made it back out of the club after the show was done.

The tour schedule also built in an open evening when we could stop back by the Treehouse after conquering New England and before riding triumphantly for New York City, New Jersey and Long Island, giving us a chance to sleep in our beds (or in the studio, in Matt's case) and catch up on our jobs while we were home. I had actually been worried about my job when I went in to tell Anna that I was going to need to be gone for two weeks while Arctangent toured, but she just nodded, said "About time, wondered when you guys were gonna finally get out on the road," and told me to make sure that I had the freelancers all scheduled and lined up to submit their work to Brennan before I left, and to check in every couple of days just to make sure the place hadn't burned down or anything. I guess she'd meant it when she said that my job at the *Advocate* was going to make it easier for me to put more of myself into Arctangent. I hadn't really been willing to test her up until that point.

I have to admit, as stupid as it seems to me now, that we were all positively giddy when the day arrived for us to pack up our equipment and hit the road, each of us secretly thrilled to be going through such a basic rock and roll rite of passage, each of us too cool to let the others know how just excited we were. Our mood wasn't dampened in the least, of course, when we piled into the back of the van and Matt pointed out the cooler of goodies he'd brought for us: a hefty bag of very fine hash, several bottles of good vodka, a couple of choice porno magazines (hardcore, underground stuff, of course, nothing you get over the counter at your corner newspaper shop, unless you lived on Times Square) and salty snacks out the wazoo. Matt noted us that beer was part of our concert rider, so we didn't need to take it with us. We thought that was swell.

Gerry and Randy came out to the back alley to help us load the van and stood there, waving, like our adoring parents or something, as we rode up to River Street, turned right and set out for our first great adventure as a touring band, Brian eyeing the porno mags out of the corner of his eye (pretending he wasn't all the while), Barry kneeling next to one of his drum cases, looking for a flat space to cut the hash, me sitting in the shotgun seat with a stupid grin on my face while Matt shouted "woo!" and "yeah, baby!" and "rock and roll!" every fifteen seconds or so.

Our exuberance lasted for, oh, I'd say about an hour or so. Then we got bored, so Barry and I got high in the back while Brian sat up front and read the van's technical manual and Matt fiddled with the radio and the air conditioner, trying to get the music and temperature just right, never succeeding. We arrived in Springfield an hour after that, hauled our gear in, waited, waited some more, drank our beer, got high in the van some more, lurked around the club trying to score, something, anything, finally got on stage, played our set for about 30 people who could have given a shit about our presence there, hauled our gear off the stage, loaded it up in the van, cruised the club, smoked some hash, got paid, drank some beer, never scored, got depressed, went back to the van, looked at the porno mags, felt weird with other guys around as we did, set them aside, went to sleep, woke up the next morning with our backs and necks in knots, pissed in the alleyway where we parked, ate breakfast at Denny's, drove on to Providence.

So being on the road was pretty much like being at home, in other words, except that we slept a lot closer to each other and didn't have to go to work during the day. Boring, sure, but it developed its own rhythms and had a certain air of mindless selfishness about it that was appealing on some plane. Until we all got sick after a week, that was, no doubt from breathing all over each other all night, sharing germs and bacteria and viruses and god knows what else that we'd inhaled in the dank, stanky clubs in which Matt had booked us or had shared while passing the dutchie on the left hand side, all around the van and back.

Fortunately, our home layover night arrived just at the point when our flu symptoms had made it impossible for us to spend anymore time together without someone killing someone else. (I was betting on Matt as the first victim, wanting to snap his neck after a couple of days every time he punched a radio station button mid-song, cursing the artist while he did it). It's important to note, though, that we had only been together for a week at this point, making my mind spin at the thought of bands that went out on the road for weeks, months, forever, together. I was pretty sure they weren't doing it in rental vans as small as ours. At least I hoped they weren't.

But the day off helped (I spent most of it locked in my room, sleeping, then showered for almost 45 minutes, using the Treehouse's entire hot water supply, much to Brian's chagrin) and our throats and nerves weren't quite as raw and irritated as they had been when we arrived home the day before. Gerry and Randy came out and went through the waving ritual again as we drove out of the alley, this time turning left on River Street and heading southward, for Poughkeepsie, for Long Island, for Trenton and—finally—for New York City, the place I'd wanted it all to start in the first place, all those years ago and all those miles away in Bridgefield.

So I was impressed with myself, in spite of myself, as Matt drove our van into Manhattan, down to the Lower East Side, finally stopping outside of CBGBs, the club where American punk began, a modern rock shrine of cosmic proportions as sure as eggs was eggs. It was a lot smaller than I'd expected it to be ("Lots of things are like that in a woman's life," Lindy had said with a shrug when I'd said that to her afterwards, although it took another couple of days for the joke to register), and dirtier, too, nastier in so many ways even than most of the nasty clubs we'd been playing for the prior two weeks.

I felt like a wuss smoking hash in the club's bathroom while the bouncer shot up, for instance, and was intimidated by the wandering, shouting street people who drifted along in front of the club, making our few Troy-based homeless folk look positively civilized and demure by contrast. Someone or something took a shit right next to our van, too, when we weren't looking. We were aghast, but the locals didn't seem to notice it, so we pretended that it wasn't there right along with them. When in Rome, right?

Right. And I was in my Roman glory that night, getting good and tightly wound before our set, working myself into an adrenaline frenzy at the thought of playing on that stage, in that city—then taking the stage and playing what I think was a brilliant, monumental set, the three of us releasing all our pent-up van loathing and spraying it out over the crowd before us, a crowd whose presence I had to infer from their breathing (early) and applause (later, once they'd warmed to us), since I couldn't see a damn thing with the low overhead stage lights blasting right in my eyes.

Which was probably a good thing, since after we wrapped up our set with a titanic "Baal" and "Editions of You" medley, the house lights went up and the stage lights went down, I puttered with my pedals, slapped Brian on the back (softly, so as not to hurt him), high-fived Barry, turned back to the front of the stage to pick up my bass—and found Kris standing there waiting for me.

"Holy shit!" I shouted, before I could catch myself.

"And 'hey' to you, too," Kris said, looking much as she'd ever looked as she said it, her hair a bit shorter, maybe an extra line or wrinkle at the corner of each eye, although I couldn't have been sure of that in the dim, smoky light of the room. I hoped those same visual impediments were as flattering to me as they were to her, although I think it would have required a complete absence of light to hide my prematurely graying hair, my love handles, my sunken, usually bloodshot eyes.

"Well, no, hey, hi, all that," I stammered. "You surprised me. I mean, really, really surprised me. I thought I was having some kind of hallucination or flashback or something." I reached out and poked her arm. "You are real, right? I'm not going to have to have Matt tie me up and lock me in the back of the van or anything, am I?"

"I'm real, it's me," Kris said. "Real as you, anyway, although none of this feels real now, does it?"

"No, it doesn't," I agreed. "This feels very, very weird."

"Yes, it is weird."

"Very weird."

"Very weird."

So we agreed on that. "What are you doing here?" I asked, figuring it was time to figure out how the weirdness had come to pass.

"I was in the City today shopping and picked up a *Village Voice* while I was eating lunch," she answered. "And I was just flipping through it when the word 'Arctangent' caught my eye, so I turned back to that page, and it was an announcement of this show here tonight. And I figured that there couldn't be too many bands called Arctangent in the world, so took a chance that this one was yours and figured I'd hang out in the City and check you guys out."

"So here you are."

"So here I am."

Brian and Barry were drifting around behind me, making throat-clearing noises that meant I needed to finish visiting and help them get our equipment off the stage so the next band on the bill could load up. I ignored them, or at least ignored what they wanted me to do, choosing to point them out to Kris instead.

"That's Brian," I said, pointing. "And Barry. And Matt, our manager, he's around here someplace too, selling t-shirts or hassling the door man or something."

"I figured out who those two were," Kris said. "Since I feel like I know them already from all the articles you sent me."

Busted. "Well, you know, I just wanted you to know what I was up to and everything, that was all," I explained, lamely.

"Right," she retorted, and the tone of that one word said all that needed to be said about that. "I thought there were four of you guys, though? What happened to the keyboard playing kid?"

"He quit a little while ago," I told her. "We may replace him at some point, but for right now we're just gonna work it as a three-piece, make a little bit more money that way, tighten things up some, that kind of stuff."

"Collie, you gotta get your bass cabinet off the stage," Barry shouted from behind me. "I know you don't want Brian doing it."

I didn't want Brian doing it, that was true. "Um, I gotta go help these guys," I said to Kris. "Can you stay? Can we talk some more? I really would like that…" I meant it, too, now that the shock had worn off.

"Sure, I can stay for a little while, I guess," Kris said. "I'll go see about buying a t-shirt or something. You come find me when you're done."

"Okay, I will, see you then."

"Okay."

"Okay," I echoed, inhaling and exhaling deeply, realizing that I was sweating, not the good, rich sweat that comes from playing an energetic concert, but a cold, clammy sweat, nerves, butterflies, puberty stuff, not pleasant at all. I helped Barry pull my cabinet off the stage and started to wrestle it out of the club, past glaring patrons who resented having to move for us as we passed. Matt and Brian were already at the van when we made it out, Matt helping me lift the stack of speakers into the back, Brian looking on, knowing we wouldn't let him help if he made any effort to do so, maybe resenting that fact, maybe relieved by it.

"Alright, get that pig in there and let's get the fuck outta here," said Barry, climbing into the front passenger seat of the van. "Shotgun," he shouted, formally laying claim to the seat he was already occupying, lest anyone challenge him for it.

"Yeah, really, man, it's time to go home," Brian agreed, pulling himself up into the back of the van as Matt clambered into the driver's seat and cranked the engine.

"Wait, we're leaving already?" I asked. "Have we gotten paid? Don't we want Matt to sell t-shirts and tapes and stuff?"

"I been outta t-shirts for two days," Matt said. "And I got your guarantee already. We could stick around and see if there's anything coming to us from the door, but the cover's only three dollars, so by the time we divvy it up, it won't be worth our while to wait for it. So I'm ready to head home, myself, and Barry and Brian agreed when I asked them if they wanted to take off."

"We didn't want to interrupt you 'cause you were talkin' to some girl," Brian added.

"Well, I want to talk to her some more," I said, an edge of panic and whining creeping into my voice. "She's a really, really old friend, someone I haven't seen in years. I don't just want to drive away. I want to talk to her some more."

"You can get laid at home, Collie," Matt said, boiling everything down to lowest common denominator as he was apt to do. "Probably easier and safer than here, in fact, since you don't know if this 'old friend' has gone off and gotten married or gotten the crabs or just gotten out of the home for criminally insane band stalkers or whatever. So just get in the van and let's go home."

"I don't want to go home," I said, stubbornly.

"All in favor of going home say 'aye,'" blurted Barry from the front of the van. "Aye!"

"Aye," said Brian.

"Aye," agreed Matt.

"Three to one, we go home," Barry concluded. "Get in the van, Collie."

I'd reached a conclusion. Probably a bad one, but I was sticking with it. "I ain't going home," I said, emphatically. "Matt, give me my share for tonight. I'm gonna stay here and then take the train back tomorrow morning."

"You're supposed to work tomorrow, Collie," Brian reminded me. "I think you should come home."

"It's the *Advocate*," I said, accurately. "I can roll in at noon and no one's gonna say a word to me. And we're done with the tour, so it ain't like I'm gonna be letting you guys down or not gonna make a gig or something. You're sick of me. I'm sick of all of you. I wouldn't be driving tonight anyway, so what difference does it make whether I'm in the van or not?"

I heard Matt counting out bills and change in the front of the van, so I knew he bought my logic. "Here," he said, handing me a wad of money. "Seventy-two dollars, that's two-fifty guarantee, plus…"

"I trust you," I said, although I didn't. "You don't have to spell it out for me."

"Fine."

"Alright, then," I continued, clapping my hands for emphasis. "I'll call Brian when I get home tomorrow to make sure y'all made it and so you know I'm safe and sound in Troy. That alright, Brian?"

Brian wasn't answering.

"Brian?"

"Yeah, that's alright, I guess," he said, finally.

"You don't sound convinced," I noted. "Is there a problem with that?"

"No, no problem," he said. "I just don't want this woman pulling you out of the band, the way that Ingrid pulled George out of the band."

"Yeah, that's true, man," Matt added. "Don't let this bitch pull an Ingrid on us, okay?"

Barry giggled from the front seat. "Ingrid Ono," he said. "Or Fuckin' Linda McIngrid, maybe." He turned to look at me, smiling. "Is this chick a photographer or some weirdo performance artist, Collie?"

"Neither," I answered, glad and grateful to Barry for trying to make the situation less heavy than it was getting. "She's a teacher. And a musician. And she's cool, really, used to live in South Carolina with me, used to go see me play all the time down there, never had any problem with me being in a band. She's cool."

Nobody had anything to say after that, so I assumed we were done. "Alright, I'll call," I told them. "See you guys tomorrow, or at least Brian tomorrow." And before Brian could sulk or fire off another snarky comment, I slammed the back doors of the van, slapped the side panel as if it were a horse and watched our first trusty road steed rumble off up the Bowery as I stuffed seventy-two dollars into my pocket and wondered if it was actually enough to get me home, much less a place to sleep for the night. Somehow the Lower East Side didn't seem like the best place to hunker down for alleyway nap or a stoop sleep, somehow.

I shoved my way back into the club and looked for Kris, finally finding her standing by the bar, back to the stage, which was now occupied by the next band on the bill, playing their hearts out and thereby making it impossible to talk without screaming. I gestured at the door and raised my eyebrows inquiringly, and Kris nodded, so we worked our way back out onto the street, the noise diminishing slightly as we did, although the night-time reek of the city streets was as distracting in its own way as way the concert inside.

"Kinda hard to talk in there," I noted, stating the obvious. "You wanna take a walk or something?"

"This isn't really the best neighborhood for walking, Collie," she said. "Don't you guys have a car or something?"

"Uh, yeah, we have a van, but it's gone now," I said, not sure how much I wanted to tell her just yet. Oh well, what the hell. "I, uh, I sent them home. They went home without me. I'm here for the night."

"Was that smart?" Kris asked, looking up and down the block as if to hail a cab, should one dare to cross by the corner of Bleecker and Bowery where we stood. "I mean, do you have a place to stay here?"

"No, no I don't," I admitted. "But I got seventy-two dollars, so I figured at worst I could just walk around all night and then take the train home in the morning. Sleep my way home that way."

"Sounds fun," she said, not sounding like she meant it.

"It won't be the first time I've traveled that way or walked all night since I didn't have a place to stay," I said. "But I just, y'know, you came out to see us and everything and I just wanted to talk to you, right? I didn't want to just jump in the van and go home and leave you standing in CBGBs, since I find it hard to believe it's the type of place where you hang out regularly, unless something's changed a lot since the last time I saw you."

"Mmmm, you're right about that, this isn't my normal hang-out," she noted. "I've never been here, in fact. I just came to see your band."

"Did you like us?"

"You were good," she said, not really answering my question. "Not necessarily my cup of tea, but I can appreciate music when it's done well, and what you guys did tonight was good. Real good. And people seemed to get into it. Plus I understand the clippings better now, having seen you myself."

Kris finally spotted a cab and walked out into the street, waving her arms, in an attempt to catch the driver's attention. She got it, the Yellow Cab executing a violent U-turn in the middle of the road then roaring back up the block, slamming on brakes and coming to a stop less than a yard from where Kris stood. He wasn't gonna let anyone get that fare before he got there, no sir. Kris opened the door to the cab and waved me over.

"C'mon, get in," she said. "I can at least take you further uptown where it's safer to walk around all night, maybe get you a cup of coffee even, so you don't get tired."

"What's the Minister gonna think about you taking care of a vagrant like me this way," I joked as I piled into the back of the cab. "Or do I count as a charity case? So that makes it okay?"

"He's not a minister, he's a theology professor," Kris answered. She hesitated before continuing. "And, to be honest with you, I don't care what he thinks at this point."

"Strong talk about your husband, woman," I chided.

"He's not going to be my husband anymore in a few months," Kris countered, matter-of-factly. "We've been separated for about eight months now. I've just got some final paper work to take care of and some property to settle before the divorce is complete. So he can go fuck himself, and his thoughts too, as far as I'm concerned. I'll take care of whatever vagrants I feel like taking care of."

I wish I could have had a motion picture camera pointed at my face as Kris spoke those words, just to capture the waves of emotions that must surely have been visible there. The first one was the "Ha, ha, I told you so" emotion, followed quickly by the "Whoa, that really sucks" reaction, then the "Gee, I kinda feel bad for Kris" thought flitted across my mind, finally being displaced by the "Man, if she ain't married, then I might get laid" conclusion. And normally that would have been the end, but for some reason, I rewound back to the "I feel bad for Kris" phase, some sense of guilt for five years worth of passive-aggressive behavior no doubt rising to the surface as I realized that she'd had some bigger, crappier things in her life to deal with than my mean-spirited posts.

"Wow, I'm sorry to hear that," I said, and I almost meant it, too. "Are you okay?"

"Now I'm fine, yeah," Kris said. "A year ago, though, things were pretty bad. I was pretty bad. It's better now."

"Can I ask what happened?"

"Would you ask anyway if I told you that you couldn't?"

I had to think through that one. "Uh, yeah, I guess I would. So what happened?"

"Mark turned into an old man," Kris answered simply. "So you were right in that regard, I guess, although he didn't really want me as arm candy so much as he wanted me as house candy. He wanted me to look pretty and play my bassoon and cook and make scintillating conversation with him around the house, but he wasn't much interested in having me do any of those things anywhere else."

"Wow, that sucks," I commiserated.

"Sucked, yes, very much," she continued. "As did our love life, after the honeymoon, such as it was, ended."

"I thought you said you wanted a relationship that was built on more than love life," I said. "I mean, at least that's what you told me, that sex wasn't as important to you when you guys decided to get married."

"I said I didn't want it to be the focus of our relationship," Kris countered. "But I didn't say I wanted it to go away entirely. And it did, Mark just really wasn't much interested in me physically, to the point where he would actually kinda get grossed out by my body when he saw it. He wanted me to wear frilly Victorian nighties to bed and to put on nice eveningwear while I serenaded him on bassoon as he read the paper each night. He wanted my shit not to stink, or if it did, he wanted me to make sure I didn't let any of it sully our bathroom when he might be around to smell it."

"You're exaggerating, right?"

"No, not much, I'm not," Kris said. "So you can imagine that it got a bit tense after a while, and I started to feel really horrible about myself, about my body, and started having all sorts of weird gastrointestinal problems from trying to regulate my colon into Mark's schedule. It was really awful. Such a huge mistake to marry this man."

"So you finally left him?" I asked, agreeing with her completely, but not wanting to tell her that. Yet.

"No, he threw me out," she answered. "He found out I was sleeping with someone else."

"Get out! You're a nasty thing, Kris Dennison, or whatever your name is now."

She smiled. "It's still Dennison, Collie. You know that. I didn't change it when we got married, since I'd started to establish a little bit of a reputation as a musician by that point and didn't want to confuse the few contacts I had," she explained, telling me something I already knew. "But I guess I was a nasty thing, you're right about that."

"Do tell."

"Ain't much to tell, actually," she said. "I just got fed up with Mark one weekend, went to an adult Bible study class that I'd been going to just to get out of the house, and maybe to take a shit at the church if I had time, started chatting up the one relatively young, definitely single guy in the group after the study, got horny—which wasn't hard since I'd been about two years without sex by that point—walked out to the parking lot with this guy afterwards, talked some more, finally asked him point-blank if he knew anything besides prayer to make a lonely old lady feel better about herself. And he got the hint."

The cab had pulled up outside the appointed address, a small café with a Spanish name in a well-lit city block in what I was guessing must have been Greenwich Village, although I didn't know my way around the City well enough to be sure. I reached for my wallet, but Kris shook her head and waved my hand away, reaching forward to pay the driver, telling him to keep the change as we slid out the door of his cab.

"This is a better neighborhood to walk in," Kris said. "I give you 50-50 odds here that you could make it through the night with 72 dollars in your pocket without being accosted. Down where you were, it was more like 90-10 against."

"Thanks, I appreciate the relocation service," I told her. "Can I buy you a cup of coffee to thank you? Or are you treating, as part of your charity plan for me tonight?"

"I suppose I can buy you a cup," she said. "As long as you don't start to think that I'm an easy mark."

"I know you too well to think that," I said. "High maintenance to the max, can't fool me into thinking otherwise with a cup of coffee and a cab ride."

"Didn't think I could," she acceded as we walked into the restaurant and took a booth in the front corner where we could watch the passersby. "You were always too sharp for cheap and easy tactics like that."

"Right. Takes more than that to buy my soul."

"So what is the going price on your soul these days, then?" she asked, almost leering as she did.

"Umm…I guess before I answer that I've gotta know what happened with that guy at your church," I said, stalling for time, trying to read and register the leer, and what it meant for the way my evening was about to unfold. "Did Minister Mark toss him into a lake of burning pitch or something when you got home that night, stinking of sex and shit and Bible study?"

"No, Mark didn't find out for a while," she said. "I kept doing my Bible School buddy for a long time, catching up on lost time, as it were, but that ended when he got a case of the guilties and went and told the pastor of our church what was going on, and the pastor of the church then felt compelled to tell Mark that I had soiled our marriage bed. So that's when Mark tossed me out."

"Where'd you go?"

"Back to Jersey City, another apartment just about half a mile from where I used to live, still close to the school where I teach. It's cheap, and you can get in and out of the city easy, so I like it there."

"Alright, then, I suppose it's safe to tell you then that the price on my soul these days is one night's accommodations in Jersey City, New Jersey, with tips on how best to get to the appropriate train station in time to make it back to Albany by lunch the next day," I said, smiling. "So are you still interested in acquiring one slightly tatty, worn around the edges soul, or shall I look for another buyer?"

"Do I get to keep the soul, or is this just a rental?"

"Let's call it a lease with an option to buy."

"Then I think I'll take it," she said.

And we were out of the coffee shop and into a cab heading for Jersey City before the café's wait staff even realized we'd seated ourselves and left.

Chapter Fifteen

"You have absolutely no business asking me these questions," said Rushton Chuta as I gaped, horrified, stupefied, during our first meeting. "You have samples of my writing work before you. I am here to be a writer. Judge my writing and hire or don't hire me accordingly. I don't care which one you want to do at this point, but I will not allow you to sit here and interrogate me!"

Brennan had announced that she was leaving the *Advocate* to seek the mother love bone in Seattle during the first week of September 1992 and Anna had decided that we could add two people in Brennan's place, one taking on her arts coverage, one focusing more on news stories, thereby perhaps adding some of the editorial heft and credibility that the paper had lacked up until that point. Since I would be working so closely with these new staff members, she gave me the opportunity to screen resumes and conduct first interviews and make hiring recommendations, which she would then either approve or disapprove based on her own second interviews with my candidates.

Of course, I'd never hired anyone before, so I wasn't sure exactly how to go about it. I figured out that I needed to run an advertisement in the *Advocate*, since some of our readers might like to be writers here as well. I also planned on going through the freelancers list to see which, if any, of them merited promotion to full time status—although I was disinclined to take that route, since then I'd have to go through a second order search for a new freelancer to ensure I didn't have to pick up extra work as a result of the change.

The advertisement brought in about three dozen sets of resumes and writing samples, so I perused them all and came up with a list of five people who I thought merited first interviews. I then drafted a list of questions to ask them, things that I'd vaguely recalled the Envirocorps human resources drone asking me all those years before at the South Carolina Military Institute job fair in Ulmer. Stuff about their backgrounds, interests, prior jobs, families, hobbies, seemingly simple, easy stuff, regular stuff that regular people wouldn't mind talking about.

Rush wasn't regular people, though. Rush was paranoid people—and three questions into our interview he exploded, daring me to ask him another, daring me to hire him on his printed qualifications alone. He scared me so badly that as a reactive defense mechanism, I assured him that we thought his writing was wonderful, just what we needed, stood on its own merits, thanks for stopping by, let me see if Anna can meet with you now, you bet. I was so weirded out by the whole thing that I didn't even bother scheduling an interview with my next candidate, Julie Kirkland, but just called her on the phone and told her to come on by for a final interview with Anna as soon as she could.

So then we were three in our little editorial office bin, and looking back on my decade at the *Advocate*, I think that was probably my favorite period, since we weren't too big, and weren't too small, but were just the right size, before Carol was brought in to either manage or replace me (depending on who you talked to) and Blaine joined the staff to make me feel old and tired and lame. Anna was Anna during both eras, of course, but I think she was also easier going and more tolerant of me during that time, since I had yet to give her any strong reasons to be otherwise. Those came later.

It was a good time to be in Arctangent, too, especially now that I could count Kris as an Arctangent fan—and not just an Arctangent target. She and I started communicating fairly regularly after that night at

CBGBs, both of us again happy to be sharing the other's company (intimate and otherwise), although both of us also leery of getting involved in anything too terribly intense, given our nasty past history in that regard—not to mention Kris' cataclysm of a dysfunctional marriage, which ended officially the same month that Brennan left the paper.

Arctangent had started playing in New York City (not to mention Montreal and Syracuse) on a fairly regular basis by this time, so whenever we were in Manhattan, Kris would generally turn out to see us and I would generally take my pay for the evening and train home the next morning, spending the night with her instead of in the van with Matt, Brian and Barry. One time, though, Kris decided to ride home with us instead; while I don't think she particularly enjoyed the trip, she was quite impressed at how the Treehouse had evolved since she'd last seen it, and Gerry and Randy welcomed her back like a long lost sister, seemingly having forgotten that at one point they'd dubbed her the bitch to top all bitches. Or was that me?

I also took Kris into the *Advocate* offices and introduced her to Julie and Anna and Rush and some of the other production and advertising staff, and she was impressed by all of that, too. Kris was still teaching music, but her own performing career had been derailed during her marriage to Mark, so she was trying to start over, once again pursuing her dream of playing her bassoon with the big boys and girls in some symphony hall in New York City.

Of course, I had spent the previous five years hoping that she had failed in this regard, but it actually made me quite sad to be confronted with the reality of the fact that she had indeed crapped out as a performing musician, through no obvious fault of her own. I told her this at some point, and she smiled, and knowingly told me that in her own mind she just took credit for all of my success, and that made it all okay. I never told her how right she was in that assessment.

I did try to include her in Arctangent's musical life when I could, though, or as much as I could without making Barry call her Kris

Ono—although since she was actually quite a competent musician, they were generally receptive to having her around during those rare occasions when she did visit the Treehouse. We actually invited her up there in the spring of 1993 when we went into the studio to take our next big step as recorded artists, laying down tracks for our first full length album—which I was still thinking we needed to have done on vinyl, but Matt assured me needed to be pressed on compact disc if we wanted anyone to buy it and play it. I wasn't quite yet ready to give up on my own massive vinyl record collection, I guess, and didn't want to play a role in forcing other people to retire theirs either. I can be accused of being many things, but visionary isn't one of them.

We recorded yet another version of "Baal" during those sessions, this one with Kris playing bassoon, giving it a deep, ominous tone so far removed—rhythmically, melodically and spiritually—from its original incarnation that I didn't even feel like we needed to credit William Blake and Hubert Parry (the composers of "Jerusalem") as inspiration anymore. Kris also played some keyboards on two new songs, "Owl House" and "Green Swamp," that the band wrote collectively in the studio while she was there. Barry was relieved to not have to handle all the keyboard overdubs after the fact during those sessions, and went so far as to suggest that we invite Kris to join the band. I demurred, since Kris and I were getting along fine at that point and I didn't want to fix something that wasn't broken, most likely destroying it in the process. I didn't want to take a pay cut, either, but I didn't tell Barry (or Kris) that.

We put "Wisconsin" on that first album, too, and "Love And Hate And Us" and "Makeup," although I made a point of recording those two when Kris wasn't around. She'd heard them live by then, but had never asked me point blank who or what had inspired them—although it still would have been too weird to have her there in the studio, watching, while I sang them over and over again. We rounded out the record with three of my other songs ("Lamprey," "Suffer Me" and "My Garish Life") and Brian's "Kill Thing" and "There But For," pretty well capturing our live set as it existed at that point, only with more overdubs.

We called the record *Arctangent*. Simple. Elegant. Eponymous. It was still pretty expensive in those days to press compact discs as an independent label (we put "Treehouse Records" on our discs just to make them sound like someone besides us cared enough to issue them), so we only produced 2,000 during the first production run, which shipped in May 1993.

I say "only 2,000 of them," but that's probably deceptive, since I can tell you that 2,000 seemed like a huge number to me as we all sat around the studio folding labels (printed by the *Advocate*'s art department) and putting together jewel boxes. I never got blisters from playing my bass, but folding and stuffing those discs by hand left me with weird, fat pus bubbles in odd places all over the sides of my fingers and on the ball of my hand. I used to think the baseball pitchers were being pussies when they claimed they couldn't pitch because of blisters. After that project, though, I was completely sympathetic.

The initial 2,000 discs also emptied out the band's coffers, but since we could sell them for significantly more than we could sell tapes or singles, Matt assured us that we'd recoup that cost in no time at all. He was right, as annoying as it was to ever admit that fact.

Brian was so inspired by the concept of "Treehouse Records," as we'd printed on the discs, that he started looking for other artists in the Albany-Schenectady-Troy market to add to our stable, making them pay us for studio space and production support, then putting our imprint on their final product (which they paid for), then taking credit for it if it broke big. Seemed like a foolproof scam, so I was all over that too, often engineering the sessions that Brian produced.

We shipped our album off to all of the usual radio stations and record companies, and sold them at our concerts as we'd always done. We went through our initial stock of 2,000 by the early fall (selling most of them at outdoor summer festivals where beer and drugs and sun tended to loosen people's wallets, if they had any money to start with), then pressed another 3,000 to get us through our hometown autumn shows and a winter mini-tour the next January. I refused to fabricate another 3,000 jewel boxes, so we actually paid the *Advocate*'s printing team to compile and assemble them this time. Worth the money, believe me.

We got as far south as Richmond, Virginia, during that tour, searching for warmth, not finding much. We probably left at least 1,000 of our compact discs with promoters, club owners, record stores, labels, groupies and other parasites all throughout the Mid-Atlantic seaboard during that tour, desperately trying to get someone interested in something other than paying us for one night of service, one evening of stimulating the business at the bar, one hour of noise for wrecked souls to hide behind. I'm sure that 950 of those discs ended up in the trash eventually, while the other 50 may still be in use as coasters or under the legs of wobbly coffee tables. It's good to know that we were useful.

The summer of 1994 brought more changes to the band, as Barry married his longtime beloved Janice in a nice ceremony up in Lake George Village. Arctangent played at the wedding reception (Matt and Brian wanted to charge Barry's parents, but I told them I wouldn't perform if they did), with Kris sitting in on a couple of tunes, banging away on an old piano we found in the back of the community center where Barry and Janice's families gathered to get drunk, eat too much and humiliate the newlyweds with terrible, embarrassing behavior.

It got so bad, in fact, that I wasn't even the drunkest, most obnoxious person in the room, which was a refreshing change of scenery for me, although mortifying for Barry, particularly when his mother performed a strip tease at the end of the evening, so anxious was she to shuck her formal wedding duds and get back to the jeans and flannel shirts that otherwise defined her wardrobe. I pretended not to watch Mrs. Swinton, since Kris was there watching me, but I have to say that Barry's mom offered a thrilling performance (or at least as best I could see out the corners of my eyes), in large part because it wasn't a bit contrived or audience oriented, but was instead the sort of natural-looking thing you'd see if you lurked around in people's backyards, watching them undress through their bedroom windows. Not that I'd know what that looks like, mind you. Ahem.

"Komputer Mike" (as we dubbed him) Koonz moved out of the Treehouse that summer too, after making his surprising multi-million dollar Microsoft sale and ordering his new condo in Orlando. We took his sudden, unexpected fortune as a great portent for Arctangent, figuring that if he could do it that summer, then anyone could do it that summer, or at least we could do it that summer.

But we were wrong in that regard, as we were in so many other regards, since we didn't get anything even closely approximating a serious nibble that summer, nor for the rest of that year, despite our continued regional promotional efforts and periodic mini-tours. And audiences seemed to like us, that was never the problem—but no one wanted to put our names on a dotted line and give us a lot of money to do what we liked to do and were already doing for something slightly larger than peanuts, but just barely.

We occasionally questioned whether we (or, more precisely, Matt) were doing something wrong, but I think that our experience was actually a lot more common and typical than Hollywood movies or music trade magazine articles about bands and their breakthrough moments would have you believe. We might have gotten a bit more attention, I suppose, if we'd been cute like Liz Phair or sexy like Madonna or photogenic like the Smashing Pumpkins, but our line-up (gangly, ectomorphic drummer with bad haircut, fragile geek guitarist with bad chin whiskers, prematurely graying alcoholic singer-bassist with bad love handles) didn't really seem to move the image makers much. Can't say I blame them. I wouldn't want to pay to look at me either.

And so we waited for the break. And waited. And waited some more. And then Barry decided that he didn't want to devote quite as much to the band as he once had, seeing as how he had a job and a wife and everything now, so Brian and I decided to capitalize on the whole "Your Name Here: Unplugged" thing that was all the rage in the mid-90s and started playing out as an acoustic duo, Arctangent Lite as it were. It went over pretty well, and allowed us to play some venues that we might not otherwise have been able to play, and made us appreciate Barry all that much more when we reconvened and played live and loud as a trio. Barry seemed invigorated by the change too, substituting quality time for quantity time at the Treehouse and on the road.

We closed 1994 playing a huge New Year's Eve show at the Paramount Theatre as part of Albany's First Night Celebration. 1995 found Brian leaving Radio Shack and taking a service and maintenance job with a computer systems consultant who let him work whatever hours he wanted for a far-better-than-average hourly wage. Alan Moorhead, the television public relations flack who had moved into Komputer Mike's pad, fled the Treehouse that year, too—complaining about, you guessed it, the noise. I told him he should count himself lucky that I wasn't living up there, since Lindy and Brian were mouse quiet compared to the way that I lived when I was a North Korea homesteader.

Angie High, a recently-divorced, probably-abused, high school dropout who worked at least three jobs at a time, was next into the third upstairs apartment, but we rarely saw her, since whenever she was at the Treehouse, she was sleeping, too exhausted to be bothered by whatever noise had kept Alan awake at night. She stayed for three years, disappearing as suddenly as she came, finally freeing her den for Dentist Dave, who's up there still, just down the hall from Lindy, next to Brian's now-empty apartment. Matt moved up from Albany to Troy in 1995, too, although we didn't let him take a room in Treehouse—or at least not an apartment, rather, since he did sleep in the Studio as often as he did in his own squat.

But he kept pushing at us and pressing our product wherever he could, until we all got so sick and tired of hearing and playing so many of the same old songs that we decided to go back into the studio in late 1995 to record an album of new tunes that we'd written over the prior three years. We had ten songs in the can by Christmas, three written by the band ("Waveform," "Box of Rocks" and "Prey"), four written by Brian and I for our acoustic outings ("Floating Mountain," "Leave It Behind," "Any Yesterdays" and "The Lingering Irony"), plus two of Brian's compositions ("Slender Machine" and "This Piece") and my own new-ish "Fingers," the lyrics of which were originally sketched out while watching Kris play her bassoon.

Kris didn't play on any of the second album's tracks herself since her bassoon-for-hire business was again going well in New York City and suburban New Jersey and (occasionally) Connecticut, and she was generally booked solid for the period between Halloween and New Year's, as restaurants and churches and party planners somehow felt the need for mildly somber, thoughtful sounds at that time of the year, something to mark the fact that they were shutting down physiologically and psychologically for the winter. And nothing captures that feeling better than a well-played bassoon, as Kris had discovered both to her emotional delight and financial gain, which in turn pleased me, as it meant I got nicer Christmas presents when Kris could finally get free to visit.

Which wasn't until the second week of January that year, but I got an excellent new portable stereo, so it was worth the wait. I got Kris some silk pajamas, since I've always loved the feel of silk against my skin. Randy cooked a special belated Christmas feast for the whole Treehouse during that visit, and he and Gerry, Brian, Lindy, Kris, the normally elusive Angie High and I stayed up late drinking spiked eggnog (and then just straight rum), listening to the new Arctangent songs until things got silly and we somehow ended up playing a game of Treehouse Hide and Seek and I hid in a great secluded spot in DMZ, where I woke up the next morning, since no one had been able to find me.

A few days later, after Kris went home to New Jersey, I was at the *Advocate* office tidying up the last of the week's business when the phone rang. It was Matt, although I didn't recognize his voice at first.

"Collie, you need to come home," he said with a tone of great urgency, which confused me, and my heart skipped a beat and I oozed a quart of cold sweat as I assumed this was someone calling from South Carolina to tell me that Junior or Sister or one of (or both of) the twins had been consumed in a house fire or something.

"Who is this? What's wrong?"

"It's Matt, you asshole," he said, and another rush of chemicals flooded through my body, anger and relief engaging in a hormonal fight for dominance, relief taking an early lead, anger winning by TKO in the eleventh round. "And nothing's wrong. We just need you at the Treehouse. Now."

"Dude, in case you've forgotten, I've got a job," I snapped self-righteously. "So don't call me here and give me orders, alright?"

"Fine, then, we'll just talk to the record company without you," Matt said and hung up.

I roared into the Treehouse's back alley fifteen minutes later, banging on the loading dock doors until Brian unlocked them and let me into the studio. He and Matt were there, although there was no sign of Barry yet.

"He's on his way," Brian said, answering the question I'd yet to ask. "He should be here any minute."

And as if on cue, the airlock doorbell rang, although instead of going "ding dong," it went "Balls! Balls! Balls!" in Matt's most irritating, drunken bar boy tone, courtesy Brian's vast technological skill and perverse sense of studio aesthetics. We rarely let the doorbell ring more than once, though, so I suppose it was an effective system in its own annoying way.

"'sup," Barry said as he entered, looking like he was ducking to avoid his head on the lintel above the door, but then staying that way once he entered the room, his awful posture seeming to have gotten worse over the years. "What's the crisis?"

"No crisis," said Matt. "Opportunity. Here's the deal: I got a call from Mammon Records in Chicago this morning. One of their reps saw you guys when we were in Buffalo last fall. He got one of your CDs, although I'm not sure whether I sold him one or whether the club gave him one of their copies or what, but in any case, he evidently took it back to Chicago and played it for somebody there and that somebody was very, very interested…"

"I never heard of this label," Brian interrupted.

"Neither had I," said Matt. "They're pretty new, one of these quasi-indie, quasi-major labels that all the big conglomerations are setting up to make it look like corporate-sponsored music is actually coming out independently. Sony owns them and ultimately pulls all the financial strings, I guess, but Mammon's been set up to run independently as an imprint label, something for people to identify with that's a bit more personal and focused than a megacorp like Sony or Polygram or whoever. And Mammon's target audience are the sort of guitar-nerd types that listen to Steve Vai or Yngwie Malmstein or that kind of stuff, really technically proficient players doing something other than straight alt-rock or pop or whatever."

"Yngwie Wellington," Barry muttered, chuckling to himself. I snickered with him.

"So anyway," Matt continued. "I got a call from Mammon about a month ago…"

It was my turn to interrupt. "Why didn't you tell us?"

Matt was getting agitated. "Fuckin' hell, will you guys let me talk?" he shouted, literally leaping off his chair as he did so. "I get calls like that all the time. Do you want me to tell you every time one comes? Or every time I make one? I haven't seen any reason to do so, since all it would do is depress you guys to learn just how many people aren't interested in you.

But if you want me to start, fine, I'll call you at the office, Collie, every time I get an inquiry, just to keep you posted on all of your rejections."

He stopped, lit a cigarette, inhaled deeply and held it, so that only the faintest wisp of residual smoke emerged when he began speaking again. "Do you want me to go on or do we need to renegotiate how I do business and how I keep you informed right now?"

"Go on," Brian said. I just looked at the floor and didn't say anything.

"Alright, so Mammon called, and I sent them a press kit and another CD and the live tape and the single and a tape of the songs you guys were working on in the studio," Matt explained. "I told them that you were almost done with a second album and that the plan was for us to release it independently this spring. But I told them that if they were interested, they could have the album, which would save them a lot of money since we've already done all the work and all they'd need to do would be to mix or master or tinker if they wanted to spruce up some of the tracks in a bigger, better studio or whatever."

I could see that Brian wanted to protest and defend his work in our own studio, but he didn't want Matt to yell at him the way he'd yelled at me, so he bit his tongue and bristled silently.

"They like that idea," continued Matt. "So I talked to them again this morning and they want me to fly out to Chicago to talk about details. Ideally, we may be able to reach some agreement in principle on a contract, at which point they'll want to have someone come here to meet you guys and make sure they're still cool and comfortable with you, and then we can do the signing in Albany, since that gets Mammon some press outside of their home town. So I'm booked on a flight tonight, I took the money out of the band fund for now but I assume Mammon will reimburse us, and I'll be meeting with them tomorrow morning to see if we can't get ourselves signed and then get the fuck out of Troy, once and for all."

I called in sick to work the next day, committing the cardinal sin of missing an editorial staff meeting in the process, so that I could be available on call for Matt should he need anything from the Treehouse during his visit to Chicago. I was actually nervous, butterflies in the gut, the whole nine yards, so I started drinking earlier than I normally would have, just to take the edge off. And I was pretty edgeless indeed when the phone finally rang at about three o'clock that afternoon.

"Collect call from Matt," said an operator's nasal voice, drilling into my ear before I could even say "hello." "Will you accept the…"

"Yes, yes, I accept, I accept," I shouted, then listened to a series of clicks and beeps as the operator turned me over the Matt. "Are you there?" I said, afraid I'd lost him in the transfer, somehow in my addled logic of the moment feeling like he would disappear with the deal if I didn't touch base with him right then, right there.

"Yeah, I'm here," Matt answered. "But I gotta get on a plane, so I can't talk much. But here's the punch-line: one record guaranteed, option for two more at their discretion, the first record with them to include your new songs plus three that they want from your first album, you guys go to their studio in Chicago for remixes and mastering, they commit to a first pressing of 25,000 copies, we get 100 G's up front, then twelve percent royalties on sales. It's a good deal. I'll explain it all when I get home. Later."

Did he really say 100 G's up front? And twelve percent on sales for 25,000 discs? I stumbled into the kitchen and fished around in a drawer for a calculator. 25,000 records sold for, let's say, fifteen bucks apiece, that was 375,000 dollars, and twelve percent of that was 45,000 dollars. So that was a total of 145,000 dollars, divided five ways (me, Brian, Barry, Matt, band expense fund), which meant almost 30,000 dollars for me. Which would double my annual income and then some. Wow.

I probably should have called Brian and Barry to share the news, but I decided to get really, really drunk instead to celebrate, which didn't take much doing, since I'd already gotten close to being really, really drunk to alleviate my nervousness. I was nearly toxic accordingly when Matt arrived at the Treehouse at about nine o'clock that night, banging on our door and asking me where the other guys were. Was I supposed to convene a meeting? Oops, sorry.

We finally got everyone together an hour or so later, Randy and Gerry joining us in the studio as Matt walked through the details—or at least his version of the details—of the proposed Mammon contract. I don't remember much of the discussion, but I do recall that some questions were raised, and I do recall that the answer to those questions was almost always something like "One hundred thousand dollar advance, then twelve percent on sales…that's all that matters." I couldn't argue with that, so I just shut up and drank some more.

Matt made arrangements for our Mammon representative, a surprisingly young guy named Terry Steele, to travel to Albany three weeks later. Matt and Terry spent most of the interim in heavy phone negotiations about this detail or that detail, none of which Matt said we needed to worry ourselves about. The plan was for Terry to arrive on Albany Saturday for afternoon meetings, then to have him watch us play a heavily promoted show at Humphrey's that evening, then to (hopefully) offer a contract for our signature Sunday afternoon.

I arranged to have *Advocate* freelance writers and photographers following us the whole weekend, just to make sure we got Mammon (and us) the local media splash that they (and we) wanted. Terry seemed suitably (or was it ironically?) impressed at being greeted at the airport by Matt, Arctangent and a scurrying photographer, attempting to capture each handshake and gesture, trailing us, flash popping, through the baggage claim area and into the parking garage, at which point I shooed him away and told him to meet us back at the Treehouse.

The Saturday meetings with Terry went well. He left five huge stacks of paper for review by our counsel (or so he said), and we nodded knowingly and set them aside on the studio console and gave Matt sidelong glances, assuming he'd know what to do. Which certainly seemed to be the case, as he was truly in his glory that weekend, brokering a deal, hosting a record company representative, schmoozing, orchestrating, managing. The very apotheosis of the music industry insider, agent, promoter, publicist, all rolled into one compact, if slightly oily, stacked-triangular-shaped package.

The concert that night was a success, too. I don't suppose that we were actually auditioning for Terry at that point, but we played like we were, acting as if the future of the band depended on that evening's performance and that evening's performance alone. So we kicked ass, and the crowd knew we kicked ass, and gave it up for us in a big, big way, Matt right there in front of them, whooping and screaming and cheerleading and clapping as if he was seeing us for the first time and we were rocking his world indeed.

Terry stopped by the ready room after the show and shook our hands and told us he'd had a great time, and that we'd played a great show—and he hoped we'd read the contracts he'd left us, since he was pretty sure he was going to be asking us to sign them the next day so he could get back to Chicago and share the good word about Albany and Arctangent with his bosses there. We all nodded and smiled. Sure, we'd read them. Sure, we were ready to sign. Where's the pen? Terry smiled and nodded back at us, and told us he'd meet us the next day at the Treehouse for the signing. He hoped we'd have some press coverage for the event. We assured him we would. I'd already taken care of it.

We gathered in the studio for lunch (prepared by Randy) the next day. A few minutes before Terry had arrived, Brian and Barry had been flipping through the paper work and asking Matt what certain provisions in the contract meant, but Matt waved their questions away, noting that record contracts were just like apartment rental contracts, filled with lots of pointless legal boilerplate that did nothing for anyone except the lawyers who came up with and tweaked the wording every now and again just so they could earn their keep. I had to take him at his word on that, since I'd never signed an apartment rental contract, Treehouse business generally being handled more casually than that.

Matt also explained that he'd been through the contract front-to-back and back-to-front and side-to-side both ways, and that it was solid, did what we wanted, gave us what we needed, got our record out, put cash in our hands up front and gave us an income source for at least as long as the record continued to sell. And given that fact, Matt noted that we would be foolish to reopen or question the contract at the last minute, since Terry had the authority to sign it, but not the authority to change it. Matt also suggested that if we challenged Terry on any of the contract's provisions, then that would suggest that we had less than total confidence in Matt's ability to represent us to the record company, at which point the company would inevitably engage in divide-and-conquer tactics that would destroy the tight musical enterprise we'd created over the years.

And we listened to him, because we'd gotten used to listening to him and we weren't prepared to do the work necessary to make such decisions on our own. Terry showed up around two o'clock, picked at the fresh hors d'ouvres that Randy had set out, staged a few grip-and-grins with us for the two photographers who we'd arranged to have on hand, then asked us if we were ready to make our dreams come true. We said "sure," as one usually says when asked such a question, took pens in hand and signed that contract with Mammon Records right there on the spot. I noted that the name under my line said "Collie Hay," and wondered if it should have said "Hutson Colcock Hay III," seeing as how it was all official and everything. I kept the thought to myself.

Terry's smiles seemed to have gotten much larger after we had signed, and he was out of the Treehouse and on his way back to Chicago within fifteen minutes of the ink drying on the paper, noting that our advance check would be cut and shipped to us within 30 days, and that he'd be in touch shortly after that to make arrangements for us to travel to Chicago so that we could get the record whipped into shape and out into the hands of the great unwashed. His Cheshire Cat grin and hasty departure left me feeling nervous, but I got over that fairly quickly when a $100,000 check arrived at the Treehouse, right on schedule, right as promised.

We had agreed beforehand that we would divide our advance per our normal practice, with one exception: we decided to buy a van with the $20,000 that we would have put into the band expense fund, thereby eliminating the need to deal with surly rental clerks and (hopefully) putting us on some better, cleaner wheels than those atop which we'd traveled in the past. That technicality cared for, we then divided the remaining spoils, and I've got to admit that one of the most thrilling days of my life was the day when I went to the ATM machine, made a $50 cash withdrawal, and was issued a receipt noting that I had an account balance of $20,912.

But not for long. Terry called a few weeks later and asked us to bring our master tapes and ourselves to Chicago. We asked if he'd be sending us plane tickets and he told us "no," noting that we needed to use our advance money for expenses like that. Which made sense, I guess, so the four of us trotted down to the Albany Airport on short notice and bought about $1,200 worth of plane tickets between us, hopped on a Northwest Airlines direct flight and arrived in the Windy City for two weeks of re-recording and touch-up of our new material, plus "Baal," "Wisconsin" and "Owl House" from our first album.

I was a bit annoyed about Mammon's insistence on including "Baal" on the new record, since I was pretty well tired of it by that point, and hated to think that the first thing we'd ever written was our best (or at least most popular) number—but Terry insisted, and "Baal" (version four) was included in the final mix. Kris' bassoon part ended up on the proverbial cutting room floor, although I was glad that she'd at least get a songwriting credit for "Owl House," since that might make her some money, which she might could use. At least I thought it might make her some money, since I was still a bit fuzzy about how the whole songwriting thing was covered in the contract.

I spent at least another $1,000 of my advance money during that trip to Chicago, partying and eating hard whenever I wasn't recording or sleeping. But that was okay, since I still felt like the richest man in the world, relatively speaking: I'd been living hand-to-mouth throughout my adult life, rarely carrying more than $1,000 in my checking account, my savings account permanently pegged at the five dollar bank-mandated minimum. So with $17,500 or so left on my hands, I could definitely enjoy the feeling of writing a check, or slapping a charge card on the table, and not worrying about whether something was going to bounce or someone was going to confiscate my plastic, for a long, long time to come.

Or at least it seemed like that should have been the case, particularly since I still had an *Advocate* check coming in each week (even though Anna was getting increasingly annoyed at my increasingly frequent absences) and could count on making money playing with the band, as we'd been doing for the past eight years. But Mammon had some other ideas: they wanted us to take a break, lay low, while they developed an image for us, wrote a bio, put together a promotional plan, then put us out on the road for real once our record hit, inundating markets from hither and yon with both us and our product, sometimes at the same time even.

So our nice new van sat in the alley behind the Treehouse while we took our first significant sabbatical since our inception in 1988. Which seemed odd, seeing as how we'd actually reached the big leagues at last, only to be put out to pasture for the moment, deep in right field. Matt assured us this was the way it worked, that he was in touch with Terry on a regular basis and that everything was trucking along fine, just the way it should be. We should enjoy our vacation, not worry about it. We'd earned the right to do so.

I took his advice, being the obedient, malleable sort, particularly when someone was telling me to take the path of least resistance. And I took it with gusto, I might add: the next time I went to New Jersey to see

Kris, to cite but one example, we went and got a fabulous, expensive, high-end room at a high-rise hotel right off of Times Square, one with a hot tub, one with a view, one where we could order multiple bottles of the types of champagne I'd only read about up to that point and have them delivered to the room by bellhops who were more than willing to kiss up to me for tips. I liked the feeling. I spent almost $1,800 that weekend alone.

Then there were maybe half-a-dozen trips to Montreal over the next eight months or so. I'd fallen in love with that city during our first trip into Canada to play, but had never really had the time to explore it as I thought it deserved to be explored when I was up there with Barry and Brian and Matt strapped on at my side. So I started driving up there for long weekends, leaving the office early on Friday since Anna was never there then and no one else seemed much inclined to narc on me, enjoying the three hour ride through the Adirondack wilderness, worrying each and every time I crossed the international border that there would be drug residue or paraphernalia in my car that was going to attract a customs inspector's attention and result in me being gang-raped in a Quebec prison, screaming "non non non" all the while.

But that never happened, and I regularly made it safe (and sound as I ever got) to Montreal, where I would stay in a different hotel each time and drink different wines and eat different foods and shop at different shops and spent Canadian money with aplomb, watching the tabs rack up but thinking it was all okay since the exchange rate was so good at that point. And besides, no matter how much it had turned into in American currency by the time the credit card bill arrived at the Treehouse, there was that much and more in my checking account, so why worry?

I went home to Bridgefield for the winter holidays that year, where I actually spent some money on some worthwhile things, or at least some thoughtful things, anyway. I bought Junior a new leather recliner so he could fall asleep more comfortably while watching professional wrestling than he could on the old couch that had been in the den since I lived there. Sister had been complaining about back problems of late, during the infrequent occasions when we talked on the phone, so I paid for her to go out and pick out a firmer mattress than the ancient one she'd been sleeping on for most of her life.

Greg and Ward were sixteen that year, sophomores in high school, and I used my advance money to get them a computer that Christmas, one of those bottom-of-the-line Radio Shack jobs, but enough for them to be able to get onto the Internet and discover the world outside of Bridgefield. Sister told me later that they still run their landscaping business on that machine, a veritable dinosaur at this point, but still enough for their purposes. That made me feel good, reminding me of how nice it felt to buy all those gifts back during the Christmas of 1996, total cost, approximately $2,500.

But it was only money, and there was plenty more where it came from, so I also started buying increasingly large quantities of pot and hash and coke from Matt when the mood hit me, since it was so easy to score, and since I had ready cash to convert into ready altered states, and plenty of time to do it, since we weren't rehearsing or playing much. So I became ever more an impresario of escapism, planning my empty evenings like a general, like a conductor, like a surgeon, starting with a particular alcoholic beverage, shifting to a certain smoked substance, snorting something or another, smoking a little bit more of that stuff again, drinking some more of something else, world without end, oblivion, amen.

I was generous with my drugs, too, even tempting sweet Julie Kirkland at the *Advocate* into joining me for the occasional toot in the co-ed bathroom behind the editorial offices. Brian had started to partake a bit more as he aged and worried less about his mother sneaking down to Troy to bust him, but that was okay, since there was plenty for him, too—and for Angie High, as well, who lived up to her name on the rare occasions when she appeared at Treehouse gatherings, sucking down pot like a Dirt Devil, with the power of an upright in her petite little lungs. I think Brian finally managed to get into her pants one night after one such community smoke-a-thon, although I doubt that he or she were in any condition to do anything about it once he got there.

This went on for over a year while we waited for Mammon to overcome a seemingly endless stream of (apparent) obstacles, detours and delays that (allegedly) plagued them as they worked (or claimed to work) towards the release of our album. Which was fine by me, mind you, although it started to bother two other important people in my life: Anna and Kris.

My publisher had grown increasingly short-tempered with my erratic behavior, frequent absences and general bad attitude about working at the *Advocate*. I figured I had grown beyond the paper, to be honest, and was just waiting until we could get out on the road and start making real money before telling Anna that I'd had enough of being a music critic, and was ready to be a full-time musician instead. So I was just marking time, and Anna knew it, and it bugged her.

Kris stopped coming up to Troy again sometime during that year, probably after that unfortunate night when I was a bit too forceful in my amorous advances on Kris after a long evening of partying. She used the words "date rape" to describe the evening when she yelled at me about it the next morning, but I think (or hope) she used that phrase wryly or for dramatic effect, since I was shooting pool with a rope, if you know what I mean, by the time of the alleged violation, and certainly wasn't capable of penetrating anything that didn't want to penetrated. That's my story, at least, and I'm sticking to it.

I still went down to New York to see Kris every now and again, but we generally started meeting each other half-way, staying in one of the many bed and breakfasts that littered the Catskill Mountain and Hudson Valley. Those were nice weekends: I generally wouldn't drink or smoke (much), she generally wouldn't feel compelled to go to church on Sunday morning, so we just relaxed and felt comfortable and increasingly middle-aged together, as we both looked into the near future and saw our fortieth birthdays lurking there, waiting to ambush us as soon as we stopped noticing them there.

But the price of those bed and breakfasts added up, too, so that sometime around May 1997, about two months before the Mammon album was finally released, my advance money ran out. I bounced six checks that month, since I didn't even bother checking my balance anymore. One of those checks was to my credit card company, which caused my balance to exceed my limit and got my card cut off and confiscated the next time I tried to use it.

I crawled back to Anna at that point, much chastised, promising that I would be good again, meaning to do so only until the royalty checks arrived. Which should have been around July 1997 as best I could figure, since that's when the album was released to stores, selling surprisingly briskly, especially since we'd disappeared from the consciousness of our former concert followers during our year-long sabbatical. But July passed without a royalty check, and then in August we went on the road for three weeks and made some money there, as we'd always done, but no royalty check arrived, and in September Mammon brought us out to Chicago (they paid this time) to play a series of dates there and in a couple of nearby cities in Illinois and Wisconsin, but no royalty check arrived, and in October we were home again, Mammon seeming to have forgotten about us again, and no check arrived.

Matt's excuses about the lack of new money were running short by this time, so he just generally walked away whenever I badgered him about it, shaking his head and calling me short-sighted or ungrateful or obnoxious and tedious, depending upon his mood, and upon the tone in which I asked him. I tried calling Terry at Mammon a couple of times, but his assistant informed me that Mr. Steele would only speak with Mr. Lawrence about Arctangent business matters, not with individual members of the band, as per the terms of our contract.

That made me nervous, as did the fact that the interest on my credit card balance was growing apace and I was feeling a significant hole in my life without drug money, meaning that I needed cash and plenty of it. And fast. So as desperation set in, I finally decided to ask Lindy for help, secreting a copy of the band's contract out of Matt's file drawer in the studio, carrying it to her apartment and plaintively asking her to help me figure out what I had to do to get paid.

Lindy told me she'd look at it when she could and get back to me, then innocently asked me who'd handled our legal affairs when we signed it, since she'd been surprised we hadn't asked her to do it then. I told her that Matt had looked at it, and Mammon's lawyers had reviewed it and said everything was order. She got a sick look on her face and waved me out of her apartment, slamming her door behind me.

I learned why the next morning. We'd been screwed, and screwed badly, Lindy told me. First off, the $100,000 advance was literally that—a loan, one that we had to repay to the penny out of our royalties before those royalties would start being paid directly to the band. And the twelve percent royalty deal wasn't all that it seemed either, since royalties were to be calculated on something called a suggested retail list price, which was set at eight dollars per disc in the contract, about half of what the CDs actually sold for in stores.

And we also weren't entitled to royalties on free copies that Mammon shipped to radio stations and newspapers and magazines, even though most of those ended up being resold in used CD shops. And fifteen percent of the number of discs shipped to stores for sale were written off for breakage, and twenty percent of the suggested retail list price was discounted for manufacturing costs, and the cost of radio marketing and promotions and those hours that we spent in the studio in Chicago the year before were all being billed to us, too, additional advance costs that had to be recouped through our royalty payments before we were entitled to receive any of them.

Then, to add injury to insult, we'd evidently signed away our publishing rights to Mammon, so that even if we'd been getting heavy spins on commercial radio, we wouldn't be making a penny from it. And finally, Lindy explained, we had been giving Matt twenty percent of all our take, all those years, never questioning his position as an equal member of our little band of merry musical men, either before or after the contract—despite the fact that industry standard for the types services he provided was typically in the five to ten percent range, as best she could ascertain.

The long and the short of which meant that unless the Mammon album (also called *Arctangent*, I suppose I should note, although to this day I can only think of it as "the Mammon album," since they owned it, not us) sold somewhere near double platinum status, we weren't going to see another penny, so deep in hock were we to Mammon by that point. I thanked Lindy for her assistance, and she called me an idiot for signing such an important document without having someone in my court to give it a professional look-see, and I told her I thought that's what we paid Matt to do, and she told me that maybe we ought to rethink that arrangement. Only we couldn't, since it was now formally codified by the Mammon contract.

I called a band meeting the next night and explained the situation to Barry and Brian and Matt, who I had expected to be filled with righteous indignation—but who instead looked as shocked and pale and shaken as the rest of us. I was planning to blast him for screwing us so badly, until it dawned on me that he'd screwed himself too, not out of any act of malfeasance towards us, but just as a result of assuming that his small-town hustler skills would serve him when dealing with an arm of the Sony Corporation. That revelation seemed to hit him awfully hard, so I chose not to belabor the point. Much.

We had another revelation to belabor in store the next month, though, when we got our first and only review in a major national publication. I was actually looking forward to receiving such a review, mind you, since as a music critic I was always fairly self-analytical about what we did anyway and was always interested in hearing what other people thought about it, as long as those thoughts were nice ones. Which, to our credit, they had been: most of our press in Albany over the years had been good to great, even when the critics writing about us weren't in my employ, so I figured we must have been doing something right, something good, something worthy, objectively speaking.

So when someone mentioned to me in passing at the office that our record had gotten a write-up in the new issue of *Spin* magazine, I was off to the newsstand in a flash accordingly, ready to bask in glories that I hadn't orchestrated. It didn't quite play out that way, though, since *Spin* music critic Nelson Wilson figured that on a scale of one (awful) to ten (wonderful), *Arctangent* rated only a very measly three. Which was bad, and which then got worse as I stood there in front of the magazine rack, wilting, reading words that might as well as have been my own musical obituary:

Arctangent, *Arctangent* (Mammon). This Upstate New York trio's press kit notes that singer-bassist Collie Hay is a leading music critic in the burgeoning musical Mecca of Albany—but I probably could have figured that out without reading about it, since Arctangent is filled with some of the most egregious examples of self-referential, forcibly-hip crit-rock ever to cross my desk. Take "Baal," for instance, a pointless remake of Emerson, Lake and Palmer's already-pointless "Jerusalem," minus the keyboards, plus a new set of ooo-aren't-we-scary lyrics about demons and war and plague and other such pretentious subjects. Could anyone but a music critic come up with anything as far removed from an original piece of work as this? Probably not, since you've got to mull and ponder for an awfully long time to come up with something so totally unappealing from a musical standpoint—and few people outside of the critical community have the time or inclination to do so. Which is a shame, on one front, since guitarist

Brian Wellington actually makes some impressive noise every now and again, but every time he seems poised to break free from the sonic sludge (see "This Piece" or "Slender Machine"), the miserable Hay drags him right back down again with another impossibly deep and meaningful look at his own navel. If this is the "New Progressive" music that Sony affiliate Mammon Records keeps writing about in the trade magazines, then I'm damn glad to count myself as a retrogressive musical reactionary.

Thanks, Nelson Wilson. Thanks for marking the beginning of the end of Arctangent in such a fine, readily definable fashion.

Chapter Sixteen

If there had ever been any doubt in my mind about whether or not mankind had evolved from some particularly nasty species of stinging, carnivorous worm, then the community bloodbath that went down after the *Spin* review removed that doubt forever.

Arctangent had thrived in Albany for a full decade by the time that review hit the newsstands, and while our press hadn't been universally glowing, it had been generally positive enough for us to view the rare off comment as the product of a critic having a bad day, or us having a bad night, or some combination of the two. And when I first read Nelson Wilson's scathing critique, I was willing to toss him into that cranky critic hopper, too, since (to the best of my knowledge), he'd never seen us perform and knew nothing about us before getting our press kit, but instead just dropped his word bomb upon thousands of readers based on one quick listen to our album, perhaps when he wasn't in the right mood to perceive it in all of its obvious glory.

I could rationalize away his dig at my music criticism as well, since I assumed it was just sour grapes: every music critic secretly wants to be a musician, I was both, he was jealous. But unfortunately, just about every other critic in the Capital Region (and a good number of musicians as well) seemed to be suffering from the same fit of jealousy, and we reaped more bad press in the ensuing ten weeks than we had in the preceding ten years, a decade of repressed bile erupting in a single spray of projectile critical vomiting, most of it aimed my way.

So what happened? Was the Mammon album really that much worse than anything we'd done before? Had musical tastes in Albany progressed to the point where Arctangent were passe, cliched, outre, all at once and all of a sudden? Had our year of quasi-retirement led to our fans drifting away, growing up, getting mad at us for not being there for them? All of the above? Some of the above? None of the above?

Maybe. Or maybe it was just the fact that everyone wanted to be on our bandwagon when we were the great gray hope of the Albany music scene, but no one wanted to ride with us once we'd been exposed nationally as a pompous assembly of crit-rock peddlers. I've also concluded, with a little bit of time to think about it, that we might not have been getting fair or accurate or representative representation over the years, in large part because a music community is a needy, incestuous being—and no one was willing to piss me off by trashing my band, since they never knew when they might need me, in my music critic role, somewhere down the line.

Those who knew me best over the years knew that I was capricious enough to have held their words against them, so the ones who were best positioned to offer constructive criticism were probably the ones most afraid to offer it. But once Nelson Wilson popped the critical cherry, all deals, bets, history and relationships were off, as the stinging, carnivorous worms that lived in my peers' heads smelled the blood between our legs and flew at us, ready to feast.

While Darwin would have predicted that frail, weak Brian would have been the first to be pulled down and devoured, the pack of gnashing, gnarling parasites seemed to recognize that he was diseased meat, not healthy enough to make a suitable, satisfying meal, so they bypassed him to instead pursue the more succulent brains of the organism that was Arctangent, which they sensed was most likely located in the same place that the band's mouth could be found. In my face, in other words, where they clacked and clattered, loud, vehement, vociferous, vile. And Barry? No one much troubled with him, since he was the drummer, and even vertical vermin know enough not to hold drummers responsible for their bands' actions.

All of which meant that by the autumn of 1997, I was pretty much ready to toss Arctangent on the rubbish heap of history, and would have done so barring one small mitigating circumstance: I desperately needed money. And while I knew that I wasn't likely to see any more cash from Mammon (who had gotten distressingly disinterested in us after the review, which also happened to be around the time that Sony was undergoing one of its periodic fits of unpleasant corporate peristalsis, making it unclear as to whether there was even going to be a Mammon anymore once the spasm worked itself out), I felt fairly confident that we could still get shows booked, still sell some merchandise, still make some cash as we'd been doing all along. There's no such thing as bad press, after all, and I could even see new listeners coming out to check us out, just to see if we were as bad as all that. I certainly didn't think we were.

Brian was willing to keep the band going, too, since he'd actually gotten the one or two positive shreds of feedback that had come out of the *Spin* review, and Barry was generally amenable to continuing as he'd been doing for a while, playing with us when it suited him and when the venue called for it, sitting out and letting Brian and I play unplugged when we could get away with it. Which posed sort of a Catch-22 for me, since we drew more people (and more money) when we played electric as a three piece, but had to split the money an extra way when we did. I opted to not take a stand either way accordingly, but to let Barry play when he wanted to play. I didn't have it in me at that point to try to find a regular, steady drummer again.

Matt, on the other hand, was more regularly, steadily Matt-like than he had ever been as we entered the winter of our discontent, shilling, schmoozing, wheeling, dealing and (probably) stealing as if his life depended on it, not in the least bit visibly dismayed or disillusioned by the way our Mammon affiliation had turned out. He was actually hoping by this point that Sony would dissolve Mammon and let all the bands on the label's roster go free, since he figured that was the best way for us to get a fresh start with fresh faces in fresh places—particularly now that we had learned enough from our first record label debacle to handle the next deal properly. Matt also believed that it would be far easier for us to land that second label, since we could note in our band portfolio that we'd once been good enough to get signed, giving us an edge over bands who had never escaped their home markets. I figured that might make sense—as long as the new label hadn't happened to catch any of the bilious reviews that the Mammon album had generated.

So we kept playing. And I kept spending money. Which meant that we needed to keep playing. So I could keep spending money. By Christmas of 1997, the venom of the summer and autumn had largely dissipated, although it was replaced by something that was almost harder to accept: apathy. We were old news by that time, and other bands were emerging as the town's new critical darlings—although I regularly used (or more precisely, abused) my position of authority to cut the legs out from under a few them, lest they start to get big heads and forget who was really running the musical railroad in Albany.

I didn't quite rationalize it that way at the time, though, instead justifying my lackluster statements of support as an important educational tool, helping up-and-coming bands learn to deal with nasty critics early in their careers, instead of waiting until the point when their first really, really bad review came—after they'd started believing that they were immune to such things.

Anna wasn't buying that argument though. "You gotta stop this tit-for-tat shit, Musicboy," she said to me that winter after reading a particularly scabrous review that I'd written about Goat's Head Group, who had recently been lavishly praised by a Troy-based daily critic who had hammered Arctangent half-a-dozen times in print earlier in the fall.

"Y'know, I have to maintain some editorial and critical integrity here, and it's pretty goddamn obvious what you're up to, both to me and to the readers."

"I thought they sucked," I countered lamely. "So that's what I wrote. I'm not entitled to an opinion anymore?"

"You're entitled to an opinion, yes. But you're not entitled to be a bitter crank who shits on people just because other people happen to like them. Your credibility suffers when you do that. And your writing, too: you're just going through the motions in these reviews, not bothering to look beyond the fact that you decided someone sucked before you even got to the concert…"

"Is that what you think I'm doing, Anna? Really?"

"Yes, I do," Anna answered with what almost looked like a snarl. "I've put up with you being late for meetings, and taking off whenever you feel like it, and stinking up the office with beer-sweats and morning-after smoke, and I've done all that only because you've been a great writer and editor, despite yourself…"

"And now?" I interrupted.

"Now you're neither of those things, Collie," she said, finger in my face, so angry that she actually used my real name instead of my usual pet moniker. "And I can't afford to let you drag the paper down as you work through your sad mid-life crisis deal or whatever it is that you're doing right now. I mean, why don't you just get over it, okay? Arctangent had a great run. You got further than anyone around here has gotten in years. Then you got a bad review. Big fuckin' deal. You've written more than your share of those over the years, and I have a hard time imagining that the people who received those reviews behaved any more badly than you've been behaving for the last six months."

"Are you forgetting the guys who broke my nose and hung me on the fence?"

"No, I'm not," Anna snapped, putting one of her perfectly manicured fingers a mere inch from the tip of my nose as she did, making her point emphatically. "You're being more of a baby than those guys were by a long shot. So grow up, Collie. Be a man. Or at least a professional, because if you can't manage that, then I'll find myself a new Musicboy. Molto pronto, got it?"

That should have been the sort of wake-up call that I needed to lift me out of my funk, but instead it just worked to push me down a few circles deeper into the hell of self-loathing, since now I'd been denigrated as both a musician and a writer, the only two things (besides drinking) at which I'd generally considered myself to be talented over the years. And as my own sense of self-worth deteriorated, it made it harder for me to get up each morning to go to work, made it harder for me to work up the energy and passion I needed to actually deliver a good onstage performance, made it harder for me to find healthy room in my life for Kris, or Gerry and Randy, or Lindy, or Junior and Sister and the twins, who I called ever more infrequently, forgetting all about them for weeks on end sometimes, at which point Sister would generally call just to make sure I was still alive. I always was, much to everyone's surprise, not least my own.

Needless to say, all of this wallowing didn't make for good interpersonal relationships, particularly between Kris and me. We spent one particularly dismal weekend in Jersey City together during that period of time, stuck in her apartment by the typically gray and chilly New England spring weather, me wanting to do nothing besides drink and smoke and fuck, she not much interested in any of the above.

"I hate to say this, Collie," she finally noted as I sat on her sofa, watching my third straight hour of MTV, hating everyone I saw on it. "But you're acting the same way you acted after your mother died, coming down here with this big ball of need that you want me to take off your shoulders, and I'm really not interested in carrying it for you…"

"I don't know what you're talking about," I said, knowing exactly what she was talking about. "I just come down here because…"

"…you enjoy my company," she finished for me. "Yes, I've heard that before. I just wish that you enjoyed it more during the moments when you didn't have me bent over the side of the bed or spread-eagled on the kitchen table." She paused. "And I wish that you enjoyed it enough to turn off the fucking television when I'm talking to you."

I looked around for the remote control half-heartedly, couldn't find it, sighed, sunk deeper into the sofa and kept watching the old Duran Duran video that was currently sound tracking our latest argument. Or Kris' tirade, more precisely, since I wasn't fighting back. "Hungry Like the Wolf" was the video, and I zoned Kris out as she went on about some slight or another, and thought instead about how the girl in the video would look with her knees up against her ears. Nice, I'll bet.

I didn't see Kris for nearly two months after that, although I finally finessed myself a return invitation in May—just after Anna dropped another bomb in the office by hiring Carol Ziomek, the buxom Bossgirl, a former music critic with a daily paper in Northampton, Massachusetts, brought in to coordinate editorial office efforts, to supervise my work, to make me expendable, if she (or Anna) wanted me to become so.

Anna's timing couldn't have been worse for such a move: Carol showed up in the office three days before my fortieth birthday, making me not only expendable, but old and expendable. I got very, very, very drunk that night accordingly, and called in sick for the next two days, then showed up in the office on my birthday, figuring that there might be some sort of celebration or note of the occasion, but none was offered.

Carol had a new work schedule for me, though, laying out my assignments as I'd been laying them out for freelancers for the past eight years. She still wanted me to schedule the freelancers, mind you, but she was going to have a say on what and who and when I reviewed, ostensibly to force me to attend shows that might inspire some creative juices to flow, instead of simply providing me with revenge options. I'd never been put on an editorial leash before, and generally didn't even ask freelancers to do shows that they weren't already planning to attend anyway, so Carol's schedule marked a significant devolution in my ability to control my own life and schedule and agenda.

Which meant that I had to see Kris for a comfort fix, although I didn't tell her that my wheedled visit was a need-driven one. Didn't need to, actually: we spent a fairly nice Saturday together in New York City—shopping, visiting museums, eating too-expensive food, me drinking only a socially-acceptable amount of wine while we did so—then returned to Kris' apartment, chatted, watched a spot of television, went to bed for what I considered to be the planned main event. Only problem was that when Kris curled up, back towards me, and I slid my hand down to caress her, I felt the bulge of a bulky maxipad beneath my fingers instead of her own inviting curvature.

I felt her tense, holding her breath, anticipating my next move and, to my own credit, I probably saved our relationship (at least for another month) by rolling over, patting her affectionately on the back, and pretending to go to sleep, although I really laid there awake for almost two hours, staring into darkness, listening to Kris sleep, wondering how early I could leave the next morning without seeming churlish. I figured ten o'clock would be good, after we ate breakfast, before Kris went to church, a ritual she'd never abandoned, her faith (or at least her own need for comforting rituals) as strong as it had ever been. I finally drifted to sleep, and dreamed that I was being chased across a vast, hot asphalt parking lot by a flock of decidedly-not-adorable little horned lambs, all sporting oversized sexual organs. Ponder that, Doctor Freud.

Kris and I had a nice breakfast together the next day, me craving cigarettes, but without the usual morning hangover to contend with, a dull ache in the groin standing in for it instead. We agreed that we could use a change of scenery next time we met, and Kris suggested that we do lunch at the Culinary Institute of America, a famed cooking school on the Hudson River somewhere near the midpoint between Troy and

Jersey City. We picked a Saturday three weeks out; Kris had originally proposed four weeks, but I insisted on getting together sooner, feigning altruism and interest, but actually just wanting to make sure that if there was going to be any opportunity for intimacy, then there wasn't going to be a maxipad or a tampon between us. Proper prior planning precipitates plenty plenty pleasure, you bet.

When I got home and went to pencil in my date with Kris, I was pleasantly surprised to note that Arctangent had one of our increasingly rare trio performances scheduled for the night before our luncheon, meaning that I'd actually have some fresh cash in my pocket to throw around when we got to the Culinary Institute. Champagne brunch, baby, instead of cheap house wine. I could see this change-of-scenery weekend shaping up to be a nice one, something to look forward to, something to get me through the dull and dry and dismaying three weeks that stretched like the Sahara between now and then, Carol Ziomek riding me like a dromedary the entire way.

I had to get through that Friday night Arctangent show at Humphrey's, too, which found us capping a three-band bill—although the scheduled late start for the evening meant that we were handling mop-up chores more than we were standing in as headliners. Matt worked the room hard all night, though, trying to move our t-shirts and stickers and tapes and CDs even while the other bands played, trying to separate audience from cash while the crowd was at its mid-evening peak, instead of waiting for us to pimp our product at two o'clock in the morning for the hardcore pack of drunks who remained to watch us.

Which was a shrewd strategy, since we (or someone) actually had a good crowd in the house around the time that Friday became Saturday. And even though we weren't necessarily the featured attraction, it felt good to see that many people in the building, all of the shouting to be heard over the bands playing in front of them, not to mention all of the other shouters. It all sounded and looked even better after I had half-a-dozen shots of tequila under my belt, lighting the hot little fire of confidence in my gut that was necessary for me to take the stage in those, our dark, post-Nelson Wilson review days.

Our performance was okay that night, I guess, if a bit rote. I had pretty much given up writing since the Mammon album was issued, so the only new material we had in our set was coming from Brian, who hadn't been terribly prolific himself: only two ("Meat" and "Truth") of fourteen songs we played that night were less than a year old. But we delivered the old standbys with something approaching gusto, and people were tapping their feet and nodding their heads while we did it, then clapping when we finished, so that felt good, even if it was the alcohol that was making them do it.

We wound up the set with the hearty one-two punch of "Owl House" and "Editions of You" (I refused to play or sing "Baal" anymore), then trooped to the bowling-alley-shaped club's dank back room for the obligatory post-show joint. Matt met us there, which was unusual, since he'd usually be trying to move last-minute product with the departing crowd, who (theoretically) would be all flush with excitement over our performance and lusting for Arctangent merchandise accordingly.

"Dudes, big news," he opened, before we'd even had a chance to fish a joint out of our gear bag, much less light it. "You all know Bud Greenleaf, right?"

"He's a promoter," Brian offered helpfully. "The guy that does all the druggie jam band shows out in Central New York."

"Think that's his real name?" Barry wondered. "Seems too good for what he does to be real, like someone sat around and tried to come up with something cool, like Stoney Potts, or Bongo Hashishian or Bud Greenleaf or something…" His train of thought drifted away as he lit up and pulled a long toke.

"I think Greenleaf is his real last name," Matt said. "Bud's a nickname, though, that would be my guess." He pointed at the burning pot trembling in Barry's fingers. "Give me that."

He took a hit, passed it on to me and kept talking. "But his name's not important. What's important is that he was here tonight to check out one of the other bands for a possible representation deal, and he saw you guys too, and he's doing his big annual Budstock show down in Binghamton, and he thinks that based on what he heard tonight, you'll go over well with his hippie kids, so he's willing to get us a spot on the bill, even though it's short notice."

"How short?" I asked.

"Real short: Budstock starts tomorrow," Matt answered. "But Bud says he's totally confident that we can move some serious merchandise if we play early enough on the bill, while people still have some money, so I think it's worth rearranging our schedules for this. Plus if we can build up some interest again in that part of the State it could help us in the long run anyway. So I told him that we'd be there."

"I'm not going to Binghamton tomorrow," Barry said. "I got plans with Janice, so you guys'll have to do acoustic Arctangent if you go."

"How early do we have be there?" I asked Matt.

"Bud said he needs to have us there by about ten-thirty or eleven in the morning if we're gonna get through security, get our gear in, sound-check, all that stuff," he answered. "We'll probably play around two or three o'clock, something like that. And I'd rather have all three of you there, I think that would be a better situation, but if it's just Brian and Collie, I guess we can make that work too." He'd learned by now that it wasn't worth arguing with Barry about playing when Barry didn't want to play.

"So we have to leave at like, what, seven-thirty tomorrow morning?" I continued, looking at the clock on the wall, which currently read 2:40. "By the time we load out and everything, we ain't gonna make it home until 3:30 or so at the earliest, and to be honest, I'm a tired mo-fo already, since I just put in a week of hard work for the lowest common denominatrix." I thought for a moment, the pot pleasantly clouding my mind. "Plus, I've got plans with Kris tomorrow. So I don't really want to change those, y'know?"

"I'd like to do it," Brian interjected. "Tonight felt good. I want to play again. And we can all use the money."

At the mention of money Matt pulled a wad from his pocket, counted out $412 and some change, handed Brian, Barry and I $80 each, took $80 for himself, put the rest into the band's travelling case for expenses. "We'll do a lot better than this tomorrow," he noted. "I think it's important for you guys to do this. And we'll lose a lotta face with Bud if we don't, since I told him that we'd be there."

"What are you doing with Kris?" Brian asked me. "Anything special? Or just getting together?"

"We were gonna go to that Culinary Institute thing down in Dutchess County somewhere," I answered. "Do lunch there, then see what happens."

"Why not tell her to meet you in Binghamton instead? It's not that much further for her, I don't think, and we'll be done by mid-afternoon, so we can bring the van home and you can ride down to Jersey City with her afterwards, then train back on Sunday."

Well, that made sense, didn't it? At least it did to my pot and tequila addled mind at that moment, eighty dollars feeling nice in my pocket, promises of more hanging before me enticingly. "Yeah, I guess I could do that," I agreed. "That could work okay. And Kris hasn't seen us play in a long time, so she should like that, I guess. I just gotta make sure I call her before she leaves in the morning, 'cause if I can't get her, and she shows up at the Culinary place, and I'm not there, there'll be all sorts of hell to pay."

"Call her when we get home," Matt suggested.

"Oh yeah, that'll go over good," interjected Barry. "I'm sure she'll appreciate being woken up at four in the morning to have her social schedule re-arranged."

"She's usually up at, like, six," I said. "I should be able to get her around then and not wake her up or bum her out."

"So you'll play?" Brian asked, hopefully.

"Yeah, I guess so," I agreed. "Assuming I can get to Kris in the morning."

We left to haul our gear off the stage and into our van at that point, then rode back up to Troy, Matt driving carefully lest we become an obvious target for the late-night traffic cops on Interstate 787, making it safely back to the Treehouse at about quarter-to-four. We decided to just leave all the gear (even Barry's drums) in the van since we'd be driving out again in a few hours. Barry didn't mind. He'd be gone when we got back from Binghamton, so we'd have to unload his gear without him, which made it more than worth it for him to have his kit make a needless trip to Binghamton, if it saved him from that most-hated chore.

After Barry drove off to Clifton Park, Brian disappeared up to North Korea, announcing that he'd set the alarm and make sure we were up on time, since he didn't trust Matt or I to do it. Matt curled up on his favorite sofa in the studio and was asleep in seconds—leaving me sitting behind the console wondering how I was going to wake myself up at six o'clock to call Kris, deciding that the safest course of action would be to just stay up and make it an all-nighter.

I left the studio via the loading dock, locking the doors behind me and walking up the alleyway to River Street, then turning inland, uphill, slowly ambling the dozen blocks between the Treehouse and the all-night convenience store up on Brunswick Avenue, enjoying the sense of being all alone in a city of 40,000-some people, lord of all that I surveyed, decaying urban mess that it was. Troy had been my home for fourteen years at that point, although I still felt (and feel) a sense of wonderment that I'd chosen lost and forgotten Troy, the famed Collar City, as an antidote to lost and forgotten Bridgefield, Bridgefield by the sea, 25 miles from Yemassee.

That childhood jingle rattled around my head for a few blocks, before I replaced it on the mental jukebox with "Co-hoes, Co-hoes, where everything dies and nothing go-roes," a more germane ditty as I looked back over my shoulder at the lights on the other side of the river. I presumed them to be Cohoes, although they could have been Watervliet or Waterford or Green Island or some other nameless ancient community for all that I knew. No matter, since I was sure that everything died and nothing go-rew over there, no matter what the address.

I purchased two 20-ounce cups of coffee at the all-night Stop and Shop, loaded them up with sugar and drifted back down to the Treehouse, the first light of sunrise brightening the ridge behind the imposing Rensselear Polytechnic Institute campus as I let myself into the loading dock, tiptoed past Matt, through the airlock and back up to South Korea. It was just after six, so I picked up the living room phone, stretched the cord out to the balcony, lit a cigarette and dialed Kris' number.

The phone rang three times before she answered. "'lo," she mumbled.

"Hey, did I wake you up?"

"Mmm," I could hear sheets rustling. "Yeah. Who'sis?"

"Collie."

More rustling. "What's wrong? How come you're calling me in the middle of the night?"

"Nothing, everything's fine."

"Then why're you waking me up?"

"'cause it's time to get up."

"Mmm," she sighed. "I don't think so. What time is it?"

"About six," I answered.

"So why are you calling me at about six?"

"I need to change our plans for today."

"Oh, Collie, don't say that," she said, suddenly sounding quite wide awake. "I was so looking forward to today. Please don't cancel on me."

"I'm not canceling," I offered lamely. "I just need to tweak things a little bit."

"How little?"

"Well, I still want to meet you today, but I need to do it in Binghamton."

"Why do you want to go to Binghamton, Collie? What's there?"

"We got a really great show opportunity that came up at the last minute," I explained. "It's important. A big promoter, big crowd. We aren't getting these kinds of opportunities anymore. We need to go."

"I don't want to go to Binghamton," Kris said. "I want to go to the Culinary Institute."

"Me too, honey, I really, really do. But this is important. We need to do this show. We should be done by mid-afternoon, so Matt and Brian can take the van home and you and I can either go to the Culinary Institute on Sunday or later Saturday night, even, if you want to make it a late dinner instead of a lunch."

"I doubt they're open that late."

"Then lunch the next day. Sunday champagne brunch. It'll be worth the wait."

"You think so?"

"I think so," I said, and I think I actually meant it.

"Alright, if it's important to you," Kris agreed. "But where's this show in Binghamton?"

"Umm, I'm not exactly sure," I answered. "Matt knows, but he's asleep downstairs."

"How am I gonna find you, then?"

I played through my limited knowledge of Binghamton, searching for landmarks. "There's a rest area on I-88, just outside of Binghamton as you're heading back up to Albany. We usually stop there when we're heading out that way. Why don't we meet there?"

"Will it be on the map?"

"Should be," I answered, although I had no idea whether I was telling the truth or not. "It's the only one out that way, so I'm sure there's signs marking it and everything. It's one of those rest areas that's in the median, so both sides of the highway can use it."

"When do you want to meet?"

"How about 10:15?"

"Okay," Kris said, then paused. "I guess I need to get up and get going, huh?"

"Probably, yeah. It's probably, like, three hours from where you're at."

"That far?"

"Not much further than from Jersey City to Troy, really."

"Yeah, but I wasn't going to Troy today," Kris noted. "I was going to Hyde Park."

So that's where the Culinary Institute was. "I know, it's further, you're right," I agreed. "But it means a lot to me to do this show, so I'm glad you're willing to go."

"Okay, well, I'll see you at 10:15 at the I-88 rest area, then" Kris said. "But you owe me a lunch at the Culinary Institute."

"Cool. It's a date," I said. "And after this show I might even have enough money to pay for it."

"Ha ha."

"Ha ha back atcha."

"Safe trip."

"You too. See you in, uh, four hours or so."

I wrote Gerry and Randy a note letting them know that I'd been home and left again, and would probably be gone for the entire weekend, then drifted back down to the studio to finish my second tepid cup of heavy-duty sugared coffee sludge. I slurped loudly, rustled papers and tapped on the console until Matt finally woke up, looked at his watch, stretched, groaned and disappeared into the bathroom, hunched over from morning wood. Brian joined us soon thereafter, looking far perkier than either Matt or I, no doubt because he had some sense of moderation when it came to drinking and smoking before, during and after concerts. We were in the van on the road to Binghamton by seven fifteen.

I had planned to snooze during the trip while Matt drove, but I had so over-caffeinated myself that I couldn't get my eyes to close, no matter how tired the rest of my body was feeling. So I instead spent the trip shaking nervously, staring at the lines on the highway, flinching as shadows crossed them or Matt changed the radio suddenly, my senses working overtime and over-hard to compensate for my brain feeling like it was shutting down beneath them.

I couldn't decide which chemical I needed to knock myself back into the normal zone: more caffeine, nicotine, alcohol, THC, cocaine, aspirin or speed? Or was it just sleep that I needed? Probably the latter, but that seemed to be out of the question at the moment, so I just chain-smoked Marlboro's instead, figuring that eventually they (or the time that it took to smoke them) would smooth me out. Kris would disapprove when she met me, but I'd explain that I didn't expect her to kiss me until I'd taken a shower and gotten cleaned up after the show anyway. She'd heard that before.

I explained to Matt that we needed to meet Kris at the rest area since I didn't know where the Budstock concert was being held. He surprised me by confessing that he wasn't exactly sure, either, but Bud Greenleaf had told him to just head towards the State University campus and follow the signs from there. SUNY was on the other side of Binghamton from the rest area, so Kris would actually have to drive farther to meet us, then double back for the show, than she would have had I known to send her to SUNY, but the extra ten miles probably wouldn't seem like a big deal on top of the 175 she'd already completed by that time.

I was feeling increasingly queasy by the time we pulled into the Binghamton rest stop, nausea now supplanting the feelings of dissociation and nervousness that had defined the earlier part of the morning. I saw Kris' car there when we pulled in, and I stumbled out of the passenger side of the van almost before Matt had brought it to a stop, desperate for fresh air and a non-moving surface beneath my feet. I waved at Kris, then knelt beside the van, putting my cheek against the cool metal of its side, hoping that would clear my head a bit before I had to talk to her. It didn't work.

"You okay, Collie?" she asked as she walked over to the van. "You look like shit."

She patted me on the head, then wrinkled her nose. "Phew…you smell like shit, too."

"Long night," I croaked, hoarse from cigarettes. "I haven't taken a shower since our gig yesterday, so that's concert stink you're getting there."

"Nasty. Hope you weren't expecting a kiss or a hug from me this morning."

"I know better than that," I said.

"Good thing."

"Hey Kris," Matt yelled out the window. "You gonna ride with us or follow?"

"What do you wanna do, Collie?" Kris asked.

"Umm…actually, I think I need to hang out for a while before I get back in the van," I said. "I'm not feeling too hot right now, kinda car sick, need to go sit in the grass over there and rest for a while, I think."

"We need to go find the show, Collie," Matt yelled again. "Bud's expecting us soon."

"I honestly don't think I can drive around looking for the place right now without getting sick, man," I answered. "Why don't you go do some reconnaissance, then when you know where we're going, come back and pick me up?"

"You want to stay here by yourself?"

"Kris can stay with me," I answered.

"Sure," she said. "That's fine."

"What about you?" Matt asked Brian.

"I can stay here, too, if you're just gonna go scout stuff out. I'll keep an eye on Collie. And the gear."

Matt was thoughtful for a moment, a fairly rare occurrence. "Well if all of you are going to stay here, why don't we just park the van over there in the shade so you've gotta place to hang?" he finally asked. "And then I'll just use Kris' car to scoot around and see what's going on. That'll be faster and easier, right?"

"I dunno about that," Kris said. "I don't usually let people drive my car…"

"Let him do it, Kris," I said. "He's driven us all over the East Coast in a van without any problems. He can handle your car for an hour."

"Why don't we just keep my car here and let Matt take the van?"

"You want me in your car right now smelling the way I'm smelling? And feeling the way I'm feeling, like I'm gonna puke any minute?"

"No, actually I don't want that," Kris acceded. "Alright, pull the van over there, Matt, and I'll give you my keys."

"Cool, thanks," Matt answered, pulling the van over under the shade of a line of sick-looking, carbon-monoxide poisoned trees that partially shielded the rest area from the southbound interstate traffic that roared by beyond them. We opened the back door of the van, and I lay down inside while Kris and Brian sat down against a tree behind our parking spot. Kris tossed Matt her keys, and he promised to be back in an hour as he drove away towards SUNY Binghamton.

Never to return.

Although I wasn't immediately aware of that emergent little problem, since I'd finally collapsed or dozed off or whatever you call the unconscious state I entered while prone in the back of the van, only to be shaken awake by a nervous-looking Brian after what felt like 10 minutes, but was actually two hours.

"Dude, wake up," Brian said, poking at me in a decidedly ungentle fashion. "Collie…it's almost twelve thirty and Matt's not back. Kris is starting to freak out. You need to get up and do something, talk to her, whatever..."

I sat up quickly, disoriented, and the sudden motion triggered the strongest wave of nausea I'd experienced yet, so violent that I barely made it out of the back of the van before emptying the contents of my stomach on the curb, dry heaves wracking my body long after there was nothing left to hurl. I finally looked up, wiping my mouth and chin on my shirt sleeve, eyes focusing to find Kris standing in the grass beside me, arms crossed, rage darkening her face.

"What has Matt done with my goddamn car?" she yelled. "You said it would be okay. He's been gone for over two hours while I'm stuck here with you puking your guts out and Brian sneaking peaks at my tits when he thinks I'm not looking."

I straightened myself out and walked towards Kris, stepping over the pool of vomit between us, but she waved me off, saying "Don't even think about touching me. Just figure out how the hell we're gonna get my car back so I can get the fuck out of here." She seemed to be too angry to speak for a moment, then spat: "I can't believe I let you talk me into this, Collie. You think I'd have learned after all these years not to let you make the plans or control any situation that I'm gonna put myself into, since that always seems to end in disaster somehow."

She was right. This was a disaster. I was a disaster. Although I was actually a slightly-better feeling disaster at the moment, the little bit of sleeping and vomiting that I'd done seeming to have cleared some of the toxins from my mind and body, leaving me feeling lucid, if not particularly sharp.

"Let's move the van somewhere else," I said, gesturing at the mess I'd made on the curb. "Then let's go get something to eat and drink in the rest stop snack bar, then we can figure out what to do."

Kris stormed off towards the rest area's service building, not willing to get in the van with me. Brian, looking abashed, climbed into the van next to me as I pulled it over to the other side of the lot, parked, and went to join Kris inside. I got myself a large milk, a large orange juice and a muffin, figuring that would be about the gentlest way to nourish myself without sending my guts into another painful paroxysm. It all tasted good. It all made me feel better. But I still had no idea what to do.

"Should we go look for him?" Brian finally suggested?

"I don't think so," I said. "He knows we're here, so unless something really bad has happened, he's gonna eventually come back here. If we go driving around, we'll never find him."

"What if we just go to the concert?"

"By the time we found it and got in, we'd probably be too late to play anyway," I countered. "Plus you and I don't know Bud Greenleaf from a hole in the ground, so I'm not sure we'd really be able to talk our way into the place and get backstage without Matt around. Particularly if there's a couple thousand kids there, since gate security will be pretty uptight about people trying to scam their way in, and I doubt that our names are gonna be on any of the access lists or set schedules at this point, given how late Matt got us on the bill."

"But maybe Matt's there," Brian persisted.

"And my car," Kris added, venom dripping from her voice.

"I dunno," I said. "I can't think of any reason why Matt would have gone to the Budstock site, parked the car and then not come back. That doesn't make any sense."

"None of this does," Kris snapped. "Not one goddamn bit of sense."

"You've made your point, Kris, okay?" I snapped back with equal vigor. "This sucks. I fucked up. I understand that. I'm sorry. I'm trying to figure out what to do to fix it."

"You'd better."

"I'm doing the best that I can."

"Then it's not very good."

"It's all I've got."

"And that's the story of your life," Kris spat, taking her coffee cup and walking out of the snack bar.

"Bitch," Brian murmured between bites of toast, and I didn't correct him for doing so. He and I spent another half an hour in the snack bar, trying to figure out the least painful course of action, finally deciding that we would wait at the rest area until four o'clock, and if Matt hadn't shown up by then, we would drive Kris home to Jersey City in the van, use whatever money we had in the band expense box (which, fortunately, Matt had left with us when he took Kris' car) to get Kris a rental car, then drive back to Troy and try to figure out what happened to Matt and Kris' car from there. Brian had suggested calling the police to see if they had any reports of accidents involving Kris' car, or Matt, but we decided that we had too much potential contraband in the van (zillions of pot seeds, at a minimum) to risk getting John Q. Pig involved in our sick little process.

Kris had bought a music magazine (not *Spin*, I was glad to see) and was sitting out by the van, reading and scowling. I shared our plan with her, explaining that we'd get her home, then take care of paying for her rental car, then deal with finding out what happened to Matt later. She thought for a moment, then noted that if Matt had totaled her car, she would expect us to pay her insurance deductible and any other costs that she might incur as well. I told her that sounded reasonable, making a mental note that any money given to Kris as a result of this weekend was coming out of Matt's share of our earnings, not the band fund or my portion.

Four o'clock arrived and still no sign of Matt, so we bundled into the van and hit the road for Jersey City. Kris wasn't speaking to Brian or me by this time, so she climbed in the back, laying down on the floor between the instrument cases to read her magazine, nap and stew in her own juices, as appropriate. I decided that I would drive the first leg from Binghamton to Jersey City, since I felt like I had my second wind up by now. I also figured that way I'd have us safe and sound at Kris' house before sunset, then I could nap like a champion for three hours while Brian handled the night-time trucking back up to Troy.

Brian and I spent the first half an hour or so of the trip diligently scanning the highway for signs of disabled cars, fresh skidmarks, blood, carnage, Matt, whatever. By the time we passed Windsor on Route 17, though, we figured we were well beyond the point where he could have conceivably driven, so we hunkered down and got comfortable for the rest of the trip, Brian coiling himself up in the passenger seat, me turning the stereo up loud to the point where I couldn't hear Kris sighing and grumbling and muttering in the back, then cranking the air conditioning to keep myself alert.

I contemplated smoking a cigarette, but figured that would probably push Kris beyond the emotional breaking point, so I just nibbled my nails and coveted tobacco instead. I was tired, but nothing too dramatic, nothing that I didn't think I could handle for a couple of hours more. I fiddled with the air conditioning and the stereo reflexively, just to have something to do to keep my mind alert, finally understanding why Matt couldn't leave any of it alone whenever he was driving during a long road trip.

The radio started breaking up a short time later as we passed behind the Catskill Mountains' broadcast shadow, so I rummaged around in the storage compartment next to the drivers' seat, fished out a tape and popped it into the stereo. Good choice: I'd picked *The Third Reich and Roll*, the Residents' fabulous parody-cum-interpretation of two dozen pop classics from the '60s. A great album, although had Kris been awake or willing to talk to me by that point, she'd have told me to take it off, since it gave her the creeps. Oh, well.

It occurred to me in a flash of sleepy, slow-motion intuition that the Residents, those mysterious eyeball-headed performers, were actually very likely musicians and music critics, just like me, and that they'd chosen to disguise themselves so that they could pursue their twin avocations without being accused of peddling crit-rock. Too bad I'd not followed their lead and disguised myself when I took to the stage for the first time to play "Baal" all those years before. Things might have turned out differently if I had done that, there in the Quail Tavern, Nelson Wilson sitting in the booth on the left hand side, the one where Kris always sat when she visited, sometimes dressed, sometimes not. I smiled at the memory of her there without her blouse on, then turned as I picked up my bass and realized that Barry and Brian and George and Steve, who were all there on stage together with me, had all been thinking ahead for me, God bless them, since they were all decked out in eyeballs, just like the ones the Residents wore. I lifted my hand to touch my own head, and it was round and smooth and soft, wet, slightly yielding, and it hurt a little when I pressed it too hard. I couldn't see my bass guitar anymore, but I knew the songs by feel, so that was okay, except that Steve was playing a rhythm that I didn't recognize, so I wasn't sure where to jump in, and then I looked back out into the audience and Nelson Wilson was in the booth with Kris, sucking her left tit while Matt watched, the bulge of his hard-on visible beneath his untucked blue and gray Arctangent T-shirt. I started to jump off the stage to interrupt the tawdry tableau, but my eyeball had somehow gotten twisted, so I wasn't looking through the pupil anymore, and couldn't see where I was going. Steve kept hammering away at a persistent, high-speed beat that I couldn't quite place, while beside me, just out of my field of vision, someone kept shouting my name over and over again, and then suddenly I could see, and I looked down, and it wasn't a bass guitar in my hand at all, it was a steering wheel, with four hands on it instead of two as Brian reached from the passenger seat and tried to pull us back over onto the highway while we thundered along atop the median rumble strip. I flinched in confusion, then concluded that I must be dreaming, then tried to wake myself up, then realized that I had done so already, then pulled the wheel hard to the right, quickly, suddenly, desperately, trying to get back onto the highway, feeling the wheels grip even as I heard Kris start screaming from the back of van, watching in horror as we bounced back onto the asphalt and slid hard to the right, crossing two lanes of traffic as we did, and I spun the wheel back to the left just as we were about to drive off the other side of the road, and suddenly we were airborne, the passenger side wheels of the van sliding out from under us as the driver's side lifted into the air, and we were upside down, hanging from our seatbelts, and there was a moment of silence and stillness as we tipped further, and then we hit the ground, hard, deafened by the sound of every window shattering and every body post crumpling and every fiberglass panel exploding, but we didn't stop, we kept rolling again, and sliding, and the sound changed, not metal on metal any more so much as metal on earth, and there was a terrible thumping and tumbling sound behind me, and then Kris stopped screaming, and we rolled some more, until we came to rest, the van resting on the passenger side, me hanging above Brian by my seatbelt and by my left forearm, which was pinched between the passenger side door and the steering wheel, so I unhooked my seatbelt, and fell, my arm twisting, then wrenched free as I dropped on top of Brian, who squirmed as I hit him, flailing, trying to get me off him, so I twisted again and slid out the narrow fissure where the windshield used to be, and fell to the ground, then stood again and reached back inside the van, and Brian grabbed my arm and I half lifted and half pulled him out, and he was dirty and bloody and scared-looking, but all of his body parts appeared to still be connected, so I looked down and counted my own limbs and fingers, and they were all there, although there was a lot of blood all over me, too, and my left forearm was swollen in a way that I'd never seen a forearm swell before. I stared at it for a moment, trying to decide if it was really a part of my body at all, or just some vaguely forearm-shaped thing that had attached itself to me while we tumbled, and my head spun, and my stomach wrenched, and the world went black and I fell on the ground, which smelled of hot oil and asphalt and blood and cut grass as my face hit it.

 I don't know how long I was out that time, but when I came to again, I could hear Brian shouting Kris' name, and other voices, too, people who I didn't recognize. I stood, shaky on my feet, and stumbled around to the back side of the van, where I found Brian and two other guys, who had evidently stopped to offer their assistance, desperately hauling crushed amps and battered drums out of the back of the mangled vehicle, and I couldn't really figure out why they were doing so with such urgency, since the stuff didn't look to be usable anymore, and we didn't really have anywhere to go. But then Brian yelled Kris' name again, and I realized that she'd stopped screaming as the van tumbled, and that I'd not dragged her out after extracting Brian from the wreckage. So she was still in there, someplace, underneath a thousand pounds or so of gear, unless she'd been ejected from the vehicle during its flip turn off the highway. I turned and looked back up at the road, which seemed to be an incredibly long way from where the van had come to rest, hoping not to see a body impaled on a sign or a tree there, relieved to spot only van, not human, wreckage behind me as I searched.

But things weren't a whole lot better when Brian and the strangers finally got to Kris and pulled her from the van: she was coated with blood, her left leg looked like it had a new joint in it, halfway between the knee and the ankle, her mouth and nose were swollen and bent, and the right side of her head looked wrong, somehow, not quite round and natural the way it was supposed to look, but like a hard-boiled Easter egg that had been dropped, then placed back atop its holder, cracked spot upwards. "So this is what a dead body looks like," I thought, in a strangely emotionless fashion, but then I saw bubbles form in the blood on her nose, and I realized that she was breathing, that she was still there, inside that wreck of a body, and my soul seemed to explode inside me, searing my insides, then extinguishing itself, leaving a pile of dust drifting around inside my ribcage, choking me, and I ran towards Kris and tried to hug her, but one of the strangers shoved me aside as I got close, and the other waved his hands behind me, and I heard the sounds of sirens, as the ambulance and the police arrived, driving down the embankment to get as close to the van as they could, paramedics leaping from the back of their vehicle and rushing for Kris, no one paying much attention to Brian and me as we stood watching them.

Until one of the policemen approached us, and asked if we needed medical attention. I certainly didn't want to take anyone away from Kris at that point, so I told him I was fine, a bit banged up, but nothing serious. Brian nodded and mumbled "Me too." So the cop asked us who'd been driving the van, and I raised my right (uninjured) hand and said "me" and he asked if I'd like to take a breathalyzer test and I said that I didn't think that would be a good idea and he waved to one of his comrades, who walked up behind me, took both my arms, slipping the handcuffs over the good one first, then the bad one, while the first cop intoned "You have the right to remain silent, anything you say can and will…"

But I just shook my head at them as they walked me to the police cruiser, since I didn't really have anything to say to anyone at that point anyway. Except maybe to Kris, but it seemed like the wrong time to apologize to her, so I just let them drive me away in silence instead.

Chapter Seventeen

So what exactly happened that day in Binghamton, and then later on Route 17, somewhere outside of Middletown, New York?

I sure as hell didn't know at the time, but over the ensuing two years (and particularly during the past four weeks, ever since Lindy told me to just hunker down and tell this story, without explaining why I was telling it), I've been able to pretty well piece the fragments together in some linear, if not logical, fashion.

So Lindy's structural suggestion has certainly helped me reach these advanced chapters of this increasingly-hefty tome quicker than I might have otherwise, although I'm not quite sure that I've gotten anything out of telling the story, since I didn't really stop to think (and then write) about what it meant to me as I did it.

And as I've said before: if I don't write it, it isn't real to me, never has been, never will be. But I guess I can at least lay claim to have gotten just the facts, man, down on black and white, which might make it easier at some later date to wallow in them again, just in case I didn't wallow in them enough the first time. Maybe at that point I can write a companion piece, *The Annotated Collie Hay*, with the story on the left-hand page and the explanation and logic and meaning and justification on the right-hand page, sort of a concordance format, validating a life poorly spent by analyzing it into substance, even when there's nothing but piffle as raw product.

Only problem with such an approach would be the fact that the left-hand plot pages would run out right around the time when Brian and the two young strangers, whose names I never learned, pulled Kris' broken body out of the back of our van. For all intents and purposes, *The Collie Hay Story* ends right there, since everything I've done and everything I've been since that date has taken the shape of a holding pattern, static lines joggling me along from here to there, holding their shape, defining my shape, pushing me through motions I've performed a thousand times, turning the mundane into ritual, forgetting the ritual as soon as it's performed. Until I perform it again, that is.

But anyway, that's just wallowing, and I suppose there are a few spare details to relate yet, some odd explanatory things that I need to get down on paper to make them real, for me, for whoever reads this sad little saga, for posterity's sake, whatever posterity is. Just tell the story, the way that Lindy said I should the last time I let her read the manuscript, fishing for compliments, not winning many. She's my attorney, after all, so I need to listen to her, even if I can't afford to pay her.

Easy things first: I fell asleep at the wheel while driving back to Jersey City, I guess that part's pretty obvious, my second wind not quite packing the gale force that I might have expected or hoped for. The police took me to the Orange County jail in Goshen, assuming that they were going to tag me for a DWI, given the stench of beer and vomit and smoke that oozed out from beneath my bloody rags, but—oh, lucky day—when I blew the breathalyzer at the police station, I registered a paltry .05 percent alcohol in my bloodstream, comfortably far beneath the .08 percent statutory limit. It had been about twelve hours since I'd had anything to drink, after all, and I figured I'd puked up or pissed out a good portion of what I had consumed, so the .05 percent was probably just the steady-state quantity of alcohol that my lifestyle kept in my blood, like antifreeze in an engine.

But the fact that I wasn't legally drunk didn't stop John Q. Pig and Company from finding things with which they could charge me: reckless endangerment, expired inspection sticker on the van, unsafe lane change (duh), excessive speed, failure to carry an insurance card (although, thank God, the van was actually insured), and, oh, maybe half-a-dozen other nits and lice, just to make sure that something stuck. They fingerprinted me, put me in the holding cell, asked me if I wanted to make a phone call. I didn't feel like talking to anyone, and I was still awfully tired, so I figured I'd just hang out in the holding cell until they made me leave.

Which, as it turned out, was at about nine o'clock the next morning, when Randy, Gerry and Brian showed up at the jail. Brian had ridden in the ambulance to the hospital in Newburgh with Kris, calling the Treehouse as soon as he got there, Gerry and Randy responding with their usual alacrity, hopping in their car and rocketing down to the hospital to save the day. Only there wasn't a lot of day to save: they stood vigil outside of the operating room where the doctors worked on Kris most of the night, trying to get her stabilized before dealing with the nitty-gritty of her fractured skull and eye-socket, broken nose and jaw, snapped leg bones, broken ribs and collapsed lung.

Only after helping the hospital administration track down Kris' emergency contact numbers in South Carolina by calling her school in Jersey City did Gerry and Randy and Brian begin making inquiries as to my whereabouts. It only took a couple of calls to establish that I was safe as houses in the jail at Goshen, waiting for someone to come claim me, since the police were smart enough to recognize that my own recognizance wasn't the most reliable in the world.

Post-incarceration paperwork complete, my court date scheduled for six weeks hence, I asked my three liberators to take me back to the hospital in Newburgh so that I could see Kris myself. They demurred, noting that it wouldn't be a good idea, but I flung myself down on the pavement in the parking lot of the Goshen Police Station and refused to budge until they took me to see her, so they relented, but reluctantly. They did make me stop at a gas station to wash my hands and face and hair, though, to get at least some of the dried blood out. I pulled about ten chunks of safety glass (which didn't feel safe to me) out of my scalp while doing it, which generated more blood, pretty much undoing the benefit of the wash in the first place.

After we checked in at the Newburgh Hospital Intensive Care Unit, I rushed past the receptionist into Kris' room, took one look at her—wrapped in bandages, wired and intubated, bruised, battered, comatose—and started screaming like a gutted pig. I stumbled across the room, tried to throw myself onto her body, but ended up on the floor again instead, which made it easier for the orderlies to drag me out and forcibly evict me from the hospital, although I wasn't really resisting all that much. I was too busy being shocked over how horrible Kris looked, how inhuman and unlike-herself she'd become since I'd taken her for a whirl in the amp-go-round. I would have been doubly shocked and horrified if I'd realized then that it was the last time I'd ever set eyes on her.

Brian and Randy poured me into the backseat of the car while Gerry made another visit to the hospital administrative office to see if they'd been able to contact the Dennisons, learning that Kris' parents were indeed informed and preparing to travel northward to tend to their wounded daughter. Their job seemingly done in Newburgh then, Gerry and Randy ferried Brian and I to the junkyard in Middletown to which our van had been hauled, sometime after Kris and Brian and I had been spirited away under our respective flashing lights.

Most of our gear, including Barry's drum kit, had disappeared between the accident site and the auto graveyard, and I had a fleeting mental image of thousands of dollars worth of musical equipment scattered alongside Route 17, waiting for passing musicians to pick it up and make it theirs. The bass that Junior had given me a quarter-of-a-century earlier was still in the back of the van, though, its neck snapped in two, its head crushed beyond repair, a dark clot of blood and hair matted in the strings, right between the pickups. Kris must have been sleeping next to it when the van started to roll.

We picked a few small odds and ends—one of Brian's guitars, some of his home-made pedal effects, our cash box (empty), Barry's drum seat—out of the van, stuffed them in the trunk of Gerry and Randy's land yacht and headed north, back to Troy, back to the Treehouse, back to reality and safety and (maybe) sanity, if we were lucky. But we weren't, and you can imagine our surprise when we drove up the back alley and found Kris' car waiting for us there.

Not to mention Matt, curled up on the sofa in the studio, unbloodied, clean, resting peacefully. Brian, of all people, tried to restrain me when he realized that our manager-parasite was there, knowing that I would undoubtedly try to make yet another misguided lunge towards yet another badly-chosen target, but I was all out of steam by then, and shook Brian off of my injured, throbbing left arm, and went and sat on the floor in front of the sofa, right next to Matt, and tapped him squarely in the middle of the forehead with my index finger.

He was up like a shot, quickly scanning the room, quickly assessing the damage, quickly doing a fairly astute bit of mental arithmetic.

"Where's Kris?" he said.

"Hospital," I answered. "Car crash. Bad."

"Was she driving?"

"Nope. I was."

"In the van?"

"Yep. Totaled it."

"Equipment?"

"Gone. Most of it, anyway."

"Huh."

Matt sat there for a moment with an odd look on his face, one that I couldn't quite peg as either confusion or guilt or shame or fear or worry or some combination of all of the above. Probably the latter. I know that's how I felt.

"So, uh, I'm glad to see that you're okay," I continued. "And Kris' car. Glad to see that it's okay, too, so, uh…"

"Yeah, it's fine, I'm fine," Matt answered, and sighed. "I'm tired, that's all."

"Where the fuck were you yesterday, man?" Brian finally blurted, asking the question that was certainly in the forefront of my own mind, although I hadn't quite wanted to ask it yet, since that might have led to another screaming jag.

"I was starring in a sad comedy of errors, that's what I was doing," Matt said. "And it would actually be funny to tell it right now if you guys hadn't ended up in an accident and everything." He stood, stretched, twisted his triangular torso to work the kinks out of his back. "How bad is Kris hurt?" he asked, contortions completed.

"Real bad," I answered.

"She's in a coma, they say," Randy added. "Brain injury…"

"Broken ribs," chimed Gerry.

"Collapsed lung…"

"Broken leg…"

"Facial injuries…"

"Real bad," I recapped. "I'm gonna have to make a court appearance in a month or so. They charged me with reckless endangerment, among other things."

"Oh jeez, man, I'm so sorry," Matt sat, in a rare display of seemingly sincere concern for the welfare of others. "I guess Kris was right when she said she didn't want me to drive her car. Although I don't think this is what she had in mind."

"You still haven't told us where you were," Brian said, hysteria creeping into his voice. "You're supposed to be the one taking care of us. That's why we pay you. You ditched us at the rest area, and that's why Collie had to drive us to Jersey City. So you've got a lot of explaining to do, man, or else…"

"Easy, Brian," Matt interrupted. "It sounds like you're getting ready to threaten me. You don't want to threaten me. I'm not in the mood to be threatened, since this whole situation hurts me as much as it does you guys…"

"Not as much as it hurts Kris," Gerry offered.

"I was talking about financially," Matt said. "You guys don't play, none of us make any money. You guys aren't a band, I don't have anything to take care of."

"We're not a band anymore, I can tell you that right now," I said. "We should probably call Barry and tell him too, I guess, after Matt gets done explaining where he was."

"I was all over fucking Binghamton, that's where I was," Matt said. "I was about two-thirds of the way to SUNY when the car started sputtering, and I looked down and realized that I was running out of gas…"

"Yeah, I forgot to tell you that," I interrupted. "Kris always lets her car get right down to fumes before she fills it. I've almost run out of gas in her car, too."

"Well, I actually did run out of gas," Matt said. "Right on Highway 17, just past the I-88 exit, so I rolled over to the side of the road, parked the car, and started walking. It took me about forty minutes to get off the highway to the next gas station…but when I got there, I realized that I didn't have my wallet with me."

"Where was it?" Randy asked.

"In the van, with you guys," Matt continued. "I was hoping that one of you would have it with you now…no such luck, though, huh?"

We all shook our heads.

"Shit, I was afraid of that. I gotta call the credit card company and cancel my Visa before someone charges Vermont on it or something," he said. "Anyway, I had no money, so I walked over to the SUNY campus, figured that would be the best place to try to panhandle some cash, although it took me about an hour to get five bucks together, since my story sounded so lame that even impressionable college students and bleeding heart professor types didn't want to give me their change."

"Then when I got to the gas station, they didn't want to give me a gas can without a credit card to put down a deposit on its return," he continued. "So it took about a half-hour to negotiate that with this inbred cretin clerk, and I had to sign away my firstborn child and his firstborn child and his firstborn child too as security on this ten dollar plastic can, but the guy finally let me walk away with it, so I had to trek back up to the highway—which took about an hour this time, since I was tired and it was uphill."

We were all interested, now, despite ourselves. Matt knew how to tell a story, I'll give him that, if not much else.

"I finally make it back up to where the car was," he said after a long pause. "And the car was gone. I was pretty sure that no one could have stolen it, since it didn't have any gas in it, so I figured that it had been towed. Which meant that I had to get back into town to find it. But I was tired of walking, so I tried to hitchhike my way into Binghamton, only hitchhiking isn't allowed on that highway apparently, so the next cop that passed pulled over and gave me the high inquisition about what I was doing on the side of road with a gas can and my thumb out. I thought it was pretty fuckin' obvious, but he didn't quite see it that way, I guess."

"So I explained what happened, and he made a radio call and found out that the car had been towed, so he told me to hop in the back so that he could take me to the lot when Kris' car was being stored. That took, oh, another fifteen minutes or so, and when we got to the towing yard, sure enough there was Kris' car," Matt went on, caught up in the rhythm of his tale. "So I poured the gas into the tank and got ready to drive the car away, when this big dude comes out of the shed at the back of the lot and tells me that I owe him $150 for towing and storage fees. I explain I don't have any money. He explains that I don't have a car, then, until I get it. I start to yell, he grabs me and tells me that I'm threatening him on his property, and that he has the right to use physical force to defend himself accordingly. I get the hint and leave."

Matt paused again, shook his head, looked up at us all and said "Jesus, I can't believe how stupid this all sounds telling you this."

"Pretty stupid, yep," Gerry agreed.

"Right, very stupid," seconded Randy.

Brian and I were silent. I felt like I was about to pass out again, and by the looks of Brian, he wasn't doing a whole lot better himself.

"Well, we haven't really even gotten to the pathetic part, yet," Matt continued. "Since after I got kicked out of the towing yard, I figured I needed to get back to find you guys and hitchhiked my way back to the rest area—watching out for cops this time, pulling my thumb in when one came into view—only to find that you were all gone when I finally got there."

"What time was that?" Brian asked.

"I think I got to the rest area at about four fifteen or so, something like that," Matt answered.

"We left at four," Brian said. "You just missed us."

"Figures," Matt noted. "But anyway, at that point, I dug some cardboard out of a trashcan, borrowed a pen from a woman in the lot, made a little sign that said 'Budstock' and went and stood by the southbound exit ramp at the end of the rest area. A car full of hemp girls picked me up a little while later and took me out to the concert, which was way the hell out in the woods someplace, at a camping area, and I talked my way onto the grounds and went looking for Bud to see if he'd bail me out."

"I would have guessed that he would have been pissed off at you," Brian said. "Or at us, I guess. At someone, anyone."

"Yeah, he was pissed," Matt agreed. "Didn't really want to talk to me by the time I found him, since he'd moved some things around, rescheduled a couple of bands to fit us in, pissing them off in the process too. But I begged, man, since I was pretty freakin' desperate by this time. And he listened, and said that there was nothing he could do until the next morning, so I should chill out and enjoy the concert."

"Did you?" I asked.

"I chilled out, but I didn't enjoy the concert, no," Matt answered. "I hate that hippie music shit, you know that."

"Right, sorry, what was I thinking…"

"You weren't," he said. "And you weren't thinking when you got behind the wheel of that van, either. Jesus. I could have predicted a disaster had you told me you were gonna do that."

"I thought I had my second wind," I explained, the excuse sounding as lame in my ears as it no doubt would to a judge when I had to justify my actions officially. "I didn't realize how tired I was, I guess."

"No, I guess you didn't," Matt agreed. "But anyway, I stayed up all night Saturday listening to this horrible music and watching the stoners twirling around in the mud and having bad trips and everything. And at about eight the next morning, Bud told me that he would give me a lift over the impoundment lot and that he'd loan me the $150 I needed to get the car. So he drops me off at the lot, which is closed since it's Sunday morning, so I wait around for a couple of hours, try to call you guys, but no one answers, then I see the caretaker of the lot walking around in the back, and I yell at him and he comes over and I pass him the $150 and he tells me that I owe another day's storage, so that the bill is $200 now."

"What a dick," Brian noted.

"Yeah, a big one, absolutely," Matt said. "So I told him again that I didn't have any money, and asked how we could settle this deal. He said he liked the look of the car stereo in Kris' car, and he figured that it was probably worth about $50, so he would give me the car if he could have the stereo. I was so desperate that I agreed, although I gotta buy Kris a new tape deck now…"

"She probably won't be too worried about it for a while," I interrupted. "Nor about her entire car, for that matter."

"Although her parents might care," Randy reminded me, ever the voice of reason.

"True," I acknowledged. "But they don't know it's up here yet, so we'll deal with that when we need to."

"Well, anyway, that's pretty much the long and the short of the story," Matt concluded. "I drove home after that, almost fell asleep on the highway myself on the way, got home, passed out here, just a couple of hours ago."

"And now here we are," Brian said.

"And now here you are," Matt agreed, as we all shuffled off to our respective showers and beds and medicine chests to sleep the sleep of the damned.

I managed to make it to work at the *Advocate* the next morning on time, and announced to Anna and Carol that Arctangent was no more, and that I would be devoting myself heart and soul henceforth and forevermore to the *Advocate*, so that Carol could stop managing me now and we could all go back to doing things the way that we used to. They didn't buy it, and Bossgirl remained, and a few months later we even added our annoying little Filmboy, pretentious punk Blaine Grenier. Oh well. It meant less work for me in the long run, since we could split assignments five ways instead of four, and Blaine did tend to get the shitty little projects that no one else wanted, after all.

I also asked Lindy, back on that first Monday after the accident, to represent me at my trial in Goshen, since she was the only lawyer I knew. She agreed to do so, but only after I did something about Kris' car, which was still sitting in the alley behind the Treehouse where Matt had left it the day before. Her request seemed reasonable, so Brian and I drove Kris' car down to Jersey City the next weekend, leaving it in the parking lot of her apartment complex, dropping the keys through her mail slot and running for the train station, lest someone see or stop us. No one did. And no one ever asked me what happened to Kris' car stereo, either, thank God.

So Lindy did agree to represent me in my court case, doing a fine job of mitigating the damage and minimizing the sentence: I got off (if you can call it that) with a five hundred dollar fine, a thirty day jail sentence (suspended for one year, so long as I remained on good behavior), eighty hours of community service and a mandatory spot in an outpatient substance abuse education program, since the Judge felt that while alcohol wasn't a direct contributor in the accident, there was enough evidence of abuse apparent that he felt it prudent to get me some schooling quick, lest I earn myself a proper DWI soon thereafter.

The judge also suspended my drivers' license for six months, allowing me to drive only to and from work and to drunken dummy school. No problem there, since I could walk to the liquor store near the Treehouse and didn't really have anywhere else to go other than work and drunken dummy school anyway.

So as the court adjourned, I though I could begin to see the light at the end of the tunnel on the whole accident thing—until I walked out of the courtroom, smiling at Lindy, thanking her for keeping me out of jail, and found my path blocked by a petite, yet determined-looking, older woman in a severe blue suit. She looked familiar, although I couldn't quite place her face. I smiled nervously.

"You seem pretty pleased with yourself," the woman said, her voice laced with a toxic mix of sarcasm, disdain and menace, her frosted silver hair flowing about her face like an inverted halo, the veins in her neck taut as she leaned towards me. "Got off pretty light, I'd say. Wouldn't you agree?"

"The penalty's not so bad, I guess," I stammered, then jumped as I recalled where I'd seen the woman's face: in a frame over the mantle in Kris' apartment. It was her mother, who I hadn't seen since meeting her briefly over a decade before in Bridgefield. My heart raced as I tried to do some verbal damage control. "But I'm still suffering over what happened to Kris, so, y'know, that's not light, that's not over."

"No, it's not," Mrs. Dennison agreed. "That isn't over by a long shot, Mister Hay, since we will be filing a civil suit against you now that this farce of a criminal trial is over."

My face was blank. I had no idea what she was talking about.

"You do understand what that means, Mister Hay, don't you? It means that we will be seeking compensation for the damages—physical, emotional and financial—that you've caused our daughter. And us, I might add."

I looked at Lindy, who just shook her head and made "let's go" motions with her head.

But I wasn't ready to go, not quite yet. "How is Kris?" I mumbled in Mrs. Dennison's direction, not wanting to meet her eyes while I did so.

"Terrible," Mrs. Dennison answered. "She came out of her coma three weeks ago yesterday, but she's confused, seems to have lost a sizable chunk of her memory, has some paralysis on the left side of her body, small stuff like that, typical brain injury fare, and since no one quite understands how the brain works when it's injured, it makes the therapy all that much more lengthy and painful and difficult." She paused. "Oh, and I forgot to mention the fact that she's going to need some extensive plastic surgery at some point to make her face look human again. But that's a minor matter compared to the other issues, wouldn't you say, Mister Hay?"

"I'm sorry," I said, and I was.

"Sorry isn't enough," Mrs. Dennison said. "Sorry doesn't pay the bills. Sorry can't put Kris back in the classroom where she belongs. Sorry won't make it possible for Kris to play the bassoon again…"

Mrs. Dennison's voice choked at that point, and she coughed, turned and walked crisply away from us, her heels snapping like chewing gum (or like bones) every time they hit the linoleum beneath her feet. She turned a corner and passed out of sight, although we could hear her heels for another full minute, at least.

"So what did she mean about the civil suit?" I asked Lindy.

"It means you're fucked," she answered, padding the punch not being part of her style.

And she wasn't kidding: Kris' parents filed a two and a half million dollar civil suit against me that fall on Kris' behalf, seeking to recover the lost earning opportunities that Kris would have had as a teacher and an orchestral bassoon player, not to mention medical and rehabilitation expenses she would incur, and the obligatory "pain and suffering" catch-all claim. Lindy explained that my insurance would cover three hundred thousand dollars worth of damages, so that if the Dennisons' suit resulted in a judgment of anything larger than that amount against me, I'd have to figure out a way to pay, lest I have my assets confiscated and my salary garnished. I made a parsley joke. Lindy didn't laugh.

I also asked Lindy why Kris' parents were filing the suit, since I had a hard time imagining that Kris would have wanted them to do so, seeing as how it was an accident and everything, and it wasn't like I had tried to hurt her. I could see Lindy thinking hard about how to answer the question before finally blurting "She's mentally incapable of managing her affairs; they say she's operating at about an eight-year old intellectual level right now." She paused again. "But the Dennisons' lawyer tells me that she remembers you, and is telling everyone who will listen how much she hates you, although she can't remember why."

"Do you think they're just saying that to help their case?" I asked, stunned, shocked, sick.

"Maybe," Lindy answered. "But in the shape she's in, if her parents keep telling her that she hates you, she's gonna hate you. So I'd operate as if that really were the case, hard as that might be to do."

Which was—and remains—pretty hard indeed, particularly given the fact that the case has dragged out over nearly eighteen months as Lindy and the Dennisons' lawyers and my insurance company and the New York State Supreme Court Justice (I was impressed, until someone explained to me that "Supreme" was the name of the lower court in New York State) assigned to the case slogged through the process of discovery and postponements and hearings and negotiations and God knows what else, while I went to work, and came home, and drank, and gained weight, and watched people drift out of my life, any force of gravity I might once have exerted upon them spent and dissipated as I directed what little karmic energy I possessed strictly towards wallowing and self-pity.

Barry was the first to go, freed from Arctangent as soon as we gave him a thousand dollars of insurance company collision money to replace his drum kit, although I doubt that he ever did so. Barry's still working in his dad's hardware store, managing the place for the old man, much as Sister manages Junior's Music, despite Junior still being around. Barry's a dad now, too; Janice gave birth to a little girl named Ariel this past spring. I got a picture of the newborn baby in the mail with the announcement: God help her, but it looks like she's got her dad's bad hair and poor posture already. Unless that's the way babies are supposed to look, I mean.

Mammon Records passed out of my life—and out of existence—a short while later when Sony finally finished twitching and reorganizing its vast holdings in some ostensibly more efficient fashion, dumping half-a-dozen boutique labels and forty-some bands (Arctangent among them) in the process. But Terry Steele survived the corporate mayhem, somehow earning a promotion and a swell office in New York City in the process, from where he called Matt Lawrence a couple of months later, asking our former manager to join the Sony Empire as a low-level lackey in the artists and repertoire department. Needless to say, Matt was gone before the ear-piece of his telephone had cooled—although his last act in the Capital Region was to close the Arctangent bank account, thereby officially putting the band to bed for good. I got forty-six dollars out of the final settlement.

Brian stuck around for a while longer, although when I decided that we needed to take the studio apart (ostensibly so we could sell the equipment ourselves at maximum profit, rather than waiting for the court to do it once I lost my civil case—although in reality I just wanted to make it go away because it depressed me), he too began to drift away from me. Which was understandable, since he had wanted to keep Treehouse Records as an ongoing concern, which meant that he needed to keep the studio as a production facility, so that he could earn money by helping other bands get to the point where they could sound good enough to sign major label deals and have their lives turned to shit in exchange for their hard work and effort. I wasn't about to be a party to that, thank you very not.

So Brian sulked around for awhile, trying to avoid me, until that got too weird and he moved out of the Treehouse altogether, taking a new apartment in Albany. He still does computer consulting work—but he's better known around town these days as the soundman of choice at the Heartland Club. Or as the hot-shit guitarist for an up-and-coming band called Slender Machine, named after an Arctangent song—and featuring none other than George Kellenberger on keyboards and (wonders!) lead vocals. I hear George sounds pretty good these days. Guess he spent the past eight years practicing. Good for him.

Which leaves Randy and Gerry and Lindy and Dentist Dave and I in the Treehouse, Lindy and I spending a lot of time together as a direct result of the court case, Gerry and Randy spending a lot of time with Dentist Dave since the three of them like to build things and hang out at the antique building supply store in their spare time. I have the *Advocate* crew, too, of course, and while things are still a bit brittle there, Anna's reasonably kind recognition of my tenth anniversary with the paper may indicate that she's feeling a bit more benevolent towards me than may have been the case for much of the past three years. God knows I'm trying to get back on—and then stay on—her good side, since I can't afford not to.

Can't afford to alienate my family either, so I went home to Bridgefield last Christmas, taking the train down, spending a week with Junior and Sister and Greg and Ward, even though I still didn't know which one was which. It was a nice visit, actually, and lately I've been trying to remember to call them a couple of times a month or so, whether I've got something to say or not, just to make sure they're still there, and they're still them, and to let them know that I'm still here and still me, too, for better or (probably) for worse. We don't talk about the legal case much, since there's nothing any of them can do about it, and they've reinvented history to convince themselves that they never much liked Kris anyway, and that I should be glad to have her out of my life.

Only problem with that is that I don't have her out of my life, and I'm not sure that I'm ever going to. I mean, there's the lawsuit and everything now, so that's a constant reminder of Kris (not to mention her mother) these days, but even if that eventually plays out and disappears somehow, I still don't think that I'm going to live a Kris-free life, because no matter how much I drink and no matter how much I deny and no matter how much I write and rationalize and explain, I still have to live with the knowledge that I destroyed a life, which on some plain is almost more difficult, I think, than living with the knowledge of having taken a life—since in the latter scenario at least the victim's suffering is over and done with.

Which isn't the case for Kris, whose once-healthy body and once-sharp mind are now damaged beyond repair because I couldn't manage to stay awake through the Residents' *Third Reich and Roll* tape. Or because I couldn't say no to the promise of a couple hundred easy dollars at Budstock. Or because I couldn't honor the commitment I'd made to Kris to go to the Culinary Institute of America. Or because I couldn't control my alcohol intake before, during and after a Friday night concert. Or because I wasn't smart enough to get a few hours of sleep before taking off for Binghamton. Or because I wasn't organized enough to actually put my bass guitar in its case when I was done with it, instead of tossing it loose into the back of the van so that it could become a projectile while I napped behind the wheel.

I've tried to figure out some way to make this all someone else's fault, mind you. I blamed Matt for a spell, since he's the one who made the arrangement with Bud Greenleaf to go to the show in the first place. And it could have been Brian's fault, since it was his greed that pushed us into accepting the booking, and since I might have been able to get the van under control myself had Brian not reached across and startled me by trying to take the wheel and gently guide us back onto the highway. Barry was guilty, of course, since he'd left his drums in the back of the van, and Terry Steele had to carry some burden of complicity since it was his awful record contract that put us in a position of having to consider such a dud booking as Budstock on short notice in the first place.

Oh yes, there was plenty of blame to be spread about, and I've occasionally tossed a bit of it here or there, particularly while drinking. But no matter how I slice it ultimately, I can't come up with a way to blame Kris, and that means that she's suffered, and continues to suffer, for nothing. Or, even worse: she's suffered, and continues to suffer, because she loved me, once upon a time, and because she was willing to humor me, to honor the things that were important to me, even though she'd had some seventeen years worth of experience in watching me honor nothing but my own whim and need and lust and addiction and self-loathing and anger. She didn't deserve what happened to her. She didn't deserve what I did to her.

So I guess what I'm trying to say is that I feel awfully guilty about Kris—and I don't think the guilt is ever going to dissipate. People say that time heals all wounds, but I'm not sure I believe them anymore: I didn't really think about Kris much right after the accident, but now I wake up in the night or early in the morning, and I imagine her laying in a hospital bed somewhere—not sure how she got there, wanting to play the bassoon, not understanding why she can't do so—and it makes me want to scream with remorse and sadness and pain, and I usually end up reaching for the Motrin or the Nyquil or the Scotch to make it all go away, or at least to render myself unconscious so I don't have to think about it anymore.

I've been grabbing my laptop computer sometimes, too, when those middle of the night moments of reflection hit, working on this book, trying to make some sense of the story, trying to make it real to me, hoping that by so doing, somehow it'll be easy to close the final chapter, set the whole thing aside, and get on with my life.

But it hasn't quite worked that way, since writing all of this down has instead put me in a position of focusing on things that I'd suppressed until now, to the point where I'm having a hard time distancing myself from the past, or distinguishing one bit of current pain from another bit of historical pain, so that my feelings about my mother's suffering and death are intermingled with my feelings about Kris' suffering and life, and the guilt I feel about destroying Kris' life is bound up in the guilt I feel about trying to take Vance's dream away from him, and the alternating feelings of inadequacy and mistrust and loathing that I've felt over the years—at Junior's Music and the South Carolina Military Institute and Envirocorps and the *Advocate*—are all jumbled up inside me into one big knot of inadequacy, Nelson Wilson sitting atop it, a veritable anti-alchemist turning Arctangent records into shit, then making me eat it.

And that's pretty much where things stand as I prepare to drop this (proverbial) pen, sit back and sigh, my written record complete, my damage done, my sad tale told, whether it needed to be or not, my messy pile of papers handed to Lindy a couple of days ago for discovery or review or whatever it is that lawyers do with messy piles of papers. Maybe they just read them. Who knows?

Whatever she's done with them, though, is finished now, and she's here in South Korea with Randy (puttering in the kitchen) and Gerry (sitting at the dining room table, polishing a new brass door knob set he found at an estate sale) and me, her red ink visible on my manuscript from all the way across the living room.

"I see you bled on my papers again," I observe.

"I figure you wouldn't give them to me if you didn't want my opinion on them," Lindy says. "Since they don't really help your case much, now do they?"

"Dunno."

"I do know. They don't help," she says. "But I'm compartmentalizing. I'm reading them as your friend and neighbor. Not your lawyer. That okay?"

"Sure," I answer, then pause to sip my beer. I'm trying to cut down on the hard liquor a little bit these days, although I seem to just end up drinking more beer, gaining more weight and pissing more often for my efforts. "So what did you think about what I wrote?"

"Well, I know I told you to just hunker down and tell the story," Lindy says, rifling through the stack. "But it all got kinda clinical for me over the past five chapters or so, as you just sort of roared through the whole band story, not really pausing to explain anything…"

"I thought that's what you suggested."

"Well, sort of, yes," she explains. "But you're just so digital, Collie, it's either all this way, or all that way, and there's probably some happy medium that would make the whole thing work together really well. And maybe you should be the one to decide, since it's your book, instead of just doing what I tell you to do, whether you think it's the right thing or not."

"Whatever, I dunno…it's a moot point, really, since it's not like I'm going to publish this or anything…"

"Maybe you should," Lindy interrupts. "You're gonna need some money, and there's no sense typing five hundred pages and then hiding it under your bed. So why not try to get it published?"

"Too much work. Too embarrassing. Too me."

I think I'm being funny, but Lindy sits forward on the coach and scowls at me. "As much as you don't want to admit it, Collie, 'too you' is actually some pretty interesting stuff. I mean, how many people go from

East Yakfuck, South Carolina to a prestigious military school, then end up playing in a rock band or writing music reviews for a liberal rag like the *Advocate*. It's an interesting story. I enjoyed reading it. Other people might too."

"You only enjoyed it because you know me," I protest. "There's nothing here to interest anyone else that doesn't know about Arctangent or the Treehouse or Junior's Music or whatever."

"Suit yourself," Lindy says. "I'm not going to argue with you about it again, but I think you've done the hard work already, and you could earn some money with this thing if you'd just put in a little bit of extra effort to market the thing to the right people."

"But if I earn the money, Kris' family is just gonna get it all when they win the settlement anyway, right?"

"Not if you earn enough."

"How much is enough?"

"Mmmm…. a lot, I guess, still," Lindy says. "I'm running out of stalling tactics with the Dennisons, and we know that the insurance company isn't gonna pay more than $300,000, and we've whittled Kris' lawyers down to about $1.2 million total at this point, so you'll probably end up owing them about $900,000 or so, assuming we can settle out of court and it doesn't go before a jury."

"Yeesh," Gerry mutters from the dining room.

"Yeah, really, yeesh," Randy agrees.

"Y'know, I've explained to them that you've liquidated most of your assets and don't have a lotta cash to play with," Lindy added. "But they're not really interested in the logic of the situation at this point, really, so they're probably going to pursue that $900,000 by garnishing your wages, ten percent off your salary, forever, until you pay off the judgment, that sort of thing."

"Yeah, you told me that," I mope. "Although I can't help but think that they're just being mean at this point, since on my salary I'm never gonna be able to get them anywhere close to that amount of money."

"Right, mean," notes Gerry.

"Very mean," adds Randy.

"Can they do that? Just to be mean?"

"Sure they can. There's no law against being mean."

"Right."

"Right. Seems like the law actually lets people be mean sometimes."

"The law is mean."

"Really."

"Right."

I turn my attention back to Lindy, who notes "They are being mean, you're right. They want you to pay, or suffer, or never forget, depending on what kind of mood they're in. Although they've offered to take a lower settlement, cash payment now, but I think they're doing that just because they know you can't pay."

"Like how much lower?" I ask.

"If you could write them a check for, say, $350,000 or so, right now, I could probably get them to go away," Lindy answers. "They could invest it, spend the interest, that sort of thing, and they'd come out well ahead financially of where they'd be if they garnished your pitiful salary forever."

"They're gonna have to garnish anyway, then," I note. "Since $350,000 is just as unattainable for me as $900,000 is. I've got, what, maybe $15,000 in the bank from the studio sale and what little bit I can save, and I figure a good chunk of that's going to pay you..."

"Damn straight it is," Lindy says. "I don't bill by garnishing."

"So, y'know, unless I find another third of a million dollars laying around somewhere, I ain't gonna be able to help you with the quick settlement deal."

"Help yourself, you mean."

"Help you help me, I mean."

"Right."

"Right."

And we all lapse into silence, each in our own thoughts, mine flitting from a pointless mathematical exercise (ten percent of thirty five thousand dollars is thirty five hundred dollars, divided by nine hundred thousand...no, wait, nine hundred thousand divided by thirty five hundred is, uh, oh fuck it, it's the rest of your life, asshole) to a brief reflection on Lindy's publishing idea (never happen) to a quick twinge of need (cigarette, another beer) to my normal, pained steady-state contemplation of Kris in her all of infirmity, real and imagined: this is your life in brain injury hell, Kris Dennison, courtesy Collie Hay, music critic, bad boyfriend, failed musician, loser, thanks for being a good sport, Kris, and playing the hospital version of our game, but that's all the time we have tonight, so sleep, sleep, sleep and dream of better days, which will never come, no matter how much you deserve them.

So maybe, when all's said and done, I've really got some pretty damn good reasons for hating myself, and being hated by others, after all.

Surprise, surprise, surprise.

Epilogue

"What'cha burning?" Randy yells.

He and Gerry are standing on the South Korea balcony, looking down at me as I stand in the alley behind the Treehouse, feeding a stack of papers into the hearty flame that I've stoked inside an old metal drum tossed out by one of our neighbors some years earlier.

"Book," I answer, without looking back up at them.

"Did he say book?" Randy asks.

"Yeah, book, that's what he said," Gerry answers. "But can he do that? Isn't it illegal to burn a book?"

"No, that's money you're thinking of. It's illegal to burn money."

"Oh right, you can't burn money."

"No, you can't, or flags. But I think it's okay to burn books, except that writers don't generally like it when people do that. Especially when preachers do it. Or dictators."

"But he's a writer."

"Right, so I don't know why he'd be burning a book."

Silence.

"How come you're burning a book, Collie?" Gerry asks, finally, when the suspense and mystery become too great for he and Randy to collectively bear.

"Don't want anyone to read it," I tell them, shoving another dozen pages of paper into the can.

"Did you read it, Collie?"

"I wrote it, Gerry," I answer as, whoosh, another handful of paper is consumed.

"He said he wrote it."

"Right, so that must be the book about us."

"And Lindy…"

"And Kris and Matt and the accident and everything…"

"Right, and he's burning it."

"Doesn't want anybody to read it."

"Didn't he let Lindy read it?"

"Yeah, but not us."

"Nope, not us."

"Wonder why."

"Dunno."

"I'm gonna write a new book," I shout up at them. "A better book. This one's no good anymore. You guys would be wasting your time reading it."

I toss the remaining sheaf of papers into the can, watching the flames and smoke dance and twist, sparks and particles whirling upwards past Gerry and Randy, past the DMZ, past Dentist Dave and Lindy's apartments, catching in the breeze as they clear the roof of the Treehouse, then blowing eastward, away, forever, gone.

My face is flushed, from the heat of the fire I've built, but also with a ridiculously intense, wholly cathartic sense of exhilaration and release. A long time ago I read an article about Buddhist monks who spend years building elaborate mandalas out of sand, one grain at a time: when they complete their work, they open the windows of their monasteries to let the mandalas blow away where they will, their painstaking craft obliterated as the first gust of fresh air enters their heretofore still and stagnant work spaces. I never really understood the rationale for such a seemingly pointless exercise—until now, that is, as I watch the only copy of the manuscript I've diligently compiled over the past year being consumed and annihilated. Next I'll toss in the floppy disc that holds the computer files and be done with the whole thing altogether.

It's a powerful experience. I feel an incredible burden being lifted from my shoulders as I destroy my exegesis—much as an incredible burden was lifted from my life on the day when Gerry and Randy casually mentioned that they'd been receiving stock options from Envirocorps since the early '80s, and that they had over seven million dollars worth of stock between them sitting in retirements accounts, so that if they cashed out $350,000 of it to settle my civil case now, it wouldn't make much difference in the big scheme of things or over the long haul as far as either of them were concerned. In fact, after they wrangled it around for a few minutes, they actually got to a point where they concluded that it would be advantageous to cash the stock out now, just as they'd once managed to conclude that they were better off having me live in the Treehouse rent free. I couldn't follow the logic, but I wasn't going to argue with it either.

When they told Lindy of their plan for bailing me out, she insisted that they formalize the gift through a written contract that put some constraints, terms, conditions and caveats on the gift. First off, she didn't want them paying her legal fees; those would have to come out of the money that I'd accumulated by selling off the studio gear. Second, she asked them to make the gift only if the amount would settle the suit in its entirety, since she didn't want me going back to beg for more from them at some point in the future. Third, she recommended that Gerry and Randy finally draft a rental arrangement that acknowledged the terms under which I lived in the Treehouse; she further suggested that it might be decent of me to agree to make rental payments of similar magnitude to those Brian had once contributed to the Treehouse coffers, since my actions had directly contributed to his departure from our quasi-communal home.

The fourth and final provision was the real ball-buster: she asked Randy and Gerry to have their gift be contingent upon me making a legitimate effort to find a twelve step or substance abuse counseling or mental health therapy program or whatever else I needed to both break my addiction issues and learn to deal with what had happened to Kris in some constructive fashion. If I failed to do so, she proposed, then their gift would be recategorized as a loan, which I would be obligated to pay off at a rate of ten percent of whatever income I was earning, same way I would have had to pay the Dennisons if Randy and Gerry hadn't come to my rescue.

They were dutifully impressed at Lindy's organization and thoroughness, and agreed to have her draft up the appropriate documents, which she presented to me one night over dinner in South Korea, Randy and Gerry signing one side of the final page, me signing the other, Lindy and Dentist Dave adding their marks at the bottom as witnesses. I have no idea how legal the whole arrangement really is, of course (you know me and contracts, after all)—but I'm willing to go along with it if for no other reason than out of sheer marvel at the magnitude of the benevolence of the people who proposed it.

I mean, I've lived a horrible, selfish, pointless sort of life—yet Gerry and Lindy and Randy are still willing to invest finances, time and energy into helping me turn what's left of it into something positive and worthwhile, even though none of them appear to get anything out of doing so, except the knowledge that they've done something good, and kind, and maybe even humane. And as efficient and single-minded as I've been over the years about looking gift horses in their mouths and biting the hands that feed me, this latest burst of benevolence has finally forced me to stop and ponder what I've done to deserve such good fortune, such good friends. Truth be told: I can't think of a single goddamn thing.

But I'm going to try to find a thing, to find a reason, I really am, and the first step in that process was the burning of my manuscript, the elimination of that sprawling wallow, the eradication of all the horrible, selfish, pointless things I'd written about myself and others, and all the horrible, selfish, pointless things I'd done to inspire them. They're gone now, leaving me with at least a symbolic tabula rasa, upon which I can write another, better story about good people who do good things, even for those who don't deserve them.

And I can write about myself, too, maybe, someday. Not about the Collie Hay that was—musician, military academy punk, bad boyfriend, lazy office worker—but about the Collie Hay that is and will be, one who hopefully will be able to define himself in some higher, brighter, more meaningful fashion, one who will make those who loved—and love—him proud, one who will return the respect that's been shown him, whether he was worthy of it or not.

Which is not, of course, to imply that everything is or will be sunshine and lollipops henceforth and forevermore. I don't know how this whole twelve step thing is going to go, for instance, although I'm planning to attend my first Alcoholics Anonymous meeting tonight, and Lindy has promised to take me out to dinner afterwards if I behave and don't smoke too much while I'm there. She told me that could be my thirteenth step. I asked her if a thirteenth step was anything was like a nineteenth hole, and she winked and said she was surprised that I'd only played eighteen to date. I like it when she winks.

I also know that there's no happy, fairy-tale ending as far as Kris is concerned, so I'm going to have to continue to live with the knowledge that she continues to live with the knowledge that I'm the one who destroyed her life as she once knew it and once wished it to be. I wish I could undo it—but I know I can't, and I know that the best thing I can do about it is to funnel my remorse into something positive, although I don't yet know what that might be. This whole "do unto others" thing is a new concept for me, see.

But give me time: I adapt, I really do.

For better or worse.

Or maybe just for better.

Maybe.

And so in that spirit of maybe, here's to a new story, one I've yet to tell, one I won't have to burn once I've told it. A story wherein I define myself afresh, wherein I make myself and my life and decency equally eponymous, I equal I, me equal me, this is that and that is good and one becomes the other.

"By my words shall you know me" (it will begin) "Collie Hay, music critic. And if people can love me in spite of that, if people can even love me for that, then who am I to hate myself?"

About the Author

J. Eric Smith is not Collie Hay. Honest. He is, however, married to a beautiful lawyer, and he has a beautiful daughter, and all of them live, beautifully, in Upstate New York, which does not include Westchester County, no matter what millions of Manhattanites might think.

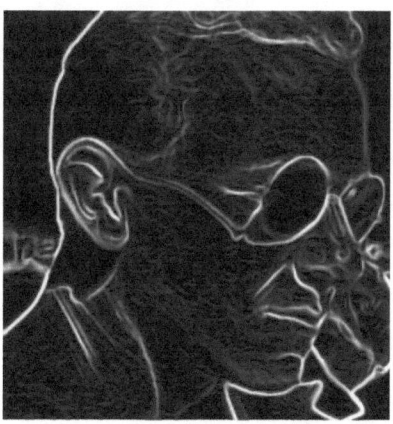

Made in United States
Troutdale, OR
07/04/2023